MW00928294

larry
CORREIA
("the shooter")

kevin j.
ANDERSON
("the boss")

d.j.
BUTLER
("the bot")

blake
CASSELMAN
("the heavy")

mercedes
YARDLEY
("femme fatale")

THE LONGEST CON

michaelbrent
COLLINGS
("the author")

Michaelbrent Collings presents

MICHAELBRENT COLLINGS IMAGINATION in a MICHAELBRENT COLLINGS PRODUCTION
starring MICHAELBRENT COLLINGS "THE LONGEST CON" KEVIN J. ANDERSON D.J. BUTLER BLAKE CASSELMAN
LARRY CORREIA MERCEDES YARDLEY with ORSON SCOTT CARD DAVID FARLAND DAN WELLS SEAN SMITHSON casting
JUDI AND MICHAEL R. COLLINGS art "THE PARROT" costume design by MICHAELBRENT COLLINGS
music by WHATEVER IS ON YOUR IPOD BOOK BY MICHAELBRENT COLLINGS BASED ON HIS AWESOME IDEA

website: http://www.michaelbrentcollings.com
email: info@michaelbrentcollings.com

**For more information on Michaelbrent's books, including specials and sales; and for info about signings, appearances, and media,
check out his webpage,
Like his Facebook fanpage
or
Follow him on Twitter.
You can also
sign up for his email list for deals and new releases.**

PRAISE FOR THE WORK OF
MICHAELBRENT COLLINGS

"Epic fantasy meets superheroes, with lots of action and great characters…. Collings is a great storyteller." - Larry Correia, New York Times bestselling author of *Monster Hunter International* and *Son of the Black Sword*

"… intense… one slice of action after another… a great book and what looks to be an interesting start of a series that could be amazing." - Game Industry News

"Collings is so proficient at what he does, he crooks his finger to get you inside his world and before you know it, you are along for the ride. You don't even see it coming; he is that good." – *Only Five Star Book Reviews*

"What a ride…. This is one you will not be able to put down and one you will remember for a long time to come. Very highly recommended." – *Midwest Book Review*

"I would be remiss if I didn't say he's done it again. Twists and turns, and an out-come that will leave one saying, 'I so did not see that coming.'" – *Audiobook Reviewer*

"His prose is brilliant, his writing is visceral and violent, dark and enthralling." – *InD'Tale Magazine*

"[N]ear perfect." – *The San Francisco Book Review*

DEDICATION

To...

the stars (not the ones in the sky,
but the real ones)...

and to Laura, FTAAE.

Special Note:

The names of the irrelevant have been changed to protect their irrelevance.

The names of the innocent and the guilty have *not* been changed. As for the innocent, everyone needs to know they *are* innocent – it's the only way to protect them.

As for the guilty… they can suck it.

1

My name is Michaelbrent Collings. This is what I do.

2

"I dunno. It seems expensive."

I sighed and squinted. "You look like you can afford it."

I tried to make it sound funny, but Bryan Cranston's eyes squinted and he looked every inch the Outraged Actor.

"Wait, back up," I can hear you saying. "*Bryan Cranston?* And he's looking at one of your books? And quibbling about price?"

You're right to be skeptical. I don't actually *know* if it's Bryan Cranston. It could be Walter White – I get them confused. I've never actually seen a single episode of *Breaking Bad*, and I always have a hard time remembering which is the name of the actor, and which is the name of the guy he plays.

"Wait, back up," I can hear you saying. "You've never seen an episode of *Breaking Bad?* Not a *single* episode?"

No. I know that probably makes me un-American, but that show just sounds too dark. From what I understand, it's a show about a guy who goes balder and balder over the course of five seasons. And some things are just too close to home – too horrifying even for a horror writer.[1]

Anywho, Bryan picked up another book. *Apparition.* "That's one of my favorites," I said. "It's so scary that –"

He cut me off with a snort. Though it was hard to hear, since he was in full regalia – gas mask, yellow suit that looks like jammies made of tent nylon (which I understand protects him from Deadly Meth Gas or something – apparently there's a lot of farting in *Breaking Bad*).

Finally, his fingers moved to my book, *Strangers.* I didn't bother saying anything at this point – just plastered my "customer = always right" look on my gob and tried to think un-murdery thoughts.

---

[1] If you don't understand why this would affect me, just take a gander at my author photo in the back. And weep with me.

Surprisingly – or not, if you really knew what kind of guy Bryan Cranston was – he suddenly shoved the top copy of *Strangers* aside and went digging through the pile of copies below it. He made a mess. Didn't seem to care.

Diva.

I sensed her before I saw her. The comforting presence that was *almost* enough to balance out Cranston's general jackassitude.

"Can I help out?"

My mom is what in bygone eras you might have called a cool old broad. Maybe a neat dame. Today, in a PC world... I dunno. Probably "a pleasant, female-identifying humyn of less-than-juvenile years."

I like "cool old broad."

She was dressed in her favorite outfit: purple dress, with a blood-red bustier over it, and a laser gun at her side.

Cranston kept ignoring her, until he found what he was looking for: the fifth book down. He looked at it strangely, then abruptly spun on his heel and walked away.

"I guess that's no sale," said Mom.

"I guess not." I waited a moment. "Ma, do you think you could guard the castle for a minute? Pee break."

She nodded and wiped her brow with a lace hanky before putting on a tall velvet top hat that had a pair of brass goggles resting on the brim.

I moved out.

The next part wasn't hard. I mean, it *was*, but I'm very good at this. It's *why* I do this. Well, that and they make me do it. I'll get into that in a minute.

I caught up to Bryan in the hall. He was posing for pictures. A gaggle of giggling girls had grouped themselves around him and were busily taking selfies. I couldn't blame them – even I had to admit Bryan looked good. The outfit, the gas mask, the baldness... it was all perfect.

I saw him eye one of the girls. Young enough to be his great-great-great-etc.-granddaughter, but he leaned over and whispered something into her ear and she giggled and I sighed because now this was getting complicated.

The giggle gaggle dispersed, leaving only Cranston and his target.

The girl was cute – exactly the type I'd heard Cranston liked. Dark hair, with the still-blooming body of someone moving seamlessly from youth to womanhood, one foot in each world. Coltish form, but starting to get the grace that comes with full maturity. She wore a red plaid, side-button mini skirt over thigh-high white socks, the whole thing topped by a tight white button-up that had been knotted at the bottom to show off a bejeweled navel.

Yep, just Cranston's type. Dirty old thing.

I wanted to intercede, but knew that would only get me in trouble. I followed them instead. Cranston looked around a couple times, but like I said: me good at job (sometimes). Much hidey-hidey, no findy-findy.

He took her to a door that led to a service hallway – the kind of place you send the help through, so the illusion that everything simply *appears* will be as unbroken as possible.

The door to the service hall should have been locked. But of course, it wasn't. It wouldn't be for him.

Actors have all the luck.

It was only partly a joke. Little secret: inside every author is a person who kinda wishes they were an actor. But we generally have faces made for typing. Often *with* our faces.

So yeah, jealous. A little.

Sigh. On to work.

Cranston pulled the door open, then went through, arm around the girl. She had melted fully into his embrace, pushing her body against him and writhing in a way that seemed more than a little obscene.

Again, I wanted to jump in. I have daughters. And there is no dad with daughters in the world that wouldn't have wanted to murder Cranston in that moment.

I waited.

The door swung closed behind the pair, and I finally darted forward, getting my fingers curled around the edge of the door in the instant before it shut. Partly so that I could go through it without it making that loud clicky noise that would have screamed "HI! JUST BUTTING IN!" and which I definitely wanted to avoid.

Partly because I suspected that Cranston would have locked it behind him if he'd heard it shut. He didn't get this old

—

(*And this bald! Ha!*)

– by making mistakes.

I held the door, my fingers squeezed uncomfortably between it and the jamb, for a full ten seconds. Then I slowly swung it open.

Cranston was bent over the girl. His gas mask pushed up, his face pressed against her cheek. She looked ecstatic, and the writhing she had done before was positively Sunday School-ish compared to what she was doing now.

Cranston's face dipped lower.

"Aaaaand, that's gone about far enough," I said. I lunged forward – I'm not a tall guy, but I can cover distance quickly when I need to. At least, in small bursts. Cardio sucks.

Cranston moved fast. Too fast. He saw me coming and lunged, too. Right at me.

It felt like I'd been hit by a brick wall that had been covered by larger, angrier bricks. My breath exploded out of me in a "*whoof*", and Cranston powered me back – right into the door I had just come through. My back hit the crash bar on that side and we exploded out into the main hall.

I ended up on the bottom, Cranston's hands around my throat. His gas mask was askew, and a small part of me noted with some pleasure that his bald head looked a bit less cool – at last.

Of course, I probably looked *much* less cool. I could feel the blood trying to make its way past Cranston's vise-like grip, and my mouth opened and closed soundlessly like a mime doing a guppy impression. My eyes felt like they were going to pop right out of their sockets.

And – wouldn't you know it – the hall was chock full. Because that was just my luck. People staring in a knot on either side of the hall, ringing us in a loose circle and wondering what to do. I got the sense that a few people took steps forward, but stopped. They weren't sure what was happening – what to *do*.

Cranston didn't seem to care. He just bore down harder. I couldn't hope to pull his hands away. He was too strong.

I didn't even try.

I just pulled the Very Long Knife from under my waistband and shoved it through Cranston's face.

3

It wasn't really called the Very Long Knife, of course. But its real name sounded like something a Klingon with a sinus infection would go mad trying to reproduce, so I liked to call it the Very Long Knife.

Whatever its name, it was effective. It was Cranston's turn to do the mimefish impression, and his eyes didn't just bulge, they absolutely *popped out*. At least, one of them did, bouncing right out of its socket on a long optical cord that, in the madness of the moment, made me wonder whatever happened to my childhood Slinky.

I took the opportunity to rip his face off.

Underneath his face, Cranston wasn't a he, he was a she. Beautiful gold hair spilled out from under the bald cap, and the latex pulled away to reveal high cheekbones that had an appropriately ageless quality to them.

Then those cheekbones split apart, too, to reveal something dark and roiling. The impression of tentacles, the sense of madness made flesh.

I twisted the knife, and whispered something deep in my throat: "*Ch'ph'throd, Yidhra.*" I was going for "Go to Hell" in the most literal sense. I might also have been calling the creature a potato.

I must have gotten it right, though, because there was a blat of hot air, the sigh of a thousand souls driven insane by torments beyond imagining... and the Cranston-thing disappeared. All that remained was an empty Meth Protection Jammies, a gas mask that fell hard on my nose, and a bald cap/latex face combo that had more or less glued itself to my right hand.

I looked around at the people still assembled. They looked shocked, afraid – a few looked ill. I knew they wouldn't have seen the monster part of the scene – the supernatural takes care of itself – but they might have seen me just murder someone.

I popped to my feet. I held the Meth jammies aloft in triumph. Grinned widely as I spun in a slow circle and shouted, "Direct from the cold reaches of space, that was the demon Yidhra – offspring of Cthulhu himself!" I shook the yellow suit for emphasis. "Now slain for your entertainment!" A smattering of applause began. I mock-frowned. "Come on, is that all you got?" The applause grew louder. My smile widened to its widest, and I shouted at the top of my lungs. "*Does FanFamFunComCon give you the best show, or what?*"

And now, the assemblage of nerds, geeks, and dorks all around me exploded into applause usually reserved for Stan Lee or William Shatner.

I bowed. "I'm on a panel on Religion in Horror Literature at three o'clock today, and you can find my books in Artists Alley in the purple aisle!" I shouted.

The applause kept coming.

It felt good.

4

The assorted nerd-folk dispersed pretty quickly after that, though a few chanted "M.. *B*... M... *B*!" which was pretty awesome. I'm not famous, but a few people know who I am.

They left, and pretty soon it was just me.

And Blake Casselman.

I'd seen him in the crowd of course – noticing things is part of what I do. But I had successfully ignored him until now.

Blake's a complicated guy. He's in high demand for conventions all over the place, and I know from personal experience he's very good at his job(s).

When people were in the hall with us, he wore his "panel organizer" face: harried, worried, put upon. He slouched like he bore the worries of the entire realm of Geekdom on his shoulders. He sweated all the time – and I mean that. *All. The. Time.* He ran around like a coked-up rabbit, trying to make sure all the artists, authors, and actors – what I call the "a-ness group" – showed up to their panels on time and had enough caffeinated drinks to get them through the comic/art/fan convention *du jour*. This last was like herding cats. Who are made of water. And have ADHD. Also, they are artist, author, and actor cats.

Blake's gray hair looked like he went to Einstein's barber, and his shirt was perpetually wrinkled. I had never seen a t-shirt be wrinkled until I met Blake.

And it all changed when the people in the hall dispersed. He pushed a hand through his hair, and it went from "vaguely slovenly" to "executive CEO." His shoulders straightened. I could swear I saw the wrinkles just falling out of his t-shirt, and the sweat literally sucking *back into* his pores through sheer Will of Blake.

This was the face that scared me. The face of my Handler.

He looked at the yellow jammies in my hand, the gas mask on the floor. He scowled as he saw the Very Long Knife, which I had tucked back into my waistband (which, P.S., is another sign of how good I am at this – do you know how hard it is to hid a ten-inch blade down your pants without cutting off your tender bits?).

"How's the sylphilis?" said Blake – and yes, you read that right. Sylphilis.

Very funny. Like I haven't heard that *one a million times.*

I didn't say it out loud, which was a good thing since Blake moved on without waiting. "You made the move without permission." Somehow, he made the *words* scowl.

I scowled right back. I wasn't as good at it – I couldn't kill birds in flight like Blake could – but it got the point across. "He had another victim."

Blake made a grand sign of looking around. "And this person is...?"

I walked to the service hall entrance and threw open the door. The girl lay beyond, face-up on the floor and crying softly.

"Looks like you didn't move soon enough," said Blake.

I threw up my hands. "What *is* it with you? Too soon, not soon enough –" I threw up my hands again. You know, for emphasis. "Will I ever get it right, Blake?"

"Probably not." His gaze shifted back to the remains of the Cranston-thing. "And you were reckless. There's no way you could have confirmed –"

"I did. I knew it was Yidhra."

Blake's arms crossed. "And how, pray, did you know? That this wasn't a real person? Yidhra's a shape-shifter, and the whole point of a shape-shifter is –"

"Yeah, I know: they look like people. But I had proof."

"What?"

"He/she came by the table and I laced one of my books."

Blake went very, very still. "With what?" he whispered.

I cursed internally. I hadn't – *really* hadn't – wanted to share this little bit of sleuthing. "Nothing, really, it –"

"With what?"

"I think we should get this girl back –"

"With *what*?" Blake's voice almost raised. I'd only seen him raise his voice twice before. People died both times.

"Uh... with the last victim's finger."

Blake's turn to look like his eyes were going to pop out – there must have been some eye-popping bug going around the con. "You shoved the last victim's finger – the only thing left of her, I might add – in one of your books and –"

"No, not the whole finger. I just grated a little off the stumpy side and sprinkled it in the pages. Then when Bryan Cranston went right for it, I knew he – er, she – was hungry to consume what he'd missed of her last victim."

Blake tried to talk. Nothing came out. It was kind of nice.

"Come on, Blake," I said. "I did the job. I found the monster. I solved the case." I nodded into the service hall. "I even saved the girl. Hooray for the good guys!"

Blake's cell phone rang. The ring tone was the Darth Vader theme from *Star Wars*. He lifted it to his ear. "Hello?"

His face grew white, and I knew what he was going to say even before he held out the phone.

"It's Cthulhu," he said. "And he's pissed at you."

5

All right, let's back it up a bit. See, I'm an author, so I know how it works: slam-bang opening, some unanswered questions for suspense, a few surprises. Then, before the audience starts getting too irritated because *what the heck is going on?*, you give 'em a bit of backstory.

Here's mine. I'm doing this so you don't get all confused and hate me forever. Also because I don't want to talk about the Cthulhu thing.

When I was a kid, being a nerd/dork/geek was a bad thing. It meant no parties, no friends, and the only place you consistently got invited was the inside of a trash can. Sure, you got good grades and the teachers loved you... but the alpha males beat the crap out of you and the desirable girls (which, to a nerd back then, meant "she is breathing") would either ignore you, or also beat the crap out of you.

A few years ago, it changed. Nerds are cool, and they kinda rule a big chunk of the world. The most successful movies are straight from the Nerd Bible. The biggest TV shows' fans are auto-nerdified somehow, and they don't have a problem with it. People buy glasses and punch the lenses out of them, because glasses are now a fashion statement instead of nice spot for jocks to aim at.

And there are comic cons.

If you've never been to one, imagine a swap meet, where everything they sell is related to movies, comic books, video games, or genre work. Now imagine the swap meet is so full the aisles become meat rivers that can easily drag you along if you aren't willing to push a bit. And every second person is dressed up as someone – or something – from a favorite book, comic, movie: "cosplaying."

That's where the monsters come in.

There have always been monsters. Most people don't know it. Most people *can't* know it – if they see something supernatural, they either can't accept it and their brains provide a "rational" explanation for it, or they simply forget about it the second it's all over – though I still try to be careful, because there's an exception for every rule.

The upshot is that monsters walk among us. Unnoticed, but real.

The one place they *do* come out and play – visibly, noticeably – is the cons. Monsters, it turns out, like to cosplay too. Only they cosplay as humans.

It's not just slumming, either. Monsters from the lowliest grubble to the highest demonic royalty have shown up at San Diego, Chicago, New York, Salt Lake City – anywhere there's a convention and a chance to dress up and mingle.

Obviously, this presents a problem. A lot of monsters aren't known for their good impulse control. For a long time – before history, actually – the Dead Ones kept them at bay. No, this isn't some super-badass anti-monster zombie commando group (though "Super-Badass Anti-Monster Zombie Commandos" would be a great name for a metal band). It's the name of the ruling council of humans who a) know about the supernatural, and b) have the magical power to keep them at bay.

I'll tell you why they're called the Dead Ones at some later date. We're already hip-deep in Exposition Land.

To summarize the rest: Monsters start showing up at cons. People start dying. The Dead Ones gear up for war. The monsters do the same.

And one of the convention organizers – not wanting the world to be destroyed or, more importantly, to lose attendee revenue – proposes a solution: the cons are a sort of "gun free zone" for monsters. They can come, but they can't do anything naughty.

Of course, we all know how when a bad guy sees a sign that says, "Gun Free Zone" he just frowns and puts away his bazooka and goes home. Not.

That's where guys like me come in.

Some humans *can* see the monsters. Some *can* process what's happening, and remember it after. I'm one of them. And when Blake Casselman – that rotten, scummy, unethical sonofahellbeast found that out, he roped me into the Wardens.

The Wardens are… well, think of them like Air Marshals: the guys who are on some airplanes, sitting there and pretending to be Normal Joes while actually packing heat and prepared to kill terrorists or subdue teens who realize their iPads have no wifi service.

So I and a few others are seeded through the cons. We're supposed to spot trouble before it happens. And if it *does* happen, we're supposed to find out what went down, and punish the wrongdoers.

Why don't the Dead Ones just do it? Because, believe it or not, the monsters have mostly lived up to the Comic Con Accords. So having the Dead Ones move in would be the equivalent of nuking China because a Chinese national knocked over a 7-11 and shot the cashier.

The Wardens keep things low-key. We're disinterested parties.

We're also expendable – a fact which Blake constantly reminds me.

6

"Are you going to just stand there like a moron?" Blake jabbed his phone in my direction again. "*Cthulhu* is on the phone. For you."

For whatever reason, I'd had it. I had gotten to the convention the night before it started – my usual deal, so I can check in and get my vendor's table all set up. I hadn't unpacked three books before Blake came up to tell me someone was already dead. He was all smiles and hugs at first – my mom was there, and she doesn't know what I do. Well, she knows that I'm an author. But she doesn't know about the whole detective/monster killer thing. So Blake was careful not to let *her* know what was going on.

I'm surprised about my situation myself, actually. Not about the monsters – I started seeing them a week after getting married. I worried I was finally losing my mind – something people had been joking about as an impending event for years. But something kept me from telling anyone what I was seeing. I didn't even tell Laura; and I tell my wife *everything*.

Well, I used to.

It turned out to be a good thing I didn't tell her. Because after some digging around and some clandestine visits to some seriously creepy people/monsters/I'm-still-not-sure-what-they-weres, I discovered that I *wasn't* crazy. There really *were* monsters.

And Laura, my wife, the love of my life, was one of them.

Don't get worried, and please don't show up at my house with torches and pitchforks. It would worry the kids.

She's not one of the "oogah-boogah scary" monsters. She's a sylph. A spirit of the trees. I go walking when I need to think. At the time I met Laura, I wasn't a writer yet, just a lawyer (yes, I'm still purchasing my soul back on an installment plan), and I was walking through a hiking trail in a state park near my house. She showed up on the trail, dressed as a hiker, and we hit it off. I couldn't believe my good fortune – though after I found out what she really is, I wondered if she had some mischief planned for me. I doubt she intended to fall in love, get married, have kids.

And, as a package deal with that last: she gave up her life as a sylph. With the birth of our first child, she fell from a grace I'll never understand, and became a mortal.

But until the kid came, she was still technically a creature of the Otherworlds. And we did the nasty (which you probably figured, based on the "kids" comment). And, surprise surprise, guess who ended up with an STD? I'll give you a hint: it *wasn't* Laura. Hint number two: it *was* me.

I didn't get itchy anywhere, and it didn't hurt when I went pee-pee. Instead, I got to see monsters. That's what STD stands for in the Otherworlds: Supernaturally Transmitted Disease. Laura was a sylph. I got sylphilis.

A few years later: I became a full-time author. Doing well enough to quit my job as a lawyer,[2] but I still have to go to cons to meet new fans and hand-sell books at the table I set up with my mom.

I met Blake at the first con I went to. He found out what I can see... and I'd tell you how he got me into this gig, but Cthulhu, the Great Old One who cares not a whit for us and could destroy all humanity with a blink of its eye, is on the line.

I looked at Blake's phone the same way I looked at toilets in airplane terminals. "I don't want to talk to him."

"*It.*"

"Whatever. I don't want to –"

"You have to."

"No, I don't."

"Michaelbrent, you *murdered* his daughter."

---

[2] You would probably not be surprised at all to know how many lawyers and judges are actually vampires, ghouls, and worse.

"*Its* daughter." Blake looked like he might go full-Exorcist on me at that quip. I put up my hands. "I'm not talking to him, Blake."

"You killed –"

"Yes!" I finally lost it. I started marching toward Blake, and without realizing it drew the Very Long Knife and started waving it around for emphasis. "Yes, I did. I killed her after she ate – and took the form of – two convention goers. *Paying* convention goers. And she was about to kill another one, which – even though I haven't read it recently – I'm pretty sure is against the Con Accords. So you can tell Cthulhu to shove it up his –"

On the last bit I apparently got a bit too close to Blake with the huge knife. I barely saw him move – he was that fast. I just blinked, and in the middle part of open-close-open I somehow went from upright and waving a long blade to flat on my back with the weapon jammed into the nearest wall. Blake had me in a wrist lock, too, and he twisted my hand hard enough I thought the little bones there would pop right through the skin.

I didn't even think about fighting back. Remember all that stuff about how hard it was for nerds when I was a kid (and we had to walk uphill in the snow to get to our Nintendos!)? Eventually I got tired of getting the tar kicked out of me and started taking martial arts – and I do mean martial arts. Every different discipline I could find, I consumed. I didn't stick around for belts, just for fighting. As soon as I could beat everyone in the dojo, I moved on. Hapkido has always been my favorite – it's why it shows up in a lot of my books – but I also like jiu jitsu, aikido, taekwondo, ninjitsu, and several others.

But even with all that, and even if I hadn't just been knocked down so fast a hummingbird would have missed it, I could tell from Blake's grip – the subtleties of it, the security of it – that I was outclassed. Severely.

There was also the fact that he had done all this one-handed. The other still held the phone, which he now held flat against my ear.

A deep, ugly thrumming sound pulsed out of the phone. The words were incomprehensible – to learn the language of the Great Old One would be to flirt with madness (plus it's really hard). But I still got the sense of it.

YOU HAVE DESTROYED MY YOUNGLING.

The anger I'd felt before was still there, burning in my gut. Blake had me locked down, so I guess I figured venting on a Great Old One would be safe. He wasn't there, right? Just on the phone. That's the secret to life in the twenty-first century: the farther away someone is from you physically, the more of a douche-mobile you can be to them.

"She broke the Treaty," I snarled. "She was going around sucking people up. And she had terrible taste in costumes."

YOU _DARE_? BREAKING BAD _IS A MASTERPIECE OF_ –

"Tell it to the stars, Octopussy."

Blake yanked the phone away from me, jerking it to his own ear. "So sorry, Lord Cthulhu," he said. "He didn't mean –"

"I did so!" I yelled. Then yelled again when Blake cranked a little harder on my wrist. Through the pain I hollered. "It's not like she's totally dead! You can't murder Cthulhu's freakin' daughter. She'll be back after a century or so, twice as pretty and three times meaner."

Blake paused. Then he said something in the gargling, guttural language of the Great Old Ones. That surprised me – but like I said, Blake is a complicated guy. Ruthless and conniving, but shallow he is not.

He nodded, then hung up the phone. He looked at me. "Lord Cthulhu wishes to convey that you are only alive because you are a Warden of the Dead Ones. He also bids you take care that *you* never stray out of the Treaty." He sighed.

I sensed there was more. "And?"

Blake shook his head, like he was dealing with a child. "I wasn't totally sure – my R'lyehian is a bit rusty."

"Yeah, I lost a lot of mine after I stopped visiting him. Pretty much all I remember is 'Where's the bathroom?' and 'Blake Casselman likes it rough with tentacles.'"

Blake yanked me – painfully – to my feet, his expression moving from irritated to angry. "Fine. He –"

"*It.*"

"– said *he'd* see you suffer for this. Before the weekend ends, you will know fear and pain."

A cold wave passed over me at that.

Blake shook his head, then went to the Very Long Knife and yanked it out of the wall.

"Think he's going to break the Treaty?" I asked quietly.

Blake shrugged. "How should I know?" he said. For the first time, he looked vaguely tired and vaguely human. Like he almost might care about something. He turned to me. "There are reasons we do things a certain way, Collings. Not just for us, but for you." He waved me off. "Go. Get back to your table. I can't stand the sight of you right now."

I turned to go. He cast a few parting words in my direction. "Don't forget your Religion in Horror panel."

"Three o'clock," I answered.

7

Back to my table. Mom had made a few sales, which was par for the course. I said she was a "nice old broad," which is true. She's also probably "slightly loony" – which actually helps at comic cons, since people think it's cool to see a seventy-year-old woman dressed in full steampunk cosplay regalia. She stands out a heckuva lot more than the seven hundredth elf or Starfleet captain to walk by, that's for sure.

She doesn't always do the Steampunk thing – she also likes to be Mrs. Claus. Though that's usually more an "at home" get-up. And yes, I do mean she actually dolls up that way at her and Dad's house, which is only a few doors down my own street.

Dad is a good guy. He seems to encourage it, though the neighbor kids do think it's a bit weird come Halloween, when they knock at her door and instead of a witch or some iteration of Jason Voorhees they end up with a giggling, rosey-cheeked Mrs. Claus who dukes a handful of candy canes into each of their trick or treat bags.

You might be thinking, "Holy cow, is Michaelbrent the *normal* one in the family?"

Yes. Yes I am.

You might also be thinking, "Does anyone actually *eat* the stuff they show on those fancy cooking shows?"

I don't know. I'm a steak and potatoes guy.

So Mom had sold some books. She sold a few more, then wandered off to buy *Dr. Who* trinkets. She and Dad love *Dr. Who*.

Dad, by the way, used to come to these things as well. He's an author, like me, though he does a lot more academic writing: code for "he's much smarter than I am."

He doesn't come anymore. I'll get to that later.

The day went pretty smoothly. I sold a lot of books, to the point that I wondered if I'd brought enough. Like I said earlier, I'm not *famous*, exactly, but I do have a fanbase. I write sci-fi, fantasy, YA, and any other kind of genre work that hits my fancy – though I'm best known for horror. People wonder how I come up with such creepy monsters.

I usually blather something about hard work and the power of imagination. I don't have the heart to tell them I've actually *met* most of the beasties that feature in my books. The ghost/demon/child-eating thing in *Apparition* still gives me nightmares.

I sold books, I autographed books ("Actually, the book is free, but the autograph costs fifteen bucks, ha! Ain't I hilarious!"), I posed for a few pictures with fans. That last part always made me feel weird. Again, I'm not exactly "photogenic." Cameras cry when I walk into the room.

Some people like pain, I guess.

One "browser" read the first sixty pages of *Strangers* (not the one with grated finger, I put that in my pile to mail to reviewers), then flipped to the end, then put it back on the pile with Cheetos stains on the pages before saying, "I don't like horror."[3]

That made Mom mad enough she actually drew one of her laser guns and pointed it as his back and muttered a very dark, "Pew, pew, pew." For my mom, who is about the jolliest person I know, that is the equivalent of taking a hit out on someone.

Other than Mr. Cheeto, things went well up to the three o'clock panel. In between selling books, I kept an eye out for illicit monster activity (IMA, in the biz). Didn't see much. Oh, they were there, but they were keeping a low profile. I went on alert when a group of Deadpools walked by.

Protip #1: if you see a Deadpool at a comic con, there's a good chance you're looking at an imp. Especially if it's a group of them. Some supernatural creatures fixate on pop icons. I don't

---

[3] THEN WHY DID YOU READ SIXTY PAGES, YOU TWIT?

know why, any more than I understand why some people give a flaming bag of turds about the Kardashians.

At least Deadpool *is* actually cool.

The Deadpools walked by – six or seven of them, and even though I was selling a book I turned at least half my attention to them. Imps aren't really that dangerous, but they do cause mischief that can snowball if you don't watch it.

These were deep in conversation. I only heard snatches.

"… do you think it'll actually happen…?"

"… dunno if the peace accord is a real…."

"… they're bullshitting. Always do…."

"… frickin' vamps…."

I perked up at that. I knew vampires would be at the con – they're at *every* con. But the imps seemed agitated. Not scared, but anxious in a way I couldn't quite grasp. It made my Spidey Sense get all tingly.

"You gonna take my money?"

I turned back to the fan who had a pair of books in her hands. Grinned at her. My grin is nice, in spite of the face that surrounds it. She grinned back and handed over a fifty. I made change and signed both books with my "author signature" – which looks like someone fell asleep while writing a capital "M."

She thanked me and did a little curtsy – appropriate for someone dressed as Belle from *Beauty and the Beast* – and disappeared into the meat river.

More sales. More books. More autographs. More fans (mine are the best!).

Three o'clock.

And this is about when it all starts to fall apart.

8

The Religion in Horror panel was a popular one – people are always interested in hearing about how God figures into the *Saw* franchise. It's a favorite of mine, because I think good horror isn't about mucking around in blood and gore, it's about redemption, about a trip from darkness to light. Horror is morality in its strictest, most Old Testament format.

People eat it up, and the RIH panels are often standing room only.

Oh, I forgot... if you've never been to a con: the panels I'm always talking about are when a group of people get together and bloviate about some area of expertise. That's the theory, at least. Sometimes there's a woefully unqualified person on the panel ("Well, I'm on the C.S. Lewis panel because I saw the poster for that Narnia movie and thought it was absolutely fan-*tastic!*"), who usually makes it hard to say anything worthwhile.

That's why I was happy to see that this panel was full of competent people. Dan Wells (*I Am Not a Serial Killer*), Sean Smithson (freelance horror guy who does pieces for *Fangoria*), a few others I didn't know personally but whose work I respected.

And Larry Correia. He grinned when he saw me, and the power of that almost knocked me off my feet.

You may know Larry as the writer of the *Monster Hunter International* series (though my favorite work of his is *The Son of the Black Sword*). Or perhaps as a gun expert – his website (monsterhunternation.com) gets millions of visitors who come not just for fiction, but to hear about 2nd Amendment rights, gun specs, the benefits of concealed weapons permits, and related things. It generates a *lot* of controversy, which he seems to enjoy – he even embraces the "International Lord of Hate" moniker which some of his liberal/Democrat very-much-*not*-fans have given him.

And yes, I'm gently hinting that you should not try to rob a bank if Larry is there. First, there's the fact that he's like six-foot-eighteen-and-a-half, and can knock down condors by focusing his chi. More important, if you try anything he will probably shoot you with his concealed Desert Eagle, then hit you again with the Mossberg he has stowed up his size 48 sleeve, then after you're down will march out to his car for something *really* dangerous and use it on your body just to be on the safe side.

For the record: my position on gun control is none of your beeswax (though I obviously use weapons in my line of work). There's no way I touch Larry for weapons expertise or for gun knowledge. Which is a good thing, since he works for the Dead Ones, too.

He's not a Warden. He's something else.

But for now, he just grinned and nodded and after I hugged and/or shook hands with everyone else he bear hugged me so hard I shrank two shirt sizes. "Good to see you, Mike!" he said in his "soft" voice, which only shattered a few windows in the next street over.

Not many people call me Mike. I go by Michaelbrent. Not because I have a solid gold stick up my butt – there are just too many "plain ol' Michaels and Mikes" in my family to go by either. My dad is Michael, my son is Michael, I have a brother-in-law and a nephew named Michael, and the list goes on. At least if someone yells, "Michaelbrent!" at the family reunion, I know they're actually talking to me (side bonus: if a person calls my house and asks for "Mike" I know it's a telemarketer and hang up).

Larry often *does* call me Mike, and it's fine. I know him, and his voice is distinctive enough there's no confusion when he says it. Plus, he's a "Mike" (or occasionally "MB") kinda guy – very middle America, who "dresses up" by wearing the nice blue jeans and the flannel shirt that he actually bought in a store other than Walmart. Very successful as a writer, very dangerous for the Dead Ones. But a real earthy guy for all that.

I sat at the opposite side of the table from Larry. Yeah, far away from my bud. We liked to call ourselves the blackhearted cookies in the Oreo of any panel we were on: we sat at either end, talked the loudest, and woe to any creamy little newb who got squished between us.

The seating arrangement was also tactical. Part of Blake Casselman's job as "programmer" is to put undercover Wardens (me!) on panels that might spark "mild controversy." Religion in Horror was popular, so the con organizers had to have it as a draw. But it had also been known to get certain Otherworlders irritated. They never made moves in such a public place, but it made the potential troublemakers easy to spot for future reference.

Larry and I sat behind the table on the podium at the front, elevated a good six feet above the audience: a perfect vantage point to scan everyone as we spoke. He would watch left, I'd watch right, and after the panel he'd give me a report of anyone he spotted.

Again, he wasn't a Warden – but he did work for the Dead Ones, and I trusted his judgment and if he wanted to help out I was hardly going to say no. I'm a kind person like that.

The panel was fun, as expected. Sean made some really good points as a Satanist, Dan sounded very smart, the others were at worst non-harmful to the panel. Larry and I stuck to what we do best: nuts-and-bolts approaches to writing, with a generally positive outlook on others' chances of developing good writing skills (though Larry often phrases his in terms of "how not to suck so much").

The con volunteer at the back of the room held up a green piece of paper: fifteen minutes left. She was young, as most of the volunteers are. A girl who looked like she was maybe still in high school, with the last bits of acne still clinging to a face that nevertheless managed an impressive level of cuteness. She was clearly thrilled to be watching the panel, and it showed on her face.

The next moment, her face was landing on the carpet in what I could only assume was an uncomfortable manner as Blake shoved in through the back door, plowed through her like she didn't exist, and plucked her green of paper out of her hand as she fell past him.

He looked straight at me, and held the green paper up. Then, still holding it up, he turned it over several times, so I could see the back, the front, the back, the front.

Dan Wells leaned in to me. "What the heck does *that* mean? Are they giving us one-minute warnings now?"

I sighed. "No." I glanced at Larry, who was already looking my way. He shrugged, then gave a small smile and a covert thumbs-up: a *have fun with this, sucka* gesture.

"Then what *does* it mean?"

I scooted back my chair. "It means I have diarrhea."

I thought Dan's lower jaw might hit the table, bounce up, and smack him in the forehead. It was hard not to laugh.

"What?" he said.

"Sorry, bad joke." I stood and spoke loud enough to be heard by the whole room, cutting off the gal who'd been speaking – one of the authors I didn't know, so I felt less bad about it. "I have to leave a little early, folks. My tummy's upset." I clutched my stomach and groaned to really sell it, then turned toward the stairs at the end of the podium before turning back to my mic and saying quickly, "You can purchase my books at my table in the Artists Alley on the purple aisle!"

Then I swept off the podium. A few people booed as I went down the center aisle toward Blake. I choose to believe they booed because they were so unhappy I was leaving. Sure.

"The International Lord of Hate calls for *silence*!" roared Larry. Everyone shut up. He amended, "Except for the panelists," then turned to the woman I'd cut off and said, "You were saying?"

I didn't hear the rest of it. Blake was already through the door and I followed him out to the hall.

I didn't bother asking him what was up. A fifteen-minute warning paper turned over several times like that was the equivalent of the Bat Signal going up –

(*I should get something like that. Maybe the outline of a bald head.*

No, that would just look like a spotlight with the outline of a lightbulb in it. Sheesh.)

– and Blake *never* interrupted a popular panel unless it was a thermonuclear war event.

Besides, we couldn't talk about it. The halls were filled with con-goers – fairies and sprites and vampires and dwarves who were really people underneath, normal families complete with sullen teens and screaming kids who were really cosplaying things from the Otherworlds, and a few groups whose identity couldn't be guessed either way. There was no telling who would overhear us if Blake and I started chatting. And even though the average person doesn't process the supernatural, the dimmest mortal will understand words like "dead" and "maimed" and "parts of his body ended up in the sandwiches they're selling at the concessions" – all of which I've heard on my job, by the way.

We didn't want the Otherworlders hearing anything, either. We handle things on the downlow, because one of the worst ways to get an Otherworlder rampaging was to let him/her/it/unsome know that some *other* Otherworlder had already started said rampaging.

So… silence between us. Well… nearly. He did murmur, "How's the sylphilis?" and then I might have heard the words "crotch rot" more than once.

Har, hardy-har.

Blake took me through the main concourse. A few people waved at me. I didn't recognize them, so they were probably fans. I waved back and hoped they would still be alive at the end of the day. Or at least that they would buy a bunch of my books before they got their tickets punched.

What can I say? Man's gotta feed his family.

I also popped a pill bottle out of my pocket, opened it, and dry-swallowed one of the tiny tablets inside.

Blake noticed. "Still using?" he said.

"Your fault this time," I said. Then tossed back another pill.

A few years ago I got into a bit of a tiff with something nasty. You know how in the movies and books and comics the hero gets shot, stabbed, punched in the nards, and then stands up because *BELIEVES* and *FEELS* and then runs a marathon so he can find the bad guy and tear out his lower intestines?

Doesn't work that way. In real life if you tangle with the wrong thing you end up getting your cervical spine fused, permanent damage in your lower back, and chronic pain that keeps you popping enough narcotics to kill Dr. House, M.D.[4]

"You should have better self control," Blake sniffed.

"Your fault," I said again. "You threw me down awful hard."

"Awful*ly*." He shook his head. "For a writer, you really don't know how to use words properly."

"Me caveman. Write books on toilet paper. Already used. Where cavewoman so me make sweet cavebabies?"

Blake didn't answer. That worried me more than anything else had. For him not to take the chance to belittle me... geez.

"What's going on, Blake?" I whispered.

He didn't answer.

We went up the stairs. There was a pretzel vendor at the top, and I grabbed one of the twisty treats, managing to only wince slightly as I handed over a twenty-dollar bill and only got fifteen back.

Ripoff.

Blake still didn't say anything when I bought the pretzel, though he did get irked when I asked for a receipt. I didn't bother telling him that this was a business trip, a business pretzel, a business expense, and so was tax deductible. He knew. And knew what the pretzel was for, so didn't complain.

He turned down a side hall. I followed, taking a bite. I love pretzels, and I'd only need to save a little of it.

The hall split off to an even smaller set of halls. As crowded as the big cons could get – and FanFamFunComCon was a big one, well over one hundred thousand attendees from Friday to Sunday – if you follow the halls to the very ends, you inevitably end up alone. People crowd together – it's one of the

---

[4] Aside: don't try to steal my stash. I only take the bare minimums to cons, and if you *do* try it either I'll kill you or I'll sic Larry Correia on you. You will prefer door number one.

fundamental laws of humanity. Normal people do not crave solitude.

Which is one reason the very worst crimes so often happen in solitary places: because normal people do not commit them. Only the truly evil, and the mad.

Blake's expression told me I was about to see the work of one or the other.

There was no question of our destination: the closed door at the end of the hall. A "con volunteer" stood with crossed arms in front of it. Big enough to juggle two Larry Correias and a bowling ball while balancing a cinder block on her fist-flattened nose.

For all that, though, the volunteer still managed to be a fairly attractive woman.

I didn't know her, but she wore a black FanFamFunComCon shirt with a red stripe that marked her one of Blake's personal retinue. Not really a volunteer after all, but one of those rare normals who saw the World – though I would hesitate to make STD jokes to someone who could probably crush walnuts with her eyelids.

She was a cross between a guard and a gofer, and she nodded and moved away from the door as we approached.

I noticed that She-Ra started to sweat as Blake reached for the crash bar. Not a good sign. The exit sign at the end of the hall started to sputter and flash as though to reinforce the already-creepy sense of the moment.

"Get ready," he said.

We went in.

10

The way Blake was acting, I expected to see blood all over the place, guts hanging like New Year's streamers from the ceiling, eyeballs squishing underfoot.

There was none of that.

Even so, a shiver ran up and down my spine.

The room was small: one of the rooms they used for panels like "Gender Inequities in Underwater Basketweaving" and "The Lost Episode of [INSERT TV SHOW WITH A FANBASE OF TWO HERE]."

No blood.

Two bodies.

The first one lay on the floor. He looked middle-aged, with brown hair that had receded to the point that the bald spot in back and the forehead in front were on the verge of shaking hands. He had the kind of skin complexion you typically see in someone who spends their life under fluorescent lights. I'd guess a banker or lawyer. Maybe someone who worked in a factory that made fluorescent lights.

He was also dressed like the cheesiest vampire ever. Vinyl cape that looked like it had been modeled after Count Chocula's Sunday best, teeth that hung half out of his mouth, at his throat a blood-red "ruby" that looked more like the sticky end of a Ring Pop.

The "vampire" man stared upward. His brown eyes were open so far that the irises were completely visible, ringed by a circle of white like strange twin bullseyes in his face. I glanced at Blake.

"Alive?"

He nodded.

I turned to the other body.

This one was a bit more serious. Definitely not alive.

She was young – maybe early twenties. She wore an outfit – but only in the most technical sense. There was nearly enough fabric acreage in her outfit to make a car cover for Malibu Barbie's Corvette. She looked like she was cosplaying as "Slutty Ninja" since everything she (nearly) wore was black, and she had a black bandana wrapped around the lower half of her face. Not sure where she would have blended in in feudal Japan, but hey! Unless you're a live-action roleplayer (aka a larper), cosplay isn't about historical accuracy.

She lay on her back, spread-eagled: arms straight out, legs spread wide enough that her belt/mini skirt had ridden well past her thighs. Certainly high enough to see the gash in each inner thigh, just below her crotch.

I looked at Blake. His eyes betrayed nothing.

Back at the girl. I reached out and gently untied her bandana.

Her face, when revealed, was beautiful in a wild, nearly feral way. Blond hair that had fallen like a broken halo on the floor around her. A face that managed to be both round and high-cheekboned, like you might see on a Native American or some Hispanics. A mutt of some kind, genetically speaking, and the results had been good ones.

When I pulled her bandana away, her neck had the same kind of gash as her legs did. I rocked back on my heels. I knew those gashes, but even if I hadn't seen them I would have known what caused this.

It was in the way she was arranged.

It was in the bloodless pallor of her face, the blue tint of her lips, the gray of a body that had no doubt once been tan and bursting with life.

Most of all, it was in the fact that my gut told me she had been killed here, but there was no blood to be seen. Not a single drop on the floor. Even her wounds were just gray slits on grayer flesh.

"Vampire," I sighed.

11

I looked at the other guy, still staring up at nothing in the corner of the room. "He do it?" I said.

"We don't know," said Blake. "One of my guys found the room during a sweep. Thank God none of the celebs found it."

I nodded. A few years ago a big name had taken a groupie to an empty room for some quick celeb-doinking. The girl ended up in therapy and the celeb ended up at a rehab center in Malibu. And he didn't finish out the weekend at the con, which *really* pissed off Blake.

"We have *any* information?" I asked.

Blake bristled a bit. "*You're* the Warden."

I took a last bite of my pretzel. "Good bye, my doughy friend," I said to it, "I barely knew thee."

Then I pressed it to the dead girl's arm, noting as I did that she had a tattoo on the back of one hand: a simple star, the kind of thing that any of a million tattoo parlors could put on.

When I pushed the pretzel to her arm, there was a slight flash. The hint of ozone in the air. I nodded at no one but me and then moved to Count Dracula's fashion-impeded brother in the corner. I pulled his sleeve back – noting that the dude had arm hair thick enough to knit a sweater from – and pressed the pretzel down again. Another flash, another hint of ozone.

"Both supernatural," I said.

Don't ask me why, if you touch a supernatural creature with a pretzel, you get a bright spark, an ozone smell, and an outed monster. Not just any pretzels, though; just the soft ones. The gourmet ones work okay, but for my money Super Pretzels get the best results.[5]

As I shoved the half-charred remains of the pretzel in my pocket, Blake said, "We already *knew* they're supernatural. That's

---

[5] If you think this is weird, just give it a couple pages and things will get *really* strange.

why we're here instead of just giving this over to the regular authorities. My question is, did he do it?" He gestured at the guy on the floor. "Or did he just get caught in the crossfire?"

"I doubt he did it. Those are vamp wounds. And he does not have the body or the hair to be a vampire. Based on his arms that only a mother could love, I'd guess he's a lycan of some kind. Can't say if he's an omega, *rougarou*, shifter –"

"I get it. You don't know anything. Situation normal."

"Pretty much." Another glance at the staring guy. "I guess he could have simulated the vampire wounds somehow, but it's unlikely. Lycans aren't usually that subtle, and it's not *the* time of the month." I looked back at the dead girl. "And I have no idea what she is. Humanoid, but she could be –"

I was interrupted as the door slammed open and one of the last people I expected to see walked in.

Dave Butler (D.J. Butler to his reading audience) was even taller than Larry – I don't know why, but I surround myself with tall friends. But he was thin, nearly gangly. He always wore a black blazer over a white button-up and blue jeans, and topped out the ensemble with a John Bull hat. He also tended to walk around with a guitar in his hands, hunched over slightly to minimize his height and singing songs he's written about whatever caught his fancy – often poking fun at his most recent book.

In addition to writing, Dave is an attorney and corporate trainer and general overachiever. He reads things like *The Religions of Ancient Israel: A Synthesis of Parallactic Approaches* and *Deuteronomy and the Hermeneutics of Legal Innovation*, often in Greek or Ancient Egyptian because he likes the challenge.

He's one of my oldest convention pals. We actually used to live a few blocks from each other and would play the occasional game of *Settlers of Catan* or *Ticket to Ride*.

But here's the thing: Dave's a normal. So he shouldn't have gotten past Blake's flunky. I resolved to make fun of Blake for this failure.

"Dave! What are you doing here?" I nearly hollered the words, and I jerked side to side as I tried to figure out which body I should attempt to hide first.

Dave reacted as most people do when confronted with a clearly dead, nearly naked girl who has been drained of her blood in the middle of a comic con while Count Chocula lays in the corner looking like he got hit with the Joker's Smilex gas: he went woozy, then stumbled back.

Then he slumped, all eighteen feet of tallness just pitching forward like a redwood cut down by a grenade.

I lunged forward to catch him. Or, more likely, to throw up my arms futilely and end up squashed underneath him. It's the thought that counts.

"*Quo.*"

When the word was spoken, Dave's tumble abruptly ceased. I was under his tilted body, my arms up and the both of us looking a bit like the picture of the soldiers hoisting the flag at Iwo Jima, if the flag had been a fainting guy with a guitar strapped to his back.

I looked over. And the lights in the room all flashed – just a quick second – as I saw *him*.

12

Everyone who reads sci-fi knows Kevin J. Anderson. Writer of the *Dune* prequels, *The Saga of Seven Suns*, and numerous *Star Wars* and *X-Files* spin-offs... along with about a hundred other books. He's sold something like eight hundred trillion books, which is nearly as many books as there are cell phones in Los Angeles. He also started a successful publishing company called WordFire Press, whose authors include, among others, the very same D.J. Butler who was now frozen at a forty-five degree angle directly above me.

Middle-aged, with an oval face that looks friendly and unthreatening. Light hair, receding at the forehead and temples, a goatee that is always meticulously trimmed. Always neatly-presented, well-groomed. Successful-looking, but not ostentatious. He has a reputation for being a smiley guy. A nice guy. A successful guy. A good writer.

Most people don't know, however, that he's also one of the Dead Ones.

I blinked, so stunned to see a Dead One that I momentarily forgot everything else. The Dead Ones *did* show up to cons, sure, but not normally. Again, their intercession was sort of a nuclear deterrent, so they generally stayed out of things. Only terrifically important events brought them to the cons. And I'm not talking about the guy who played Gimli in *Lord of the Rings* being interviewed by Tolkien's daughter's maid's great-granddaughter.

Big, *big* stuff.

"Why are *you* here?" I said.

KJA barely looked at me. He whispered something else, and Dave went from acute angle to ninety-degree-upright. Another muttered word, and the queasy terror disappeared from my friend's face.

"Uhh..." I looked at Blake. "What's –"

"Shut up," said Anderson. Smiley and nice my ass. He probably used magic to sell so many books, too.

Anderson leaned close to Dave and whispered something in his ear. Dave blinked again, and now his whole persona seemed to change. His slouch disappeared, and he stood to his full height. His face, which normally bears an expression of restrained amusement, went blank of all emotion.

He slid to the side, moving past me in a graceful movement that, again, was at odds with what I knew of my friend. He's not a klutz, but he doesn't move like a dancer, either.

"Hey –"

Dave ignored me. He went to the dead girl, then knelt beside her. I had a horrified moment to wonder what was going on, then an even more horrified moment as Dave leaned toward the dead girl's crotch and then stuck his tongue into one of the gashes in her leg.

I'm pretty sure someone screamed at that point.

I'm pretty sure that someone was me.

"Dave, what are you doing?" I finally managed. "You're... you're *married*!"

Yeah, dumb thing to say under the circumstances. But I've stayed at his house, I've met his wife. I couldn't imagine any world where she'd be okay with Dave licking a Sexy Ninja on the upper thigh, alive or dead.

Plus, ew.

Dave licked the other wound, too, then repeated the motion on the gash on the girl's neck. He sat up straight, then stood. He walked to the guy in the corner. There was no bloody gash this time, so he stuck his tongue into the guy's ear.

"Dave?" Dizziness threatened to overwhelm me. To find out that my friend was some kind of licking necrophiliac was too much. "Dave, what's going on?"

Dave ignored me. He turned to Kevin Anderson, and said in a dry monotone, "The woman is dead. The man is alive. Both are lycan."

I gawked. "Wait, how –"

Anderson held up a hand. "Any hits on either of them? Anything in the girl's wounds?"

Dave shook his head. "I will have to continue my analysis with a full-body investigation, but there are no matches with known Treaty Violators on her wounds." The words all came in that same creepy, expressionless voice.

"Can you tell what subclass of lycan they are?"

"Yes, but I will first require time to process the information I've received."

"Anything else?" said Anderson.

"No, sir."

I barely registered anything past "full-body investigation," wondering with horror if that meant my friend was going to spend the next minutes licking both bodies from head to toe. I think I would have killed myself.

Thankfully, that didn't happen. Anderson waved a hand, and Dave took a huge step back. He remained expressionless, body oddly rigid as he took a position near the wall.

I finally found my words. "Uh, what's going on?"

Anderson looked at me. "More than you know."

"Obviously." I turned to Blake. "You know what's happening?"

Blake looked confused, too – which I found oddly comforting. He looked at Anderson, who was staring at the dead girl.

Anderson cursed in a low voice. Turned to me. "Find who did this, Warden."

"Sure." Still off-balance, I added, "Were you worried I wouldn't?"

Anderson turned his gaze fully upon me. It was the first time I'd really been stared down by a Dead One. I didn't like it.

Imagine you're an ant. Now imagine a mountain threatens to step on you. Now imagine the universe explodes.

I was the ant in this scenario. Anderson's eyes held power, purer and deeper than anything I'd ever seen. I suddenly understood how the Dead Ones had held back the combined weight of the Otherworlds for so long.

I took a half-step back, then managed a subdued, "What's happening?"

Anderson ignored my question. "Could he have done it?" He pointed at the staring man on the floor.

I shook my head. "Lycans are team players. They don't attack each other. Ever. If you're not a wolf then all bets are off, but they watch each other's backs." I squinted. "You already know that, sir. Why are you asking me?"

Anderson shook his head. "I know, I know. It's –" He looked around suddenly, like he was worried someone might overhear us. It was just Blake, me, the blank-eyed Butler, the dead wolf girl, and her lycan friend.

"What I'm about to tell you stays in this room, you understand?" Blake and I nodded. Anderson stared at the dead girl, at the slashes on thighs and neck. "This con is incredibly important."

I had to quell the urge to spout, "Of course it is! FanFamFunComCon! The place where *fans* and *fams* go to have *fun*, so *come* to the *con!!*" Instead, with manly and highly impressive restraint, I simply said, "Oh?"

"The vampires and lycans are here in force. Both royal courts. They're sealing a peace treaty tomorrow night. And...."

Blake whispered something that sounded like a prayer. I agreed completely.

Vamps and lycans don't like each other. They've been at each others' throats for the entirety of their existences. For them to enter into an actual peace treaty was just... unreal.

And yes, I'm using that word in the context of vampires and werewolves.

But what would happen if, on the eve of the treaty, it was discovered that a vampire had killed a lycan? At best, the peace talks would be over.

At worst... war.

14

"Here are the marching orders," said Anderson. He looked at me. "You. Find who did this. Fast." At Blake: "You. You know what your part of this will be." Then to both of us, he added, "And no one finds out about this, okay? The only hope the peace treaty has is for us to find out who did this, and bring them to justice." He looked back at me. "I'll give you free reign of Butler, and I'll contact Correia to let him know the Dead Ones have need of his services, with you as our point of contact."

"Yeah, about Dave." I looked back at my friend. "What exactly is going on there?"

Anderson looked pleased. "You like it?"

"Not especially, no. Is enchanting people to lick the dead just *your* thing, or are all the cool kids doing it now?"

Blake stepped forward, his expression clearly showing I was about a breath away from being tossed to the floor again. "Collings," he began.

Anderson's own pleased look fell away, revealing a cold expression beneath. "Neither, Mr. Collings."

I know. The guy could kill me with a glance. He could turn me into a chicken and make me walk straight into a deep fryer at McDonalds. He could make me listen to *boy band songs played on bagpipes*. And I'm sassing him.

I couldn't help it. I'm sarcastic at the best of times, and fear makes it come out even worse. Plus, there were all those *books* Anderson had sold.

Has to be magic. He's enchanting his readers.

I am a jealous ass. I admit it.

"Mr. Butler has been… retrofitted," said Anderson.

"What does that mean?"

"It's technical. A *layman* wouldn't understand the details," said Anderson, somehow managing to make "layman" sound more like "low-functioning, brain-dead microbe." Blake smirked. "The end result is that Mr. Butler has become a walking repository containing information about all known supernatural species. He can do limited on-site analyses, which you saw –"

"The licking."

Anderson kept on as though I hadn't spoken. "– and he can gather evidence and match it to any DNA samples the Dead Ones have gathered over the years on treaty breakers or other criminals. He also makes my coffee."

"Oookay." I eyed Dave. "So he's part of the World now?"

The World was how we who could see reality – all of it – referred to ourselves.

Anderson shook his head. "No. You activate him with a key phrase, and he shifts to this state. Another phrase, and he goes back to himself. He doesn't remember a thing." He eyed me hard. "So no chatting about the details of this case with your pal."

That surprised me a bit: I hadn't known Anderson was aware of my friendship with Dave. I hadn't really known he was aware of *me.*

"What are the words?" I asked.

"'Gepetto's work begins' activates him. 'Pinocchio is a real boy again' returns him to normal."

I nodded, then froze. "How long ago did you do this?"

"A couple years."

"About the time when Dave wrote *The Adventures of Clockwork Charlie?*" It was a book about robots, steampunk clockworks and automatons – and something of a departure from everything he'd written before.

Anderson didn't answer. I said, "So, you've turned my friend into a magic robot who writes about magic robots and licks dead Otherworlders' thighs?" I waggled my eyebrows. "Is this some kind of Freudian projection, sir?"

Anderson gritted his teeth. "Just figure out what happened here. Keep Blake updated."

He turned and left, just like that.

15

I saw my first dead body when I was eight. My first *violently* dead body in my teens.

Even before I got hit with Monster-Vision,[6] I had an interesting life. And by "interesting" I mean "saw way too many dead people."

It *does* get easier. You don't want to puke as much. You can focus on the job that has to be done.

But each one leaves a mark. As a Warden, I was there to clean things up. Just a mop on the great, gritty Floor of Life. But funny what happens: the cleaner the floor, the dirtier the mop.

This one was no different. I could move around the floor, could look at the body, and I knew nothing showed on my face. But there was a part of me screaming in the mental background, hollering that I needed to get out *now*, before it was too late.

I looked at the man first. Dressed in that cheesy outfit, looking like a high school production of *Dracula! The Musical!* or something. I'd never seen him before.

The girl seemed familiar. Not a friend, but someone I'd seen in the background. Someone…

I turned to Blake, and pointed at the upward-staring man on the floor. "Hey, errand-monkey. Pat him down and see if you can come up with a wallet or ID."

Blake bristled. I held up a finger. "Remember what your boss said." I did my best Kevin J. Anderson impression. "You. Help the amazing and strangely attractive Michaelbrent however he needs."

"He didn't say that," Blake growled.

"Close enough."

I turned to the girl, content that Blake would do what I'd told him. He had my number – not just the fact that he could

---

6 ™, patent pending!

kick the crap out of me at will, but the terms of our contract meant he could all but kill me without repercussion of any kind.

But Anderson had *his* number. And Anderson had given *me* that number. And two plus two is four, so by the transitive property....

I lost my train of thought at that point, but I was pretty sure it came down to "Blake is your bitch." A nice change. I had to stifle a laugh.

Then I turned back to the girl, and the laugh that I'd stifled died a quick, ignominious death.

Yeah, each body leaves a mark.

This one was worse than most – which was strange, considering how bloodless the area was. Even her cuts were empty slits.

Maybe that was *why* it was so bad. The violence had been there, and then stolen not just life but any trace of its passing. Death comes for us all, but it should not come as a thief.

No blood, just a few gashes across arterial junctions. It all screamed vampire. Bad mojo for the peace treaty.

I did find a few brown crumbs beside her leg – the blood hadn't simply congealed, it looked like it had crystallized. No liquid content left, just base minerals that crystallized on the floor a few inches from her knee.

I patted the girl down. Not too hard to do, considering the ratio of clothing to flesh I was working with. I didn't turn up much. Just a card, and two con passes.

Everyone who goes to a convention has a pass – usually hanging on a lanyard around their neck. Those passes range from "I barely get in and you can treat me like dirt" level to "VIP all access and if I ask for your firstborn you should offer me the next kid as well just to be on the safe side."

The girl had two. Instead of being on lanyards, they were stuck down the front of her shirt, one peeping out over each breast. When I pulled the cards out, one was the aforementioned VIP-give-me-anything level, the other was for vendors – the passes they gave to artists, authors, and other people selling their wares on the con floor.

The fact that she had two wasn't all that unusual: I had two myself – a vendor pass and a "Special Guest" pass that let me into everyplace but the few rooms reserved for highly famous and/or attractive people.

But most people didn't have a vendor pass and a VIP pass. The vendor pass came free with a vendor station, and it basically got you into almost everything that a VIP would have done. Why have two?

I put the question aside for a moment.

The only other thing I found was a business card. It was thick stock, clearly expensive. My business cards were nice, but this was the kind of thing that screamed, "I can buy your soul!" Black, matte finish, and a single word embossed in gold letters: "NESPDA."

I showed the card to Blake. "You know what this is?"

He looked away from his own investigation. Took the card. "Nespda? What's that?"

I resisted the urge to close my eyes and count to ten out loud. "I don't know, Blake. I just asked *you* that. Let's start again. Do you know what this is?"

Blake shook his head and handed the card back to me. "No idea."

I stared at it for a moment, then looked around the room. "You finding anything?" I asked Blake.

"This guy is in serious need of a professional waxer," he said.

"Was that a joke, Blake? I didn't know you had it in you." I looked at Dave, still standing motionless against the wall. Processing whatever information he had gathered while licking the dead. I thought I saw his eyeballs flicker, like there were sparks going off in that big brain of his.

I showed him the card. "You know what this is?"

Dave blinked and stood forward, still moving with that strange grace. He took the card from my hand. "I have no knowledge of N-E-S-P-D-A."

"It's called *Nespda*, Dave." I rolled my eyes theatrically.

He didn't seem to notice the joke. Too busy shoving the card in his mouth.

"Aw, geez, are you going to do that with everything?"

The card popped back out and Dave handed it to me. I took it. It was dry, but between all the death and the licking and mouth-examinations, I felt like I needed to burn the card and then jump in a vat of hand sanitizer *stat*.

"There are no registrable traces of offenders on the paper," said Dave. "Though the DNA on the card does match that of the victim."

"How weird, since she was holding it and all."

"Ah-ha!" Blake held up a laminated card on a string. "His pass!"

"Way to go, Columbo." Before Blake could say something mean and hurt my little feelings, I said, "What level?"

"VIP gold."

"Same as the vic."

The door opened then. A pair of guys dressed as Ghostbusters came in. Their costumes were impressive – they even *looked* like Venkman and Egon.

More impressive, though, were their proton packs. Complete with lights and sounds, and one of them had the *Ghostbusters* theme playing from a small speaker hidden in the back. But when they shrugged off the packs, each hit a button and the packs split apart to reveal what was underneath, and what they *really* were.

I had seen them before, but I had no idea who Venkman and Egon really were, or if they were even human. They never talked to me, never so much as *nodded* when they walked in a room. Just got down to business.

Inside their proton packs, each held analytic machinery – both technical and magical – that made them walking forensics labs that would have been the envy of anything you ever saw on a crime procedural.

Dave was still standing near the girl's body, and he stepped out of their way as Venkman approached. When he did, I saw a flicker of emotion on the Ghostbuster's face for the first time. He shot a look of mild disgust at Dave. Fast – blink and I would have missed it – but real.

Apparently the supernatural world didn't like being automated out of a job any more than steelworkers in Nebraska.

I moved out of the way, too. I'd gone as far as I could go with the dead girl (*Augh!* Forget I said that!), and these guys would forward me any further info via Blake.

I looked at the two passes I held, and at the Nespda business card. I handed the passes over to Venkman.

"Run an analysis on that. Let me know if you find anything."

Venkman looked pointedly at the business card. I pocketed it, glancing at Dave, who was still standing there staring off into some beautiful electronic dreamland. "I already had this one looked at," I said.

Venkman scratched his head with his middle finger, the motion slow enough for the subtext to really slap me in the face.

I sighed. It's hard being so loved. "Usual run up, okay? I especially want both these folks ID'd, and I need the time of death to the minute."

Venkman scratched his head again, even slower this time.

I shrugged. "Let's go, Dave," I said. He stepped obediently behind me. I resisted the urge to see if he would Hokey-Pokey for me.

"Where you going?" asked Blake as I moved to the door.

I looked around. "There's nothing in here."

"You don't know that." He gestured at the Ghostbusters – Venkman was taking a skin sample from the girl, and Egon was murmuring an incantation over the wide-eyed lycan male. "They could –"

"Yeah, they could. But I don't want to wait for that. Places to be."

Blake frowned. "You don't have another panel for several hours."

I pointed behind him. A black orb hung from the ceiling in the far corner of the room. "CCTV feed," I said. Then turned back to Dave. "Come on, Gort, let's go to the security office."

I went out the door, Dave close behind me. A few steps into the hall, though, I stopped. Robot Dave said nothing, just stood there like a good member of the Borg and waited.

She-ra still guarded the door, massive arms crossed against her chest, but she was no longer paying attention to me.

I didn't move. Something was making the small hairs on the back of my neck stand at attention. I looked up and down the hall, but there was nothing there.

Even so, there was no denying the disquiet that stole over me. The spot between my shoulder blades itched and burned.

"Has anyone been in here?" I asked She-ra.

She shook her head. "The person who found them, and the ones you saw in the room. Why?"

I shook my head and said, "Nothing. Not important."

She-ra looked at me for a moment, her head cocked. "You feelin' all right?" she asked.

I smiled. "Fine."

I walked away. Feeling the lie. I didn't feel all right at all.

I felt *watched*.

16

We didn't go to the security office. Not directly.

I was heading there, then peeled off abruptly. Dave didn't say a word, just followed evenly.

"I know, you want to know where we're going," I said. Dave showed his agreement by not saying anything at all. "Okay, okay, I give up. I'll tell you. We're going to see Mercedes. If you want to know more, stay quiet." Dave was quiet. I shook my head. "Well, you can't. It's a secret, and you talk too much."

Every con has similar layouts. Not the details, but the same general pieces are always there: a con floor, rooms for panels and workshops, concessions.

They almost all have several places off to the sides, with chairs and tables or at least just floor space – somewhere for people to rest and get away from the furor without actually leaving the convention.

FanFamFunComCon had three such spaces. I bypassed the closest, and went to the one on the second floor. The security office was on the fourth floor, so it wasn't terrifically out of my way – though Blake would have had a fit watching me amble past the signs proclaiming *Zombie Laser Tag!* and *Nerd Speed Dating!* and *24-hour Game Room!* (con organizers *really* like their exclamation points!). "Where are you going, Collings? Get moving!" he would have said.

I almost laughed. Blake all but owned me, so if I could tweak his nose – even in my imagination – I would do it.

Of course, that thought led to just how much he *did* own me.

"And now I'm sad again." Dave didn't respond, of course. I held up a hand. "No, don't cry for me, old friend. Some day I will have my vengeance. I so swear, by the skull of Grobthick and –"

"*Michaelbrent!*"

I was bummed because the word drowned out the rest of my Skull of Grobthick speech, but I was happy because of who said it. I turned away from Dave and only just barely managed to jump to the side fast enough to avoid Mercedes' outstretched arms.

And when I say "jump to the side," I *mean* it: I launched myself to the right, bounced off Dave (who I forgot was there), then flung myself to the left and back and managed to turn "headlong fall" into "attempt at a shoulder roll" with only a minimum of bruising and curse words.

It's not that Mercedes is unattractive – she's actually very cute, with a pixie face accented by beautiful eyes and hair that she cuts in any of a thousand different styles depending on her mood. She also tends to wear brightly-printed dresses that are bookended by even brighter lipstick and still brighter footwear – which could be anything from six-inch stilletos shaped like the *Aliens* xenomorph to purple Wellingtons that squeak as she rushes you like an affectionate linebacker. Hardly subtle in appearance, but nothing ugly to speak of.

But no way in hell am I ever going to let her hug me.

Mercedes' arms dropped to her sides. A ukelele dangled from one of her hands, and the people who had been listening to her serenade them with Hawaiian-sounding versions of *Suicide is Painless* and *Don't Fear the Reaper* shouted angrily at me for interrupting their concert.

Mercedes turned to them and curtsied. "Thank you, kiddos! Don't worry, I'll be right back!" Then back to me, watching as I scramble/crawled back to my feet. She pouted. "No hug?"

"You know the rules, Mercedes." I dusted myself off. "I read *Pretty Little Dead Girls*, by the way. Fantastic."

She curtsied again, then reached to hug me. "Mercedes!" I yelled.

She giggled. "Just kidding, MB. Glad you liked the book, though!" She glanced at Dave. "Are you going to introduce me to your friend?"

I smiled internally. "Dave, Mercedes. Mercedes, this is one of my oldest friends, Dave."

She squealed and, predictably, threw her arms around Dave. Then the squeal dribbled off to something like a quiet wail. She didn't let go, but stared almost angrily at me. "What's wrong with him?"

"He's a robot, Mercedes." I shrugged. "For the moment, at least."

She still didn't let go. Looked up at Dave, who was staring straight ahead into the air a few feet above Mercedes' head. "Huh," she said. She let go, then turned to me and stamped a foot – she was wearing bright green combat boots under a dress that would have looked "Housewife Circa 1950" if it weren't for the decapitated poodle burying its own head printed on the front. "That's not playing fair."

"There's no playing fair with women, Mercedes. You know that."

She smiled at the joke. Mercedes is a good soul, even if she technically doesn't have one.

You may have gathered that she's another writer friend (we writers do tend to stick together – probably because everyone else thinks we're slightly off). And if you gathered that, way to go! Gold stars all around! She writes absolutely wonderful, whimsical, fun horror. I know those adjectives don't usually go together. Mercedes makes 'em work.

I love her work, and I love her as a friend.

But I will never let her hug me.

Because you don't do that to a succubus – not if you want to keep your mind the way it is.

She was staring at me now, and I could see she knew I wasn't here for a social call. "What's going on?" she asked.

I looked around. Lots of people. I took her elbow and drew her off to the corner of the rest area. The people she'd been singing to shouted their opposition. "Don't!" "You just got here!" "Play *Master and Servant*!"

Mercedes blew a kiss at them, then let me pull her away.

I can hold *her* safely. It's just bad if she puts her arms around me. Not that she'll drag me off for a round of boot-knocking: all that stuff you hear about succubi is pretty far off the mark. They're not really about sex at all.

Incubi – the male versions – are definitely horndogs, and the very definition of "non-discriminatory": male, female, old, young, whatever race, ethnicity, crack whore or congressperson... if you're breathing, you're fair game for an incubus.

Actually, you don't even need to be breathing. But they probably *wouldn't* bang a congressperson – even incubi have standards.

Your body is safe from succubi, though. Because what they do is far scarier: they specialize in *emotional* seduction.

The way they do it is pretty nifty/terrifying: they hijack your own emotions. In other words, an incubus will seduce you (unless you're a congressperson!). A *succubus* will wrap you in a cocoon of your own memories of love and affection, and use the power those memories hold to make you her slave.

Interestingly, this means a happily-married man like me is in some of the greatest danger from a succubus. If Mercedes ever actually got her arms around me, she could pluck every memory of my wife, every wonderful moment we shared – the very best times of my life – right out of my head and use them to lead me around by the nose.

Or she could just overload me. People are built to want happiness, but the reality is we can only deal with so much at one time. Maybe in Heaven we'll be retrofitted to handle absolute bliss, but right now if Mercedes grabbed all my favorite memories of experienced love, then packed them in a tiny ball and punted them back into my brain... well, I didn't want to know what that might do to me. I'd be lost, one way or another, adrift in nothing more than memories of my favorite moments.

The succubus: the world's most powerful selfie-stick.

As soon as we were away from everyone – except Dave, who followed us with his too-even tread – I let go of her. "A girl's dead, Mercedes."

Mercedes' hand went to her mouth and she said, "Oh," in a small, surprised voice. "An Otherworlder?"

"Yeah. Lycan."

Mercedes' hand moved away from her face. "Surely you don't think that I –"

"No, Mercedes. The victim didn't have a smile on her face."

Mercedes relaxed visibly, though something still simmered just behind her gaze. "What is it?" I asked.

"If I'm not a suspect, then why are you here?"

"I just wanted to know if you knew her."

"Why would I know her?"

"Because you know *everyone*, Mercedes."

She smiled, but it was weak. She looked ill. I couldn't blame her, really. I hadn't let her grab me out of reflex and an over-cautious nature, but the reality was that other than some low-level singing spells when she performed with her ukelele, Mercedes hadn't used her power on anyone in over a decade. She had married a normal, and they had several kids together. She had elected the life of a human, though for some reason she hadn't lost her powers when she had a child, the way Laura did when she had our first. I'd asked Mercedes about that once, years ago. The look she gave me told me it was a forbidden area of inquiry; that I should let it go for both our sakes.

She didn't want to be "Rcham Bt'Agra, Spy of Samael, Slayer of the Living," the name she had gone by for thousands of years. She wanted to be "Mercedes Yardley, wife, mother, author." She wanted to forget everything that wasn't that woman.

But it never works like that. We can try to put our deeds behind us, but the nature of time mandates that the past will always follow us.

Mercedes didn't work her succubus mojo, but she still had a sense for people, a feel for who was happy and who was sad. It made her a great writer. It also made her someone others sought to be with. And given the fact that the dead girl had been wearing a vendor pass, there was a good chance she had been to a lot of these conventions – the kind of girl that would eventually, inevitably, end up chatting with Mercedes.

"What did she look like?" asked Mercedes.

Wardens aren't allowed to take pictures while on duty. The Dead Ones and the monsters who are part of the Con Accords worry that one of us will sell photos to the *National Examiner* or something. I contend that would work out for everyone – the Wardens will make a little side money, and the Average Joe will believe even *less* in the supernatural.

So I couldn't just flash a photo of the underdressed ninja lycan. Didn't matter, though. I said, "Blond hair, exotic features. Lycan, dressed like –"

"A ninja."

I nodded. "You knew her?"

"No." Mercedes shook her head. "Not really. Just… I've seen her around. I talked to her once. She seemed sweet."

"Vendor?"

"I think so." Mercedes shook her head. "I'm not really sure."

A few of Mercedes' musical admirers shouted at her to hurry up. She turned and held up a finger, *One moment*. Then back to me.

"What can you tell me about her?" I said.

"Not much. The one time I talked to her was a year ago, maybe more. She was nice, but reserved. She never even took off that mask." She laughed, a sound without humor.

"What was her name?"

"She didn't say."

"She say where she came from?"

"No." More shouts from the crowd on the couches. Mercedes started to sidle back toward them. "I should go," she said.

"One more thing." I pulled out the business card I'd found on the victim, and showed it to Mercedes.

She turned the black card over in her hand. "What's Nespda?" she asked.

"I was hoping you could tell me."

She shook her head. The movement was strangely jerky, and when she handed the card back it almost felt like she was trying to shove it as far away as possible.

Mercedes eyed Dave, then moved away. Her smile reappeared after only a few steps, and by the time she was back to the couches she was grinning and singing, a jaunty song about a psychopathic peacock.

I watched her go, then said, "What do you think, Dave?"

"About what?"

"Why do you think she didn't want to talk about what she knows?"

"I have insufficient data to respond."

"Yeah, that's the same way I feel." I started moving again. "Come on, let's check out the security footage of the room."

I moved to a nearby stairwell, and tried to pretend I didn't notice Mercedes glancing at me over and over.

She was scared.

But of what?

17

The convention center had several security offices. One was for processing paperwork and holding onto trouble makers until the real cops could arrive. Several were basically just break rooms where security staff could kick back between walking around and looking as thugly as they could.

The last one was the surveillance room. That was where I was headed.

Sort of.

Good procedure would have been for Blake to call the office and let them know I was coming, and have everything ready for me ahead of time. But the way Blake looked at it, the normals in the surveillance room weren't likely to know or have seen anything useful.

"But what if the bad guy worries they *did* see something useful?" I asked him once.

Blake grinned that cold grin of his. "Then you'll have to solve that many more murders."

He then told me in no uncertain terms that the whole point of the Wardens was to keep anyone else from finding out about the little – ahem – *niche audience* that showed up at the cons; and so letting them know that something had happened by putting them on an investigative alert was a bad idea.

I didn't argue the point. Partly because it was Blake, and partly because I thought he might be right.

Still, that meant that whenever I did something like this, I went in blind – no information, no way to know if I was going to be in danger or put *others* in danger through my actions.

The door to the surveillance room had a card reader, which wasn't a problem. One of the perks of being a Warden was a master card. It was actually just one of the magnetic room key cards for the adjoining hotel (*my* room key, actually, to my very cheap and very small hotel room). But every time I checked in at a con I gave Blake my key card, and an hour later he handed it back and something had been done that would get me through every electronic card reader. Not just in the building – it usually worked on every reader in a five-mile radius of the con. I didn't know whether this was accomplished through magic or tech, just that it worked and that it made me feel rather James Bondsian when I used it.

I lay the card against the reader, and the lock clicked quietly. I opened the door and, trailed by Robot Dave, stepped in.

The surveillance room was pretty much what you've seen in a dozen movies or TV shows – four guys with rentacop outfits staring at screens and watching for Evil Afoot.

Well, *one* of them was staring at the screen and watching for Evil Afoot. One of them was playing Candy Crush on his phone while shoving a powdered donut into his face, one of them had a boot off and was very industriously using a pocket knife to shave bits of callus off his heel, and the third was rocked back in his chair with noises like you'd hear at the elephant Bean-Eating Contest coming out of his mouth. I assumed they were snores, but didn't get too close to the wind tunnel, just in case.

The three awake guards lurched to their feet when I walked in – though the skin-picker almost slipped on the little pile of heel-shards that had accumulated below his chair.

"What are you doing here? Who are you?" demanded Donut Face, bits of pastry shooting out with each word. He sounded enraged, though whether that was because I was trespassing or because I had interrupted his kingly feast, I couldn't say. I just tensed as he stepped toward me.

Before I got a chance to answer, the one guy who'd actually been doing his job held out a hand. Face Full of Donuts stopped in his tracks. Guy Does His Job (I would be great at making up Native American names!) turned to me and said in a soft voice, "Sir, this is a restricted area."

"Really?" I looked around in confusion. "Isn't this the how-to workshop on Self-flagellating Erotic Pinecones?"

Guy Does His Job cocked his head at that. Man of Shaven Foot looked over at the boss, waiting for direction. Face Full Of Donuts growled irritably.

Snores Like Elephant Farts just kept on snoring.

Guy Does His Job (he had a nametag that said "Jimmy," but who needs *that* for a name?) took a hesitant step forward. His voice was still mild, but his eyes were narrowed, and his tone was flat. "Sir, you'll have to –"

"Guys, I just need to get somewhere. If you'll all relax, this'll be over in a second."

That must have been enough to convince Guy Does His Job that I was off my rocker enough to be a threat. He turned to Elephant Farts. "Marty," he said.

Elephant Farts (or "Marty") woke in a thoroughly disquieting way. He went from full asleep to on his feet and totally aware in less than a second. Only certain kinds of people wake up like that, and they're mostly either mothers of small kids, or people who are Very Dangerous.

Marty-Farty was definitely not a mom.

He didn't wait for Guy Does His Job to speak further. Just moved toward me with one big hand reaching for me, the other pulling a black baton from his belt.

Maybe it was getting beaten up by Blake. Maybe it was pent-up stress from the fact I'd been threatened by a Great Old One after killing his –

(*Its!*)

– offspring. Maybe I was more worried than I'd known about the threat to the vamp/lycan accords.

Whatever the reason, I felt myself looking forward to what was coming.

I didn't let that show on my face, though. I shrank away as Marty-Farty closed, and said, "No, I'll leave, just –" in a whiny, high voice.

Marty-Farty grinned as he grabbed a wad of my shirt, then hoisted me up to my toes.

Marty-Farty, in case I didn't mention it before, was *huge*. Easily two hundred-fifty pounds of rock-hard muscle.

That's why I was glad he grabbed me.

Why I *smiled*.

18

Don't grab people.

It's more than just wise words from your mommy; it's actually a good idea when about to get in a fight. Why? Well in simplest terms: it means your enemy has two hands free, and you have only one.

Grabbing does have its place – some good chokes and joint manipulations start with grabby moves. But you don't just go in and grab a hunk of the other guy's shirt to scare him. If you do, and you're unlucky enough to grab someone who knows what he's doing, then this is what happens:

Marty-Farty grabbed me. He shook me. Lifted me.

With my first free hand, I very calmly poked him in the eye. Not hard – I didn't want to permanently blind the guy, but the eye is one of the most sensitive parts of our bodies. My oldest daughter scratched my cornea when she was a baby, and her one-year-old strength was more than enough to send a man in his thirties into a gibbering, whimpering fit of hysterical pain.

So: boink! I hit Marty-Farty in the eye with one finger, then flicked the nail sideways. Not hard. It didn't have to *be* hard. Just a light eyeball-raking between friends.

Marty-Farty screamed, dropped me, and his now-free hand clapped over his eye. The other hand slammed his baton down toward my head.

A scraped cornea messes with your balance, depth-perception, and state of mind. So the guard's attack was clumsy, and I nullified it by slamming the knife-edge of my palm against the inside of his bicep. The baton clattered against the floor as his arm went numb, and he howled again.

I took the opportunity to do something semi-gross, but kinda fun, and *very* effective.

While it was open in a pre-scream, I jabbed my still-pointing finger into his mouth, then hooked my finger sideways and yanked his cheek, *hard*. Marty-Farty could either stumble in the direction I wanted him to go, or have his cheek torn wide open.

Again, a small thing, but surprisingly painful.

There was a tiny, circular table in the back of the room, and I used my finger like a mouth bit on a horse, guiding Marty-Farty to the table and then jerking down until he flopped into the seat that waited there. He wasn't screaming anymore – I really *hadn't* hurt him seriously, just scared him and took the fire out of him – just wheezing and whimpering a little and trying to get his still-numb hand to join his other one over his eye.

I took my finger out of his mouth and wiped it on his shoulder, then turned to the other guards. None of them had moved. Just three open mouths (one with white powder around it), five shoes on six feet, and three expressions that struggled to figure out how terrified they should be.

Guy Does His Job suddenly realized he was armed, and his hand darted toward his weapon.

"I wouldn't," I said. There must have been something convincing in my tone, because his hand stopped long enough to allow me to sit down on another chair beside the still-moaning Marty-Farty. I began rubbing his shoulders. "Easy, big guy. You'll be fine."

"What are you doing to him?" Man of Shaven Foot ("Alan") tried to sound gruff, but his voice cracked. Not sure if he was afraid of me *per se*, or if it was the idea of a mad attack masseusse entering his domain that freaked him out.

"Guys," I said, still kneading Marty-Farty's back, "I'm *supposed* to be here." I put on a pouty face. "And you go and attack me like this? How rude." Marty-Farty moaned as I found a huge knot in his shoulder and bore down on it. "You carry a lot of stress here, big guy," I said, then turned to the others and continued, "I'm here on a matter of National Security. I need to deputize you before I can continue my work for The Man Beneath the Iron Mountain. Raise your right hands."

The three guards looked at each other, then Donut Face and Shaven Foot started to raise their hands. Guy Does His Job looked flabbergasted – even more so as the still-moaning Marty-Farty tried to use his left hand to raise his numb right one.

"Stop! This guy ain't –" Guy Does His Job looked like his head was going to blow up. So did everyone else.

Perfect.

I stomped down. Three hard thuds on the floor with my feet, then a quick soft-shoe flourish for good measure.

Guy Does His Job went for his gun again.

And, again, stopped.

Not because of me this time. It was the sight of the three-foot-tall dwarf who popped his head through a hatch that opened in the middle of the security office floor.

The dwarf had thick black hair that lay in heavy waves on his shoulders. His beardline started so high it looked like he probably shaved his pupils to get ready for work. He wore a filthy t-shirt with the Playboy logo on it, size XXL so it would stretch across his barrel chest, then cinched in the middle with a garish gold belt so what had been a shirt now became more of a toga.

The dwarf saw me, and growled, "Blake didn't say there was anyone coming."

"Does that surprise you?"

The dwarf growled, then noticed the four security guards, who were staring in shock. He probably also noticed Dave, but didn't seem to care as much about him.

"Well, it must be pretty big to –" He broke off, then frowned, looking from me to the stunned guards and back again. "Don't do it, Collings."

"Gentlemen," I said to the four security guards, ignoring the dwarf. "I really will need to deputize you. Raise your right arms."

All of them did – even Marty-Farty, who must have been getting feeling back in the right side of his body. A strange, dreamlike quality had come over them. "All right, repeat after me: I promise."

"I promise," they all repeated in unison.

"To do whatever Secret Agent Michaelbrent instructs, to uphold the letter of the Constitution of the United States, to assist old ladies across the road, to punch anyone who texts during a movie, and to always dress to impress, so help me God, *e pluribus unum,* and this oath has been brought to you by the number '2' and the letter 'J.'"

They repeated it. Word for word. I wasn't the least bit surprised.

I'd put them off guard when I came in. Confused them, then disturbed them, then scared them. Threw in a dash of adrenaline with a short fight. It all created a powerful combination of emotions and physiological reactions that primed the pump for the appearance of a supernatural creature.

Remember when I told you that people couldn't handle the supernatural? That they either didn't see it or rationalized it away after the fact? Well, if you got them in the right mood, you could tip the situation in certain helpful ways.

I pointed at the dwarf, his head and shoulders just above the hatch in the floor. "This is Gandhi, the dwarf. But you can't handle that, so what sounds better to you?"

In a dreamy voice, Man of Shaven Foot said, "Is he one of those spy robots I saw in a movie?"

Guy Does His Job shook his head, trancelike, and said, "No, it's a dog, right? One of those spy dogs they train with nanotechnology to plant computer viruses in top secret military bases?"

I looked at Guy Does His Job admiringly. "Nice, Guy."

Marty-Farty grunted his suggestion. I didn't understand it, but gave his shoulder an extra-approving rub.

Face Full of Donuts coughed out, "Sputnik monkey!"

I looked at Gandhi the Dwarf. Grinned. "Don't," said Gandhi. I chuckled. "Collings –"

I cut off his yell with a nod and a loud, "That's right, Face Full of Donuts. Below this floor hides a specially-trained Soviet monkey. I am a member of the NSA, and am attempting to turn him to our side. So whenever you see me or my tall, quiet compatriot," I said, indicating Robot Dave, "you will see two NSA agents. You will give us total access and support whenever we come in here, and will ignore our discussions with Gandhi the Sputnik Money, because as deputy-trainee NSA agents, you know that anything you see must be forgotten. It's the patriotic thing to do."

The four security guards nodded like their heads were attached to the same string. I gave a last squeeze to Marty-Farty's shoulder, then said, "All right, man. Why don't you go get your nap on?"

Marty-Farty nodded and went back to his chair in the corner, tipped it back, and was sleeping again in an instant.

To the other three, I said, "Thank you, men. Your country salutes you. Go about your business, and remember: there is nothing to see here."

They all nodded and turned back to what they'd been doing. I stopped Shaven Foot and whispered, "The monkey eats feet. You might want to cover up. And never ever ever do the feet-cutting thing again. Ew."

It didn't make a *lot* of sense, but in his highly suggestible state, it was enough to make him cram his foot in his other boot and I knew he'd keep his shoes on while at work from now on.

"Thank you for your service," whispered Donut Face. I didn't know whether he was talking about my super-duper-top-secret NSA work, or the fact that I'd just saved him and his buddies from watching the world's most horrifying medical pedicure.

Gandhi was still glaring at me. "I hate when you do that, Michaelbrent," he said.

"What? Before you had to hide under the floor. Now you can come out anytime you want."

"Because they think I'm a monkey they're supposed to ignore! A *monkey*!"

"You can steal their food this way."

Gandhi thought about it, then clambered out of the hole and to the mini-fridge in the corner. He wore mismatched shoes that looked like they'd been stolen from Baby Gap (dwarves have tiny feet). The light in the fridge flickered when he opened it.

"Crappy wiring," he said to himself. To me, he added, "The electrical surges here are a joke. Been messing up my Netflix feed all day."

The fridge had a leftover Domino's pizza, and he ate what was left – including the box – in three large bites.

It seemed to mollify him a bit. He still glared at me, but said, "Come on," in a slightly less-peeved voice.

He dropped into the hole in the floor. I followed.

The hole was too small for me – way too small. But when a dwarf invites you into their home, you find there's always enough room for you. I didn't exactly change size – I don't *think* I did. More like the hole and the rest of the universe somehow became a bit more... *accepting*. The rules of physics, of mass and volume and relative size, were still there, but simply didn't care quite so much about their jobs in this moment.

I fit. I was still bigger than Gandhi, but he was looking me in the eye now. I wasn't sure if I'd shrunk or he'd grown.

Magic. Wondrous, awesome, brilliant, shocking – all wrapped up in a delicious, slightly creepy, package.

Gandhi waved me to a nearby chair. It was one of those inflatable ones you see in college kids' rooms – the kind that look fun, but turn out to be incredibly hard to sit in because you keep sliding off with a skin-curdling squeak that sounds like two balloons rubbing their nails against a blackboard.

I sat in it, planting my feet as best I could to keep from shooting off the seat. A moment later, Gandhi waved at something beyond my line of sight. I heard a thud and realized he had invited Dave in as well. Dave sat down, too, but not on the blow-up chair. Instead, he just bent his knees and sat on nothing at all, holding himself in a seated posture by muscle and/or magic alone.

Gandhi eyed him. "That's weird," he said. He rummaged under his shirt and pulled out a squashed Twinkie that, to him, was the size of his forearm. Two big bites and it was gone. He belched, then glared at me. "What do you want, Collings?"

"I need to see the CCTV feeds for one of the con rooms."

What, you thought I wanted the *upstairs* surveillance room? Are you *nuts*?

CCTV works fine if you're looking for a murderer or a terrorist, or if you're making fun of that guy who picks his nose and eats it when he thinks no one's looking. But it's not so good for spotting Otherworlders.

There are some, like vampires, whose images just don't capture well on video. Others, like poltergeists, tend to hijack electronics and make them scream and weep blood rather than do what they were designed for.

Sure, if a werewolf rips someone's throat out or a Yeti pees on the wall outside its favorite bar, regular CCTV is fine – though human watchers, again, won't be able to process what they're seeing and will either miss it completely or explain it away as Hollywood effects, which is why *Insidious* came out as a horror movie instead of showing on the documentary channel.

Which brings us to Gandhi. Like all dwarves, he is perpetually hard up for money. All that stuff about them being rich miners is hooey. You ever meet a dwarf with more than ten cents in his pocket – a pocket he or she probably stole – you're looking at the equivalent of royalty. Mostly they have to steal things to get by: food, shelter, clothing. You know how all your left socks seem to disappear? Dwarves.

They *do* live under things, though. Not just mountains. They'll bed down anywhere the sun isn't shining on them:

beneath mountains, yes, but also in storm drains, sewers, and under floorboards.

They don't forge legendary weapons of power, either – but they're very good at tech. They're savants, and can fix or flat-out build anything from a wagon wheel to a Cray computer.

Blake always hired Gandhi to work the cons with him. Gandhi thought they were "partners," though I suspected the dwarf had been roped into service the same way I had – a way that involved little pay and absolutely no "partnership" whatsoever.

Blake paid Gandhi to move into a con a day or two ahead of time, get into the floor beneath the surveillance office, and tie into their CCTV feeds.

"Hey!" you're yelling,[7] "I thought you said the CCTV wouldn't work on a lot of monsters!"

Very true, young Padawan. They don't. Until Gandhi soups 'em up. He hijacks the feeds and runs them through his own setup, and what comes back at that time is pure gold. Even vamps show up on his feeds – though they appear as a black, smoky outline. Still, that's more than anyone else has ever managed to get. Gandhi is a dirty, ill-mannered genius among dirty, ill-mannered geniuses.

"You want to see the CCTV feed for a room?" Gandhi said thoughtfully. "Which one?"

I told him the number. The room we were in was about what you'd expect for something under the floorboards – mostly bare wood, sawdust, conduit, and piping lit by a flickering bulb that hung above the tiny space. But one side of it held a computer desk (again, I wasn't clear if the desk had shrunk, or the room somehow just accommodated it). Four tablets were propped on the desk. Three of them showed different episodes of *Downton Abbey*, and the fourth just had white flickering across it.

---

[7] You should stop doing that – people are starting to stare.

Gandhi grabbed this last one and stared at the tablet. The flicker changed as he watched it, and slowly began to resolve – not really a blank flicker at all, but the CCTV feeds from the entire convention, being routed into this one tablet and flipping past so fast that someone like me saw them simply as a white-gray light.

Gandhi could see them all, though. He could binge-watch *Downton Abbey* on three screens at once, and would still have enough brain space left over to monitor every event in front of every camera in the convention center.

The pictures began to resolve as he concentrated his magic on the tablet, but before they became fully visible to my eye, he frowned and clutched the tablet to his chest.

"Why should I?" he said.

"Because I'm working for Blake, and I need to see what happened in that room."

Gandhi shook his head. "That's between you and my partner. I don't see anything between you and *me*."

I dug in my pocket and pulled out what was in there.

"What's that?" Gandhi poked a stubby-fingered hand at my pain pills.

"Nothing you want, G-man," I said.

"How do you know what I want?" He sounded offended.

I shrugged. Popped open the bottle and spilled a few Norco onto my palm. "Fine. Have one." He reached for the yellow pills. "Of course, you probably won't have the concentration to follow your show."

His hand froze. "What?" he whispered.

"You'll never find out if Mr. Bates reunites with his beloved Anna."

"The horror," whispered Gandhi.

"Indeed. But...." I peeled away several layers of pocket lint to discover the chewy center beneath. Sometimes it pays to have kids who constantly cram stuff they don't want into your pockets. "Behold!" I pushed forward the fuzzy upper half of a Gummi Bear.

Gandhi darted for it. I yanked it out of reach. "Not so fast. Do we have a deal?"

"Yes, yes, just give it over!"

I kept the candy in my fist. "Are we... *partners?*"

He glared at me. "Just for this con," he said.

"You drive a hard bargain, G-man." I sighed as though in pain, then handed over the sugary gunk.

Gandhi popped it in his mouth and belched again. He's an equal-opportunity belcher. Then he looked at the tablet. "What was the room number?"

"287-B."

"No problem."

Without physical motion on his part, the flickers on his tablet slowed as he magicked his way through the images, zeroing in on the right one. I saw vendors, guests, artists, and celebrities flash past almost too fast to see – though I will say I spotted one of the cast of *Firefly* doing something truly weird with a potted plant.

The flickers sped up again, and I saw Gandhi's brow furrow. "What is it?" I said.

"Been through all of 'em," he answered.

"Well, where's mine?"

He didn't answer for a moment, then began chanting, "Not here not here not here *not here not HERE!*" in near panic.

"Hey, Gandhi!" I reached for him. Shook his shoulder. "What is it, man?"

He turned a pair of eyes on me that had gone from slightly crazy to straight-up *haunted*.

"The room's not here," he whispered.

"What do you mean, 'the room's not here'?" I shook my head. "I just came from there."

"No, no." Still looking terrified, Gandhi shook his head. "Not the room. The *image*. The *picture.*" He shook the tablet like an Etch A Sketch, then visibly restrained himself from throwing it against the wall. "Someone got into my system and stole the feed from that room. Stole it from *me*."

He said it like the world was ending; like someone outfoxing him technically was one of those End of Days moments that happens right before the trumpet sounds and everything literally goes to Hell.

I was inclined to agree with him.

I told you dwarves are tech-savvy. That was an understatement. By the time she's two, a dwarf baby should be able to hack NATO's secure databases during breakfast. Industry secret: Steve Jobs didn't invent the iPod, he stole the plans from a dwarf school science project. An *elementary* school science project. Made by a dwarf who, as they say, "had to take the short yellow dragon to school."

And Gandhi was the best of them.

No one should have been able to mess up his system. But someone had.

That meant someone had gone to some serious expense. Serious time. Well beyond what you'd see with a simple murder.

Gandhi shivered.

I did, too.

19

"Okay, G, let's figure this out."

"There's nothing *to* figure out!" Gandhi was nearly hysterical. "Something stole the feed!"

"Right, G, right." I held out my hands placatingly. "But how? And is there anything else gone?"

With an effort, Gandhi looked at the tablet in his hands. The flickers brightened for a moment, and when he looked back at me a bit of his old expression had returned. "Nothing. All present and accounted for."

"But not room 287-B." It wasn't a question.

He answered anyway. "No. It's missing."

"In what way is it missing?" Gandhi looked at me like I also rode my own short yellow dragon to work.

"*Missing* missing. Not there. Gone. Kapoof."

I shook my head. "No, I mean – is the feed corrupted somehow? Is the signal there, but just static?"

"Can't you see?" he said in disgust, shoving his tablet at me, it's jumble of images almost nauseating to watch.

"Not like you, no," I said. "It's running on Dwarfspeed, pal."

He furrowed his brow, and the images on the tablet slowed, slowed... stopped.

The screen was black.

"This is the feed for 287-B?" I said.

"No. It's the *lack* of feed for the nothing between 282-A and 296-C." Gandhi sighed at my blank look. "Each feed has its own information carrying through. Each time I switch over from one feed to the next, there's an instant where the liquid crystals are activated and polarization offset results in a darkened phase output."

I tried to put that one together. "So... every time you switch to another screen, the screen goes black in between?"

Gandhi rolled his eyes, but nodded. "Yes. In Moronland."

I'm a dad. A patronizing attitude has no power over me. I just roll with it. So I nodded and said, "Yep, I'm the mayor of Idiotville. So explain this to me: is what I'm looking at now," I said, holding up the black screen, "all that's left of the feed from 287-B?"

"No, you don't understand. There *is* no feed. It hasn't been erased, it's like it never *existed*. And not just 287-B: everything within a hundred feet of that spot is just *gone*. It's why I didn't notice the loss – there was no blurring or phase shift to put me on notice that there was a hole in the camera feeds. They just disappeared."

"What could do that?"

Gandhi didn't hear me. He was turning the tablet over and over in his hands, and now he squinted and looked at it more closely.

"What is it?" I said.

He went to his desk. Opened it and pulled out a magnifying glass with a light built into it. He activated it, shining it against the back of the tablet. I moved to look over his shoulder – or perhaps his shoulder moved under me; I told you, things are spatially weird in a dwarf's lair.

Either way, I saw what he was looking at, though I never would have seen it with my naked eye the way he did. The corner of the tablet had a small mark on it - one of those tiny scratches these gadgets tended to get on their corners over time. To the naked eye, it was just a smudge. Under the magnifying glass, it was more than a smudge, though hardly terribly impressive:

"You drop it while you were on the john?" I whispered, not quite sure *why* I was whispering, but there you go. It was a whispery moment.

I reached for the tablet, wanting a closer look, but Gandhi yanked it away as he shook his head. "I've never dropped a machine in my life."

I believed him. "So how'd that get there?"

He shook his head. A voice sounded, and both Gandhi and I jumped. "May I assist you?"

I'd almost forgotten Robot Dave was in the room, but he'd risen from his air-chair and joined us, looking down over both our heads (or our heads looking up from under his – dwarf perspective!) at the crack in the tablet. His eyes seemed to flicker. He bent down and, before Gandhi or I could say anything, licked the tablet screen.

"Hey, don't, that's disgust –"

Gandhi's shout was interrupted as Dave abruptly went limp and pitched forward directly on top of me and the dwarf.

Gandhi screamed and rolled to the side. I valiantly tried to catch my friend, then instantly regretted it as his full mass landed on me. My back shrieked in rage, and something popped in my neck, but I managed to keep him from falling nose-first to the floor.

We settled for shoulder-first. Both of us.

We both ended up laying in the dust, face-to-face on the floor, my arm thrown over his shoulder like we were about to have the weirdest pillow talk in the history of pillows. Or talking.

Dave's eyes were blank. Open, but his brain-hamster was definitely asleep at the wheel. Then he blinked, and a semblance of conscious thought came back to his expression.

"Michaelbrent?" he said, and squinted. "What are you.... What the hell haaaaughaughaugh~"

"Happened" turned into a long, drawn-out scream as Gandhi climbed onto Dave's torso. Gandhi started to scream, too – who wouldn't? – and fell off my pal.

Something on the screen must have reset his circuits, turned off Robot Dave and left only Normal Dave (as normal as he gets, at least) behind. And as nice as it normally was to have my friend around, this was less than optimal.

"Gepetto's work begins!" I shouted.

Dave went immediately silent. Gandhi didn't. "Get him out of here!" he shrieked. "He comes in here and messes up my stuff and –"

Dave stood, then looked at the tablet the dwarf still held. He reached for it.

"Dave, that's probably not –"

Robot Dave ignored me, plucking the tablet from Gandhi's fingers. I braced for impact.

Nothing. Dave stayed upright.

"Why aren't you falling?" I asked.

"The tablet seems only to object to my invasive lingual analysis," said Dave.

Invasive lingual analysis. That's about the right term for tonguing things all the time.

74

Out loud I said, "You ever see something like that before?" to Gandhi.

"Get him out!" was all I got in reply. "There's sensitive equipment in here! My life's work endangered because you choose to bring this... this...."

"Robot," I supplied.

Gandhi's mouth slapped shut so hard it made his beard rustle. "Robot?" he said in a hushed voice. He leaped to his feet and started prodding Dave, who didn't seem to notice. "That's so cool! I mean, who is it... how is it... what is it...?" Then he was just muttering to himself as he yanked up Dave's shirt and poked him in the tummy.

Dave giggled – apparently even robots can be ticklish – but never stopped turning the tablet over in his hands.

"Do you see anything?" I asked him.

"A great many things," said Dave. "But none pertinent to this investigation."

Gandhi looked at me, his hand still on Dave's belly. "Can I keep him?" he said.

"It's not a lost schnauzer, Gandhi. And no." Gandhi's expression fell. I resisted the urge to pat his head. Things were already weird enough.

"Okay, so we have a disappeared magical camera feed, a scratched tablet screen, and a robot who passes out when he licks it. Which brings us to...."

"What?" Gandhi looked excited.

I jammed my hands in my pockets, and felt the "Nespda" business card that still lurked there. That and two con passes, now this... not a lot to work with.

The thought of the con passes sparked something, though. I turned toward the hatch in the ceiling.

"Where are you going?" said Gandhi.

"Up," I replied. Dave moved toward me, but I held up a hand. "Stay here, Robot Dave. Help him," I added, gesturing at Gandhi.

Gandhi looked both thrilled and piqued. "I don't need help!" he protested.

"Maybe not. But if you let him help, won't that be just like if you had your very own magic robot?"

Gandhi's eyes lost their irritation. "What can he do?"

"I don't know. Ask him. He's got tons of info, though, and the base he's built from is plenty smart to begin with." To Dave, I added, "Help Gandhi."

"With what, precisely?" asked Robot Dave.

To both, I said, "Find the missing feeds."

"I told you, they're gone," said Gandhi.

"Yeah, but 'gone' doesn't always mean 'gone forever.' Find it, Gandhi. I don't have time to bring you in on all the details, but there's a LOT riding on this. Get me video of what's happened in 287-B." After a moment, I added, "And figure out what happened to your tablet."

"You think they're connected?"

"It'd be weird if they *weren't*, don't you think?"

A moment, then Gandhi nodded. I went to the hatch, and by the time I had it open he and Dave were involved in a very serious conversation about "nematic phases" and "electroplasmetic pulse surges" and a bunch of other things I understood even less.

They didn't say goodbye, though when I asked for Gandhi's phone number he did at least scribble it down on a sheet of scratch paper.

I programmed the number into my phone, then went up into the surveillance room above the surveillance room. The four guards there pretended not to notice me, though one did give a quick nod. "The other agent?" he whispered.

"The other officer remains below for a time. With the Sputnik monkey."

In other circumstances, I would have paid big money to utter that sentence. Now, however, I just said it so I could get out with the minimum of fuss.

The guard – Man of Shaven Foot, who, I noted happily, had kept his boot on and seemed uninclined to start hacking at his heel callus again – nodded and turned pointedly back to his work.

I slipped out of the office with a whispered, "Your country thanks you," then headed with purpose toward the main con floor.

Murder is all about motive. To find who killed someone, you always ask, first and foremost, who stands to gain? Obviously that doesn't apply to rage-killings or spur-of-the-moment attacks. But when looking at a murder – intended, and planned for – that is where you start.

Who stands to gain?

That had been bugging me, since it's hard to know who will gain when you don't even know the name of the person who's died.

And I still didn't know her name. But in Gandhi's lair I thought I remembered something. I thought I remembered where I had seen her before.

And I thought I might know who to ask to find out who she was.

20

The WordFire Press booth was on the way to where I was headed, and I stopped there for a moment on the way. I wanted to give Anderson a status update, and I figured the best place to find him would probably be at his own booth.

There was a line around the WordFire Press area – a long one. Not unusual, considering that some of the biggest writers can often be found there, autographing books and talking about how great it is to be famous while their fans hurl sweaty piles of cash their way.

Me? Jealous? Not at all.

I fought my way through the line, elbowing a few people aside. Three people knew who I was, which was a win, but two of *them* just informed me that my books were terrible, which really took the wind out of the moment. The third didn't mention my books, just yelled, "Hey, author guy! You're mom's hilarious, man!" Then he extended both pointer fingers at me and went "Pew! Pew!" which I found about as strange as everything else that had happened that day.

After kneeing two Captain Kirks, elbowing one Darth Vader, and throwing very dirty looks at a pair of *Pokemon* characters, I finally made it to the front of the line. The person there – a thin teen dressed as Bart Simpson, and whose mulchy body odor and crazed eyes attested to the fact that he'd been here for hours – wept openly as one of the WordFire Press employees put the finishing touches on a sign that said, "Author Signing Delayed."

I wondered who the author was. Butcher? Sanderson? Farland? I had my suspicions about the WordFire business model, and suspected that at least a few of the other major authors who hung out there might be bigwigs in the Otherworlds – Wardens, Otherworlders, or perhaps even other Dead Ones.

If you hadn't noticed by now, authors tend to have at least one foot in the Otherworlds. You think it's a coincidence that the earliest stories are about monsters? *Beowulf* wasn't a story by some bard – it was a how-to manual for dealing with a monster, written by someone lucky (or unlucky) enough to see the whole of reality.

If you're wondering if that means a lot of your favorite books are actually true... well, I'll say this: there is a reason Edgar Allen Poe was addicted to drugs and eventually went nuts – you would, too, if you'd seen what he did. Lovecraft developed some of his more "charming personality quirks" because when you spend that long among the Old Ones they tend to rub off on you.

And you don't want to see what Stephen King has in his basement.

Back to the task at hand. "Where's Kevin?" I asked the WFP employee.

The employee – a twenty-something girl with enough pins in her face to be an acupuncturist's practice dummy – said, "Who are *you*?"

I placed my hands carefully on several of the books on the table, then leaned forward conspiratorially. "I'm Mr. Anderson's illegitimate son. Can you tell him Mom has herpes again, but she's not sure if she was the 'giver' or the 'receiver' this time?"

The employee turned around and walked away. For some reason I doubted she was going to get Anderson. Which made me doubly surprised when he came out from behind a tall stack of books a moment later. The crowd behind me erupted in a roar.

Anderson raised his hands. "People, please! Just five more minutes, I promise!"

Sounds of despair. Anderson used his happy go-lucky smile to good effect, and soon everyone looked merely sad instead of desperately crestfallen.

As soon as he'd taken all necessary suicide-prevention steps, Anderson gestured for me to come to the far end of the table with him. I did. He stayed on his side, I stayed on mine.

"What is it?" he said.

"That was really impressive," I answered, gesturing at the crowd. "That could have gotten ugly." He didn't respond, and because I'm incredibly bright I deducted that he had heard about the herpes joke.

I told him what had happened, bringing him up to speed so far. He seemed unimpressed. "That's it?"

"Well, yeah, I –"

"And for that you interrupt me, force me to come away from my work?" He gestured at the fans, and his smile was as wide as ever, but I sensed he would rather have been crushing my skull.

"Well, I also wanted to ask if there are any other Wardens who could –"

"Can't even do your job, eh?" The new voice was far from pleasant, and I was far from happy to hear it. Blake had appeared as though by magic (perhaps actually *as* by magic), and now took up position at my elbow. "Probably late-stage sylphilis."

I ignored the oft-repeated non-joke. "Blake, my *job* is to write and sell books."

"Not according to this." He held out a hand, and a scroll appeared in fingers that had been empty only a moment before. A flick of the wrist, and it opened. I didn't look at it. I knew what was there.

A few years ago, Blake found out I could see into the Otherworlds, could see the world of the real. And he also discovered that I had certain skills that would be useful to him. I didn't know what he was really like, and I bought his buddy act hook, line, and sinker. Before I knew what was going on, I was drunk off my gourd and involved in a high-stakes poker game.

For those who don't know me that well: neither of those should have happened. I don't drink *at all*. Not even rum cakes at Christmas. And as for gambling, the last time I did that was for a kitty of Jolly Ranchers at a poker game during Boy Scout camp when I was twelve.

I don't remember the details of the night – everything's foggy, so I can't recall how Blake Casselman set the whole thing up. I suspect that he gave me a magically-spiked drink, and set me up at a game with a couple sharks. Maybe people from Bacchus' court, or even some of the Argonauts – those folks really know how to fleece a guy.

Maybe even (shudder!) Blake himself.

Whoever it was, I ended up signing up as a Warden. And here's the real punchline: I think that signature is actually what makes Blake hate me so much. Because even though I don't remember the night, and even though I was clearly not myself, there was one bit of "genuine Michaelbrent" that slipped into it all.

I looked at the scroll now, and pointed at it. That sweet spot. Right above where I signed in my own blood. "Well, let's hope I can get this all wrapped up by tomorrow at midnight," I said.

Yup, that's right. At the last second I'd managed to insert the words "MbC Does Not Work Sundays" – also written in blood, I might add. And I think it was that – the fact that I'd managed to get something even moderately good inserted into my one-sided contract – that really made Blake rage. If he ever offered to make a deal with the devil, I'd have to tell Old Scratch to check to make sure he still had his pitchfork after it was over. Blake was that shrewd.

Blake snarled and rolled the scroll away again, making it disappear with a snap of his fingers.

I looked back to Anderson, who was still waiting. "Kev-kev, there's something very bad going on here. I could use some backup."

"Based on what?" asked Anderson. "You don't have any information yet."

"Actually," said Blake, "the MMEs[8] just let me know that they can't find what did the victim in, though they guess vampire. And they have a time of death, around ten this morning, give or take an hour.

"Great, thanks." I returned to Anderson. "Point is that someone's gone to a lot of trouble, and you yourself pointed out the timing with the treaty." I looked around. "It just feels –"

"You're not paid to feel, Mr. Collings," said Anderson. He never lost his smile – the paying fans were still there, looking on only a few feet away. "You're paid to get results."

He turned to walk away. "Technically, I'm not paid at all," I muttered.

Anderson stiffened, then turned back. "Costs are tight," he said, and nodded at Blake. "Blake knows that. Speaking of which...." He gestured, and the same employee I'd seen before appeared. Anderson whispered into her ear, and she nodded. Walked down a ways, then grabbed a pair of books off the stacks and brought them back. "These are ten dollars each," said Anderson.

I blinked, nonplussed, then realized they were the two I'd leaned on earlier when talking to the employee. "You're kidding," I said. "You're going to make me buy them just because I –"

"Don't come back here again, Mr. Collings," said Anderson. "This is an incredibly important convention, and I don't have time to listen to you bring me up to speed on your lack of accomplishments." Anderson walked away. "Make sure he gets a receipt," he threw over his shoulder. "He's an author, so those books are tax deductible."

---

[8] Monster Medical Examiners. They were dressed like Ghostbusters, but if there's something dead... in your convention hall... who you gonna call? MMEs!

Blake smirked. The employee waited with her hand out.

I considered just leaving without buying the books.

Then I considered what kind of magic Anderson could command. And the fact that he was still staring at me.

I reached for my wallet. Paid. Pinhead handed me the books and walked away.

"Oh, you might want to know," said Blake as soon as she was gone, "There's a lot riding on you figuring out what happened."

"Yeah, I know." I sighed. It was only the first day of the convention and I already felt burnt out. "The treaty –"

"The treaty will absolutely fail if we don't get a satisfactory answer to what happened," interrupted Blake. "I hope you know what that means to *you*."

Something about the way he said that made my skin prickle. "What?"

He shrugged. "Just that if everything falls apart, the only hope the Dead Ones have for keeping humanity out of the fight will be to admit we knew about the murder first, and didn't say anything because we hoped to resolve the issue and bring the murderer to justice."

"But...?"

"But we failed." He was still wearing his "public face" – harried, messy hair, wrinkled clothes. But the real Blake showed in his eyes. "And the only thing we can do at that point is show our remorse by turning over the one who failed to find the culprit."

"That won't stop humans from being hurt," I said in a weak voice.

"Maybe not," agreed Blake. "Or maybe it will. Maybe it will make the Otherworlders feel better and that will be the end of it." He winked, then added, "I know it would make *me* feel better." Then he clapped me on the shoulder. "Either way, have fun," he said. "Don't let your sylphilis get in the way of having a wonderful day."

He melted into the crowd and I was – again, already, and as always – on my own.

21

"COME AND PLAY" – the words were printed on a twenty-foot-long banner that showed a variety of girls dressed as characters from television, movies, comics, and literature. The banner itself was hoisted on poles nearly thirty feet tall, so the words and the images danced well above most of the other displays, visible to almost everyone in the convention hall no matter where they stood.

I headed to the Come and Play exhibitor space with more than a little dread. I looked down at the books in my hands – *Dune: The Butlerian Jihad* and *Jedi Search: Star Wars Legends*.

I sighed. There was a convention volunteer nearby, and I grabbed him. "Can you take these to Purple-25?" I asked. He nodded and grabbed the books and disappeared. He might actually take the books to my table, he might not. I didn't much care.

The Come and Play booth waited.

Booth babes are something most con-goers know about. Attractive young women dressed in outfits that ranged from "tight" to "not-quite-there" were very typical additions to a lot of large exhibitor booths. Video game companies, major publishers, some of the big comics artists – they all knew the magnetic power of a pretty girl (and, sometimes, a handsome guy).

The Come and Play booth was a waystation for a lot of the booth babes, and several of the professional cosplayers. These last were celebrities of nerddom who dressed up as fictional characters and often got paid for it – sometimes acting as booth babes, sometimes just being paid to show up and make nice with the masses. The girls pictured on the huge banner overhead were pro cosplayers all – people with names like Arya Stryker and Lady Pixela and Miss Sterious.

Come and Play should have been bustling – there were always girls there, chatting and signing autographs. That meant there were always fans there, chatting and having autographs signed.

But the booth was – for the first time in my recollection – completely empty. And I'm not even talking "empty as the space in front of my table" empty – I mean *empty* empty. The lights that normally illuminated the banners were off, and there was no movement or sound within three feet of the place. Even the crickets seemed uncomfortable about the silence.

"You looking for flesh?"

I looked around for the sound of the voice. Found it in a wizened lady sitting at the next booth over – which was woefully small in comparison to Come and Play She was apparently selling some kind of *Lord of the Rings* armor – only instead of plate or chain mail, these all looked to be crocheted out of thick yarn.

It takes all kinds.

"Yes," I managed. "Uh… flesh." I shook my head. "What?"

She gestured at the empty space beside her. "The harlots. You looking for them?" Her expression told me in an instant exactly what she thought about people who looked for "the harlots."

"Yeah," I managed. "You know where I can find them?"

She sniffed and went back to crocheting a bright pink leg greave. With flowers on it. "Why do you want them?"

Because I need to solve a murder, you weirdo.

I knew that wouldn't work. She'd undoubtedly think I was trolling for flesh. Instead, I looked at the booth, poked a finger in my throat, then mimed spitting. "I need to tell the harlots to their faces that their harloty harlotnishness is not welcome here."

The old woman brightened. "They said they all had to leave. Good riddance."

"Agreed. But still, I'd love to tell them what I think of them. All… fleshy things."

"They said they went to the Green Room." I turned to go. The Green Room was where celebs went for downtime between con appearances. They usually didn't let me in as an author – authors tend to bring the average attractiveness level of the room down far too low for the beautiful people's comfort – but as a Warden I had full access.

"Tell them! Tell them all! Fleshy harlots! That's sixty-two dollars." I turned back, confused, then saw she had addressed that last to a customer: a similarly ancient person dressed as an elf who was looking at a floppy shield-doily. The crazy coot with a flesh obsession caught my eye, then added, "Oh, and one of the harlots mentioned it was the *other* Green Room."

A shudder ran down my spine.

The old woman had said it with the wrong inflection. It wasn't the other Green Room.

It was the *Other* Green Room.

22

"If you're going to the Other Green Room, you might want to take backup," boomed a voice behind me.

I turned and saw Larry Correia standing there, big as life and dressed in a black trenchcoat that nearly merited "cape" status. Normally that'd be enough to coax a smile out of me, but right now all I managed was a nod and a quiet, "Yeah."

He grinned, then opened his trenchcoat for me.

No, Larry's not a NY Times-bestselling author who moonlights as a flasher. When he opened the trenchcoat, he was showing off his big guns.

That sounded weird. Forget I said that.

I think I mentioned earlier that I'd get around to Larry's connection to the World. In "regular" life he's an author, a gun enthusiast (or gun nut, depending on your viewpoint), and the International Lord of Hate.

In the World he is one of the top supernatural arms dealers around.

No one knows how Larry entered the World. I've met his wife, and I don't think she was anything supernatural, so an STD was out. But there aren't a lot of other ways for a mortal to enter the World, short of magic use. And Larry was definitely not a magic-user – he veered more toward "blowy uppy" than "wandy incantationy."

I don't think *anyone* knew how he got his first look into the realm beyond the real. If you asked him about it, you got a steely look and a very pointed tour of the features of his newest firearm. To say "sore point" was an understatement.

Whatever the reason, he *was* in the World, and he made some of the coolest weapons around, good for killing anything with or without a pulse. He was a freelance contractor, but he had a standing retainer with the Dead Ones.

"What do you think?" he asked as I stared at what was under his trenchcoat.

All I could manage at first was, "It's beautiful, man." I pointed. "But what's that knobby thing?"

He slapped my hand away. "Don't touch that! It's primed and could go off if you handle it wrong."

Magic guns. All kinds of them hung from a plethora of straps beneath the coat. Large ones, small ones, long ones, short ones. Ones that glowed and ones that seemed to suck light *into* them. One under his arm looked a bit like a lava lamp with a trigger, what appeared to be an Area 51-style alien fetus hanging in the middle of it.

"What's that?" I asked. "And that? And that? And that?" I pointed at a pointy thing; a metal thing; a round, silver thing; and a spoonlike thing.

"Ectoplasmic renderer. Crystal focus blaster. Toy for my kids. Spoon." I cocked my head at that last, and he pulled the spoon off its leather thong and a yogurt out of one of his pockets. "You think I got my fabulous physique without eating right?"

"Concession's out of pizza and hot dogs, eh?"

"Damn right."

He shoved an unhappy spoonful of yogurt in his mouth, then yanked one of the guns off its holder and handed it over. It had a ring of LED lights around the barrel, but there was no hole in the muzzle. It was just a solid block of something. And on close inspection, the trigger was a piece of the gun's body – not a separate mechanism, but an unmoving part of the gun's frame.

"What the heck is this, a toy?"

"It's all you can handle." Larry grinned, then the grin soured with the next spoonful of yogurt. "Gonna have to tell Bridget I hate peach."

"How do I shoot it? The trigger's superglued."

Larry leaned in and his smile widened: a kid with his coolest toys. "You *order* it to shoot. Just whisper 'fire' and point it at something you want dead... then take cover."

The gun had a belt clip, and even though it really *did* look like a toy, I hung it at my waist with a great deal of care. If anything, Larry tends to *understate* his weapons' destructive power.

A few people looked at us during the exchange – we *were* on the con floor, after all. But few seemed to care, beyond the occasional rude comment about the poor quality of our cosplay. At least *that* part of being a Warden was easy: just pretend you're playacting, and you can get away with a *lot*.

Larry gestured with the spoon. "Shall we go?"

I nodded, even though my entire body wanted to run away and hide. We began our swim through the meat river, though I have to admit it was much easier with someone Larry's size clearing the way.

The Green Room is where the celebs go. The *Other Green Room* is where there be monsters. It's part of the Con Accords – a room where creatures from the World can take off their faces and just let their hairy, slimy, tentacley, whatevery selves hang out for a few minutes. Something of a pressure release valve.

It's actually kinda cool in a way: all kinds of monsters congregate in the Other Green Room, many of them natural enemies. In spite of this, there's never been a single recorded monster-on-monster violent incident in one of the Other Green Rooms.

Which is also kinda sad: what kind of world is it where the monsters can figure out how to get along for a few hours – but we humans still haven't managed something like that?

Speaking of humans, the monsters are at cease-fire status in the Other Green Rooms, even more so than at the cons in general. There are magical and political protections in place to guarantee it, though they've never been invoked to my knowledge.

Humans, though, do not fall under that protection. If you're a normal and you venture into the Other Green Room... the Con Accords has a specific exemption for anyone who does that, referring to this not as "treaty violation" but rather the equivalent of someone getting out of their car when passing through a wildlife sanctuary: you don't punish the animals when stupid people wander into their home.

Larry and I tromped up to the top floor of the convention center – passing as always the posters (*Tattoos of Tattoine! Nerd Speed Dating! Zombie Apocalypse Raffle Under the Stars!* Exclamation points everywhere!) and then proceeding down dingier and dingier corridors until we reached *the* door.

There was no guard. The celeb Green Room had people posted outside to make sure you didn't go in unless you were supposed to. The Other Green Room just relied on a spell: a cold spot right in front of the door that was frigid enough you had to really *want* to get past it for it to be worth the trouble.

I pushed through, gritting my teeth so Larry wouldn't see me shiver because Manly Doesn't Cold.

I pushed open the door.

Went in.

Prayed.

23

I will not describe what was in the room – even if I could do it justice, you wouldn't believe me. I will mention the smell, though: it was like a zoo took a dump on a skunk.

I'm not judging – a lot of the things in here were slimy, hairy, moldy, rotting, or all of the above. No surprise that it would be a bit gamey in here. Still, it was bad enough that I almost stumbled back into Larry.

"Easy, hoss," he muttered.

I grunted. "Sorry, Little Joe."

I tried to imagine I was just dealing with my youngest's stinkiest diaper and pushed through it.

The other thing I'll mention: the silence. Every trace of sound died away from the room when Larry and I entered. They say "silence of the tomb," but it has a whole other meaning when you're staring at some things that clearly died a few centuries ago. And, more to the point, when they're staring back at you.

One of the things slithered my way. It looked like a hairy slug with mange, with a bunch of snakes sticking out of its head/frontal area. I'd never seen something like this before, and I wished Robot Dave was here to lick the thing so he could tell me what it was.

"Norp slorp thorp dorp," said the thing. It sounded like two people with postnasal drip humping in a sewer.

"Yeah," I said. I tried to push past, but a mummy stood and walked ponderously over.

"He doesn't like you," said the mummy, gesturing at the slug.

"I'm sorry."

"I don't like you, either."

"Are you wanted men who carry the death sentence on twelve systems?" Larry guffawed at the *Star Wars* reference, but the mummy didn't seem amused. It took a step toward me and started mumbling something distinctly curse-sounding.

Mummy's curses never end well for the cursee, so I grabbed for my Hasbro Monster Shooter.

Larry was much faster. Much *much* faster. Before I'd even touched the plastic stock, he had what looked like a five-barreled shotgun resting on the mummy's head. Unlike my gun, his was made of cold steel and bore a distinctly unpleasant look.

"Don't," was all he said.

"You wouldn't dare," answered the mummy. Its jaw sagged off its hinges in shock – literally.

Larry just pressed the Shotgun King a little harder against the Otherworlder's face. He spared a sideways glance at me, then said, "Aren't you glad Anderson sent me your way?"

That was a surprise. I almost said, "*Kevin* Anderson?" Then realized it wasn't simple kindness that motivated the Dead One: I'd probably be billed for Larry's services, with a markup for a finder's fee.

I looked around.

"Hairy, hairy, slimy, something-I-can't-describe, hairy, hairy, tentacles," I muttered as I looked around the room. Then finished, "Ah! Flesh!"

The cosplayers and booth babes who should have been manning Come and Play were sitting in a dark corner of the room, huddled together in a mass. Even so, I almost didn't spot them. They looked *very* different.

I wonder if the average nerd would be so interested in hugging a scantily-clad Sailor Moon who was hiding two extra limbs and looked like a seasick roach under the makeup? Because that was the *best* looking of them. I only spotted them because I recognized several of the costumes they were wearing from the banner above their exhibitor space.

Actually, one of them looked significantly better than the others: a Wampus cat. Wampus cats are descendents of a woman cursed by an aboriginal tribe to become half human, half cat. She looked like the other Wamps I'd seen: languid and elegant and strangely sensual. I singled her out and addressed myself to her, not so much because I'm shallow and attracted to cat-flesh, but because she was one of the few at the table with an actual face I could talk to.

I also recognized her from the Come and Play banner. "Pixela?" I asked. Lady Pixela was one of the bigwigs of cosplay, with hundreds of thousands of fans willing to pay to see her dress up as anything from a fairy princess to Freddy Kreuger's hot sister. I'd actually become aware of Pixela through my sister, who was a fan, and I kind of liked her on principle. Where a lot of booth babes were stick-thin girls with overstuffed cleavage, Pixela had real-seeming curves and seemed more like a legit nerd girl having fun playing dress-up than someone just cashing in on the very real combination of low self-esteem and sexual desperation that afflicts some in nerddom. (I'm not judging. I'd been there.)

Pixela may have been a legit nerd, but she definitely *wasn't* merely a girl. She looked at me through dangerously-slitted eyes. They flicked over my shoulder to where Larry was still stuck in his standoff with the mummy, and narrowed still further.

"What business have you here, human?" Her voice was a pur, every bit as leisurely and dangerous as the rest of her.

"I need to ask about one of the girls you work with."

"The dead one."

It wasn't a question. Apparently we hadn't managed to keep this as under wraps as we hoped. I covered my surprise with a nod. "Yeah.

"Yessss...." Her voice trailed off with a hiss, and I realized she – and, from what I could tell, the rest of the babes – was hammered. There was an open pot of something that looked like simmering socks, and as I watched, the roach babe slurped one of them up and then sighed and started looking at her forearm as though it contained the secrets of the universe.

Pixela leaned forward. "What do you wish to know, human?"

"Her name, for starters."

Pixela shrugged. "We knew her only as Prostitute Ninja. Sometimes she appeared as Schoolgirl Phantom of the Opera." She ran a paw over her features. "Always masked. Always... elusive." She ran a pink tongue over her canines.

"She have any friends? Relatives? Stalkers?"

Pixela shook her head and then began to lick the fur on the back of her paw. She was clearly under the influence of the sockpot as well, but more under control than the others. "None of these, my treat. She was ever alone, even when surrounded by admirers – of which she did have many."

"Any in particular?"

Pixela shook her head.

I fished the Nespda card out of my pocket and showed it to Pixela. "What about this? You ever see it before?"

"I know nothing of this," said Pixela.

"You didn't even look at it."

"We do not *truck with that FILTH!*" She roared the words, shattering the silence of the room and making me step back.

"What filth?" I finally managed. Then, louder, "What filth?"

Pixela refused to answer. I looked around, holding the Nespda card high. "Who can talk to me about this?"

None of the onlookers spoke. Some looked at me with undisguised hatred, others stared at the card with expressions that I gradually realized were disgust.

What *is* Nespda? I wondered.

A moment later, I turned back to Pixela. "Please," I said. "She worked with you. She was one of you."

Pixela's eyes caught the room's lights and cast them back in twinkling shards. "Where did you get that?" she finally managed, nodding at the card.

"Off your friend."

The Come and Play girls all reacted as one, drawing back and making various sounds that ran thick with revulsion. A slime bog monster nearby actually threw up. Then ate what came out. Then threw up again.

No one spoke, though, and when the initial reaction faded they all glared at me with open anger.

"If she carried this card," said Pixela, "then Prostitute Ninja was no friend of ours. She was no friend of *any* of ours," she added, taking in the whole room with a nod.

At this point one of the other babes – a ghoul dressed in an awkwardly bright Supergirl outfit – abruptly launched out of her chair. She ran past me with a terrified shriek, blasting through the room. She beelined for the door, though she swerved to give Larry a wide berth – not that I could blame her.

"Hey!" I shouted, and turned to follow her. People don't react to me that way as a rule, so it was a pretty sure bet she knew something. I lunged in the direction she'd gone, then stopped short.

"Don't rush out, my delicious," Pixela said softly.

I didn't look back at her, but said, "You remember something?"

"Yes," she said. "I remember that you should not be here."

The reason I didn't follow SuperGhoul out the room, the reason I hadn't moved an inch in the last few seconds, was because the configuration of the room had changed. Larry still had his gun against the mummy's head, and neither he nor Imhotep had moved.

But everyone else had.

They had moved slowly – I hadn't even noticed it, and I didn't know if Larry had, either. But they were now spread out in such a way that I was completely cut off from my friend. And, not to put too crass a point on it, from all his guns.

Everyone took a step toward me. I held up a hand, "Sorry, but if you want autographs you'll have to come to my table on the purple aisle."

One of the Otherworlders made a slobbery, gruff noise that sounded a bit like a laugh and then muttered, "The one with a humorous old lady in steampunk garb."

His friend, a tall, thin person who I was pretty sure was an aswang, nodded. "Indeed. I laugh with great abandon to look upon her."

"That's my mom!" I almost shouted, but knew that no matter how they felt about *her*, I was in mortal danger. The aswang is a charming creature whose upper half detaches from the lower and it uses its intestines to strangle its prey, which are mostly unborn babies. You do *not* want to know how it gets to them.

As I watched, its waist started to elongate and pinch off at the middle. And regardless of its preferred "food," I got the feeling it was going to make an exception for me.

No one oriented on Larry, just me. I couldn't tell if that was because they knew who he was and knew how well-armed he'd be, or if it was just because I'd been the irritating one with all the questions. Regardless, the attention was more intense than I cared for.

A goblin lurched forward. I grabbed my toy shooter and hoped it was as good as Larry said it was. I pointed it at the goblin – a sickly-looking thing with a distended belly and a bunch of boxes on it painted to look like a toddler's attempt at an Optimus Prime costume – and whispered, "Fire."

The results were anticlimactic. The goblin halted; not hurt, but surprised as the lights on the gun flicked out on the ends of fiberoptic cables. They started to spin like a fan, and the lights spelled out, "Game Over" in red. The noise Pac-Man makes whenever a ghost gets him sounded from somewhere in the gun.

What happened next was a bit hard to process or describe. You ever pop a zit? Don't lie, no one's listening and we both know you have. Ever get one that burst with a bit more force than you were prepared for?

The goblin did that. He turned white, then his already-bloated form distended further. He had time for a short scream of agony, then he exploded in a gray mist of pus.

Everyone fell back. They looked at the greasy spot on the floor the goblin had occupied, then back at me.

"You dare break the rules of the room," breathed Pixela.

I pointed my gun – lights still spinning – at her. "The rules say Otherworlders can't kill each other," I said. "As you were about to demonstrate, they don't say anything about you killing me, or me killing you." I swung the gun in a slow circle. "Next person to move gets it in the –"

Pixela whispered, "Get him, Trixy Cuddles!"

"You people really have to work on those names."

No one listened, least of all Trixy Cuddles – who was a very undainty scab of a creature wearing a Jean Grey outfit.[9] She darted one of her three heads at me.

"Fire."

Head number one did its Clearasil commercial imitation. Trixy Cuddles fell.

Then got up. The whitened stub of her exploded head twitched. Then two more heads appeared.

Hydra.

Trixy Cuddles moved a bit closer. I resisted the urge to shoot – what would that do? Hercules had defeated a hydra by calling on his friend Iolaus to use a hot iron to cauterize the stump of each head he cut off – but I had no hot iron, and I was no Hercules.

Trixy Cuddles took another step toward me. Pixela growled, and moved forward on hands and knees – managing to make the movement as much sexy as frightening, which somehow made it *doubly* frightening – as three-inch claws sprung from her paws.

---

[9] Original Jean Grey, not *X-men* movie Jean Grey.

"Larry?" I glanced at him. He still had his shotgun against the mummy's brow, and now held what looked like a miniature bazooka in his other hand, pointing it at one beastie after another.

"Busy, MB," he said.

I tried to step toward Larry, but a halfling, a minotaur, and an *ammeona* moved to cut me off. The *ammeona* is a Japanese creature, a spirit who can create rain, and a light mist began to form around her.

"Don't, or we'll lose our deposit," screeched a rock monster in a voice that sounded like tectonic plates doing the lambada. The mist ceased, but apparently the *ammeona* could control more than rain, because small bolts of lightning began flickering around her.

I spun wildly, trying to point my gun at all the creatures moving close to me – an impossible task. I sensed motion in Larry's direction, and suspected he was doing the same.

No way out.

24

First thing I did was reach into my pocket. In one motion I grabbed the rest of the pretzel I'd bought earlier and crushed it to bits, then threw it at the assemblage. Pretzel bits flew, and there were a dozen sparks and a dozen whiffs of ozone.

It wasn't a great attack – or an attack at all, really, but it made most of the monsters fall back for a moment. That created a moment of chaos. Even Trixy Cuddles and Lady Pixela – the two closest possible implements of my doom – halted their approaches for a moment, though neither of them had been hit by any of my flying pretzel.

Still, it gave me a moment – and a moment was all I needed.

I shot two of the creatures in the room. They were standing next to each other, and when they exploded I ran directly for the spot they had been standing. I flew through a gunky mist of pus, punching through the hole they had left in the line of creatures between me and Larry. I darted under his arm and grabbed one of the items in his trenchcoat, then turned with it held aloft in my hand.

I thumbed a switch, and the silver ball whirred and lights blinked along its circumference.

"If I go, we all go!" I shouted.

Everything stopped. Larry murmured, "Don't," under his breath, but I murmured, "Shut up," under mine and he went back to swinging his guns back and forth.

Lady Pixela looked at me, and at what I held. "I know that thing," she murmured.

The ball began to beep. "Not surprising," I said. "Since it was developed by a Catholic, Buddhist, and Unitarian partnership and is designed to keep nasties like you at bay." I held it toward her, and took a step. She shrank back with a hiss. "It's got a dead man's switch. I let go of this – like, because you kill me – and it goes boom. And even if you're fire-resistant, the explosive base is silver fulminate, with a combination of holy water, garlic, and wolfsbane built into the shrapnel: a big fire with enough iconic power to destroy a legion of vampires. Might not kill all of you," I nodded at the rock monster, "but are you really willing to take the chance that you're going to be one of the lucky ones?"

The assemblage stepped back. Then the rock monster – who literally had more stones than anyone else in the room – stepped forward. "I'm not afraid of you," he said.

At that point, six Otherworlders leaped in front of the rock monster. A variety of claws, fangs, and ectoplasmic tentacles barred his way. "Don't provoke him," whispered a ghost.

"He's bluffing," said Pixela, but she sounded unsure.

"We don't bluff," said Larry. "Ever." He had more steel in his eyes than in his hands. The assemblage took one more step back.

I turned and lobbed the orb at the door. "Oops, dropped it!" I shouted.

Everything – *everything* – shrieked and dropped back.

Except Larry and I. We dove after the rolling ball. Larry barreled into and through a zombie, which must have been a really old one because it fell to pieces. Something else grabbed for me, getting a hand on my shoulder. I didn't look, but I delivered a spinning back kick and prayed it was something kickable behind me.

It was. There was an "uff," the grip on my shoulder loosened, and then Larry and I threw ourselves out the door.

25

Okay, *I* threw myself out the door. Larry contented himself with a little hop-skip-leap thing that took him beyond the frame, but I did the full-on commando roll, reversing mid-roll and coming up with my gun pointed back at the door.

The fact that my gun still looked like something you'd pull out of a plastic bubble from a candy machine only lessened the coolness slightly.

Okay, maybe a lot.

I came up staring at the empty door, sounds of screams filtering through the cold spell. There was no fire, no explosion, no supernatural flesh seared by religious symbology.

A second later, the shouts ceased. Pixela, the rock monster, and the slime bog creature appeared in the doorway, naked hatred in their eyes.

The stone monster picked up the ball I'd thrown. It was no longer beeping. Instead, an electronic voice shouted, "Time's up!" over and over.

"I told you he bluffed us," growled Pixela.

I hadn't known the toy Larry had bought for his kids was Electronic Hot Potato, but it looked vaguely like the thermal detonator from *Star Wars*, so I had taken a page from Princess Leia's book.

"Nicely done," said Larry under his breath. The rock monster crushed the toy, and he added, "You owe me twenty-nine bucks." Then Larry chuckled. "Though the kind of grenade you described was really cool. Let me run with it and get a design prototype with those capabilities moving forward and we'll call it even."

"Go nuts, man."

Pixela took a step forward, moving from the Other Green Room to the hall. As she did, she changed from her cat form to the curvy cosplayer that so many people adored.

If they only knew, right?

Actually, she'd probably get even *more* fans. While I struggled to sell fifty copies a week at these things. Sigh.

I took a step back as she moved into the hall. "Remember the Treaty," I warned.

Her eyes still had the same cat-sparkle. "I remember," she said. "But you should remember, too: it only holds within these walls."

She went back into the room, becoming the cat again. The door shut behind her.

"Fantastic," I murmured.

My cell phone rang. I held up a finger to Larry – holding up a finger makes you not be rude! – and answered.

"We have found no further clues," said Robot Dave.

"No 'Hi, how are you?'" I said.

"No." Robot Dave had a terrible sense of humor.

"Hey, how'd you get my number?"

"It was in my phone." Of course it was – Robot Dave was just Dave with more monster info and significantly less fun. For some reason, remembering that Robot Dave had my buddy inside him made me feel a bit better. "Are there any further investigative activities in which you wish me to engage?"

"No. Yes!" I added, nearly shouting the word. "Check out the Come and Play exhibition space. Do it fast, too – the girls are all in the Other Green Room, and it might be easier to poke around if they're not there."

"Affirmative," said Robot Dave. "Is there anything specific you wish me to examine?"

That was a good question. And I had no good answer. Sending Dave over there was a fishing expedition in blackest night. Other than maybe looking for the SuperGhoul who'd run away, I had no clue what to do next. "Keep an eye out for a Supergirl," I said.

"I have recognized eighteen Supergirls in the convention," said Robot Dave. "Which one do you wish me to note?"

Another good question. I had no idea what the ghoul would look like in her human guise. "Just... find something," I said, and hung up before he could ask me yet another question for which I had no answer.

Larry eyed me sympathetically. "Rough day at the office, huh?"

"Yeah. And this," I added, shaking the toy gun at him. "I thought you said it was all I could handle. It's just a zit-zapper."

Larry shook his head. "No, I said it was all you could handle. Anderson said you'd be footing the bill for it, so...." He shrugged. "I figured I should keep it in your price range."

Ouch. "How much is it?"

He told me. Double ouch. "Do you want to make a return?" he added. "That way I'd only have to charge you for ammo."

I thought about that. "Can I return it after the con?" I asked.

He clapped me on the shoulder. "Sure," he said. "Anything for a friend. But you break it, you buy it!" He glanced at his watch. "I gotta jet. Panel on Getting the Most From Your PR Team."

He was gone. I barely noticed – though I did register that I hadn't been invited to that particular panel. Instead I had my own appearance – "Getting By on a Shoestring Budget."

I clipped the Monster Blaster (from Mattel!) to my belt, and ran to my next appearance. But after only a few seconds of running – enough to get me panting because, again, cardio sucks – I stopped short.

The same feeling that had gripped me after I left the murder scene caught me again. The same hair-raising, prickly sensation that I wasn't alone. That I was being watched.

And just like at the murder scene, I could see no one else in the hall.

So why did it feel like I was anything but alone?

I shivered. And ran – for more than one reason.

26

Turned out that Getting By on a Shoestring Budget was being held in a room next to Dave Farland's panel *The Runelords Experience*. That and the fact that Larry had a big panel on Getting the Most From Your PR Team, plus the fact that Nerd Speed Dating! was starting now meant I could look forward to a totally packed room.

In my dreams.

Everyone was either geeking out to Runelord lore or learning how to utilize their massive, multi-million dollar PR team or getting their love on. There were five people on my panel – none of whom I knew. There were *four* people in the audience.

Dan Wells was there. He doesn't have to Get By on a Shoestring Budget – his John Cleaver books are incredibly popular both in the U.S. and internationally, so I knew he was just here to support me. Authors are generally a supportive bunch, willing to sit through panels they hate to help someone feel a bit more loved, and I was strangely touched to see him.

I was about five minutes late – the introductions had already started when I ran in. Still, I shook Dan's hand and whispered, "Thanks for coming," as I went by.

"How's the diarrhea?" he whispered back. That flabbergasted me – until I remembered the way I had bowed out of the Religion in Horror panel.

"Fine," I managed. I also wondered how many people now knew me as the Mad Pooper.

The day just got better and better.

I took my spot on the panel, introduced myself quickly. "Sorry I'm late. I'm a writer, and we all know that's Latin for 'generally incompetent.'" That got me a laugh from three out of the four audience members. I think the fourth was just using the room as a quiet place to make some important tweets about what he'd had for breakfast.

I went through the rest of the panel in a funk fugue. Barely noticing the moderator's questions, barely able to put together the most mediocre answers. Whenever I'm on a panel I usually shoot for "second dumbest in the room." It's a low bar, but I figure that if one person is impressed by me, at least I might make a sale and/or fan out of that person.

Today, at this panel, I utterly missed that goal. First dumbest by a mile.

I was too busy mulling over what I'd seen and heard. Mercedes' actions seemed weird – she'd seemed nervous to the point of fright. I'd have to talk to her again.

The rest, though... I had a vendor pass, a VIP pass, a dead lycan Slutty Ninja, another lycan dressed like Dracula's tacky cousin who was unable to talk because he was in a trance of some kind, and the Nespda card.

Something had been eating at me during the investigation. Not the odd sense that I was being watched. Something more.

I nearly slapped the table as I realized what it was. I'd seen plenty of Otherworlders at this con. Not just during my investigation, but before that as well. Cthulhu's kid, gnomes, elves, faes, a Leshi, a cockatrice... all the usual suspects and more.

But outside the murder scene, I hadn't seen a single vampire or lycan. Anderson had said they were signing a treaty, so wouldn't that mean they were here in force? And shouldn't there be a few lycans wandering the halls looking for friends who had suddenly disappeared?

I resolved to talk to Kevin Anderson about it. He'd be pissed at another interruption, but this felt like something important.

Laughter erupted from the room beside us as Farland told a joke on the other side of a partition so thin you could practically see through it. I like David Farland – nice guy, smart, good writer. But when his enormous audience burst into laughter so loud it overpowered the moderator in our room – again – I wanted to murder him. Just a little.

Not all his fault there's no one in here. There's Larry, and Nerd Speed Dating also –

I sat up in my chair, becoming fully alert for the first time, and said a word my mom would not have liked.

"What was that?" said the moderator, a girl with glasses who looked like she'd just graduated from college with a B.A. in Poor Makeup Application.

I blinked, and started to stand. "I'm sorry, I –" I was about to make some excuse for leaving, but then... you ever have something you desperately *don't* want to say, but as soon as you open your mouth that's exactly what comes out? When I stood to beat a retreat from the panel (as fun as it had been!), I caught Dan's eye, looking at me from the audience with concern. To my horror I heard myself say, "I have diarrhea! Crap." The last part was because I couldn't believe I'd said the first part, but it certainly didn't help the moment.

"Uhhhh...," said the moderator. She wiped her eyes as though she couldn't believe she'd just seen what she heard. Mascara slid across her face in a greasy stain. She now looked like the Joker, which made it hard to concentrate.

"Sorry," I mumbled. Then left.

Dan reached a helping hand as I walked by – worried, no doubt, that I would pass out on the way to the little boy's room and be found in a puddle of my own offal by some unlucky member of the janitorial staff. I high-fived his outstretched palm, then moved out of the room as quickly as possible, trying to ignore the fact that I was pretty sure someone muttered something about "poop boy."

Then I was, thankfully, into the hallway. More laughter erupted from Dave Farland's room. "Bless you, Dave," I said.

Because I knew where I had to go.

Well, I hoped I did.

27

Nerd Speed Dating! was in the biggest hall, with so many costumed people inside it looked like the Justice League had thrown a block party. Chairs ringed the hall, with another ring just inside them. They faced each other, and nerds of all stripes and walks of life chatted with each other to see if they could connect in thirty seconds or less.

The middle ring was for the girls. A few years ago, there would have been about six seats taken, with ninety percent of the people in the room members of the male nerd persuasion. Both rings would have been peopled by exquisitely desperate people.

I sincerely believe that one of the greatest tragedies of human existence is the huge number of people whose biggest fault is they don't recognize how amazing they are. I've never met someone without a great story to tell, never met someone who wasn't interesting if you dug far enough. Even the monsters were fantastic on more than the obvious level – evil, but amazing.

For a long time, the biggest problem with nerds and geeks – myself included – was that they knew without a doubt they had nothing valuable to offer. How does society benefit from people who dare to dream of dragons and dwarves, of adventure and treasure?

No wonder we were marginalized for so long. Not just because society thought we had little value, but because we *believed* that lie ourselves.

Now, however, nerds know different. Know *better*. We *are* the dreamers – but dreams are nothing more than hopes for a better future. Fantasy, horror, and sci-fi are the ways we discuss not what the world can never be, but the way it truly *will* be.

So the people in the room were mostly happy, upbeat folks with the exuberance of shared dreams and the upright posture of people who knew they mattered. Sure, there were a few who looked like this was their last, best attempt at human contact – but you've got those with any group.

I was proud of my people.

Unlike a lot of the presentations at the con, Nerd Speed Dating! was run by an outside party. Ten dollars to get in *And Find the Dweeb of Your Dreams!* The group that ran the event was Sweat Dreams (and yes, I spelled that correctly – say it out loud and you'll get the joke), and there were a group of attractive twenty-somethings congregated around a table full of checklists and raffle tickets. An electronic timer dominated the table, counting down from thirty seconds.

One of the Sweat Dreams girls detached from the group and came over. She smiled a smile from a toothpaste commercial. "Sorry, we've already started." She pouted a well-practiced pout, then brightened in an equally polished manner. "But if you want, late tickets are available for only fifteen dollars! And you've still got half an hour – what a bargain!"

I could *hear* the exclamation points in her sentences, and wondered if she was the company's sign designer.

"Sorry, honey, I'm not here for the dating."

Her smile cracked a bit. The hint of a snarl could be seen behind the pearly whites as she said, "Then I'm afraid I'll have to ask you to –"

I pulled the Nespda card out of my pocket and showed it to her. I hadn't realized what it was until I was complaining to myself about Farland's and Larry's panels eating up any possible audience I might have had. Them... and Nerd Speed Dating!

<u>Ne</u>rd <u>Sp</u>eed <u>Da</u>ting!

Nespda.

The girl froze. A strange look crossed her face, then the smile returned. She bowed, an oddly archaic gesture, then said, "Of course, sir." She held out a hand. "Right this way.

I followed her. Glad I had figured out what the card meant, but still completely clueless about what was actually happening.

We stepped into the hall. The girl looked at me and asked, "Before we go, can I get you anything? Beverage, food? Or will you be... eating there." The way she said "eating" was genuinely weird.

"Uh, no thanks," I said, and hoped the ambiguity would cover everything.

She moved on, and as I fell into step behind her my phone rang. I glanced at the girl. She hadn't seemed to notice or care, just kept walking forward.

I looked at the caller ID, then picked up.

"I have information to provide," said Robot Dave.

"Spill."

"There is no spill, though I did find considerable hair."

"Care to explain that?"

"I discovered an astonishing number of personal hair care products at the Come and Play booth."

"Not so astonishing – girls are girls, regardless of the, uh, species." I glanced at the Sweat Dreams girl again, falling back a bit so she couldn't hear what I was saying. "Why is that important?"

"Though I can make an immediate assessment of supernatural species through my invasive lingual analysis –"

"You've *got* to stop saying that."

"– I cannot distinguish between subspecies of lycan without a genetic sample acquired during their transformative period."

"That sounds like a TED talk." I pressed a hand on my forehead. This was all giving me a headache, and my back was starting to feel the effects of my GI Joe roll out of the Other Green Room. I checked the phone display clock. Time for another pain pill. I dry-swallowed one, then said, "Give me the quick version: what did you find?"

"One of the hairbrushes clearly belonged to a lycan. Given that it lay beneath a ninja sword, I extrapolated the likelihood that it belonged to the murder victim and determined a ninety-two percent probability. I performed an invasive lingual analysis –"

"*Stop* that!"

"– and was able to determine that the hair on the brush did in fact belong to our victim. There was also fur present on the brush."

"She used the same brush to comb her hair and her... pelt?" That seemed gross for some reason.

"Correct. Utilizing the fur –"

"If you say invasive lingual analysis I will find you and cut you."

"– I was further able to determine the victim's lycan subgroup."

My pulse quickened. This might not seem like much, but each different branch of the lycan family has its own quirks and characteristics. Knowing what the vic had been would give me a *much* better chance at figuring out where she had probably been during the con, as well as helping me know about her personality.

"What was she? Omega? Skinwalker? One of the –"

"Lycaon."

I dropped the phone. Picked it back up and hurried after the Sweat Dreams girl, who hadn't noticed the momentary halt and was now a good twenty feet ahead.

My attempt to pick up the phone wasn't helped by the whisper I heard nearby: "Guy who poops," someone said.

Great. I had my own Native American name.

I fumbled the phone back to my ear and said, "You sure?"

"Of course."

"Not ninety-two percent?"

"Negative. There is no margin for error during this phase of an ILA."

"ILA?"

"Invasive ling –"

"Never mind!" I shouted. Ahead of me, the girl had drawn up short and was waiting. This stretch of hall was a bit out of the way, but still quite busy given that this was where the bathrooms were. "Did you find anything else?"

"Further ILA turned up nothing, and after I attempted an ILA on the rest of the objects I was unable to unlock any further information of significance."

"Ugh," I said. Pithy. "Okay, why don't you just... go sell books or something. I'll let you know if I need you." Then I added, before he could mention his tongue anymore, "Pinochio is a real boy again."

Nearby, a Power Ranger pumped his fist and said, "Hells yah he is!"

I ignored him. On the phone, Dave's – the *real* Dave's – voice came over. "Anyway, Collings," he said, "that's why I figure Neoplatonistic *allegorisis*, though no longer practiced with the frequency of the seventh century, still exerts widespread influence over everything from contemporary hermeneutics to the board layout of *Settlers of Cataan*."

Apparently when Robot Dave was in charge, Real Dave just got to have whatever conversation his heart desired. Too bad I had no idea what he was talking about.

"Well, you've swayed me," I said. Because I'm agreeable that way.

"Cool. I gotta go. See you later."

"Most likely."

He hung up. I put away my phone and tried to ignore the cold sweat running into the small of my back.

Lycaon. The dead girl was *Lycaon*.

Lycaons are the big bad of the werewolf world. Some lycans literally change into wolves during their cycle, just big animals with no human thought in their angry little skulls. Others remain bipedal during their shift and retain at least some basic human intelligence. Strength varies, too, as do their weaknesses.

The Lycaons are lycan royalty. Literally. Descended from Lycaon, King of ancient Arcadia and the first true lycan, his direct descendants transform to upright wolves, with super strength and incredibly powerful senses, but unlike most lycans they retain every shred of their human knowledge, awareness, and cunning. Perhaps worst of all, they are one of the only kinds of lycans who can change at any time. Most lycans are either cyclical – like omegas, who only change during the full moon – or require some external stimulus – usually a spell or incantation – to change.

Lycaons shift when and where they wish. You can play chess with one, then he shifts and now you play croquet with a big hairy wolf. Then he bites your throat out. Not because he *must*, but because you beat him at both games and he hates to lose. Very human, wrapped in a big, super-powered fur coat.

Simply put: the Lycaons rule the lycan world. There aren't many of them, either – thankfully, they rarely breed.

The Sweat Dreams girl was still waiting for me, standing in front of a unisex/family bathroom. She didn't seem at all hurried or perturbed that I hadn't kept up with her. Just flashed a smile with more caps than a typewriter and said, "It will be just a moment."

I nodded, trying to look like I knew what she was talking about.

A few seconds later, there was a muffled flush. A harried-looking mother came out, dragging a pair of kids who looked like they wanted to be anywhere but here and were not amused at the fact Mom had stuffed them into Raggedy Ann and Andy outfits, and pushing a sleeping infant whose face was covered in green paint.

"Sorry," she grimaced as she went by.

We waited until she had passed, then my guide went into the bathroom. "This way, please," she said, gesturing for me to come in.

I still didn't know what was going on. I hoped Nespda wasn't some horrible website for people who liked hooking up in bathrooms that smelled like diaper.

I glanced around to make sure no one was looking in my direction. The Sweat Dreams girl hadn't seemed to care, but it certainly mattered to *me* if someone saw me following a girl into a single-occupant bathroom. I'm already Guy Who Poops, I don't need to be *Philandering* Guy Who Poops.

When I thought no one was looking, I stepped into the bathroom. The girl closed the door behind me, locked it, then took my arm and walked me to the hand dryer on the wall. She didn't punch the button though.

Like everyone at the con, she wore a pass on a lanyard around her neck. When she flipped it over, there was a barcode on the back. She held it under the exhaust port of the dryer, and a laser flickered across the black and white lines.

The floor dropped out from under me.

28

It started out as an "AAAAAAAUGH!" but quickly turned into more of a "WHEEEEE!"

Part of being a parent is killing time: there are hours in the day that are black voids, where the chores have been done and school is over and the minutes limp by with all the speed of a sloth stapled to quicksand.

That's where McDonald's and Burger King come in helpful. Laura and I pack up the kids and take them to one of them – both are near our house and, critically, both have those indoor playgrounds where kids get to run around something that looks like a giant hamster habitat. The older kids read, the younger ones scream and play, and Mom and Dad avoid first degree murder charges. Everyone wins.

Every time I go to one of those, I get jealous. *I* never had cool hamster habitats when I was a kid. The McD's near my house just had *food*. And how lame is that?

So when I realized I wasn't falling directly into the earth's core via business-class hand dryer, but was instead slipping down a big yellow tube slide, terror turned to exuberance.

So there, kids!

I didn't know where I was going, but the ride was sure fun. Fun enough that when I hit the bottom, I was more than a little bummed that my fall was over. I took solace in the fact that I landed in a huge ball pit, though, with balls the size of cantaloupes so they were perfect on an adult scale.

I swam out of the ball pit, and here's where things got weird – which, in the context of all that had already happened, was saying something.

First of all, Miss Sweat Dreams was nowhere to be seen. Apparently the floor hadn't dropped out from under *her*, just me.

Second, and far weirder: I was in a bordello.

There was no other word for it – not "house of ill repute," not "brothel," not even straight-up "whorehouse." *Bordello*.

Red and brown were the predominant colors – thick layers of red velvet draped over chairs and desks of dark cherry and oak. Teak floor shined to luminosity. Hurricane lamps sat on mantels and in sconces in the walls, and the walls themselves were covered by beige wallpaper with flowers and stems writhing across them. If Laura Ingalls Wilder grew up, moved away from her little house on the prairie, and became a hooker, this was where she would go.

The only thing this bordello was missing: women. There were plenty of men around: some looking through large books that I assumed had pictures of "the goods," some sitting on red easy-chairs with prostitutes on their laps, some drinking cognac and smoking cigars. Most of the men were middle-aged, but there were a few who were older, and a few teens.

No women.

Prostitutes, yes, but no women.

Every single prostitute was an Otherworlder. They slithered, they slavered. They crept and crawled. All of them wore "sexy" outfits: teddies, bustiers (very few of which actually covered anything remotely bustlike), lace panties, garters in abundance. But the outfits were filled out in ways that would have made Victoria wish she knew fewer secrets.

In spite of the abundance of monsters, none of the humans seemed in the least worried. In fact, not only were some of the monsters perched on men's laps, now that I looked closely I could see that some had their suckers and/or lips planted firmly on the lips of the man beneath them. Others played rousing games of Tentacle vs. Tongue, and one in the corner –

I looked away. Fast. That sort of thing should *not* be legal.

I understood now why I had gotten the reaction I had when I showed Pixela and the others the Nespda card. This was a place where the Otherworlders came – not to feed or even to congregate. This was where they came to do whatever the humans asked. To debase themselves in return for human coin. And though there *were* monsters who would seduce a human for fun – incubuses, for example – the power always flowed in the direction of the Otherworlder. To voluntarily play the part of sex toy... you think prostitutes are looked down on in *human* society? You ain't seen nothing, I guarantee it.

A woman – blessedly human – approached. "And what are you looking for today, sweetie?" She gestured at the men flipping pages of the book I'd seen. "Do you know what you want, or would you like to browse a bit?"

She was older, maybe late fifties, with black hair drawn from her face and held in place by a gold comb. Very classy, which somehow made the whole scene even creepier.

"I'm actually looking for someone specific. Cute lycan, blond hair, kind of exotic looking, with a little star tattoo on her hand. Dressed like a ninja or maybe Schoolgirl Phantom of the Opera."

The madam nodded. "Lani. One of our most *talented* girls, and very popular."

Lani. Finally, I had a name to go with the face of the dead girl.

"Is she... uh... 'on' today?"

Of course, I knew she wasn't working here. She was too busy being dead dozens of feet above. I was fishing – not the sign of a great investigation, but that was all I had.

By the way, for those of you wondering how there could be a big hole and a slide in the convention center: is that *really* the hardest thing to believe about all this? Just trust me when I say that – as you already saw with Gandhi the dwarf – magic makes everything a bit more pliable. Even space and time.

The madam was shaking her head. "No, Lani hasn't shown up today." She pouted. "Which is too bad: she's one of our finest girls." The pout disappeared, and a glint that was half sales pitch, half naked greed, appeared in her eyes. "But not our absolute finest. I'm sure I can interest you in –"

I wasn't interested in having some tentacled monstrosity touted to me. "Sorry, lady. I'm not here to buy." She frowned, and gestured toward several parts of the wall, which detached and began walking toward me: mimics.

Mimics are about six feet tall, broad in proportion. They look fairly human, except their heads. The head of a mimic looks like the inside of a garbage disposal: just one row of spinning teeth inside another. No face, no features. Just a grinding whirl of toothy death. They're often used as bodyguards and, occasionally, assassins, because they have the ability to blend in with their surroundings. It's not perfect: if you look straight at one you can usually spot it, but if you're not aware you can walk past a lamp or a section of the wall without even being aware of the presence of what amounts to a chameleonic rock chewer.

The mimics' teeth started to whir, the blades rasping over one another with a sound like a bunch of orgiastic dentist drills.

At the same time, a short girl stepped out from behind a bar. Her fingertips glowed: a witch. That scared me, a lot. Witches are very mean, and *very* tough. Almost nothing can take them down, and the one thing that can hurt them is something I most definitely wasn't carrying.

No one in the room seemed to take notice of the sound, or the threat. Too busy canoodling.

I glanced at the mimics and the witch, debated pulling my Hasbro McShootsalot, then decided I'd *really* get out the big guns.

I leaned in close to the madam and stage whispered, "Before things get bloody, I should tell you: I'm a Warden."

Now everyone – and everything – in the room took notice.

The madam froze, then nodded at the mimics. They had stopped moving, too, and now they slunk back to their walls and seemed to disappear. The witch slid back behind the bar, but had a bit more gumption: she glared at me the whole time.

The madam had gone rigid. I didn't know if she was gearing up to run or fight. I didn't want either to happen, so I held up an open palm.

"I'm not interested in your little business," I said, trying to keep the disgust out of my voice. Call me un-PC, but I definitely think there's a point where "love conquers all" bows out to "eww, yuck, yucky that's just *wrong.* "I just need some information."

A few people had stood and begun moving to a door that I assumed was the exit. They were hampered by the fact that they were clearly trying to look like they *weren't* fleeing with tails between their legs (in some cases literally).

"How dare you? How dare you come in here and...."

"And what? I haven't done anything. Yet."

The madam's eyes narrowed. "What do you want?" she asked.

I knew I had her. Though saying I'm a Warden doesn't get me far in a lot of places, this was a whole other ball of banana peels. If they hurt me, the Con Accords would be violated. And if the inevitable investigation turned up the existence of this place, it wouldn't just mean her business. It would mean both the Dead Ones and the governing bodies of a good dozen Otherworlders would join together to exterminate everything connected with the place: the clients, the employees, and the boss.

"Just information," I whispered. "And then I get out of your hair and forget this ever happened."

She muttered, "Come with me," then looked at the group. "He was kidding," she said loudly. "This is one of our more eccentric clients. Into roleplaying." A few of the Otherworlders and a few of the humans relaxed a bit. Then a few more when she said, "Sorry about not warning you." She glared at me. "I can assure you it will never happen again."

I nodded. "You betcha," I answered, in what I hoped was a roleplay-esque voice.

Still, there were more upset people/things than not. Until the madam added, "The next hour is on the house, and my girls will get double pay from me, so get ready for a *very* good time."

Sex – or mucus mingling, or whatever they called it here – was a big motivator. Everyone settled into their respective fun zones as I followed the madam. We went behind the bar, and the witch there glared at me.

"How's your sister under the house?" I murmured.

She murmured right back, "I'll see you again, Warden." So apparently she wasn't fooled by the pretense or mollified by the bribe.

"Sure," I said, in a tone I hoped was very manly and brave. The fact that my voice cracked like a cheap mirror didn't hurt that at all, right?

The madam went through a curtain of beads behind the door. I followed, feeling like I was being attacked by a horde of ravening Tic Tacs as I passed through the curtain.

Behind the curtain was a stockroom, and past that sat a small office. Nothing fancy, just a desk, a laptop, and a safe, all illuminated by a plain Jane fluorescent desk lamp.

The madam sat down on the office chair that was the office's only furnishing. She did not offer to find me a chair.

"What is it you want?" she snarled. She opened the desk as she spoke, and yanked a Hostess fruit pie out. She started eating it.

"Some information," I said. "You should slow down on that."

She ate the rest of the pie in one big gulp. Cherry filling dripped down the side of her mouth, making her look very vampy. "I'm trying to quit smoking," she said. "Sugar makes me less cranky. What do you want to know?"

"Everything you know about Lani."

"Why?"

"Because she's engaged to my brother." It was meant as a sarcastic, not-your-business answer.

The madam took it at face value. "Then you probably know as much as I do."

With a moment's thought, I realized the "engaged brother" angle might work for me. What else would a Warden be doing here, if not trying to close the place down for some Treaty violation (and I'd never seen a place like this that *didn't* violate the Treaty in some way). She was hardly going to open up about her business, but if I played it right....

"I didn't know about this place," I said, and put what I hope was the right amount of restrained disgust and surprise into the words. The tone of a man finding out something hideous about the girl his brother loves.

The madam grinned, the first genuine smile I'd seen on her face. "Oh, you didn't?" she purred. Her tone scared me. More when she leaned forward and said, "Then let me enlighten you."

"She was popular," said the madam.

"So you said." I frowned. "I gotta admit, I keep thinking of you as just 'the madam.' Do you have a name?"

She smirked. "Like I'd tell you." She pulled a package of Hostess Donettes out of her desk and as she unwrapped it she said, "The madam is fine."

I shrugged. "Okay, so tell me about Lani."

"She was a popular girl."

"Meaning?"

"Meaning she never failed to make money. And never failed to make *me* money. People lined up to be with her." She popped a Donette into her mouth.

"Why?"

The madam looked at me dryly. "Have you seen her?"

She *had* been pretty. Even beautiful. Not the prettiest girl I'd ever seen – that spot was completely and forever reserved for my wife – but I could understand why people would want her on their arm for esthetic value if nothing else. But.... "That doesn't explain why she's popular. This place doesn't really cater to 'pretty.' What was she?"

"Lycan."

I'd known this, but the secret to getting information is first asking easy questions, and those questions should be ones whose answers you already know. If they lie, you get to show them you know more than you've shared, and it breaks down their inclination to lie further. And the easy, "harmless" questions get them into a conversational flow. I'd learned about this as a lawyer, examining and cross-examining witnesses at deposition and trial. Just never thought I'd put it to use in a monster bordello.

Life is funny, eh?

"What kind of lycan?"

She shrugged. "We don't ask, we don't tell. She could change whenever she wanted, so that narrowed the the possibilities, but I didn't worry about it too much. As long as she could do the job, I didn't care."

"Where did she live?"

The madam eyed me the same way you'd look at an exceptionally stupid piece of balsa wood. "Doesn't your brother know?"

Oops. Thinking quickly, I snarled, "He knows her *human* home, you slut-peddler. But you and I both know she's got somewhere else. So *where is it?*"

The madam's grin was back. "We don't exactly ask those questions on the employment form. No W-2s here."

"How did you pay her?"

"Cash."

"And which of your," again, I curled my lips, "other 'girls' was she friends with?"

The madam frowned a bit at that. "None," she answered, and either she was telling the truth or she was the best liar I'd ever seen. "She came in, she did the work, she got paid, she left. I knew nothing more about her, and I got the feeling she was happy with that arrangement."

"So no one knew her, no one knew anything *about* her, and yet you say she was popular? What was it that made her so popular, exactly? "

"Her rates, and her willingness."

"Why would her rates make her popular?"

"She was cheap. I let my girls set their own hourly rates – taking a small commission, of course –"

"Of course."

"– and the laws of supply and demand ensure everyone gets what they deserve." She leaned back contentedly. "We are perhaps the last and truest free market on the planet."

I frowned. "But you said both you and she made money."

The madam smiled, a dangerous smile. "Yes, I did."

"So how –"

"You ever shop at Walmart?"

A guy trying to make it as an author while supporting a family of six? I felt like I *lived* at Walmart sometimes.

"Sure," I said nonchalantly. "What does that have to do with anything?"

"Lani made money the way Walmart does. She dealt in bulk: she worked more than any two other girls. Even pennies add up when you save hundreds of them. *Many* hundreds."

That made no sense. I'd said Lycaons were royalty, and that they bred more rarely than most lycans. That meant they had small families, and most of them got tributes from other lycans. They were rich – the poorest of them could buy and sell me several times over. Then why did she do it?

I suspected I knew, but I asked the question anyway. "You said she was popular because of her rates and her 'willingness.' What did that mean?"

The madam was still holding the Donettes package. I saw her fingers tighten around it, mashing the nuclear-proof cake slathered in nearly-chocolate-flavored "frosting"[10] to pudding. Her grin widened, and I knew she was delivering the *coup de grâce*.

She leaned toward me. "She would do anything. *Anything*. There was no request too awful, no instruction too foul." She licked her fingers clean, then added with exquisite pleasure, "Tell your brother she was a whore."

I knew she expected me to react, so I did. I gritted my teeth in rage, understanding that she'd told me this as revenge for my intrusion: a proud woman who couldn't stand being threatened without reprisal. She couldn't hurt me – not directly

---

[10] For the record, I have it on good authority that Donettes "chocolate" frosting is made of a mix of carob and ear wax. Also crack cocaine, because once I start I *can't stop eating them*. Nom-nom-nom.

– but she could certainly hurt my "brother" by letting him know what kinds of things his fiancée did.

"Why would she do all that?"

The madam shrugged again. "Because she liked it," she said, delivered in that same smug, nasty tone.

I clenched my fists in mock anger. "Who?"

Her eyebrows rose. "Who?"

Through gritted teeth I said, "Who saw her?"

She waved a sticky hand. "They *all* did, my dear."

I leaned in close. "Who saw her the most?"

She told me.

I reacted in the only rational way: mouth open, a look of ridiculous surprise crossing my face. "Are you serious?"

"As poison." She leaned in close, and I smelled something unpleasant come off her. Maybe too many Hostess snacks without brushing her teeth.

Most likely, it was just the smell of a rotting soul.

"Where can I find this guy?"

Again, she told me. Again, I said, "Are you serious?"

She didn't bother answering the question, just said, "I hope your brother enjoys his new life. I truly do."

I turned to leave. There wasn't anything here for me. I could come back if I needed – try to interview some of the other girls, but I sensed that the madam had given me all anyone knew.

The madam cleared her throat. I turned back to her. "One thing I forgot to mention," she said.

Something about the way she said that made my body tense. "What's that?" I asked quietly.

"You came here," she said. She waited, and I finally nodded. "You questioned me," she said. Another pause, another nod.

Sometimes my kids screw up. Nothing unusual there: even the best kids (which are mine, FYI) mess up. Even the best kids need a good lecturing occasionally. When they *really* pull a humdinger of a dumb decision, I talk to them like the madam was talking to me. One sentence at a time, waiting for them to acknowledge each thing individually.

Being on the receiving end like this, I didn't like it at all.

"I just wanted to make sure you knew," she said. That purr was back in her voice.

"Knew what?" I said when she, again, paused.

"Why you've made an enemy."

Her words and her tone chilled me. I actually took a step back before remembering our situation.

"You do anything…." I let the threat trail off.

She waved it away. "Yes, you and I both know what will happen if my little enterprise is uncovered during an investigation." She sat forward, and I suddenly realized the pupils of her eyes had widened, consuming the irises and leaving nothing but black pools surrounded by pure white. The madam was a creature of the Otherworlds. I didn't know what, but she was more than she had seemed. That rarely meant "less dangerous than she looked."

"You and I know what will happen if you're killed in a way that will lead to me," she said again once she'd seen my reaction to her change, "but you and I both know that Wardens aren't Wardens all the time. Just as it's impossible for any person to look over their shoulder all the time."

She sat back. "You can see yourself out," she said. She smiled, but the smile was cold, and the look in her eyes told me that I had made an enemy… and that sooner or later we would meet again.

30

I had a name: Lani.

I also had some facts that put me more ill at ease than I'd already been. Not just because they painted the picture of an Otherworlder with extremely unusual appetites, but because that picture just didn't fit with any other Lycaon I'd ever met. The murder victim – Lani – seemed like more of an enigma than when I'd first been brought onto this job, with more questions than ever: not a good thing for someone whose job it was to find answers.

Though knowing about Lani's predilections and the way she spent her time did give me at least a few possible suspects.

First: the other hookers. Could one or several of them had been angry about her/their business being stolen by Lani? I didn't think the madam would be involved – her happiness to have Lani as an employee, or contractor or whatever you called it, seemed genuine. But could one of the other "girls" have gotten mad enough about lost income to kill Lani?

Second: the clients. Could one of them have gotten jealous? Twirled his black mustache between finger and thumb before snarling "If I can't have you then no one shall" and then tying Lani to a railroad track (figuratively speaking)?

I rejected the idea that one of the girls killed her. It was possible, yes. But not likely. It didn't look like the bordello was short on clients – and the sophistication of the Nerd Speed Dating! front, along with the mode of entry (that slide would have been expensive, let alone the magic required to make it work) indicated the madam was running a place with more clients than it needed or could handle.

So no, there was money to go around. And though there are always people who have enough but are willing to kill for more, it didn't sound like Lani had taken the jobs anyone even wanted.

No, not the girls. *Probably* not.

And the clients? I'd gotten one name from the madam. Perhaps eventually I'd have to go back and get some more names from her if this one didn't pan out with something useful. But that would probably mean revealing what I was really there for, and I wanted to avoid that.

So for now I was stuck with what I had: one name, and one location. It was a place to start, at least.

I thought about stopping at my table to see if I'd actually sold any books, then thought about calling Laura to talk to her and the kids.

I rejected both. The table would take care of itself for now; heck, the way things had been going, Mom probably would sell more books *without* me. And as nice as it would be to talk with my family, the clock was ticking. Word had already gotten out about the murder, and I wanted to stay ahead of that as much as possible.

So I just continued on to the gaming room.

Most major cons have at least one room set aside where people can go to play board or card or roleplaying games. Dice roll as people battle orcs and goblins, cards fly as players pit Japanese monsterlings against one another, bright-colored boards represent conquests of worlds both real and imaginary.

I don't generally end up in these places. Not because I don't like board games or RPGs, but because I'm just too busy. And I suck at most of them. Enough that I don't want to inflict my terrible playing on all the nice people who love the games.

Still, I'd been in a decent number of rooms like this, and one thing I almost always noticed was the presence of an Alpha Nerd. While most of the players in gaming rooms gather evenly around the tables, sitting next to each other but with plenty of elbow room for effective dice rolling, the Alpha Nerd is always the center of a different seating configuration. He or she (usually a he) sits at the table, true, but the table isn't his main focus. He throws off-handedly, puts down cards without really thinking about it.

Most of his attention is on the people who crowd around him. Listening as he holds court, speaking on subjects that range from the proper way to hold a tablet while playing Clash of Clans to the reason the world is circling the drain – along with precise instructions on how all such matters should be properly dealt with.

The court mutters approval. They nod. Every once in a while one of them tries to add something to the conversation. The Alpha Nerd is usually a benevolent overlord, so he allows this person to finish a full two sentences before he breaks back in and returns to his topic as though the Lower Nerd had never spoken.

The Alpha Nerd is, in a word, kind of a dick. But he's a dick with a strange charisma that attracts a certain kind of person.

The Alpha Nerd in this room was even more obvious than most. His table was the largest one, and made of higher quality plastic. The people playing against him always put down a slightly less powerful card than he did – though it was often an exercise in creative play to find such a weak card. The group following the Alpha Nerd was larger than most, and crowded closer around him, hanging off his every word.

The Alpha Nerd himself was also stupendously proportioned. It was hard to tell exactly how tall he was while he sat there, but I *could* tell he was probably just as tall laying down. His huge belly hung not only over his belt, but over the table itself, creating a rounded shelf that I could have balanced a champagne flute on.

He had a beard, which was so dark black it had to be dyed. Ditto his hair, which looked like either a weave or the most unfortunate hairline of all time. His eyebrows and sideburns, however, were auburn, giving him a patchwork appearance. As though God had gotten halfway through the project, sighed, and then let his intern finish the job as "good practice."

True to form, the Alpha Nerd was deep in single-sided conversation. "That's why the new rules regarding *Star Trek* fan fiction are totally bogus, especially when measured against what Lucas allows the *Star Wars* fans to do. *Lucas!* I mean, the guy's –"

One of Alpha Nerd's entourage broke in, a whiny, almost fearful interjection: "But doesn't Disney own the *Star Wars* franchise now? So Lucas –"

"Lucas sold the *franchise*, my friend. The *franchise*." Alpha Nerd tossed down a card with a power level of two and somehow still won the hand. "But the tradition is already embedded in our culture, and tradition is stronger than –"

He broke off as a small, twitchy kid entered the room and beelined to the big table. The kid was dressed as Wolverine, the effect of his costume – which was actually pretty good – more than slightly compromised by glasses so thick and round I expected to see goldfish swimming inside them.

Blind Wolverine knelt beside the Alpha Nerd, who held out a hand. One of the fat fingers had a Green Lantern ring, and Blind Wolverine kissed it.

"The rumors are true," I whispered, and I'm not ashamed to say there was more than a little awe in the words.

When the madam told me Lani's best customer was a guy named Harold Kumar, and that he was the gaming room Alpha of this particular convention, I was stunned. First, because he *was* a gaming Alpha Nerd. The madam's bordello was an upscale, exclusive club, and though Alpha Nerds are the Jedi of the game room, once they leave its confines their charisma dissipates and you're usually left with nothing more than the underlying annoying twit. Hardly the kind of person who would be able to find and afford the hottest commodity in an underground brothel.

More important, Harold Kumar, in addition to having maybe the worst name of all time, was a *legend*. Not just an Alpha, but *King* of the Alphas. Rumor had it that he had invented *Dungeons & Dragons*, had provided original code for *Skyrim*, and had once used Patrick Stewart's bathroom.

These rumors, obviously, were false – at least some of them, anyway – but the fact that they kept making the rounds showed that Kumar was something special. At the very least, he had a PR department the envy of any movie studio.

One rumor that I heard enough to think was true: he wasn't just the Alpha of Alphas, he was also something akin to a Godfather. Everyone who used a bathroom to change into their cosplay outfit did it with his blessing, or did it not at all. Those who crossed him ended up with the decapitated screen of their laptop – and nothing else – in bed with them the next morning.

All of that was confirmed by Blind Wolverine's posture: head bowed as he kissed Kumar's ring. Actually, he kissed several of Kumar's kielbasa fingers before he finally found the ring. Someone really needed to get the kid some better glasses.

Kumar daintily removed his hand from the kid's slobbery lips, then leaned back. "You come to me at last?"

"Yes, Nerdfather." Blind Wolverine spoke with head still bowed. "I was foolish to resist your...." He gulped. "Very reasonable request."

"Good, I'm glad you've come to your senses, my friend." The Nerdfather nodded at one of his cronies, who produced something wrapped in a flat plastic bag. The crony passed it to the Nerdfather, and I saw it was a Spider-man comic. Probably a first edition, mint condition, based on the way Blind Wolverine quivered. I wondered if it was written in braille.

The Nerdfather held it out to Blind Wolverine, who reached for it. The Nerdfather pulled it back at the last second. "When I do a favor for my friends, I expect that they will do a favor in return. That is the way of friends, is it not?" Blind Wolverine nodded, looking like he was about to wet his pants.

"I am glad you remember this, my friend," said the Nerdfather. He looked at the comic, safe in its plastic sheath. "If we are friends, I can protect you and yours. If not?" He shrugged. "I cannot guarantee your safety. As it was, I barely managed to restrain certain uncouth individuals from having their way with this beautiful *Amazing Spider-man* Number Ninety-Nine from August nineteen seventy-one." He sniffed. "Why, had he not known that you and I are such good friends, I feel secure that he would have removed the comic and read it with his bare hands while eating fried chicken, thus changing its condition from Gem Mint to merely Very Fine, or perhaps simply Fine."

Blind Wolverine moaned. The Nerdfather held out the mylar package. Blind Wolverine took it in shaking hands. The Nerdfather clapped him on the shoulder and said, "I am glad we are friends. Very glad. I trust I can call on you for a favor, now that our friendship has been cemented?"

"Anything," sobbed Blind Wolverine. "I'm your man now, Nerdfather."

"Good." The Nerdfather cocked a finger, and three of his cronies lifted Blind Wolverine to his feet and escorted him to the door.

The Nerdfather followed his progress and, since I'd been standing off to the side of the door, he saw me.

The wide smile he lavished on me was at odds with the reptilian look in his eyes.

"Ah," he said. "I see fate and fortune have brought me...." He licked his lips. "A new friend."

31

He said the words in the same way you or I might have said "my next pizza slice": excited, and more than a little hungry.

I am a grown man. I am a horror author of some (very moderate) success. I have seen Very Bad Things. Most of all, I'm a husband and a father. All of these combined would typically make me unworried about the opinions or actions of a Gaming Room Alpha.

But this guy was different. Possibly dangerous. I was going to have to disavow him of any notions of adding me to his roster of close personal buddies.

I strode forward, put my hands under the plastic lip of his table, and heaved the whole thing over.

Cards flew everywhere, and though no one cried much about the lost game – hard to care about the outcome when your only job is to enthusiastically lose – there *were* a number of shrieks about the dangers of intermingling decks.

I sat down on one of the seats absented by a girl who was now on hands and knees, frantically scooping up her deck before it was defiled by contact with competitors' cards.

I put my right ankle on my left knee and sank back, trying to look casual and unafraid. The chair was an uncomfortable folding chair, aluminum and plastic and hard in all the wrong places, and it made my back start to throb immediately. I ignored the pain, smacking a big grin on my face and waiting.

The Nerdfather's normally flushed complexion had bleached of color, except for two red highlights on his jowly cheeks. He looked like a pug with a fever.

"May I assume you wish my attention?" he asked. "Or is this merely a strange way to commit suicide?"

I said nothing.

The Nerdfather clearly wasn't used to people ignoring him. "I would pay a bit more respect if I were you."

"If you were me, I bet the only thing you'd want to do would be to look at your feet without a mirror."

Those last two spots of red disappeared. The Nerdfather's lips pressed together, a gray-white line. He hissed out, "You *dare*?" He spoke in a whisper, but it carried easily in a room that had gone utterly silent, utterly still. "Your comic books, your unopened movie action figures, your still-working Atari 2600... whatever you have, it's gone. You hear that? You've made a powerful enemy, and –"

"I came here to talk about Lani."

The words didn't just shut him up, they physically rocked him. His seat creaked dangerously as he pitched backward, and it took three of his cronies to catch him and keep him from falling.

"Lani," he said hoarsely. "What do you know of her? Where is she?"

This was why I had come in and spilled his table. This was why I'd treated him with a disrespect he clearly rarely – if ever – encountered. With a man like the Nerdfather, you need to trade for what you want. He has no real friends, which gives you two alternatives: you can either trade as his subject, or you can position yourself as an enemy. If you're his subject, you'll give much and get little. If you're his enemy, you might get even less... but if you can position yourself as a bit more powerful, and out-Alpha the Alpha, you might come out with something good.

I looked casually at the people still clearing their cards, the rest of his entourage still clustered around him.

He understood.

"Out," he said hoarsely.

Most of his cronies started moving. A few of the people gathering their cards from the floor didn't seem to notice what was happening.

The Nerdfather hove himself to his feet. A surprisingly dainty foot lashed out, catching one of the nerds in the stomach hard enough to send the kid's breath exploding from his lungs. The kid spun across the floor, and the Nerdfather screamed, "Get... *OUT!*"

Everyone moved now. Not just the Nerdfather's entourage, but the people at the other tables, even the guy who was selling game dice at a small table in the corner.

I upped my estimation of the Nerdfather. It was one thing to threaten a comic book. Another to lash out physically. And though the gamers seemed terrified as they left, none of them seemed surprised.

Just before they all left, the Nerdfather said, "Vin." A bald, muscular guy dressed in a wife-beater and black leather pants turned back. The Nerdfather nodded, and "Vin" closed the double doors to the game room as he left, leaving us alone in the room.

I didn't know what the look to Vin had meant, but I suspected it was either, "Wait until he leaves, then beat the crap out of him," or "Go get some more muscle, then beat the crap out of him."

Either way, my crap was in danger.

I tried to ignore the problem for a moment. One thing at a time. I turned back to the Nerdfather. He had settled back in his chair, and now stared at me across six feet of empty space.

He waited. Cool customer, and a good negotiating tactic: you talk first, you show what you want, and how bad you want it.

Typically, I can out-wait people. Again, I'm a dad, and after a few years of learning to let your mind go to a Happy Place after watching the fiftieth repeat of a particular *Teletubbies* episode, you get pretty good at waiting.

Unfortunately, I didn't have a lot of time. I was under a gun from the Dead Ones, I had to get ahead of whatever rumors had to be spreading at this point, and there was the possibility

135

of Vin's return with enough muscley nerds to give me serious problems.

"You know Lani?" I said casually. Of course, I knew he did – that was the reason I was here. But I wanted to see his reaction. Before, when I mentioned her name, he'd been rocked. I wanted to see what happened when he was ready for the subject.

Still rocked. He was already sitting down, so he couldn't fall into the chair, but he did seem to fall a bit deeper into it. "Where is she?" he asked.

"I'm asking the questions, bub." Yes, I actually said, "bub." So sue me. "How long have you been giving that poor dog your bone?"

Okay, let's pause here. I'm not typically a mean person. But sometimes you gotta push buttons. I didn't have time to chat nicely, and whether we like it or not the fastest way to get something done is sometimes the meanest one.

In a related topic: sometimes the meanest way to get something done turns out to be the worst idea possible. Like now.

The Nerdfather didn't make a sound, and he moved so fast I didn't even see it coming.

We talk a lot about nerds like they're one thing. A lot of people only think in terms of that one thing, like every nerd is a pimply, skinny, four-eyed dork whose heavy lifting regimen involves occasionally moving a Pizza Pocket from the microwave to his desk.

It's a lie. Nerds are fat, thin, tall, short, beautiful, ugly, weird, cool. Some are slow and weak, others fast and strong.

The Nerdfather, in spite of his bulk, was very fast and very *very* strong.

I'm pretty good in a fight, but I didn't even have time to get my hands up before he lunged across the space between us and backhanded me. I tried to pull out of the way of the strike, but all I managed was to get hit on the shoulder instead of the side of the head.

Good thing, too: the blow would have broken my neck. It felt like every bone in my body jarred to dust when he hit me, and I flew out of the seat and hit the ground in a tumbling spin that rolled me a good ten feet across the floor.

I stopped facedown against the leg of a table. Everything below my hairline hurt. I tried to roll back over, but before I could a huge hand wrapped around the back of my neck and hauled me to my feet.

I didn't bother going for a joint lock. Those are effective, non-lethal courses of action in a lot of situations, but when the joints in question are surrounded by so much flesh I couldn't encircle them with both hands, those kinds of moves lose a lot of efficacy.

So I went dirty. I punched the Nerdfather in the throat.

He didn't move. Just took the hit. And smiled.

And backhanded me again.

Pain blasted down my spine, hit the bottoms of my feet, rebounded to my skull, then went back for a second lap. I would have screamed, but my teeth were gritted too hard for sound to escape.

The Nerdfather hadn't let go of me when he hit me, so I was still dangling from his grasp. He hit me again – an open palm to the other side of the face, this time. I felt blood well out of my mouth. I managed to make a noise this time – a very dignified "*bloofg*" that sounded like a harp seal vomiting. More blood.

He still held me in the air. In the *air*. You see that in movies, but usually it's B.S. Holding someone in the air means either they're a pixie or you're a freak. The Nerdfather fit in category number two, and I realized that what I'd taken for fat was just slabs of muscle so thick they had lost any semblance of normal form.

He leaned in close enough that I could smell his particular aroma.[11] He cocked the fist that wasn't holding me up, and I have never seen *anything* look so huge.

Everything started to get dark, which was actually nice. The pain started to fade behind a black curtain, and I allowed myself to hope that I might be unconscious when the Nerdfather beat me to death.

"Where is she?" he asked. "Where's Lani?"

I could barely breathe. Consciousness fading. Time for a single word. I didn't think about it, it just came out.

"Dead," I rasped.

Then the black curtain fell.

---

[11] In case you wondered, it smelled like a combination of Hot Pockets, Monster Energy drink, and rage.

32

Fortunately, I didn't die.

Unfortunately, I *did* wake up.

The first thing I realized was how much pain I was in. Putting all my wordsmithing skills to use, I said, "Ouch." Actually, I said, "*Nngoaho,*" but I think we can all agree that I meant "ouch."

Pain was running hopscotch drills across my bones, leaping from joint to joint with sadistic screams of ecstacy. My neck felt like someone was using it as the barrel of a flare gun.

"Ouch," I said again, and this time I actually *did* say "ouch."

That's when I noticed the second thing: the crying. Deep, wrenching sobs around what sounded like a copiously running nose. Purest heartbreak.

I still hadn't opened my eyes. When I did, there was a moment when the light stabbed me in the face and I couldn't see. The blindness fought the pain in my neck for attention, and the neck pain won. The blindness retreated, allowing me to see the game room.

Trashed. Completely wrecked. The tables were all overturned, many of the chairs had been twisted into pretzels, and there were holes in several walls. Between the sobs I could hear voices, and I realized they were coming from the other side of the door.

"I don't *care* who he is," said one. "I'm the facilities manager here and –"

"Look, you don't want to mess with the Nerdfather," said the second. Actually, it came out "Jew don' wanna mess wid da Noidfadduh," like the speaker had watched *Goodfellas* way too many times.

First voice: "Get out of my way, you spastic –"

Then the sound of flesh hitting flesh, of meat hitting carpet. The voices ceased.

The sobs didn't. I finally looked at Harold Kumar. The Nerdfather was sitting on the floor, slumped against a wall and legs splayed out in front of him. Tears wet his face, his black beard dripped with them.

I know he's a scumbag – a guy who hogs every conversation; who won't let anyone else win at *Pokemon*; and who, from what I'd just seen, is more than willing to hurt other people in the real world, as opposed to just knocking their hit points out in a fixed *D&D* game. Still, my heart kind of broke a little, watching him there.

I rolled to my hands and knees and crawled over to him. I patted his shoulder. Awkward, I know. But sometimes you do what you do because it's the right thing to do when you do it. And you can quote me on that (though I hope you won't – looking at it now it doesn't sound nearly as cool as it did in my head).

The Nerdfather blinked. He wiped his nose with the back of his hand, then wiped the slime trail on his dark shirt where it glimmered brightly.

"She was my everything, man."

"I'm sorry, Kumar, er, Harold, er, Nerdfath –"

He waved at me. "What does it matter?" He buried his face in his hands. "She was everything to me."

"You knew what she was?" I asked. His expression hardened, and because I didn't want to find out what round two with this guy would be like, I put up my hands. "I mean... you know she was a lycan?"

He nodded. "Lycaon, actually. 'Course I knew."

"How did you come into the World?"

He shook his head. That wasn't a question he was going to answer. In fact, it looked like his whole expression suddenly fell into itself. What had been an open book of bereavement slammed shut. Left behind was only coldness; calculation. He looked around at the wreckage.

"They're going to toss me from the con, maybe even press charges," he said.

"Probably," I said.

"Unless I get someone else to take the blame." He looked hard at me, and it wasn't tough to figure out what he was thinking.

"You know your girlfriend was Lycaon," I said. "You know what *I* am?"

"No. And I don't care." He started to get to his feet, which for someone his size was a fairly detailed process. "But I do care about how all this looks," he said, gesturing at the room and at me. "About how it looks to have a guy come into my hood and challenge me and walk out without a scratch."

I thought about pointing out that I was *covered* in scratches. Instead, I said, "You can get me in trouble –"

"I can put you in the hospital. Or the morgue."

I grimaced. "Yeah. But then you'd get in even more trouble." He spared a wicked glance in my direction as he finally got to his feet. He loomed over me. I shrank back, wondering what he was planning. Knowing that whatever it was, it couldn't be good for me.

He took a step toward me.

I got to my feet as well – faster than he had, but still far from my best. Everything hurt too much for speed.

He reached for me.

I shrank back and said, "You hurt me and you never find out what happened to her!"

His fingers stopped an inch from my neck, which was doing spasms in anticipation of another throttling.

"Is that a threat?" he said quietly. "Now's not a good time for you to threaten me."

"Not a threat," I said. "I'm the guy trying to find out what happened to her. Who killed her."

He remained motionless. "I don't believe you."

"Believe it, man." More voices came from the hall. Angrier, louder. Something rattled the doors, which sounded as though they'd been locked by one of the Nerdfather's people. I mustered every ounce of sincerity I had and said, "I'm a Warden. Maybe you don't know what that is, but –"

His jaw dropped. "You're a Warden?"

I smiled. "Yeah, and I –"

He punched me. Not his hardest – I could tell because I just swayed instead of flying back through the wall and into the next room. Still, blood gushed from my nose.

The Nerdfather grabbed me as I slumped and hauled me to him. "It's people like *you* who made us have to keep our love a secret. People like *you* who threatened Nespda. People like *you* –"

The banging at the door got louder. I croaked. "I don't care about any of that. Just want to find who killed her."

His fist drew back again. Huger than ever. Scarred knuckles that must have slammed through many pairs of glasses, broken many nerd noses.

Slamming at the doors. They started to buckle.

The Nerdfather jerked me close. "They're gonna put me away." I didn't say anything. "But I know people. Not just here, *everywhere*. I'll walk in two days." He let go of me. I crumpled to the ground. "You find who did her in and we're friends. If not, I'll be waiting at the exit for you."

He started toward the door just as it opened. Three husky guys with "SECURITY" stenciled across yellow jackets flooded in. They looked from the huge body of the Nerdfather to my own wrecked form, and it was easy to tell who they'd rather tangle with. But the evidence was clearly in favor of Kumar being the guilty one in the room.

The security guards gulped. Stepped toward the monster-sized man. Then "Vin" said, "Nah, id wadn't him it wad da liddle goy on da groun." I translated that to, "No, it wasn't him it was the little guy on the ground."

I'm not little.

Shut up. Not important right now.

The guards figured out what he said a moment after I did, and stepped toward me with clear relief.

The Nerdfather inserted his bulk between them and me. Then, slowly, he held his massive arms forward, wrists together. "It was not his fault," he said. "I accept full responsibility for this unfortunate occurrence."

The guards looked at each other. They were big guys, but all three of them probably wouldn't add up to one Nerdfather. The bravest of them finally reached out with a pair of cuffs, then failed to put them on since they weren't big enough to encircle Kumar's wrists.

The Nerdfather shrugged, then gestured for the guards to lead the way. They turned and as they walked to the door I got up – trying to ignore the pain that wracked my frame – and lurched toward them.

"Wait!" I shouted. I grabbed the Nerdfather. "I need to know about her. Tell me what you know about La –"

"Don't speak her name," he said. The words were quiet, but strong. I shut up. He leaned in close and said, "I loved her, and she loved me. That is all you need to know from me."

"I need more," I whispered. "You want me to find who did this to her, I have to get more information."

"Ask her family," he said.

"Who is her family?" He didn't answer.

One of the con security guards stepped hesitantly closer. "Uh, sir?" he said to Kumar. "We should leave." The Nerdfather glared, and he added, "If that's all right with you, of course."

The Nerdfather turned back to me. His eyes were bright, tears again trying to make an appearance. "She loved me," he said. "She said she was going to leave him for me."

I don't even know if he was aware he said it. Sometimes grief is so strong it becomes a waking sleep, and everything we see or feel or say or do becomes just one more part of the nightmare of our lives. That was how Kumar sounded right now – dazed, drifting, unaware of most things around him.

"What?" I said. "Who was she going to leave?"

He snapped back. Blinked away the tears. Now he looked angry. "It was him," he said. "He must have found out about it. Must have known she'd never go to him."

"*Who?*"

He spoke the name. "Eustace de Vesci."

My legs went out from under me. I would have fallen, but Kumar grabbed my elbow and effortlessly kept me upright.

"That's a joke, right?"

He shook his head. "I never joke about my old lady or how big my dice are." The tears threatened to come again. He blinked them back.

"Then her real name wasn't...." He'd told me not to say "Lani," so my voice drifted away.

He shook his head. "Yes, *it was*," he said fiercely. "It was the name she used with me. The name she used when she was happy. The name she used when she was *free.*"

"What was her... uh... other name? When she wasn't with you?"

He hadn't let me go. And when he spoke again, his grip tightened slightly, as though worried I would fall once more.

"Calista."

He was right. The only thing holding me up was the Nerdfather. I could barely *see*, I was so shocked.

"Calista?" I asked.

He nodded, then drew me close. "Eustace did it. I know he did. That bastard will kill what he can't keep." Grief and rage battled for control of his face. Rage won. "You kill him," he whispered into my ear. "Kill him, and you and I will be friends. Or you can let *me* kill him, and then...."

"Then what?" I said, trying to sound braver than I felt. "Then you kill me, right?"

The rage didn't disappear from his face, but it all funneled into a smile so grim it would have made Satan run for the hills. "Yes," he said. "After I show you what it feels like to have everything you love murdered." He licked his lips and added, "And I'll do it right in front of you."

I decked him. It was automatic, and I couldn't help it. This bastard had just gone over the line; had just threatened my *family.*

The punch had no effect on him whatever. One of the convention security officers moved toward me, but the Nerdfather held out a hand and the guy stopped as though he were Kumar's direct employee. Which he probably would be by the end of the day.

Kumar just smiled at me. He set me down carefully. "Find him," he said. "Kill him."

Then he left. The guards spared only a few glances at me before following him, and behind them straggled the Nerdfather's cronies. Last out was Vinnie, who flipped me the bird.

Then they were gone.

My pulse hammered against my skull, the sounds of the convention filtered in through the open door. All I heard, though, was Kumar's threat.

And the names.

Eustace de Vesci.

Calista.

Oh, dear Lord, no.

I walked out the door and yanked my cell out of my pocket. A few people stared at me as they walked past, and I realized I must look quite the mess, so I headed to the nearest bathroom as I dialed.

It rang… and rang… and rang. Still ringing as I pulled a bunch of paper towels out of the dispenser and tried to mop up some of my blood. It hadn't gotten on my clothes very much, so that was good, I'd stick out like a sore thumb if I didn't get the blood stopped.

The phone clicked. "What is it?" said Blake.

"I need to get Kevin Anderson's number."

Blake snorted. "Like I'd give that to you. You'd probably crank call him at two in the morning about –"

"Is he there? Are you with him?"

I could hear Blake frowning. "Yes, but he's busy."

"Get him on the phone, Blake."

I could hear noises. They did sound busy, all right... but not "working" busy. Someone was moaning... low, light tones that could have been pain or pleasure, or maybe both.

What the hell is Anderson –

"He's *busy*. He's determining spell logistics for the rest of the con and –"

"I don't care if he's got an unreleased script for the next *Star Wars* movie and is reading it in funny voices, Blake. If you don't want everyone at this convention to die, *put him on!*"

Something in my voice – probably the raw panic – convinced him. There was the distinct sound of plastic being passed from palm to palm, then the moans cut off as Anderson came on.

I knew what "determining spell logistics" sounded like. It usually didn't involve moaning and panting. Only the names the Nerdfather had given me –

(*Eustace.*

Calista.

Holy hell.)

– kept me from making a crack and trying to find out what Anderson was doing. I knew he was a tightwad, but this sounded like he had a foot strongly in "pervy guy" territory, too.

Anderson snarled, "You better have the murder solved, and a bow around the killer, or I'm going to make you sorry you were ever born."

He could do it, too. Normally I'd have worried. Now, though, I just snapped right back at him. "I need you to meet me at the Ice Cream Room. Now."

I ended the call before Anderson could threaten me.

Then I ran.

33

I arrived at the Ice Cream Room at the same time Anderson and Blake did. Both men were huffing and puffing, and both looked mad enough to commit a murder or two themselves.

"What is this?" demanded Blake. "What makes you think you –"

I ignored him, moving to the Ice Cream Room door and yanking it open.

Most convention centers have freezers and refrigerators: big, industrial things to keep vendors' foodstuffs safe and sanitary. They can have anything from fresh fruit to twenty-gallon kegs of salad dressing, to enough hamburgers to put a McDonald's to shame.

In the old days, that was enough. But when the Otherworlders started attending cons, a bit more was needed. Some of the Otherworlders' culinary needs could not be assuaged by a crisp salad or a foot-long hot dog.

Some of them needed *real* dogs – preferably alive and still barking. And things got weird from there.

So during cons these days, you look hard enough and you'll find what the organizers call the Ice Cream Room. Half of it's a freezer, the other half a pantry. And in it you will find everything from fresh viscera to twenty-gallon kegs of blood, to enough raw chicken beaks to *also* put McDonald's to shame.

The freezer side is also where the con organizers stash any bodies. It's cold, so decomposition is slowed. It's out of the way; there are numerous wards set up so that anyone who doesn't belong to the World can't stumble onto – or even get to the place. And, if push comes to shove, some of the things being held in the cages for later consumption are pretty good at doing the consuming themselves – very handy if you need to make a body disappear.

When we walked into the Ice Cream Room (and please don't ask me why it's called that, I have no idea), there was Lani. The guy she'd been found with – the other lycan who'd been discovered in a magical trance and wearing a five dollar excuse for a vampire outfit – wasn't there. No surprise; Anderson undoubtedly had someone working to wake him up.

Or, if he didn't, I suspected he'd get on it soon.

The girl was silent, of course, but I knew more about her now. Nowhere near *enough*, but what I had already found made her more of a person. One of the primary reasons we as a species are able to hate one another is that we are able to be ignorant of one another. The more you know of a person, the more you understand, the more you eventually *love* that person. I knew this girl better, and so her death hurt me more now than when I had first seen her in the room where she was murdered.

"Lani," I murmured.

Kumar had said that wasn't her name, but I hoped he was lying. I preferred this to be Lani – even if I didn't know who that was. Because I *really* wanted this to be anyone but the person he had named.

"I need you to check for a glamour," I told Anderson.

He frowned. "Why would I? Why would *she* have a glamour?"

A good question. In the nineteenth century, the term "glamour" meant something used to improve one's appearance. *I.e.*, makeup. But before that, it was known for what it truly is: a spell used to change something's appearance. They're rare, though. Not only are they hard to cast, but most glamours only work when the caster is concentrating on them specifically. In other words, if the caster isn't actually thinking *about* the spell, it instantly dissipates. And the worth of an appearance-altering spell is lessened significantly when the first time the caster notices something else – something as small and mundane as an unusual pattern on the carpet – the spell disappears and leaves all as it truly is.

The only people who have the ability to cast spells that work better are certain families with gypsy blood, and even then they have to actually embed the glamour in something – a ring, an amulet, a circle of precious stones embedded in the floor. The glamour requires a powerful mix of thaumaturgy, alchemy, and incantation that few wizards or Otherworlders can manage.

Blake snorted. "The MME already examined her. She wasn't wearing a glamour or he would have told me."

I ignored him. "Check her," I told Anderson.

"Why?" he demanded. "You pull me away from something important, yank me down here without any kind of explanation and now you think this *girl* is –"

I told him. "I think she's Calista."

Anderson and Blake instantly grasped the implications of that. Blake looked ill, and Anderson's fists clenched.

"Where did you learn that? Who told you that?" asked Blake.

I didn't answer. Anderson was already starting his spell. He chanted – low, unintelligible sounds under his breath. I couldn't hear what he was saying, but I could feel its power. It felt like the onset of a summer storm: the air grew heavy, somehow thicker and harder to breathe on a primal but very real level. The Ice Cream Room grew dim, but Anderson's figure was outlined in radiance. He was pulling power from the air, from the very light that had been in the room a moment ago.

He reached down and touched the dead girl's forehead. Her eyes snapped open, and for a moment I thought Anderson might have somehow raised her from the dead. But it was just the power in his touch, causing nerveless muscles to clench in a momentary semblance of life. Her eyes were still clouded, gray and sightless.

The eyes closed. The muscles relaxed.

Another light joined Anderson's nimbus. I turned over the dead girl's arm, revealing the star tattoo on the back of her right hand. It was glowing, liquid fire tracing the outlines of the dark ink.

There was a rolling table nearby, cluttered with kitchen utensils. I grabbed a small, sharp knife and pushed it into the center of the star.

The girl had been exsanguinated, and even if she hadn't been sucked dry, she'd been dead long enough that any fluids left would be settling to the bottom of her corpse. So the small gash I made in the center of the tattoo brought up no blood, just created a slit in rubbery flesh.

That's not to say nothing happened, though. The second I pierced her skin – more importantly, the second I ruined the integrity of the tattoo – there was a flash of light joined by the smell of burning plastic. As the light faded, Lani's body seemed to melt. Her features sagged like candle wax before a bonfire, drooping away and then suddenly pulling back into a new configuration.

"The *tattoo* was the token," said Blake.

I nodded. It was what I had expected, but it was still surprising – again, tokens for glamours were usually rings, necklaces. I'd never seen one made via tattoo. This was cool. Cool, and very powerful.

Lani, the blond girl with the exotic features and a body you could see on any fashion magazine in the supermarket, was gone. In her place was someone with dark hair, thicker and more wavy than the blond tresses had been. Her body was still beautiful, but the dimensions had shifted from those of a Playboy model to those of a young athlete in her prime. Lean muscle overlay her arms, corded in her shoulders. The legs were those of a sprinter: trim without being stringy, muscled without being thick. It wasn't at all hard to imagine this girl as a she-wolf.

"Calista," said Anderson.

"Yeah," I said. I felt a new pang of sadness, and the fear that had followed me throughout the investigation intensified. "And guess who else I found out is here today?"

Anderson didn't even have to think about it. "The de Vescis."

The way he answered told me that he had already known as much. Did he know Calista would be here, too? Calista and the de Vescis together....

Wow.

I looked at Blake. "So what do you think? Was this important enough to get you guys down here?"

Blake growled. Anderson held up his hand. "This is not the time." I wasn't sure who he was talking to, Blake or me. He thought a moment, then said, "Get to the WordFire Press station, Blake. Get Card and any other mage you can find. We need to put up a Containment. A big one."

Blake nodded and ran off, dialing his phone as he left.

Anderson turned to me. "You know what she was here for?"

I nodded. "I'm pretty sure. The princess of the lycans' Great Pack," gesturing at Calista's body – *Princess* Calista's body, "and members of the High Court of the Vampires are here to sign the treaty. And one of them's dead, which is going to seriously screw up the signing." I shook my head. "This isn't just a murder; it has all the markings of a political assassination."

Anderson shook his head. "I don't think they were here to simply sign an treaty. I think they were here to *seal* the signatures."

It took me a moment. Then I looked at the girl – Princess Calista, lovely even in death, and representing the hopes of her race. Understanding dawned. "You think she was here to *marry* Prince de Vesci."

It wasn't a question, but he nodded and said, "Correct. The only way to stop hostilities between the lycans and the vampires would be to merge the two camps with something more binding than a mere signature." He looked woefully at the body.

"Maybe it's a good thing if they don't 'merge,'" I said. "If the vamps and the lycans ever *really* teamed up, there wouldn't be much hope for us as a species."

"Perhaps so," said Anderson, and to my surprise I saw real sadness on his face. "That's one of the things the Dead Ones have worked to thwart for centuries. But *this* High Court, and *this* Great Pack... we actually thought there was a hope for peace. Not just between them, but between them and us as well."

"Well, you might want to rethink that." I told him what Kumar had said about Calista's fiancée: that she had planned to leave the vampire prince for the Nerdfather. "And even if Prince de Vesci didn't kill her because she had fallen for someone else, he might have done so anyway, because of how she was spending her off hours." Anderson cocked an eyebrow, so I clarified, "When she wasn't princessing, she moonlighted as an interspecies call girl."

I told him about Nespda, about what it was, and how Calista was involved: not just with the Nerdfather, but apparently with any human willing to pay the fee – with preference given to the ones who asked for the weird stuff.

Anderson suddenly drew himself up. He cocked a finger, and a solid wall of air pushed me forward, bringing me almost nose to nose with the Dead One. His expression was calm, but there was no disguising the set of his eyes or the power in his gaze. "You will tell no one of this," he said. "Not about the princess, not about the prince, and certainly not about the accusations some thug of a gamer has brought against them."

"It's gonna be hard to do my job without a *few* people knowing about it."

He shook his head. "No. It won't. You're off the job."

"Someone needs to tell the families. Someone needs to find –"

"Someone *does* need to tell them!" Anderson roared. "But that someone will not be some poor excuse for a Warden who can barely find his shoelaces in the morning!"

"I actually wear slip-ons so –"

Anderson's look shut me up. "Go to your table. Go to your panels. Sell books. And keep your mouth shut." I nodded. "Where's Butler?" he asked.

"I sent him back to his table, or wherever he is when he's not licking stuff for you."

Anderson growled something incomprehensible. He stormed out, and I was alone in the Ice Cream Room. Just me and a few creatures waiting to be consumed, and the body of a princess whose death might trigger a supernatural war that could consume the earth.

Just another Friday.

34

I was back on the con floor when "it" happened.

The change wasn't major... unless you were part of the World. Everyone else probably sensed it as a sudden ripple in the air conditioning, or maybe they built up a bit of static electricity that discharged when they grabbed a loved one's hand.

I felt it like someone dropping a bucket of ice cubes down my back.

I'd known it was coming, so I was able to resist shivering outright, but I saw a few people – well, not *people* – who weren't waiting for it. Magically-created "faces" or latex masks that jerked upright as something strange infected the air.

The Containment.

This was something I'd never seen before, and just one more thing that scared me about today. It was enough to make me miss the straightforward cases – like Cthulhu's daughter eating people, followed by swift, straightforward action by My Li'l Stabby Friend.

Containments are a big deal. They require numerous wizards to erect – not even someone as powerful as Kevin Anderson or Orson Scott Card can put up a ward like this on their own. It acts as something like a supernatural electric fence: any Otherworlder venturing out of the Containment area is going to feel like it has stuck its finger (or tentacle, or misty-misty parts) into a psychic light socket. The farther out they go, the more it hurts, until they either give up and turn back... or until they just die. The same thing happens the other direction, if an Otherworlder on the outside tries to get in. It's a very nasty spell.

And it's the equivalent of moving Soviet missiles into Cuba: a last step before magical thermonuclear war. I'd never seen this happen because I don't think *anyone* alive in the last century had seen it happen.

It showed how serious the situation with the dead Princess Calista was: it was going to make everything non-human in the con very cranky, and that much more inclined to break the Treaty. Beyond that, word would spread through the World, and many of the creatures out there were going to agitate for aggression against humans in general and the Dead Ones in particular. Essentially, the Dead Ones had risked all-out war with Otherworlders in order to make sure the killer didn't escape. Pushing the world to the brink because to *not* do so would be to ensure it went right over the edge.

That's probably why I didn't end up going to my table. I walked by close enough to see that everything was all right, but then continued on after making the "sorry, I'm working my butt off at panels and whatnot" signal to my mom. She saw it and nodded, otherwise busy handing over a stack of books to a buyer. I saw she was pushing *The Colony* and *The Sword Chronicles*, which were her favorites. I pointed at the seemingly-untouched pile of *The Haunteds* and mimed her to work those. She nodded again.

Then I kept walking, not even really sure what I planned to do until the Come and Play booth hove into sight.

It was still empty, which surprised me. I figured that Pixela and the rest of the "cosplayers" would have finished grieving for Calista/Lani by now, and would be back to business.

No one.

I sagged a bit. I'd been hoping to find SuperGhoul, the Come and Play "babe" who had bolted from the Other Green Room when I started asking questions. A lame idea, I knew, given how fast she had run off: people who flee in abject terror don't tend to go back to the easiest place to find them. But hope springs eternal. Or something.

Other than SuperGhoul, I had no real reason for being here. Robot Dave had already tossed the place, and I knew Real Dave well enough to know that he was excruciatingly thorough.

The chances of him missing anything of note in either guise were slim.

"They went again. Came and went after they went back from coming."

That little bit of sagacity was from the armor-crocheting old lady at the next booth. She sniffed. "Good riddance. Maybe they went to buy some real clothes."

"You think so?" I said absently. I didn't really like this gal, but she was certainly chatty – and chatty people often have something to say, in between all the *nothing* they say.

She shook her head. "Nah. Maybe they went to all have the sex with that tall guy who came by. Maybe smoke some of the pot."

In spite of the seriousness of everything around me, the way she said "the sex" and "the pot" almost made me giggle. The idea of Dave being covered in amorous monster sexpots got me even closer to laughter. The thought of what his wife would do to him if she found out sealed the deal.

The old lady squinted at me. She had a good face for squinting. "What's so funny, boy?"

I managed to suck back the laughter that wanted to come, recognizing that it was hysterical as much as motivated by any real humor. "Nothing," I said. Her expression said she clearly didn't buy that. "Just, uh, thinking about them having the orgy all the way to the dying and then going to the Hell together."

I couldn't help myself.

She didn't blink. Just nodded. "The truth," she mumbled, and even cracked a smile herself. Not at the joke, but at the idea of people going to the Hell.

I really didn't like her.

"But they're not going to the Hell," she said. She sniffed and squinted again. Her face was also made for this combo. She had a face of many expressive qualities – all of them apparently sour or patronizing.

"Where are they going?" I asked.

"To see facilities management." She nodded at the Come and Play booth. "Power's out."

I looked closer and realized that the spotlights that usually highlighted the huge banner above the booth were in fact still dark, as were the strings of LED lights that ran up the poles holding up the booth. "They *all* had to go?" I murmured.

The question was rhetorical. Lady Crochetsalot answered: "They were *really* mad. It's the fifth time it's happened today." She sniffed again. "The universe's judgment on whoring, you ask me."

"No one did," I murmured under my breath. I don't think "whoring" is a great idea either, mind you, but I suspected my definition of it was a bit narrower than hers. Not to mention that people – or ghouls, or whatevers – who end up in the worst end of that particular spectrum are most often not doing what they want, but what they have been forced to do.

"Been gone a while, too," she added.

She sniffed, but before she could say something nasty I interjected, "Maybe they got the lost."

"Flesh peddlers are *born* lost."

So much for my attempt to sidetrack the conversation. She had a one-track mind, with a train that apparently ran only from Judgment Station to Hell Terminus.

I moved toward the booth, then around the side and into the Come and Play exhibitors space.

The booth was basically a square with three long walls, no wall at the back because there was no need for one. The front and side walls were plywood, about waist high, painted white on the outside so the semi-lurid pictures of girls in costume that had been lacquered over them would show up better. Each length of plywood was screwed to a PVC corner post – also white, with clear LED lights writhing around it – that went up thirty feet to the banner overhead.

The outside was eyecatching, inside was a lot more spartan. The wood was unpainted, revealing the mad criss-cross grain of industrial plywood. There was a shelf built into the back of each length of wood. Nothing fancy, just a long piece of wood attached at a right angle to the booth walls – somewhere the girls could rest on, or so they could lean forward and tease visitors with better views of their cleavage, depending on the girl.

I'd seen these kinds of booths before, and though this was a bit more extravagant, it pretty much followed the usual makeup. There was one major difference, though if you weren't looking for it, you'd likely miss it: Usually booth babe/cosplayer exhibition spaces have piles of clothes, makeup kits, various personal effects, some drinks and bits of whatever food they'll pretend to eat while working with the normals.

I knew that Robot Dave had found these things, but now there was nothing. I wondered why, then realized it was probably because of me. I'd come around asking questions, and they must have gotten paranoid that I'd find and then poke into their personal effects without asking.

That made me feel oddly conflicted. Hurt because they would think such a thing about such an obviously nice person as me, and triumphant because I'd had Robot Dave do just that before they had a chance to hide their stuff.

"What are you looking for?" The lady next door was leaning over the booth, a crochet hook held in one hand like she was planning on stabbing something.

I realized the woman was a hooker. Ha!

I decided not to share this with her. She probably wouldn't be amused.

"I don't know," I answered. "Maybe a phone, or even better, a log of all the girls' activities." I spoke for my own amusement: I didn't know a woman of *any* species who would voluntarily leave behind her phone, and folks like the Come and Play girls weren't likely to keep a diary of daily activities.

Once more, even though I didn't expect it, the Crocheting Wonder answered. "Nah, the big guy took all those things."

I froze. "What?"

"The giant. The one who moved like a robot."

"That's impossible."

Again, I was speaking to myself. Again, the crone answered with a squint and a scowl. "You calling me a liar, boy?" The scowl deepened. "Hey, you said before that *you* were after flesh." She shook her head, and I could practically *see* visions of myself in the Hell dancing in her eyes. "You interested in one of those *menageries* or something?"

I began to suspect at this point that the reason the woman was so crotchety about the Come and Play booth was that she secretly wished she had been invited to be an honorary booth babe, and further that she had some weird repressed dreams about participating in her own "menageries."

I was also more than a little sick of her, I had to admit. Which was why I said, "Yes. Oodles of menageries with as much fleshy fleshness as I can get my own fleshiest parts on. Also, I'm a man-whore."

That shocked her silent – for a moment – and then she began hollering at me, damning me to Hell and Sheol and Hades and Be-er Shachath and a surprising number of other versions of Outer Darkness.

I tuned her out, though. Just remembering for a moment.

"Nah, the big guy took all those things."

That didn't make sense. Dave had said….

"Dammit," I muttered.

"That's right! Damned to Tit ha-Yaven and –"

I looked around. Searching for a lock box, something built into the housing of the booth itself. Nothing. Just wood.

He could have meant a makeup kit, I thought. Or some kind of briefcase.

But what if…?

I pulled out my phone. Dialed. As the phone rang I went ahead and told the old lady that she was technically a hooker and had just said "*Tit* ha-Yaven."

She continued not being amused.

The phone picked up. Real Dave spoke. "Collings, I'm about to close a deal –"

"Sorry man," I interrupted. "But Gepetto's work begins."

The line went silent. I heard someone else saying, "You all right? Do you want to talk about a five hundred thousand dollar advance or not?"

Friggin' everyone *is becoming a millionaire but me!*

"How may I be of assistance?" Robot Dave's comforting monotone came on the phone.

"You said earlier, when you found the fur on the comb –"

"I did not say comb. I said I discovered a hairbrush, and that it lay beneath a ninja sword."

I looked around, just to make sure I hadn't missed something *else*. Nothing was there. Nothing at all – which didn't mean there was nothing more to be found. "Stupid," I muttered.

"My IQ in this augmented phase is beyond your comprehension," said Dave.

"I was talking about myself."

"You are slightly above average on the Wechsler Intelligence Scale – though, it should be noted, that measurement is used on children."

I gritted my teeth. "After you mentioned finding the brush, you said you found nothing else, right?"

"Incorrect; my wording was...." He seemed to hiccup, then said, in a slightly scratchy voice, like his voice was coming from an old-fashioned Victrola, "Further ILA turned up nothing, and after I attempted an ILA on the rest of the objects I was unable to unlock any further information of significance." Another hiccup, and a female version of Dave's voice said, *sotto voce*, "Recording ends."

Oh crap. Oh crap oh crap oh crap.

"When you said you couldn't unlock anything else, you meant you licked a bunch of stuff, but there was no more supernatural information, right?"

"Correct."

The word came as a huge relief. For a minute I thought I had done something truly idiotic.

And then... relief dashed as Robot Dave added, "The only information that might remain is that on the smartphone I discovered underneath the brush."

"You said you couldn't find anything else!" My voice was shrill enough to shatter glass.

"Incorrect. I stated there was no further information I could garner via invasive lingual analysis. The phone is purely scientific. And there is a password lock which prevents further investigation."

"WHY DIDN'T YOU TELL ME THAT EARLIER?!"

Another hiccup. This time I heard a Dave who sounded weirdly like Michaelbrent. "Ugh. Okay, why don't you just... go sell books or something. I'll let you know if I need you. Pinochio is a real boy again."

I had cut him off before he reported everything, then turned him back into Real Dave and cut off any chance for him to tell me later.

I would have kicked myself if it had been physically possible. And if I had had time.

"Get that phone to me. Now!"

Robot Dave answered, "Affirm. Your location?"

I told him. I heard him get up. I also heard that other voice on Dave's side of the phone say, "Fine. You don't want half a million dollars, you don't have to have it. We have other authors waiting for this kind of advance, you know!"

I vowed two things: never to assume anything, and never to tell Real Dave what our little conversation had cost him.

I'll make it up to him.

Sure. And pig demons will fly out of my butt.

I took solace in the fact that, given how everything else was going, that last was a real possibility.

35

Robot Dave was there fast enough that I barely had time to ask the old lady if she dreamed about trains a lot. She didn't understand the question, and I was about to inquire whether she'd ever dreamt she was a donut sitting on top of a tall tree, but Dave showed before I had the chance. Life is full of lost opportunities.

We left the booth and walked into the con floor. I took a last quick look around, hoping without hope to see SuperGhoul, but she was still a no-show. Not surprising – I certainly hadn't acted competently so far, and it was understandable that the universe wouldn't be in the mood to toss me any easy pitches.

Dave and I wandered aimlessly, passing everything from a guy who made Captain America shields out of the pull tops from soda cans, to a girl who painted you... and I mean painted *you*. Music thumped from a truck owned by a local radio station. There was a full-sized boxing ring in the middle of everything, where you could pay five hundred bucks to go *mano a mano* with people who used to be American Gladiators.

Cons as usual. Weird and wonderful and more than a little overwhelming.

Robot Dave handed the phone to me as we swam up the meat river between displays. It was about what one would expect from a princess/interspecies hooker/booth babe. Late model, silver, with a pink case that had a bunch of rhinestones spelling "Easy Rider" on the back.

I turned on the screen. It showed an innocuous blue background, asking for the passkey. No numbers, though: it must need a particular pattern swiped on the surface. I swiped my fingers across it in a few random patterns: a star, a fish. I turned it sideways and did my best "up, up, down, down, B, A" attempt.

It stayed blue and unopened. Maybe I could get someone to magically unlock it – though I doubted it. This particular manufacturer had a *really* good security unlock system, and even magic could run into trouble with something like this. I'd probably be better off just fondling the screen as often as possible and hoping to get lucky.

Wow. Yeah, I just said that.

"Anything else?"

Robot Dave looked at me. "The question is vague."

I held up the phone. "Is there anything else you have discovered but not yet disclosed that is of evidentiary or potentially evidentiary value as pertaining to our current investigation?"

Robot Dave went still, standing there like a stone in the current of people. He was big enough he could get away with it, and I hid in his shadow so as not to get swept away.

"Negative," he finally said.

I nodded. Gave him the keyword to unlock Real Dave. As before, the spell that returned him to his normal self apparently filled in whatever blanks necessary to keep him unruffled. He mumbled something about Homeric principles, then moved in the direction of the WordFire Press booth.

I kept playing with the phone. It kept quietly mocking me. When I got to the point where I had to choose between putting it away until later or flinging it to the ground and stomping it to itty bitty bits, I made the right choice and shoved it in my pocket.

I stood for a moment – well, I ambled in the direction the meat river directed. For the first time today, I had nothing to do. I had no further leads, and Anderson had all but told me the case had moved beyond my abilities – my "above average when compared to children" abilities.

Nothing to do.

A moment later, I began laughing.

Nothing to do?

How about your job, dingus?

I could actually be at my table. You know, *making money.*

I beat it over there, really looking forward to interacting with buyers, maybe a few fans – people who rarely tried to kill each other or, more importantly, me.

I noticed from pretty far off that my mom wasn't at the table.

That in and of itself wasn't too unusual. Like all beautiful women, my mother never has to go Number One or Number Two (I thought they did, but that was before I got married and my wife let me know what's what). But she does occasionally visit the Powder Room, for reasons both mysterious and unknown to Man. So when I saw the unmanned table, I figured she had just taken a Powder break. Usually there are two of us at the table, so if one or the other has to leave for some reason – Powdering of some kind, or solving a supernatural murder that could lead to the end of the world – the other person just guards the fort.

If there is only one person at the table – as had been the case for my poor ma almost the whole day – you just leave. This is a cool thing about conventions: if you're at a swap meet or even a mall kiosk and you leave hundreds – or in some cases tens of thousands – of dollars in stock with no one watching, you can be assured that you'll come back to your table to find that people had assumed the five-finger discount was in effect.

Nerdkind, however, seems to have a greater percentage of people who have mastered basic respect for others' things. Maybe it's because they all have a treasured piece of art, or book, or bitchin' video game console that they would hate to see abused or stolen, and that gives them greater empathy. Maybe it's because the Kingdom of Nerd was so long besieged by bullies who could steal their lunch money with ease and without reprisal.

Whatever the reason, most of the con vendors are happy to leave their stuff for a short time so they can get food or do their Powdering. All they do is tell the person at the table next to them (who is usually a complete stranger, as well), "Can you keep an eye on my stuff?" That suffices.

Usually.

But now... as I got closer to my table, I saw that Mom wasn't the only thing missing.

My books were gone. All of them.

I couldn't fool myself for an instant that I had just sold out. I never do that on the first day. Never. I'm just not that popular, that cool, or that good-looking.

No, my books hadn't been sold, they'd been *stolen*. The racks they sat on were askew, the table covering was messed up. It looked ransacked.

There *was* one book still on the table. It sat in the middle of the destruction, its cover missing. Seeing that, I knew that whoever had stolen my books wasn't looking to resell them (good luck with that) – they were looking to send a message.

But what message was that?

My table was bordered by a another table laden with small iron sculptures, and a vendor space whose owner sold manga comics and anime DVDs. I couldn't remember either of the vendors' names – I hadn't been at the table long enough to really set them in my mind.

I went to Mr. Manga. "Where'd my stuff go?" I said.

He looked confused. "Who are you?"

"I'm...." Words failed for a moment. All I could do was point over and over at my table. "*Me!*" I finally managed.

That was enough. He looked at the table, and when he looked back at me, there was a strange light in his eyes. Fear?

"I don't know," he said. "I went to get a burrito, and when I came back it was like this."

He wasn't telling me something. "What aren't you telling me?" I asked. Direct, that's me.

"Nothing," he mumbled, looking away from me.

"Hey, man, I –"

"I don't know *anything!*" He snarled the words, but still didn't look at me. Yeah, that was fear. Fear masks itself as anger a lot of the time – maybe most of the time. That's why wars start, not to mention gang disputes, fist fights, and nasty words over a Monopoly table. But I could see his dread in the set of his shoulders, the way he kept grabbing DVDs off his table and then returning them.

I thought about pressing. Decided to move on. Maybe my other neighbor would provide answers.

The gal who made the iron figures was just as vociferous. She really underlined her point when, after asking me in perfect English if I wanted to buy anything and then hearing me ask about my table, she pretended to only speak what I think was Cambodian.

I moved away from her, too, when she grabbed a dragon sculpture the size of my fist and made it clear she was about to chuck it at me.

I get into it with Otherworlders. And sometimes Blake Casselman. But mostly I try to avoid actually physically assaulting normals. Not only can it get me in jail, it just isn't cool.

I moved back to Mr. Manga. He got ready to snarl at me, but I held up my hands. "I'm not going to ask you about the books." He waited, tense. "I just want to know... where's my mom?"

This was the question that really worried me; the one I'd avoided because, for one of the rare times in my life, I didn't want to know the answer.

What if something happened to her? What if whoever took my books and roughed up my table and scared the other vendors had also carried her away? Forget about how horrible that was for me personally, I didn't know how I'd tell Dad if something happened to her. That could literally kill him.

But Mr. Manga's face relaxed, and I did, too – a bit. "Oh, the old lady at the table?" He actually smiled a bit. "She's a riot. 'Pew, pew!'" He made a gun with his fingers.

One of the people at the WordFire Booth had done that, too. I wasn't sure why, but seeing another person do it exactly the same way gave me the creepies.

"Where is she?" I repeated.

He shrugged. "I think she went to the bathroom."

"How long ago? Before or after...." I gestured at my table.

His eyes got cold again, darting away from me. "I don't know," he said. "I don't know *anything* about that, you get me?"

Not good.

Not good at all.

36

"You need some help?"

At the sound of a female voice, I almost turned and embraced the woman behind me on the slim chance it was Mom. I managed to quell the urge, which was good since Mercedes already had *her* arms out.

Again: Mercedes hasn't used her succubus powers on anyone since getting married. But again: Why take the chance?

She pouted a bit at my response to her, then shrugged. She was holding a plastic bag in each hand, obviously doing some shopping on the con floor. A strap held Mercedes' ukelele on her back and what looked like a pair of Wonder Woman boots peeked over the top of one bag.

She nodded her chin at my table. "What happened, MB?" she said

"I don't know." I tried to say something else, but found I couldn't. I was scared – maybe more scared than I'd ever been as a Warden.

It's one thing to tangle with a tentacle, to kill a Kraken's cousin. But that's *me*. My family is another matter.

Mercedes saw my face. She moved forward and almost put a hand on my shoulder, stopping a foot away. I could tell she *wanted* to hold me, but wasn't going to.

In spite of everything else going on, I really liked Mercedes at that moment. She usually played a bit, teasing at grabbing me. Not now. She knew when the time to tease was past.

"Did something... happen?"

The way she said the last word was clear: she wanted to know if an Otherworlder had taken Mom.

"I don't know," I answered.

Worry creased Mercedes' face. She knows Mom. They like each other – a lot. They're very similar in temperament, with personalities that shine brighter than a quasar. Not to mention the shared enjoyment of "eccentric" wardrobes. So I could see that Mercedes had caught my concern and made it her own.

I turned to the table. Nothing but the racks, the skewed tablecloth. The book.

I grabbed it. Looked through the pages. And felt simultaneous relief and dread.

Nothing on the title page of the book – which was *Crime Seen*. I wondered if the choice of what book to leave behind meant anything. I turned the page.

Yes, it did.

The second page had a *Pokemon* card taped to it. And below it, a symbol I knew: the circle bordered by two parallel lines that was the symbol of the Green Lantern. Small – about the right size to be the imprint of a man's ring.

"The Nerdfather," I said.

He had said we could be "friends" if I found – and killed – whoever killed Calista. Apparently he had decided to motivate me a bit, by giving me a small taste of what would happen if I didn't do what he'd asked me to.

I tore the *Pokemon* card away from the page and looked at it. Normal on the front – it actually looked like a pretty decent card, one that my oldest son would enjoy adding to his deck.

The other side, though, ruined it as a playing card. *Pokemon* cards all have identical back sides, so as not to reveal what they are before they're in play. This one had been defaced, rather noticeably.

On this one, someone had written my address. My *home* address.

"Message received," I said, crushing the card in my fist.

Mercedes hadn't seen what was on the card. "Can I help?" she asked.

"Yeah," I said. "Can you stay here?" I nodded at the table. "I want to see if I can find Mom, but I don't want to miss her if she comes back here."

Mercedes nodded gravely. "You betcha." She squeezed between the tables without another word and sat on one of the chairs behind mine. She laid her swag on the floor and swung her uke around so she could pluck absently at it.

I had another thought. "Mercedes, is there a cashbox under the table?"

She lifted the table skirt and checked. Nodded.

"Can you give it to me?"

My cashbox was fixed to the table with a cable barely long enough to reach me. But it did. I keyed in the combo on the lock and opened the box.

My money was there. There hadn't been much to start with, and I could see that every penny was present and accounted for. That chilled me even more. There was no way the Nerdfather could have done this personally – he was either in a holding room in the convention center, or on his way to the local police station. His lackeys had done all this. And they had done *only* what he told them, clearly evidenced by the very specific ransacking and the fact that they ignored the cashbox.

The Nerdfather wasn't just a gaming Alpha. He had troops, and those troops did what he told them to.

I looked at the crumpled card in my fist.

I called home, dialing as fast as I could. I got Laura's voice mail. I texted, and a moment later she responded.

> we R fine. #3 kid started throwing up.
> Probably won't call 2nite because barftrain keeps loading.
> UR lucky to be gone. ;o(

I stared at the text. There was no doubt it came from Laura. She was safe.

So why didn't I feel any better?

"I'm sure she'll be fine," said Mercedes, and I liked her that much more.

172

"Yeah," I said, then I turned and hurried toward the nearest bathroom. Behind me, I heard the Mercedes plink out the first notes of *Where, Oh Where Has My Little Dog Gone?*

Don't stress. Maybe she did *just go to the bathroom.*

A lie, I knew it.

Mom wasn't in the women's bathroom. I know, because I just barged right in. A twenty-something dressed as a woodland fairy and another one adjusting her Harley Quinn makeup both screeched as I came in, looking ready to call security. I couldn't blame them – I caught a look at myself in one of the mirrors and saw a ragged, crazy-eyed person who was sweating like he had just worked out with The Rock. *I* would have called security on me.

Harley's eyes widened, and she whispered something to the fairy. I thought I heard, "He's sick, he has to get to the closest bathroom," to which the fairy whispered (very loudly), "This is *him*?" and Harley said something quiet enough that I couldn't hear it, but which I suspected was some variation on "that guy with all the attacks of diarrhea."

Whatever, I didn't care. I just wanted to find my mom.

I moved past them, and opened the first stall. No one. Second stall was empty, too. The third and fourth were occupied, and I dropped to my knees to see if I could do a foot-based identification on the occupants.

"Uhhhh...." Harley started edging for the door.

I ignored her. "Mom?" I called out. There was no answer. "Judi?" Still nothing, and the feet (and the clothes wrinkled around the girls' shins) below the stall doors belonged to a Batgirl and a whatsername from *Game of Thrones*.

At this point, something hit me on the back of the head. Hard. The pain I'd already been feeling thanks to my scuffle with the Nerdfather tripled, then doubled again.

I hadn't realized that the fairy had a wood staff. Now I did, because it was crashing repeatedly down on my back.

"Get out of here!" she was shouting. "Get out, you perv!"

This was really *not* my day. I put my hands up, shielding the back of my head as well as I could. Then ran, hunched over, for the exit. The staff rained down on me the whole way.

I ran out of the bathroom, hoping that if I left her domain the fairy would simply allow me to disappear into the crowd. Alas, it was not to be. She followed me right out of the bathroom, screaming at me at the top of her lungs. I ran, bent over and half blinded by the blows that kept falling on my back and head.

I was concerned I might be the first recorded case of "Death by Bathroom Fairy."

I worried more that this would draw some serious attention: we were three steps into the con floor, and a wood fairy beating a harried horror author half to death is the kind of thing people notice. Though I had a lot of latitude for certain things as a Warden, I wasn't acting as a Warden now, just a concerned son. Something like being found peeking under the women's restroom stalls could get me tossed out of the con.

Would that be a bad thing?

I quickly told that part of my brain to shut its hole. Yes, it'd be nice to be out of range if this murder case blew up, but there was always the slim possibility I might be able to help with the pesky "entire Earth at risk of supernatural destruction" thing.

Plus, if I left I'd just be eating all the travel expenses and wouldn't be able to offset them with sales.

Sales of what?

Then the staff hit me again, and any semblance of thought went out the window for a second. The wood fairy whacked me on the back of the skull, and my vision went blurry – though not before I saw Harley Quinn coming at me with a massive cosplay hammer that looked all too heavy and hard.

I braced for impact. Closed my eyes. Then opened them just as quickly – I'd rather see my death coming, I guess.

That was why I saw what happened. Saw rescue coming from the least expected quarter.

Blake appeared at the edges of the con floor, emerging from between several people (who still hadn't noticed the kerfuffle, thank goodness). He saw what was happening – what was *about* to happen – and he *moved*.

This was the first time I'd seen Blake at full speed without being on the receiving end of it. And even though he wasn't moving to thrash anyone, he still moved like an oil slick, sliding over the floor with near-inhuman grace.

He darted forward, reaching into his pocket at the same moment, and came up with something in his hand. I didn't see what it was, but he hurled it over me.

There was no "poof" or "bam" or anything like that. Just silence... which itself told a lot. No one was attacking me. The next blow of staff or cartoony hammer didn't put out my lights.

I risked a look at Harley and the fairy. They stood totally motionless, matching faraway looks on their faces, as though they stared at a divine sunset over some faroff shore that only they could see.

"You... you saved me," I managed to stutter, still half-crouched with my hands trying to shield the back of my head.

"Don't sound so surprised," said Blake. "Anderson wants you."

I blinked. "I thought he said I was done."

Blake shrugged. "I'm just the messenger. Now get going."

I looked back at the fairy and Harley, and now I noticed the fine, twinkling powder that still floated gently around them. I smelled the lilac.

I looked at Blake, impressed. "A Forget-me-not?" I asked. Blake nodded.

Forget-me-nots are basically mental reset buttons. Prepared by only a few of the most powerful witches, they cause those effected by the spell to forget everything that's happened in the last few minutes. The caster – literally, since the powder has to be thrown – can either leave the victims with a five minute gap in their memories, or he can suggest an alternate memory that will seem perfectly reasonable and convincing when the first effect of the spell wears off.

A very nifty spell, though very hard to find and very expensive even if you *did* find it. I also thought it was funny that it was called a Forget-me-not, seeing as how its base was lilac powder. But that's witches for you: they like flowers, and they like misdirection.

Well, they like *most* flowers. Which is another part of the misdirection, I suppose, considering the whole *Wizard of Oz* thing. A lot of people don't know that L. Frank Baum, the writer of the original *Oz* books, was threatened by a witch, and actually forced to put the bit about poppies in as a way of embedding the idea that poppies are dangerous to people. And they are... but they're more dangerous to witches. About the only thing that can take down a witch is a serious concentration of *Papaver somniferum* – the opium poppy. Which, seeing as how it's illegal in the United States to cultivate opium poppies, is not something I carry around with me on a typical – or even atypical – day.

I digress. The point is that Forget-me-nots aren't something you typically just carry around. But Blake had some. I wondered whether he'd gotten it from Anderson, or had acquired it himself. I didn't *really* know all that much about Blake, just that he was fast, cunning, and had an extraordinarily painful right hook. I didn't even know if he was an Otherworlder, some kind of human mage, or something even weirder.

Almost as though he sensed me thinking about him, and didn't want it to continue, Blake spoke. He directed himself at the fairy and Harley and said, in an authoritative tone, "You two saw what seemed to be a man in the bathroom. But it was just a woman who was really bad at cosplay, and she ended up looking like an ugly white dude with no hair." Harley and the wood fairy suddenly relaxed even more as the Forget-me-not did its work. They wouldn't report me, and there would be no further hassle, other than that they were going to give me very weird looks in the future. I glared at Blake, but he ignored me as, ever the panel programmer, he added, "And you both will definitely go to the Medieval Fighting in a Modern World panel at eight o'clock."

The girls nodded like their heads were controlled by the same puppetmaster. Which they more or less were.

Blake turned to me and reiterated, quietly so as not to intrude with the last bits of the spell, "Anderson wants you."

I finally managed to stand up straight. My back let me know it was angry at me. I told my back to shut up. "Blake, now's not a good time. My mom's missing and –"

"I don't care," he snarled. "Get your butt to the hotel. Room 902."

"Hey, I really can't –"

Blake must have seen something in my eyes, because even though he cut me off with a gesture, his own gaze softened a bit. Just a bit. "What's up with your mom?" he said.

"I can't find her."

He nodded, then pulled a walkie-talkie off his belt. All the con runners had one, as well as the heads of security and some of the more trusted volunteers. Blake activated his and said into it, "Orrin."

A deep voice that *screamed* "I am burly" said back, "Yo."

"I need you to detail ten people to go looking for someone."

"Uh-huh." Orrin was a talky one.

"Older lady, late sixties, dressed in purple steampunk with a top hat. Probably going 'pew, pew' and shooting people with a golden gun as she wanders around."

"I know her. That woman's hilarious!"

I gaped at Blake, surprised at his description of my mom. I mean, I knew he knew her, but I wouldn't have thought he was so aware of her he could describe her with such specificity.

He saw the look, "What?" he practically snarled. "Unlike my feelings for you, I *like* your mom." Then he added, "Now get to 902. Fast." I remained rooted to the spot for a whole second, so he screamed, "*MOVE. NOW!*"

I moved.

38

In case you don't remember: the hotel was connected to the convention center via a covered walkway, so getting there wasn't a problem.

The only thing of note on the way over was that I got a few serious glares. I didn't understand it at first, then I recognized some of the cosplay costumes: they were Otherworlders I'd seen in the Other Green Room. One of them - a guy dressed as the Stay-Puft Marshmallow man and whom I was fairly certain was the rock monster, mimed slitting his throat.

I was making so many friends!

Room 902 was on the top floor of the hotel. Normal shlubs from the peasant levels shouldn't even have been able to get there, since floors seven through nine required a special key card to access. Of course, my key card worked for every door, but even so when I got to the elevator a man dressed in the hotel's uniform was waiting.

Interesting. Anderson knew I had an all-access pass, so either he'd forgotten about it – unlikely – or the invitation to room 902 didn't come from him. Just relayed to me through him.

I wondered who could have made one of the Dead Ones do his lackey work. It was a short list, and other than Anderson's agent, everyone else on the list was an Otherworlder… and very scary.

The kid at the elevator must have been given a description of me, because he jumped forward and bowed several times (seriously: *bowed*), then thumbed the elevator's call button and as soon as one arrived he swiped his keycard over the security reader and hit the button for the ninth floor.

The guy was jumpy enough that it made my teeth itch. Things didn't improve when he said, "Good luck," in a warbling voice as the doors closed, then ran away at top speed.

Blake hadn't indicated what was on the top floor, only that Anderson wanted me there. I had an inkling. My inkling almost started *me* inkling, right down the leg of my pants.

The elevator opened to a small antechamber with a door at one end, also secured by an electronic lock that could only be opened if you had the right key card.

Again, someone was waiting for me. A woman this time, but dressed in the same livery as the man downstairs. She shouted, "Hold the elevator, please!" as the doors opened. I put my hand on the doors to keep them from closing. At the same time, the woman slid a card over the security reader on the door to the main part of the ninth floor.

A green light blinked on the security reader. I realized what she was going to do, and even though my magic key card would have gotten me into the hall beyond the door, I automatically lunged forward to yank the door open at the same time as the woman lunged *back* to throw herself into the elevator.

Apparently she'd been told to wait and to open the door for me. Which she had. And she wasn't going to wait a single instant beyond doing that.

I saw her slump against the back of the elevator before the doors closed. The door to the ninth floor was cracked open, the handle in my right hand, and I seriously debated letting it close and then running downstairs, finding my mom, and bailing on this whole situation.

Of course, I couldn't. There was the Containment, and even though I wasn't an Otherworlder, I *was* in the World, so there was a decent chance the spell would catch me if I tried to leave.

Also, staying was the right thing to do.

You go ahead and pretend that latter one was the big reason I stayed. I want you to think well of me.

So I didn't leave. I pulled the door the rest of the way open and stepped into the ninth floor hall.

My mom and I were staying on the third floor: a basic room with two beds, a television, a bathroom (shower only!), and not much else. The hall alone on the ninth floor was about ten times nicer. I mean it: the carpet was probably softer than my bed, and the view out the panoramic windows was nicer than any television show.

I was where the rich folk walked. It felt totally wrong.

902 came upon me too quickly. I felt like it had leaped out of the wall and shouted, "Boo!"

I turned as soon as I saw it, though, and raised my hand to knock without any hesitation. Not being brave, I just knew that if I *did* hesitate, I'd grow old and die trying to work up my nerve.

So: the hand went up.

The hand went down.

It didn't hit the door. Instead, I went blind.

It took me two very fast heartbeats to realize that my eyes hadn't stopped working. Instead, someone had grabbed my arm to keep me from knocking on the door, and someone else had dropped a dark hood over my head.

I tried to scream, but another hand went around my neck and gave it a gentle squeeze. By "gentle" I mean that I nearly passed out.

A voice hissed in my ear. It was strangely sibilant, like a snake had taken human form. I half expected it to encourage me to eat the apple. "If you resist or shout for help, I will tear out your throat and drink you."

The inkling feeling that I'd had earlier intensified. I may actually have peed a little. (Don't tell anyone.)

I was jerked roughly to the side, then I heard a door open, and the hum of an elevator. Doors click-clicked open.

I expected to hear the tap of a button being hit. Instead, I heard a metallic jingle that I identified after a moment as being a keyring.

"Hey, guys, if you smell something in here, I will admit ahead of time that it was me."

That earned me a sharp cuff on the back of the head. My neck yelled at me for being a smartass. I told my neck I was sorry and vowed never to do it again. Though I crossed my fingers behind my back. Which, by the way, earned me another cuff.

"Don't move," snarled that same voice.

Metal scraped on metal.

The elevator began to ascend.

Yes, I *did* tell you the ninth floor was the top floor, thank you for paying attention! But still... up, up, up we went.

And that could mean only one thing.

The doors opened. I was pushed forward, then we turned. Turned again.

I heard murmurs. I couldn't hear any words, but there was the sense of that same sibilance that had marked my captor's words.

The hood was jerked off me. I still couldn't see, though, since bright sunlight blinded me. My eyes squinted, tears squeezed out the corners – not only from pain, I think I was just that scared.

A group.

All speaking in hisses.

Bright sunlight.

Bright. Sunlight.

All of this could only mean one thing: I was standing before the High Court of the Vampires.

39

Sunlight doesn't kill vamps. Quite the opposite: it's a powerful narcotic to them. Which is why they generally avoid it like the plague, since vampires are both hunters and (occasionally) hunted, and nothing will get someone in that situation into more trouble than wandering around like an idiot.

It's also why the High Court is always – *always* – held in a place of bright light. Vamps are naturally aggressive – the hunter part. To the point that holding diplomatic meetings or rendering evenhanded judgment is nearly impossible. So they use the sun to their advantage by holding court under a huge canopy that travels wherever they go. It shields them from direct UV so they don't turn into morons, but enough sunlight filters in that it... *mellows* them a bit. Enough so they don't just skip to the throat-tearing part of every conversation.

And it *is* the direct UV that's a problem – specifically, the UVB that's part of sunlight. Which is why vampires can move around hotels and convention centers with impunity, since window glass nowadays all blocks UVB.

End result: vamps like cons. And though the members of the royal court don't care about what floor they're on, they *always* make sure they get roof access.

I was standing outside the canopy, which I suspected was intentional. The vamps might be a bit more mellow under the wide stretch of canvas, but that didn't make them like humans in general or me in particular.

There were no thrones, no sconces with eerily flickering flames. The vampires were thoroughly modern. A group of them milled on either side of me – perhaps thirty or so, total. The only obvious reason I could tell who the royals were was because they were actually seated. Nothing fancy: they sat on folding chairs whose only nod to frivolity or ostentation was a red cushion on the seat.

Still, there was no mistaking the royals once I spotted them. I had never met them, but I knew their names and positions, and it was easy to place names to faces.

There were four of them. First was a strikingly handsome man dressed in black slacks and a simple white button-up. He appeared to be in his forties, but an extremely fit forty-something. He had blue eyes, but as with all vampires that iris had a ring of dark red around it. His beard was threaded with a few gray streaks – not enough to make him seem old, just dignified – and he had a body that was visibly powerful and fast, even in repose. King William de Vesci.

Next to him, on his left, sat Queen Borga. She looked about the same age – forties – but like him she was stunning. Long-limbed under the short black skirt, white skin that fairly glowed with energy beneath her own white blouse. Her hair was blond, bound up on her head by an intricate series of pins that gave the hairdo an Asian feel. A tiara rested on her forehead.

Beside the queen, Princess Roberta sat. Unlike her mother and father, there was nothing relaxed about her, even under the influence of the narcotic light around her. She sat alert, almost rigid, and when I saw her she leaned forward and bared her teeth, the canines growing visibly and the ring in her eyes widening until her blue irises almost disappeared in red as her anger soared. Even so, she was as gorgeous as her parents. Slimmer than her mother, with the body of a girl in her early twenties. She had hair that was a mix of both parents – light brown. But where many women with that color hair must get used to hearing it described as "mousy," Roberta's hair shone like a lion's mane. Nothing mousy about her; she seemed like the most dangerous of the three.

Next to Roberta was a younger man: Prince Warine, which in my opinion was about as terrible a name as I'd ever heard. Warine looked a few years younger than Roberta, and had the same facial features, hair color, and complexion as his sister. But even at first glance, if I'd had to pick the calmer, steadier of the two, he was the easy choice.

There was one more chair, on the right side of King William. I wondered where Prince Eustace was hiding.

The rest of the assembly – the royal court – murmured and hissed among themselves, and several threw me sideways glances. They quieted, though, when Queen Roberta leaned forward.

"Thank you for coming," she said.

"Sure. I'm always at the service of people who kidnap me." I shrugged. "By the way, with the hood: *really*? Were you hoping to keep me from knowing how I got here? Because it was an elevator. To the roof."

The princess snarled, but the queen laughed. King William just looked bored. I wondered if he'd been sunbathing before I got here.

"We don't wish to hide our location," said Queen Borga. "As you say, it is no secret. But...." Her eyes narrowed to slits, and I thought I saw a hint of fang in her mouth. "We know what you are, Warden. And we have no wish to have you hunting any of us for stealing you away. The hood was to protect those who came for you."

"I would have shown up with a 'please,'" I said.

She shook her head. "Doubtful. And in any case, you were already on your way to the Great Pack." She leaned forward. "I wanted to speak to you first."

So the vamps knew what I had suspected: that 902 was the penthouse where the Great Pack – the lycan equivalent of the High Court – was staying.

"Okay, you've got me here," I said. "What do you want?"

The princess leaped out of her chair, and I'm not ashamed to say I cringed. She wanted to kill me, I could tell. Maybe kill every human alive. "Why do we waste time?" she shouted. "The whore-princess is dead. Let it be."

"And when war comes for us?" said the queen mildly.

Roberta bared her teeth again. "Let the dogs and bitches come. We will tear their blood from their veins."

William made his first entry into the conversation: he sighed. I knew that sigh: I made it all the time when *my* daughter verged on going overboard. Though usually *my* daughter went overboard about bedtimes and not being allowed to watch her favorite show, and not about bloodlust and the desire to murder whole species.

Maybe when she gets to be a teenager.

"Roberta, please," he drawled. Then he actually closed his eyes and seemed to fall asleep.

Roberta glared at him. He didn't see it. She glared at me. I did see it.

Borga waved, and the princess bowed slightly and settled back in her chair. Borga gazed at me. "Calista is dead," she said.

The way she said it surprised me. I mean, that they knew wasn't too big a surprise – no matter how hard you try, people are going to find out about things that big. But she said it with what sounded like genuine sadness – even grief.

The emotion got me to say what wild horses might not have dragged out of me: the simple truth. "Yes," I said.

Roberta hissed, a triumphant sound. Again, Borga silenced her daughter with a gesture. "We weep with the Great Pack," she said. At this, Roberta laughed.

Borga stood. Her husband opened an eye at the movement, but didn't seem inclined to get involved.

"Walk with me," she said. An attendant handed her a parasol – beautiful, with lace edges and a handle that looked like it might be obsidian.

She stepped away from the canopy. A few people – obviously guards – stepped toward her. She stopped them. "I'll be fine," she said.

"Lady," answered one of them, a heavily-muscled man with green irises barely peeping out from under their ring of red. "The king –"

Borga simply looked toward her husband, who opened his eyes and said, "Rathton, let the queen play her games."

Rathton nodded – though he didn't like it – and stepped back into the crowd of attendants. He glared at me as he did, and I could tell I'd just made another enemy. He didn't like me, didn't like what I represented, and perhaps most of all didn't like that I was walking around like an equal instead of like a skin-wrapped smoothie.

Have you ever walked hand-in-hand with an alligator while it smiles at you? If so, you might have a small idea of what I felt when Borga put her arm through mine, then drew me away from the court. She was beautiful, and when she looked at me it was with a smoldering, sensuous gaze. Her smile was genuine, too – near as I could tell.

But she was dangerous. To be the vampire queen was more than just a birthright. It could be challenged, taken by those more "worthy" – meaning more able to kill. By very nature of the succession, the king and queen were killers beyond understanding.

And yet when she she spoke, there was no hint of animus or threat.

"Forgive Roberta," she said. "She has opposed the treaty since the matter was broached."

"You don't say."

She took my words at face value. "No, it's true. Roberta is a good girl, but sometimes she lacks...." She searched for the word.

"Impulse control?" I said.

Borga took no offense. She smiled a bit wider and said, "I was going to say, 'vision.' But you speak truly as well."

"Why am I here?" I asked.

We'd drawn about forty feet away from the court, in bright sunlight on a tarpaper roof. Small stones embedded in the tarpaper crunched underfoot, and I couldn't help but think of someone crushing my skull with each footfall. Now Borga stopped, drawing me close.

"The vampires are not united. We are an independent people, and one of the reasons we have not risen up to take our place as masters of all is simply because no one agrees how to do it, why to do it, or even if it must be done." She sighed. "There was, as you can imagine, great opposition to the idea of treating with the wolves." The way she said "wolves" brought another surprise: there was none of the rancor I would expect to hear from a vampire talking about its mortal enemy. She just said it as another group of Otherworlders; as....

Equals?

I shook my head. That was almost impossible to believe.

"So why'd it happen?" I said.

"Because I know it is the right thing to do," she said. "And I generally get my way." At this last, her expression changed subtly and I had to resist the urge to run and take cover. The dangerous hunter she was had reared its head, if only slightly.

"So... that still doesn't explain why I'm here."

"You were the Warden charged with finding Princess Calista's killer, yes?"

I nodded, then said, "But I've been taken off the case."

She shook her head. "Consider yourself back on it."

"Uh, I don't think –"

"You misunderstand. Even if not following as Warden of the Dead Ones, you are now called to act as Envoy of the High Court." She leaned close, her eyeteeth suddenly long as my pinky. "And I charge you to find who killed my friend."

I almost lived up to my Man Who Poops moniker at that. "Your... your friend?"

She nodded. "Yes. Calista was my friend, and she was the reason I was able to reach out to the lycans. She and I together explored the possibility of a treaty. Without her, there would have been no possibility of peace."

"So you want me to find the killer because she was your friend?" I was still having trouble with the concept.

Borga chewed her lip – which actually required a bit of skill to do without turning her lip to hamburger, given the state of her teeth. But even as I watched, the eyeteeth receded and returned to "normal."

"The friendship is not all," she said.

"What else?"

A moment's hesitation, then she said, "I said the vampires do not accord easily, or often. I had to use all my influence to push this treaty upon the court, and upon my people. Should it fail...."

I got it. "You'll be challenged. You could lose your place as queen."

She shook her head. "There would be no challenge. William would execute me and take another in my place – someone who had not failed so completely. Likely Roberta."

I started. "Isn't she his – your – daughter?"

Borga chuckled. "The Children of the Sun do not live under the same rules and taboos as do your kind. Yes, William would marry her, and bed her, and perhaps raise another girl-child to take *her* place someday. If Warine ever challenged their father and succeeded to the Kingship, he would then take Roberta as his own."

I successfully resisted the "*Ewwww*" that really wanted be said. I settled for, "Huh. Uh-huh." And then one more, "Huh," to really drill the point home. Then, "What does King William think about your possible resignation?" I had noticed she didn't mention the possibility of *Eustace* challenging his father. Because he was off-limits since he was going to be married off as part of the treaty? If so, would his inability to ascend to the throne be reason for him to put a stop to the treaty, even if he had to murder someone to do so?

"My husband thinks nothing of the treaty – rather, he shows no preference." She shrugged. "He was on the fence about the possibility of a treaty, but he thought my arguments had more merit than those of Roberta. Barely. So he took the way of any true politician: he let the person of greater power get her way, then distanced himself enough from both sides that no matter who wins, it will seem that he supported that person in the wisest way, by letting that person forward without impediment, while at the same time keeping a watchful eye on the other."

"Would Roberta have gotten staked if the treaty hadn't worked out?"

Borga shrugged. "I don't know. Her failure would have been great, but she is several centuries younger, and that may buy her some leeway."

"I guess, that – Wait, 'buy' her some leeway? Are you still hoping for the treaty to go through?"

"Of course. If we – you – can discover who killed Calista, and point the blame elsewhere, then the treaty still has a chance at going forward. Even if not sealed by a marriage between the lycan and vampire houses, such a treaty would still be a great step toward peace between us."

"So Princess Roberta hates the treaty, King William is trying not to have a dog in that fight, and Prince Eustace is the insurance policy for the treaty's efficacy. What about Prince Warine?"

The queen's eyes grew distant. "Like his father, Warine does not intrude, though he, too, hopes for my failure and my fall."

I shook my head. "Sorry, your highness. But I don't see the lycans just saying, 'Oh, no worries, our princess is dead but we'll still sign the treaty.' Especially not if the person who blames someone else is an Envoy of the High Court. That doesn't really say, 'fair investigation,' does it? It'd be like Al Capone being checked out by his number one hitman."

Borga grimaced and nodded. "Which is why you will interview any of us you wish, except the king. I cannot secure his cooperation, but you are free to speak to anyone else. And you have my guarantee that you will have their cooperation. That way you can not only find who did this horrible thing, but assure any who ask that the first suspects were those of our court."

I asked the big question. "Do I have a choice in this, uh, huge honor?"

She just bared her teeth – very long again – and I watched her eyes turn completely red, the ring of blood swallowing not only iris, but white. Just a vast expanse of crimson with a single dark spot at the center.

Answer enough.

I dove right in. "Where were you this morning?"

"Listening to Stan Lee's opening ceremonies speech."

That probably covered the time of the murder, but.... "Everyone here was listening to Stan Lee. That's a big room, so I don't suppose you saw anyone who could vouch for you being there the entire time?"

She shook her head. "No, but I was in the front row. Fifth from the right of the center aisle. I'm sure the security cameras could see me easily."

Sure, if they were even working, I thought, remembering the electronic cloak that had fallen over the place where the murder occurred.

Borga misinterpreted my expression. "I know, I know. I won't show up on the camera. Just an empty chair. But surely your dwarf friend will be able to find me in spite of that fact."

Yet another surprise: she knew about Gandhi. Whoever or whatever was in charge of the court's intelligence, it was someone very good at what they did.

Still, what she'd said was true. "Do you mind if I verify your alibi?"

"I would expect it."

I pulled out my cell and dialed a number. Gandhi answered with his customary politeness. "What is it?" I could hear the sounds of a *Minecraft* game in the background.

"Hey, G-man, I have something I need you to do."

"Why should I?"

"Because we're partners, G. I gave you half of a very precious Gummi Bear."

He harrumphed. "I'm not stupid. I *know* you have the rest of it somewhere."

I sighed. "You caught me. But you get nothing until I'm satisfied with our partnership."

Contrite, he said now, "What do you want, *partner*?"

"First, did you find the feeds?" I was still standing with Borga, but I hoped she wouldn't be able to figure out what "find the feeds" meant. Alternatively, she might already know about them – she knew about everything else – in which case it made no sense to hide the information from her. She couldn't get much from a one-sided question.

"Nada," said Gandhi. "They're gone."

"I told you I need you to look harder than that, G-man. I –"

"I know, I know!" He stopped and the noise of Gandhi chewing something – probably a microwaved burrito or some Bagel Bites – sounded loud and clear in my ear. Through a full mouth, he said, "I didn't find the feeds, but I did find something."

"What?"

More chewing. "You remember that little mark on my tablet?"

"The little crack?"

"Yeah, only it wasn't a crack."

"What was it?"

"Still not sure. More of an etching than a crack, though that's not exactly right either." Chew, chew, burp through mouthful of cheese and meat substitutes, chew, chew. "It's magical, though."

That was interesting. "A spell token?"

"Not that I can tell. And get this: the same mark was on the cameras covering the rooms I couldn't pick up on my monitor."

I didn't ask him how he'd gotten into those rooms – especially the one where the murder had occurred – without anyone seeing. Dwarves have their wily ways.

"Same exact mark?"

He burped again, a truly amazing sound from someone his size, then said, "Yeah."

I didn't know what that meant. That someone had tampered with the feeds was already obvious, but I didn't know how this fit in, or how it would gain me anything useful. I moved on. "Okay, G-man, can you bring up the feeds for the opening ceremonies?"

"Sure, what are you looking for?"

"Who was sitting in the front row, fifth from the right of the center aisle?"

"Which right? Viewed from the back or the front?" Before I could answer he said, "Doesn't matter, I see it."

"What?"

"Vampire. Empty seat, fifth from the right as viewed from the stage."

"Can you get a picture of who's there?"

"I can try. Just give me...." He grunted, doing his thing and coaxing more out of the picture than anyone else in the world could have done. Then he whistled. "Hottie."

"Can you give me details?"

"Almost, just give me a –" He whistled again, a different kind of whistle. "Queen Borga is a fan of the Stan? What a cool chick."

"I'll tell her. Can you see if she was there the entire time?"

"Stan the Man's talk, or the entire opening ceremonies?"

"The whole ceremonies."

A short pause, then, "Yup. She was there, no bathroom breaks or anything. She cheered about when Stan talked about Captain America as an Agent of Hydra, though." He sounded disgusted about that.

"Can you tell if the person actually *was* Queen Borga? Check for spell auras or nearby runes?"

"Harder. But yes." After a moment he said, "Nothing. At least, nothing I can see. There could be something I haven't spotted, but that would be some serious mojo."

"Okay, G-man. I will send a package of Gummi Bears."

"A *package*?" he breathed.

"For services rendered, and as a retainer for the rest of the con. Deal?"

I actually *heard* him nodding.

I turned off the phone, pocketed it, and looked at Borga. The queen had waited patiently during the entire exchange. Now, she arched an exquisitely-shaped eyebrow. "Far as I can tell, your alibi's good," I said. "Though I'm going to revisit it if I need to."

"Of course." She nodded seriously, then gestured back at the court, the canopy above them flapping in the light breeze on the roof. "To whom would you like to speak now?"

I thought about it. The king was off-limits, Borga had said. I didn't have to ask why: if he was apathetic to the treaty, and wanted to distance himself from it, he wouldn't likely participate in an investigation that would have a major impact on its outcome. And it's not like you can subpoena the frigging Vampire King. He answers, or he doesn't. At *his* whim.

There was Roberta, of course. But before I checked her out, I realized there was someone else I needed to talk to.

"Where's Eustace?" I asked. "Where's the prince?"

40

"Why do you wish to talk to him?"

"Murders – even between Otherworlders – are most likely to be perpetrated by someone who knew the victim. The first person normal police always check out is the spouse, or, in this case, the fiancée."

"I beg you not to intrude on his grief."

I shook my head. "Gotta do it. If you really want this to be a balanced investigation." I frowned. "Is there a problem?"

She didn't answer my question, saying only, "I will take you to him." Surprisingly, she didn't turn toward the canopy or even toward the small structure beyond it that housed the elevator. Instead, she headed away from that side of the roof. It seemed to get hotter as we walked, the tarpaper reflecting the sunlight.

It was getting late, but it was still summer. And summer in this here parts means that the hottest time of day is six in the evening; the sun doesn't got down until after ten. I was acutely aware of this as I walked, the sweat springing from my pores and quickly running down the back of my neck.

The farther we went from the edge of the roof, the more air conditioning units, ducting, and other equipment were in evidence. It turned into a slow-moving obstacle course.

We passed two hulking air conditioning units, and Borga stopped. Without looking at me, she said, "Roberta is not my daughter."

I shook my head – confused at both the statement and the motivation behind it. "I thought you said she was."

"No, *you* said she was. I did not correct your assumption, because as a general rule, we of the court do not disclose our social or familial links to Wardens." She smiled. Her teeth were normal. "I'm sure you can understand."

I nodded. Waited.

She went on, "I am William's fifth wife, the fifth queen of his reign. Roberta is the child of his fourth wife. These facts do not endear me to her, or vice-versa."

"Sure."

"But what makes it worse is that she is William's firstborn. She believed that – in the unlikely event William died of natural causes, I would be set aside and she could ascend to the throne."

"Wait, how does that work?" I'd never heard the rules of vampire royal ascension. It was confusing, to say the least.

"It does not matter, Michaelbrent." Hearing her say my name creeped me out a bit. Like the boogeyman under your bed confirming your address before he massacres you. "What matters is that she believed she would rule the world of the vampires. Then the treaty came about, and she realized that not only would Eustace become king, he would be king of a greater domain than any she could have imagined."

"She hates him."

"Yes. But he loves her. As he loved Calista."

"He sounds cuddly."

Borga looked at me reproachfully. "He is a great man. He is my son. And he is grieving. So, please, be kind." She leaned very close to me. "Or his mother may take offense."

I gulped. Borga turned and moved toward a huge white box that hummed loudly but whose purpose I couldn't guess at. I followed her around the box.

Sitting on the roof on the other side was the prince.

With a name like Eustace, I fully expected to find a thin man, immaculately groomed, perhaps with the supernatural equivalent of a pocket protector in his shirt. Okay, I admit it: I'm a name bigot. I'm probably a bad person, but if I hear of a Nermal, or even a Winston, it conjures up a certain "type."[12]

---

[12] For the record, I do have a friend named Winston. I've told him not to hate me – he should hate his *parents*.

Eustace ranked high on the list of names that called up images of socially awkward weirdos.

But my idea of what he might look like was wrong on all counts. Eustace might be a slightly unfortunate name these days, but it must have meant "I am a badass" when he was born – which from what I knew could have been centuries ago.

His face was that of a kid barely into his twenties. But he already had the thick musculature of a mature man, with a strong chin covered by enough stubble to make him a candidate for a Wrangler jeans commercial. He would be just as good-looking as the rest of the family, under normal circumstances. But these weren't normal.

It had only been a matter of hours since Calista died, and even less time since he could have found that out – assuming he wasn't involved – but he looked as rumpled as if he'd been wearing the same clothing for the last week. His blond hair was wild from nervous hands running through it repeatedly. His body was loose, nearly limp. He sat cross-legged, leaning against the box at his back. But even with the structure for support he looked on the verge of spilling over to one side.

He had no shelter from the sun. His eyes were half-open, but I could see they were nearly colorless: the ring of blood had faded away almost completely, and the irises had gone gray. An effect of the light.

He was wearing a dark red Armani shirt, and that was lucky. It masked the blood. Borga gasped as she saw the same thing I did.

Crosses *do* hurt vampires. Not just any crosses, but those borne by faith. You don't have to be Catholic to wield one, but you do have to believe the cross will work. No doubt can be in your mind. That's why I don't use them. I believe in God, but I don't believe much in two sticks pasted at right angles. Just not something I was raised with, so it's not something I can put all my faith in.

You won't typically see vampires using crosses, either. They don't have faith in a deity – or maybe they do, I've never sat down to talk theology with them – but they've all heard enough about crosses that they fear them, and their utter assurance that a cross means danger is usually enough to activate the weapon. A vamp handling a cross would be like you or me handling a live coal barehanded.

That was what shocked both Borga and me. Prince Eustace had rolled up his right sleeve and was very carefully using his left index finger to trace crosses on his bare forearm. The lines sizzled as he completed each cross, the skin splitting and bleeding copiously for a few seconds before the wound sealed and left unmarked skin behind.

It obviously hurt, even through the near-stupor the prince had fallen into, but he didn't stop. Just gritted his teeth and drew line after line, cross after cross, blood after blood.

When his mother gasped, Eustace looked up. I could tell he'd been crying. A lot.

It took a moment for him to fully focus on her. He smiled, a wan, unhappy smile. "Mother," he said, and the vampiric teeth were not in evidence. His eyes slid over to me and he said, "Who's this?"

"This is the man who will find Calista's killer."

The prince began to weep. That fast, he went from a doped-up masochist to a soul torn asunder by grief. Borga leaned over and hugged him tightly. I felt uncomfortable – not just at the grief, but at the familial affection. It was as though I were intruding on something secret, even sacred.

A lot of people had lied to me about everything going on. But either Borga and her son really loved one another, or they both deserved to sweep this year's Tony, Emmy, and Academy Awards.

Even in the midst of tears, Eustace reached for his arm and started tracing another cross. Borga held her son's hand tight, but he pulled away and completed the figure. It tore, bled, and healed.

"The pain dulls the pain," he said. And I knew just what he felt. Memories of some of the worst days of my life – losing my job and my ability to take care of my family, the day I found out my daughter would die, the day she did – clawed their way to the surface of my mind in the face of Eustace's agony.

Eustace traced two more crosses, and Borga let him. Then the prince looked up, and in spite of the direct sunlight the red was back in his eyes. "You will find the killer?" he whispered.

I nodded. "I'll try." And for the first time it wasn't just a job. Monster or not, no one deserved the kind of pain the prince was feeling.

What it looks *like he's feeling. It could be an act.*

Be careful.

The prince nodded, then surged to his feet in a fluid movement. "Find him," he said. His canines extended faster than cats' claws. "Find him, and tear the beating heart from his still-living body!"

Then he sagged again, so fast and hard Borga barely caught him. She guided him back to the roof, and looked at me. "Ask your questions," she said.

"I don't think he's in any shape –"

"Ask them," she said again, and her voice brooked no disobedience. "Ask them now, so you can see my son loved her."

"Did you?" I said, turning to the prince. The question was a bit of a surprise to me: not your standard opening question for an interview of a potential murder suspect.

But he looked at me, and said, "Yes." I knew then why I'd asked the question.

Love – real, true, deep love – is almost impossible to feign. I love my wife, and there are many people who have commented on the way we are together. The way I look at her. I know exactly what that look is, because I can feel it on my face when I wake up at night to realize I'm having a never-ending slumber party with my best friend. I can feel it on my face when she teaches our children, when she takes care of me in an offhanded way that says her service is no sacrifice, but part of all the life she has chosen to lead with me.

Best of all, I have seen it on Laura's face, looking back at me. Don't ask me *why* she loves me – it truly baffles me. But she does, and I know what her face looks like when that love is closest to the surface.

It looked like the look on Eustace's face. Again, either he was the world's greatest actor, or he truly loved Calista.

"Where were you this morning?" I already didn't believe he'd killed his fiancée, but I also wanted to be thorough. Could I have been fooled about his apparent love for the princess? Sure, there's a first time for everything.

He thought – clearly a bit harder of a process for him than usual. "I was on the Cosplay & You panel from nine to nine-thirty. Then I was on Medieval Fighting Techniques from nine-forty to ten-thirty. Then...." His gaze swam a bit. He jerked himself back to the present, though with difficulty. "Then I was in the Green Room."

"The Other Green Room?"

"No. The one the normals use."

"How'd you manage that?" I asked. The prince was good-looking enough, but certainly not a celeb in the human world.

He shrugged. "I wanted to meet the cast of *Fringe*."

He said it like, "I wanted it, so it happened. End of story."

Must be nice.

"Okay, so both of you have alibis," I said. "I'll check them out more carefully, but...."

Now I was at a crossroads. I'd bet my *own* eyeteeth that the prince really did love Calista. But, again, I could be wrong. What if the prince had never really wanted the treaty to move forward? What if he had started out wanting them, but changed his mind? Would murder solve that problem? Even if he *did* love the lycan princess?

And what about if he discovered, say, that his bride-to-be was an interspecies prostitute who moonlighted as a booth babe? How much would his opinion of her change?

A long moment, with me deciding whether or not to ask if he knew about that.

I had already done a bad enough job this far. It was time to start earning my lack of pay.

"What do you know about Nespda?" I asked.

There wasn't so much as a flicker in the prince's eyes. No recognition whatsoever. That could have been because he was just *that* stoned, but it seemed like he simply hadn't ever heard of it before.

The queen, however, responded quickly and forcefully. She was still under her parasol, but the sun's mellowing rays suddenly had no effect on her. She snarled and nearly dropped her son as she leaped to her feet. The eyes were red, the teeth were bared.

Vampires are nothing if not mercurial.

"Disgusting," she said. "It should be laid waste to."

"What is it?" asked Eustace, his grief momentarily outweighed by his curiosity. Borga whispered into his ear, and he jerked with a mixture of shock and disgust. "Why would you ask me about such a thing?" he asked breathlessly. "What could a trafficker have to do with an innocent girl like my Calista?"

I could have told him, but asked instead, "Trafficker?"

Borga still looked angry. "You have sex traffickers in the human world, don't you? Why would the Otherworlders be any different?"

"And Nespda is a trafficker?"

Borga nodded. "They steal Otherworlders from their homes as children. Train them to do..." and her nose wrinkled, "... what they do. They *make* them do it, either because of fear or through magics or drugs."

"What does this have to do with my fiancée?" The urgency, confusion, and concern of the moment were driving out the relaxation and dissociation the sun had imparted to Eustace. His senses were sharpening, and with them came sharper pain.

"I have it on good authority that she was seen there," I said. Evasive, but I didn't want to play all my cards now.

"Never!" shrieked Borga. "She couldn't have been forced into that life. No member of the Great Pack would let that happen to one of their ruling class. They would die first."

True. Vampires didn't get along very well – internecine warfare was one of the greatest checks to the danger they presented to others. Werewolves were polar opposites: loyalty was their first and greatest value. Loyal to their families, to their clans, to their rulers. No lycan would let the princess of the royal family be taken away without hunting down the kidnappers. And they were *very* good hunters. Any such kidnappers wouldn't last long, and if a princess were taken she would quickly be returned.

But, again, there's a first time for everything. So could she have been roped into that life against her will? Blackmailed physically or mentally to perform for the pleasure of people like the Nerdfather? Was her stated love for him real, or was it part of the service?

Or did Calista *want* to be at Nespda? Did she want – for whatever reason – to play a role only the most desperate Otherworlders would find themselves in?

Too many questions. No answers at all.

Eustace started sobbing again. I wasn't done talking to him, or to Borga either – not by a long shot. But I decided to let them be for a moment. A lot of successful interview technique is knowing when to lean on someone, when to ease up. It was time to ease up here.

"I'd like to speak to Warine."

"That bastard?" said Eustace, and anger muted his sadness, made his eyes redden and made him seem less destroyed. Not powerful, but not broken, either. "What could he possibly tell you?"

A new line of inquiry. "He didn't approve of your marriage to Calista?"

"He doesn't approve of *me*." Eustace slashed the air with an open hand. "If you set me afire, he wouldn't piss on me to staunch the flames."

I looked at Borga to see what her reaction was. She nodded. "Warine is the middle child, born of the same Queen Mother as Roberta. He has always hated Eustace – he sees him as an interloper in his father's home. And he hated him still more when the treaty was announced."

"Why?"

"Because Roberta might perhaps someday have been Queen of the High Court, for she is the eldest. Eustace, through the treaty, will govern over a greater kingdom still, even though he is the youngest. Warine will never have call on any kingship, nor any place of importance other than that given him by others."

"He could challenge for kingship," I said.

Eustace snorted. "He would never do such a thing."

"Why?"

"Because he would lose. And he knows it."

Again, Borga nodded. "Warine is not a fighter. But he is sly, and cunning."

She let that hang there. I got it. Warine, she was saying, might well have meddled in the treaty. Perhaps even killed to stop it?

"Okay, so that's all the more reason for me to talk to him. Then Roberta."

The queen nodded. She leaned down to pull her son to his feet, but he jerked away from her.

"You can't stay here forever."

"I can stay until sundown."

Borga looked like she wanted to argue with her son. But I saw she didn't blame him for wanting to remain as dead to his emotions as he could for as long as possible. Perhaps she, in a small way, wished she could hide from the world, as well.

She touched her son's shoulder, her fingers lingering until he reached up to clasp her hand. Then his hand dropped away and he resumed drawing crosses on himself, smothering one pain with another.

"Come," said Borga. The queen didn't look at me when she said it, nor did she look back to see if I followed. She set off at a speedy pace. I caught up to her only when we were nearly back to the pavilion.

"Queen Borga," I said.

She kept walking, didn't turn, but said, "What?" in a clipped voice.

"You need to tell me what you know about Nespda."

"I have."

"You told me how it gets its employees. I'd like to know how you know that. And whether you knew that Calista had been there."

She stiffened. "Of *course* I didn't. Do you think I would associate with – *ugh*." The sound she made wasn't very queenly, but it effectively communicated her anger and disgust.

"Okay, then how did you know about Nespda? About Nespda in particular, not just places like it."

"I make it my business to be aware of such things." I thought she would keep talking, but she said no more. Instead, she halted so quickly that I slammed right into her back. It was like hitting a tree. Vampires are strong, and the queen felt like an exceptional example of her people.

She didn't seem to notice me piling into her back. But the second I managed to pull away from her, she was marching forward at top speed once more.

I saw why.

The Longest Con

There was a werewolf standing in the pavilion, and he and Princess Roberta looked to be on the verge of killing each other.

41

The lycan was in wolf form, a massive creature standing on hind feet and towering over Roberta. Even for a lycan he was enormous, easily eight feet tall and broad in proportion. He had a slim face, with long snout and way too many sharp teeth poking out between thin lips. Even so, there was a cast to its eyes that left no doubt: inside the wolf lived a cunning creature capable of both unrestrained ferocity and careful thought. The most dangerous pieces of two separate worlds.

That he was Lycaon was without question. I couldn't see him traveling around the convention center looking like Chewbacca's angry big brother, which meant he was able to shift at will. A self-controlled shifter, with human intelligence. Add that to the regal aura around him, and "Lycaon" was the only feasible conclusion.

Roberta didn't seem to care that she only came up to the thing's chest. She had changed, as well. Eyes that were completely red, fangs that curved well over her lower lip. Her fingers were more bony than they had been, less like human hands and more like the talons of a creature who could live in the day... but who thrived in the darkest night.

The Lycaon reared back and I thought he was going to strike Roberta; was gong to snap his huge teeth around her and shake her like a toy. Vampires and werewolves are pretty evenly matched if you're talking about one race vs. another, but I've never seen a vampire that could successfully engage in a one on one fight with a Lycaon.

That fact was obviously lost on Roberta. She launched forward as the lycan reared back. The treaty that had been endangered by Calista's death now seemed on the verge of shattering – what would happen if a Lycaon were killed in the middle of the High Court? Or if he killed one of the princesses of that court?

A blur whipped past me. Something shoved Roberta so hard she crashed into the members of the court who stood a good fifteen feet away. She blasted through the first row of courtiers, then the second row. The third managed to grab her, stopping her from flying back even farther.

Borga stood in front of the Lycaon, panting and looking feral. She was the one who had shoved Roberta, and she stared at her step-daughter with obvious rage. "Don't touch him," she snarled.

Roberta shrieked and righted herself, then flew forward. There was no question about her intent: she had wanted the Lycaon's blood before, but now wanted to kill Borga.

The queen faced the charge with outstretched hands, claws, fangs.

At the last second, King William finally moved. He was every bit as fast as his wife – faster. Watching him glide through the air in that moment, I could see how he had managed to ascend to the kingship, and how he had managed to hold his crown for so long. Every step he took was a study in efficient motion, and bore the clear threat of death for those who got in his way.

He inserted himself between Borga and Roberta, one hand held toward his daughter, who stopped at the last second. Her chest pushed against his taloned hand, and dark blood welled from the five points where his claws had punctured her breast.

"You will not raise a hand against the queen," he said quietly.

Roberta raged. "I will raise a hand against whomever I choose! Especially if she dares defend a murdering lycan."

"Do you Challenge her then?" Again, William's voice was soft. But the words drew a surprised hiss from the court.

Roberta looked past him, at her stepmother. Borga grinned, exposing not just her canines but all her teeth, which suddenly seemed sharper and whiter than they had.

Roberta was clearly considering it. She could Challenge Borga, could try to take the crown from her.

She shook her head. I didn't think she was afraid. She just wanted to wait until circumstances favored her more than they did right here, right now.

Borga turned her back on both William and Roberta, a contemptuous move that made Roberta snarl again, but William took it in stride. He just moved languidly back to his folding chair, leaned back in it, and closed his eyes.

I have to admit, I kind of liked his leadership style, which seemed to be "wait until something *really* needs doing, then kick ass." It was dangerous, yet couch potatoey. Real man stuff.

Borga bowed low before the lycan, who was still growling and staring at Roberta.

"My Lord Pallas," she said. "Please forgive the rudeness of Princess Roberta." She straightened, then added, "And allow me to place myself at your service."

The Lycaon, Pallas, growled a bit louder, then gave a very doglike chuff and changed.

I'd never seen a Lycaon change. Werewolves' modes of metamorphosis vary – anything from a painful, shrieking, full-body shift to the body of a wolf; to a baying, ecstatic shift under the light of the moon, drinking the night like the most exotic wine.

Lycaons, though – they shifted with beauty, with grace. Pallas held his hands out as far as he could, his fingers stretched out as though he might hold the world in his hands. A golden glow surrounded him, and each hair on his body seemed to catch fire in the light. It created a golden nimbus so bright I could barely watch – and what I did see was blurred through a thin veil of tears that made everything seem somehow celestial.

The hairs burned away. They flared into ember, looking like countless dandelion seeds tossed into a bonfire.

Then Pallas the wolfman was gone, and Pallas the man was all that remained.

He was tall – not as tall as he was in his wolfy form, but still well over six feet. I thought he would be a thick and heavily-muscled young man. Instead, he was a whip-thin man of middle age, with hawkish features and hair that was starting to gray even as it pulled away from his temples and forehead. He wore faded jeans that looked built for work, not for admiration. A flannel shirt hung on his shoulders, which were broad enough they strained at the confines of the shirt. The shirt was only buttoned halfway up, letting me see a chest packed tightly with ropes of lean muscle and pocked by numerous scars. He looked almost like a farmer, someone who has spent his life working hard and expects to live the rest of it working even harder. The only things that didn't fit with that image were that he wore no shoes, and and that he wore trendy, hispster horn-rimmed glasses over his deep brown eyes.

He pushed his glasses up as high as they would go on the bridge of his nose, and nodded at the queen. "I totally thank you, Queen, for your courtesy to the max," he said. His voice was so deep it sounded unreal – he was obviously the love child of Darth Vader and the guy who does the Allstate Insurance commercials. It almost overshadowed the surfer vibe his words conveyed.

"You are welcome, Lord Pallas." Borga went to the empty seat on King William's left, and sat down. William didn't say anything – a vampire of little words, he was – but he was for the first time sitting up and forward and on full alert.

Actually, I suspected that he was *always* alert, no matter how he appeared, but right now he looked the part. The simple chairs William and Borga sat on seemed to gain in prestige and importance, and I realized that people like this needed no thrones. Wherever they sat became a place of royalty.

"How may we be of service, friend Pallas?" said Borga.

Pallas growled, "We totally need to speak with the Warden. Totally."

"Do you speak of our Envoy?" said Roberta, clear mischief in her eyes.

Pallas' eyes darted to me. It wasn't a happy look. I put up my hands. "Whoah! No one speaks for me but me."

"Are you, like, the Envoy of the High Court?" said Pallas.

I glared at Roberta, who blew me a kiss with ruby red lips. "I am interested in solving the murder of your princess," I said.

"That answer blows, my man," said Pallas.

"That's the only answer I'm inclined to give, Chewy."

He frowned, then returned his gaze to Borga. "We sent for this dude."

"Yes?"

"He never quite managed to arrive at our room." Pallas said this with a sarcastic nod.

"My apologies, Lord Pallas," said Borga. "We required his presence ourselves."

Pallas inhaled, and his body visibly swelled. Dark hairs started reeling out of his skin, and the muscles of his chest and arms strained at his shirt. The golden nimbus returned – not as strong this time – then faded and he was his lanky "human" self again.

"The Great Pack values your friendship, Borga. But do not interfere in our business. Fer realsies."

I noted he dropped the "Queen" part of her name. So did Borga. Her cheeks flushed slightly, and I saw her hands clasp together with white knuckles. She pushed back her anger, and she nodded.

"You are right, of course, Lord Pallas. Forgive me, and believe only that we wished to talk to the Warden for the same reason we suspect you do: to find who killed our beloved Princess Calista. And to send that killer to an early grave."

211

Pallas smiled at that, with a mouth that held far too many teeth. "Maybe not to a grave," he said. "Maybe to something way worse."

"Of course," said Borga. "We shall defer to the Great Pack's judgment of what must be done to the criminal."

Pallas' look clearly showed he didn't know who the criminal was, but that just about everyone in the High Court all ranked high on his personal suspect list.

The tall man turned to me then, and said, "Come on." He strode toward the elevator.

I didn't move. I needed to speak to the Great Pack – and I suspected that Anderson would be waiting there, too – but I wasn't done here. And I don't like being ordered around.

Pallas turned back after a few steps. He snarled. "Now, man."

I turned my back on him.

I walked to Borga. The vampires of the court gasped, though I wasn't sure if that was because I had turned away from Pallas, or because I had approached Borga without permission.

Probably a bit of both. Several vampires stepped forward, including Rathton, the well-muscled vamp who had tried to follow her before – I guessed he was the captain of her personal guards. Or, just as likely, he simply hated me and wanted an excuse to massacre me.

Borga held out her hand, staying the others. I leaned close, and as I did she murmured, "No closer, or they will take your head, and there will be nothing I can do to stop them."

Okay, *some* orders I follow. I halted. Then whispered, "I will need to speak to Roberta and Warine."

She nodded. "Of course. Return when you will and I will have them presented." To the group, she said, "This Warden has my Blessing. He shall return when he shall return, and he shall receive every courtesy and shall be given all things he desires."

The words had a ritualistic sound, and that was confirmed when Borga lay a careful hand on my left shoulder, then kissed my right cheek. The crowd was silent, but I could feel their surprise: the queen had just given me the Blessing of the High Court, and to my knowledge that had never been bestowed upon a normal before, let alone a Warden.

I also appreciated her calling me "Warden" instead of "Envoy of the High Court," since it was clear that last didn't go over well with Pallas. But any gratitude faded when, after kissing my cheek, she whispered, "You have two days. Find the killer by the night of the treaty, or I will find *you*."

I shivered as I withdrew.

On the plus side, though, that gave me through Saturday night. And since I didn't work on Sundays, that was all I planned on needing to figure things out.

Yeah. Sure.

Pallas waited. I went to him.

"Mush, husky!" I said.

42

Pallas didn't respond to my joke – which was probably a good thing. He led me to the elevator, got in, and swiped a key card across the reader, then hit the button for the ninth floor.

A werewolf with a hotel keycard in an elevator. It sounded like the opening to a terrible joke. Which said a lot about my life.

We got off on the ninth floor, and Pallas used his card again to open the door to the hall, then gestured me to go through ahead of him. I nodded, walked through, and stopped on the other side. I pulled my cell out.

"Move it, human," Pallas growled.

"Sure, sure," I said, and held up the single finger that is a universal sign for "gotta take this call, so go screw yourself."

The phone rang, and Gandhi answered. "Hey, partner!" I said. He growled, which I chose to interpret as him saying, "Lovely to hear from you!" so I continued, "Same to you, bud! I need you to check on some people." I told him about Prince Eustace's various alibis, gave him the locations and asked him to check if the prince had actually been there. "Can you see if you can find Prince Warine and Princess Roberta, too?"

"Why not just ask me to locate King William, while you're at it," he muttered.

"Good idea. Do that."

More muttering. I asked him to call me back, then hung up.

Pallas was growling – *literally* growling – deep in his throat. I repeated the finger gesture. Called Blake. "Collings," he practically shouted as soon as he picked up. "Where in Cerberus' feces are you? Anderson keeps calling me and he is *pissed*."

"Cerberus' feces?" I decided to tuck that gem away for future use. Maybe in a book. "Blake, I just wanted to know if you've found my mom."

The long silence was answer enough. "We're still looking," he said. He must *really* like my mom, because he sounded nearly human – like he had a soul and everything. "I'll call you as soon as we find her."

"Thanks." I hung up.

Pallas' growl had subsided. He looked at me with what looked like pity. "Your mother is the hilarious steampunk lady, yeah?"

Geez, my mom should be the writer – she's more famous than I am.

I nodded. Pallas made a sound I couldn't interpret, then led me to 902.

But not until I got *another* call. Again, I hadn't been super popular on the actual "author department," so I knew this would be more murder stuff. Or, in technical terms, "Bad News."

I took the call, receiving more looks from Pallas that would have maimed toddlers and caused strong men to cry.

"Michaelbrent pool hall, who in the hall do you want?" I asked. Someone grunted, and that was enough for me to identify the voice: "Blake, didn't we just talk? Do you miss me so much? I *am* married, but Laura and I might be open to –"

Blake started yelling very fast, and very loud. A bunch of naughty words and many repetitions of "sylphilitic, scumsucking shmuck." When he actually started to make sense, the upshot was that he had gotten a very angry, very short call from the Great Pack, which wanted Calista's body back asap.

"So do it. You're a big, strapping man, so it should be easy."

"We *can't* do that!" he shrieked. "It's part of the investigation."

"And nothing's been found on or about it, with the exception of my own brilliant discoveries. Give it back."

"I...." A heavy silence emerged from the phone. "I can't. It's gone."

"*Gone?*"

"Look, how was I to know a them was going to get out of its cage?" he snarled.

"A them was going to get out" etc. sounds like poor English. But "them" was the species of a monster that, you guessed it, the giant ants in *Them* was based on. A them looks nothing like a giant ant, but it is buglike. Three feet long, segmented, bright orange, with six pairs of legs and a mouth that no sane mother could love. Rock monsters like to eat thems[13] - when they eat a them it's a real treat for them. The eating them, not the eaten them. For that them it's no fun (though for the them who eat those thems, again, it's a hoot).[14]

However, the problem with putting bodies in the Ice Cream Room is: what if one of the things intended to *be* eaten get out of their cage and start eat*ing*?

Oh, man.

I took the hero's way out of this one: "Not my problem, bud. You figure it out."

I hung up.

As soon as I did, Pallas turned to the door to 902. He didn't knock or anything – just stood there. I don't know if they smelled him or heard him, but after less than five seconds the door opened and an old woman with a shawl draped over her shoulders beckoned us both inside.

Pallas went in. I followed. I saw Kevin Anderson, who was standing next to the wall and very obviously imagining ways to murder me. I also saw *why* he was standing where he was: it was the only available floor space.

The High Court of the Vampires rules with dignity and with danger. The royal family were all gorgeous physical specimens, and other than the grieving Prince Eustace I hadn't seen a single one with so much as a hair out of place. Everything about them bespoke a desire for beauty – from the designer

---

[13] "Thems" is the proper plural form for "them."

[14] This *does* make sense. Read it again.

clothes they all wore, to the way they stood; even the way King William leaned in his chair had a subtle artfulness to it. The danger of the court even added to that beauty, in much the same way that a tiger's beauty is augmented by the air of threat that surrounds it.

The Great Pack held an analogous position among lycans, but the two groups were nothing alike. Everyone I saw in the room was dressed similarly to Pallas: jeans, flannels, and sweats were the norm. They didn't look slovenly, but completely at ease: people – or creatures – who acted like they were home no matter where they were, because the entire *world* was their home. Wild creatures who brought the wilderness with them.

The lycans were mostly in human form, though there were a few who walked in the huge, hulking shape of transformed Lycaons. Regardless of what form they took, though, they sprawled everywhere. This was the front room of one of the hotel's two penthouse suites, and the lycans had made it their den; and like most creatures who shared a den, they lay close to one another. The sofas, the chairs, the floors – even the wet bar and coffee tables – were all covered by a living, chuffing, growling blanket of flesh and fur.

"Wow," I said. These were dangerous creatures, possibly *the* most dangerous in the world, pound for pound. And I could tell from the looks that some of them shot me that many would be happy to have me as a light snack. Still, there was a feral allure about the way they held each other close. The way they clung to one another as though life meant nothing without the company of their fellows.

The surreal beauty of the moment ended when Anderson stepped over a sleeping teen with a shaggy mane of blond hair, nearly tripped over the grandmotherly woman who had settled down on her haunches after letting me and Pallas in, and then did a really nifty lurch/jump combo to finally join me in the small empty space near the room's door.

"Where have you been?" he said. He didn't sound angry, but I suspected that was because he didn't want to irritate or goad any of the lycans. Anderson is a big-time wizard (who uses magic to sell books, I *know* it!), but anyone with their right mind would try to keep tempers cool in this room.

"I came as soon as I could." Anderson frowned and looked pointedly at his watch. "Really," I said. "I came right here and then –"

"Do not chastise the Warden, Brother Kev," said a soft voice. "We hope he will find the ass-bite who kiped my baby."

The speaker was short, but compact. He looked like a block of steel that had been pounded roughly into human shape. Not unkind, just strong, unyielding. Certain of what to do, and then doing it. Always.

He looked to be about the same age as Pallas – maybe mid-fifties. Vampires and many other Otherworlders don't age the same as humans, but lycans do. This man probably remembered Ronald Reagan's presidency, but he certainly hadn't gone to Vietnam.

He was also holding a sitar, of all things, and plucked a few twangy notes before leaning it against a table.

I knew the names of the Great Pack's leaders, just as I had known the names of the High Court of the Vampires. Knowing the names of people like that is the same as knowing the name of the President of the United States or the crazy dwarf in North Korea.[15] You know them because they're part of world news.

So even though I'd never seen him, I knew who this was. I bowed. "King Haemon," I said. "I thank you for your kind invitation."

I hadn't been invited to the High Court of the Vampires, and my resentment spilled over onto how I treated them. The

---

[15] Note: the North Korea nutter is not a real dwarf. Gandhi would kill me if I didn't clarify that.

Great Pack – through Anderson – *had* invited me. Or at least, they hadn't sent someone to chuck a black hood over me and force me to go with them. So I was inclined to play nice with King Haemon. For now.

Haemon bowed at the waist, then clapped me on the shoulder. "Can I get you a drink? Perhaps a blackberry-hibiscus smoothie? Or would you rather scarf something? We have steak – organic, of course."

I wasn't really sure what an *un*organic steak might be – perhaps one fashioned out of a mix of plastic and glue? Then I realized that the few people who wore shoes in the room were all wearing either Crocs or Birkenstocks. I saw how many people had dreadlocks. I noticed the large number of necklaces sporting either a flower or a peace symbol. Several of them were also playing sitars, and one transformed Lycaon was softly shaking a tambourine with one hand while tapping a bongo with the other.

I'm still learning. I've only been a Warden a couple years, so is it any surprise that I occasionally get caught flat-footed? Like now, when I realized – to more than a little horror – that Pallas hadn't spoken like a surfer after all. No, he spoke like a Lycaon. And apparently all Lycaons were tree-hugging hippie types.

Nope, not a surprise at all (not!).

I shouldn't have laughed though.

The guffaw just flew out. I literally clapped my hand over my mouth to try to stop it, but a laugh escaped is a laugh not easily recaptured.

Haemon's eyes narrowed. "What's your bag, man?" he asked.

The expression – right out of a *Mod Squad* episode, or maybe *Austin Powers* – made it even harder for me to stop the laughter. I was exhausted, I was scared for my mom, I was scared for *myself*. And I hadn't sold jack or done well on any panels. It all exploded in inappropriate mirth.

"Sorry," I gasped. "No, nothing... nothing at all...."

"His mom is missing," said Anderson.

I was shocked that Anderson knew that. Had I told him?

Is it possible he... cares?

No. Some things would be just too weird.

"Ahhh," said King Haemon. His attitude changed completely, becoming sympathetic understanding. "The hilarious old steampunk chick."

Who doesn't *know about her?*

Haemon's brows knit together. "You want we should find her, man?" He snapped his fingers, and two kids - both girls, both about twelve years old – disentangled themselves from the mass of the Great Pack and stepped forward. They were dressed the same as Pallas and Haemon: jeans, flannel tops, no shoes.

"No," I said, "that's all right, I don't need –"

Haemon held up a hand. "Please. Don't harsh my aura." He whispered something to the girls, and they immediately leaped toward me and began smelling me. And yes, that is exactly as weird as it sounds.

They looked at Haemon, and he nodded. "Go, my bitches."

That shocked me, until I realized it must be a term of endearment when coming from a lycan.

The girls opened the door and ran into the hall. As they did, I muttered something – it was too easy an opportunity *not* to say it.

"Bitches leave."

Haemon started laughing. "*Robocop*. Excellent movie." He leaned close to me. "The remake was a bad scene, though."

"I liked it."

Anderson shoved in. "Should we get to business?"

Haemon actually sagged a bit at that, as though the words knocked some of the strength out of him.

"What have you found about Calista?" he said.

I cocked my head. "Can I ask you a few questions first?" Haemon nodded. "Does everyone here, in this room –"

"The Great Pack."

"Yeah, do they all know about the treaty?"

He gestured widely. "Of course. No secrets here."

I resisted the urge to point out that if that were true, they either had utopia or a whole bunch of villages with missing idiots. They may be lycans, but part of every lycan is a person, and I've never met anyone without a secret or two. Not that all of those people are bad. People simply keep silent about certain things: secret shames, yes, but also secret services and silent personal triumphs.

Instead of telling Haemon this, I said, "Okay, so if there are no secrets, then can you tell me who might have wanted your daughter dead?"

"The High Court –"

"Other than them," I specified. "You say you have no secrets. Fine. But that doesn't mean you all agree. So does anyone in the Great Pack hate her enough to kill her?"

Again, I was using my bull-in-a-china-shop investigatory method. I saw Anderson roll his eyes, but I've found a surprising number of situations where just asking people is the best way through a puzzle. Even murderers have a need to unburden their souls – and if I can do it the "efficient" (what my wife calls the "lazy") way, then I will.

Haemon backed up my theory by responding instantly. "Of course there are some who are totally not tight with the vamps, and even less fabbed about the treaty. But there's only one whackamole who I would think capable of going all Manson on Calista." He nodded to another kid – this one a boy of about nine who was a dead ringer for Alfalfa from *The Little Rascals*. "Go find her," he said. Alfalfa left the same way the two girls had, but I couldn't come up with a witty way to see him off. "Bitches leave" didn't fit.

Life is full of lost opportunities. Put *that* in your fortune cookie and smoke it.

Haemon waited until the door was closed, then gestured for me and Anderson to follow him into the next room.

"Why did Blake even put you on this job?" whispered Anderson as we followed him.

"Because I get results and am amazing with people," I whispered back. "Plus I think I might be the only Warden here."

"Anyone ever tell you you're insane?"

"My wife. But she married me, so her judgment's suspect."

Anderson harrumphed, then was silent as we left the living/dining area of the suite and went into the bedroom.

It was like transitioning from a zoo to... well, a quiet bedroom. No one else was in here, and the bed (which was the size of my entire hotel room) looked as though it had never been slept in. I suspected it hadn't – Haemon and his people probably didn't use beds.

They're not organic. Dig?

I almost giggled again.

A sofa and two chairs were placed against one wall in the room, and Haemon gestured for us to sit as he took the couch. We did.

"I just want to say again how sorry I am," said Anderson. "How sorry *all* of us are."

Haemon nodded slowly. No tears, but I could feel sadness covering him like acid-free mist over a field of organic kale. "Yes. Calista was...." He gestured absently, trying to find words. "She was my little paper shaker."

I didn't even know what that meant, but Anderson rolled with it. "I am sure of it," he said. "And as I said, we will have our people – good people, the *best* people – look into this." He said "best" very pointedly, and glared at me so I'd know I was not a member of that club.

Haemon contemplated Anderson. Turned to me. "You were the pig assigned to the case?" I translated that: pig meant "cop," and in this instance he must be asking if I was the Warden on the case. I nodded. "What's your vibe on the drama?" he said.

I told him. Not the details – I didn't tell him about Borga's concerns about the crown succession, or anything about Nespda. But I told him about some of Gandhi's findings; the probably good alibis of Borga, Warine, and Roberta; and the fact that she had been interacting with humans.

"Did she have a fascination with normals?" I said. "I mean, other than as food?"

Anderson reached toward Haemon. "You don't have to answer that, your majesty. Like I said, we have really competent people who will talk to you." Again, emphasis on "competent." Grrr.

Haemon considered me. He didn't blink, but it wasn't creepy; more like he'd conquered the part of Zen meditation that provides mastery over your eyelids. I was scared of all of them, but I decided that if push came to shove I'd prefer to have a lycan on my team than a vamp.

As though he heard my thoughts, Haemon nodded. He leaned toward me and inhaled deeply. "I like this one," he said. "This pig will continue as my personal preferred pig."

"*WHAT?*" Not sure if that was me or Anderson. First the vamps made me the Envoy of the High Court, now the king of the lycans makes me his personal preferred pig. I didn't know whether to bow, laugh, or run away screaming.

Anderson *was* sure what to do. "I don't think that's such a
–"

Haemon held up a hand. He had enough hair on the back of it to make a toupee for Donald Trump. "I like him," he said to Anderson. He looked at me and added, "He has a trustworthy scent."

"That's Irish Spring," I supplied, smirking at Anderson. "It was on sale at Costco."

"Right on." Haemon nodded again. Then sat back and said, "You can beat feet," to Anderson.

Anderson stood. Not planning on going silently. His eyes flashed and I felt the air grow crisp with gathering power. I don't think he was going to try to fry Haemon – that *would* start a war – but I suspect he was going to do something to remind everyone he was not just a wizard, but a Dead One – and one who had written incredibly popular *Star Wars* tie-ins to boot.

The door opened, and in came several lycans. They didn't rush, but they didn't saunter, either: it was clear they had sensed a burgeoning hissy fit and wanted to be there to stop it.

Anderson didn't even seem to notice them, but he got himself under control and said, "Fine," under his breath. He dug in his pants pocket, then handed me a paper.

"What is –" I goggled. "A *bill*? You're *charging me* to let me come back on the case?"

"Standard reinstatement fee," he said, and returned my earlier smirk with interest. "And my going rate for consultation, since you couldn't possibly have gotten in here without an introduction."

"What if I don't *want* to be–" I began, sensing a way out of this situation.

"The fee will be paid by the Great Pack," said Haemon. "My Finance Bitch will settle the accounts in the other room… as you leave. Now, later, Brother Anderson."

Anderson huffed, then left. The other lycans followed him out, so it was just me and Haemon in the room.

"King Haemon," I said.

"Just Haemon, please, Brother Michaelbrent."

"That's a mouthful, Haemon. Call me MB."

Very chummy. Covering discomfort with small talk. He was worried about his daughter's murder investigation. *I* was worried about getting eaten or turned into a lycan. Or a hippie, which might be worse.

"So who was the kid going to get?" I said after a moment.

"I don't wanna say. You can grill her when she shows, and draw your own conclusions."

"Okay... who else is missing?"

Haemon didn't miss a beat. I could tell he knew I was asking about the other body: the Lycaon who was found beside Calista's corpse. The one who was in a magically-induced coma, but who so far had remained nameless. But he didn't answer the question. Instead, he said, "You do have a trustworthy scent." I nodded, a bit embarrassed that we were discussing my b.o. "But," he continued, "trustworthy doesn't mean the same as 'forthcoming.' You're bogarting the info on this case." It wasn't a question. I nodded again.

Haemon inhaled, a deep breath like a yogi might do during warm-ups. "Let's do this: I'll give you the chance to fill your little slam book on happenings here, but one question at a time."

I didn't understand the first part, but I was pretty sure I understood the last bit. "Great." One question at a time was fine, right? I didn't know how else you really *could* ask questions without a flux capacitor or a Time-Turner, so this wasn't a tough condition. I knew there was more, though.

"And between each of your questions, I will ask one of mine. You can choose not to answer, but then our rap session will end." There was no hint of threat with that sentence. I didn't get the sense he was telling me he would eat my eyeballs out of my head or hump my leg after he'd torn it off my body. Just "the end" to our talk.

I didn't have a whole lot of options. I nodded. "You get first ups," he said. "And for your turn, I'll answer the question you already asked. The other cat's moniker is Aseas," said Haemon. "Now my ups: Is Aseas dead?" Before I could answer, the lycan held up his hairy hand. "One more thing." He closed his eyes and took another one of those deep breaths. "I can smell lies." The eyes opened, and now there *was* threat in them. "And they really hack me off."

I nodded, trying not to show my fear, then continued. In for a penny, in for a pound. "No. He's not dead. Who is he in –"

"Not dead? Where is he then? What happened to my man?"

I waggled a finger at him. "No asking out of turn, Haemon." I waited, a bit worried he might decide to tear my waggling finger off. He didn't. He nodded.

"Fair's fair, man."

I continued. "As I was saying, who is Aseas in the Great Pack? I mean his position or relation to you."

"You're trying to sneak in several questions, man."

"I used to be a lawyer," I said by way of explanation.

Haemon actually smiled. "Another kind of wolf," he said. Then he added, "Aseas is the Great Pack's Peacemaker, and brother to Pallas, the big dude who got you from the High Court."

The guy dressed like a *Munsters* reject was the Great Pack's *Peacemaker*? That made me reel, even sitting down.

Peacemakers were a combination of judge, executioner, and master-at-arms. Lycans are inherently loyal to the pack and their clans and to each other in general, but that doesn't mean there are no problems among them. Usually those problems are chalked up to fits of passion or unchecked wolfiness that can be easily dealt with by the clans – or occasionally by Pack Justice (which, yes, sounds like an awesomely bad Steven Seagal movie).

Occasionally, though, the problem is too big or too complex or just too dirty for your everyday lycan to solve… and that's where the Peacemakers come in. They sniff out answers (often literally), bring lawbreakers to justice, and when needed they dispense that justice themselves.

Peacemakers are the toughest lycans alive, each one a combination of werewolf, cop, and the *entirety* of Seal Team Six. Single Peacemakers have been known to take on half a dozen vampires, ten ghouls, up to fifty zombies at a time.

And the only one standing at the end – always – is the Peacemaker.

And this guy, Aseas, is the Peacemaker – the only Lycaon Peacemaker, and the one who's supposed to be the toughest of them all.

Aseas and Calista had been found together. It was highly unlikely that anyone had snuck up on them and whammied Aseas before whacking Calista. Even less likely that it happened in reverse order. You just *couldn't* sneak up on a Peacemaker. Not with magic, and certainly not by putting on your black outfit and just trying to walk on sneaky feet.

That meant one of two things: either whoever did that to them was a friend... or Aseas had murdered Calista himself, then somehow put himself into a trance to avoid suspicion.

Haemon waited for me to think about what he'd said, then asked his own question. "Where *is* Aseas?"

"I don't know." Haemon looked unhappy with that answer, and the beginnings of a growl started to rumble in his throat. I held out my hands. "I'm not lying. I really don't know." Then, in the interests of diplomacy (and it had nothing to do with the fact that I didn't want to get shredded like a scratching post, promise!), I added, "You're asking the wrong question. You should be asking what happened to him."

Haemon nodded appreciatively. "What did happen to him?"

I shrugged. "Not too sure about that one, either. He was found with Calista, dressed like the cheesiest vampire ever, and in what looks like a magical trance."

Surprisingly, Haemon threw his head back and laughed. It was a throaty, manly laugh. If you could bottle it as a smell, it would have a name like *Eu d'Lumberjack.*

"I'm missing something," I murmured. He didn't stop laughing until I said, "Did Aseas oppose the treaty?"

The laughter wound down, but Haemon kept slapping the arm of his chair. "No," he said, gasping out the word between chuckles. "No, never. That's why I laughed: it's perfect that Aseas was dressed that way."

"What do you mean?"

Haemon didn't seem to notice me questioning out of turn. "He was the main *supporter* of the treaty. The one who brought the idea to me, and who convinced Calista to play her part. He was probably dressed as a vampire to show support for the treaty, and a willingness to give love to the vampires."

A new idea occurred. "Could she have wanted to back out? So he killed her?"

"Why would he do that? Even if she did want to back out, what would killing her gain him?"

"I don't know. Maybe he could have done it just for revenge, as payback for her spoiling his plans. Or maybe because he thought if he got her out of the picture, he could find someone else to take her place as Prince Eustace's bride."

Haemon finally stopped laughing. He wiped his eyes. "No, no, no. Aseas was not a vengeful man. He was a good person. Righteous. He loved his family, his clan, his people. And he loved Calista. If she had wanted to quit the treaty, he would have supported her and searched for someone else to serve as a suitable partner to the vampire prince. And if he had killed her, you would find no evidence of the crime at all. He would make it seem an accident." He spread his hands. "Besides, Calista was completely in love with Prince Eustace. To the point that we were all sure she had been bewitched or enchanted or had her mind torn by a succubus. She hadn't, though: she just truly loved him, in the way that only a good, pure girl can love a man."

During this last, I was busy thinking if Haemon would have come to that conclusion if he knew that Calista worked at Nespda, or that she had promised her affections to at least one human – Harold Kumar, Nerdfather of the Game Room.

"If Aseas loved Calista so much, could he have killed her to keep her from being with anyone else?"

"Nah." Haemon chuckled. "His love for her was more Donny and Marie than Sonny and Cher. And like I said, he loved his family. He worshipped his old lady, and his kids were more priceless to him than a cherry ride."

Haemon suddenly sat back and said, "You gave me several questions out of turn. Which I will totally forgive, if you'll just answer me this one. And be very careful about it, my brother." He started to glow, and I sensed muscles trying to rip free of the skin that bound them, sensed claws and fangs that wanted to explode into being and then be used to rend and tear.

"What question?" I asked.

He leaned toward me. Very close. I could feel his breath, which smelled nothing like blackberry-hibiscus smoothie and very much like something that probably screamed as it died. "Why would you think that Calista wished to quit the treaty, dude? What is it about my little angel that makes you think she'd ditch her responsibility, or ever break a promise?"

Before I could answer, the door slammed open and raw fury walked into the room.

43

"What is he doing here? This, this... *human?*"

The woman was dressed as a *Star Wars* stormtrooper, covered head to toe in white plastic armor with a complete helmet on top. I could only tell it was a woman because of her voice, and there was also....

"Aren't you a little short to be a stormtrooper?" I drawled.

The woman had screamed first at Haemon. Now she wheeled on me, screeching, "Who invited you? What are you doing here? Can't you humans just keep your noses out –"

"The man is my guest," said Haemon. He didn't raise his voice, but it still cut through her screams, which were loud enough my ears had started ringing and a pain was developing in my temples.

The woman tore off her helmet and threw it against the wall. I immediately wished she hadn't done that. Not the throwing the helmet against the wall bit, but the part where she took it off at all.

I don't want to sound shallow, but this woman was a serious uggo. I thought she was young, but that was total conjecture. Her hair looked like someone had gone at it with a chainsaw. Her skin didn't have a bad case of pimples; it was more like her pimples had a slight case of skin. Her hands and feet were subtly wrong – too big and knobby and just *hard*-looking: something you'd see on a bulky farmer named Big Joe. Her snaggle teeth looked like a game of Pick-up Sticks, and the cherry on top was that her eyes were slightly mismatched – both in size and in the direction they stared.

The fact is that most people live in a house somewhere on the big bell in the middle of the "Pretty to Ugly" scale. The sad fact is that a few of them – like this gal – had been cursed with ownership of a three-walled outhouse on the Ugly side.

"Wow," I whispered. I'd like to think it wasn't just me being superficial; that the word was simple amazement about her tantrum.

She wheeled on me. Fangs exploded from a face which started to lengthen out into a muzzle. Neither of which helped her looks. "What did you say?" she shrieked. Spittle flew from her thinning lips. "Did you say I'm *UGLY? REPELLENT? A SCURVE BAG?*"

I managed to refrain from speaking.

Haemon rose and put a hand on the girl's white-clad shoulder. He half-guided, half-pushed her down onto the couch. "This is my personal pig," he said. "Don't harsh, just answer his questions." He nodded to me.

This was certainly turning into Awkward Interview Day, but I dove in. "What's your name?"

"Don't answer that," Haemon said to the woman.

I glanced sharply at him, but shrugged and said, "Okay, do you know Calista?"

The woman snorted. She had changed back to her human shape, but the features still looked lupine. "Of course I do."

"Don't like her?"

"Are you a moron?"

"I'll take that as a yes."

"You can take it *up* the yes."

I don't have to tell you what it sounded like when she slurred "the yes" together, do I?

"Charming." I stared at the woman. She looked like she was ready to kill me. "*Why* don't you like Calista?"

"She's a bitch."

"So are you."

The woman actually laughed at that, if only a little. "I'm not talking the righteous kind of bitch. She –"

"Be careful how you twitch out the dead," Haemon said to the woman.

231

I think he was telling her not to say nasty things about Calista. I mostly ignored him – easy to do when I only understood half of what he said. "She what?"

The woman – she looked to be in her mid-twenties, though it was hard to tell since snaggle teeth and a receding hairline did tend to age a person – spat to the side. "She wants to go all the way with vampires, for one thing."

"You're talking about uh... her *consummating* the treaty?"

She shrugged. "Gross. That anyone would let a vampire ball her...." She shuddered so hard I could hear the pieces of her plastic armor clack together.

"Are you against the peace, too? Or just the marriage?"

She glared at me. "There can't be any peace when vampires are involved." She sniffed haughtily, then looked away. "Your question is stupid. Like your face."

I had a wild urge to say "So's your mother!" but decided not to stoop to her level. For once.[16] Instead I said, "So you wanted to kill Calista."

That got a different reaction than I'd expected. The woman's anger completely disappeared, dissolved in the tears that streamed from her eyes.

"Kill her?" she cried. "Why would I want to kill my sister?"

So now I knew who this was. King Haemon's wife had died years before, under circumstances cloaked in mystery. A few of the Dead Ones had looked into it – always a good idea to keep tabs on the family of one of the most important ruling classes of the Otherworlds.

The investigators they sent *did* return. But without any information. And without their noses. Haemon sent their noses back later – along with a witch who could reattach them good as

---

[16] *See*, Laura? I can be mature! (I will stick my tongue out at you when I see you next.)

new. The message was still clear: don't stick your noses into this business.

Haemon's wife left behind two young daughters. A baby, Calista, and a young girl named Moonbeam. I knew that a lot of Lycaons took Greek names, honoring the original Lycaon, the first werewolf. But I had assumed "Moonbeam" was in honor of the moon that gave so many lycans their power. Maybe that she was beautiful as a Moonbeam.

Wrong on both counts. Moonbeam was just the hippie name of something not in the least bit beautiful.

"Okay, Moonbeam," I said. Haemon nodded like I'd done a good job by figuring out the identity of the girl. He had a low bar, apparently. I might actually keep him from getting mad at me. "You say you love your sister, but you are also, uh...." I searched for the right word, "grossed out," that earned me another appreciative nod from Haemon, "by lycans who stick it to vampires. Or, I guess, *get* stuck by vampires. So does Calista gross you out?"

An expression flashed across Moonbeam's face, too fast for me to decipher.

"No," she said. Her voice was strangely hushed.

I cocked my head. "What aren't you telling me?" I asked. She didn't answer. I asked, "What was the star on her hand?"

She jerked a little. "Star?" she asked.

Lying.

"Yeah," I said innocently. "Little star?" I traced one on the back of my hand. "Little tattoo right here?"

"I don't know."

"You don't know what it was, or where she got it, or that she had it?"

"All of them."

I glanced at Haemon. He was frowning. "Problem?"

"I've seen it," he answered. Then, to Moonbeam: "How is it you haven't?"

She made a passable impression of pretending to think about it. She scrunched up her face. "Oh, you mean her tattoo?"

"Yeah. That's why I used the word tattoo."

"Oh, sure. We got that in Cabo."

"Spring break?"

Another weird smile. "Something like that."

I sat back. "Why are you lying, Moonbeam?"

She exploded forward, too fast and too surprising a move for either me or Haemon to do anything about it. I found myself pinned against my chair, the complete weight of a fully transformed Lycaon against me.

I wrote a scene in one of my books[17] where a guy gets pinned by a huge dog. I resolved to rewrite that scene, because I hadn't described the level of fear even closely.

"You dare call me a liar?" she growled. Ropy drool hung from the corners of her mouth, twisting down until they almost touched my chest.

"Maybe not a liar, but you're not telling me everything."

She transformed back. Fast as three clicks and "There's no place like home." Moonbeam's even scarier human face stared at me.

"You don't know what you're talking about," she said. There were tears in her eyes. And this time... this time I suspected they were real.

Moonbeam turned away. "I –"

My phone rang. I ignored it. "You what?"

She looked like she was trying to pull herself together. To say something.

Damn phone kept ringing. It stopped as Haemon pulled his daughter back, and held her to him.

---

[17] *The House That Death Built*, no longer on sale on the purple aisle because the Nerdfather is a douche, but don't worry! You can still get it at my website, michaelbrentcollings.com.

"She was going to tell you our secret," he said. He looked at his daughter, who nodded. "Her life would be forfeit. We do not fink to outsiders." His eyes lasered into and right through me. "I'll lay it on you, Brother Trustworthy."

Friggin' phone started ringing again. I pressed the ignore button without looking. Nodded to him to go on.

"We lycans are a righteous lot," he said. "But we're dying."

I gawked at him. "Dying?"

He nodded. "Our bitches ain't easy, they're real old-fashioned. You've already probably found out enough about Calista to know that."

I nodded. When someone's baring their soul in an investigation, you don't tell them their daughter is the equivalent of a supernatural hyper-slut. You shut up and listen.

"That can be overcome. But the fact is, even when we get it on, we lycans don't breed very often. Lots of people know that we Lycaons aren't much in the baby-maker department, but it's *all* lycans. We hardly breed with each other, and we *can't* breed with humans. Add to that the fact that we don't have that groovy Goth cool the vamps have a lock on, and the fact that even most of the lycans we do have only get their real power once a month, and we're in trouble." He breathed in, then out through puffed cheeks. "When Aseas came to me last December and was like, 'My man, treaty, right?' I knew the nitty-gritty of it was that this was our last hope. No way Calista would do anything to mess it up."

He let that hang there.

The phone rang again. I didn't even think about answering it. Haemon was now staring at me with eyes that had turned yellow. "You know the secret, man. You fink it and I'll put you in so much hurt you will tenderly remember the dreams where you have your balls cut off and fed to you."

"I've never had that particular dream, but message received." I thought for a moment. "There was this one time, though when –"

"Two days."

"Huh?"

Haemon repeated it. "You got the rest of today and tomorrow to figure this out. Come the time set for the signing of the treaty, if you haven't figured out who mangled my baby, I will mangle you." The gold glow enveloped him. He was no longer short, he was the biggest Lycaon I'd seen. "Not fast. I'll make you know the pain I feel, and the pain I *will* feel every day for the rest of my life without my baby."

Great. Now I had *three* sets of radically powerful people on my case – the Dead Ones, the vamps, and the Lycaons.

The phone rang. *Again.*

And this time, I made the mistake of glancing it.

"I further promise –" began Haemon.

"I have to take this call," I interrupted. I answered the phone. "Talk to me."

Mercedes' voice rolled out, fast and jagged. I heard a crash in the background as she said, "I'm in the third floor hall, beside the LARP demo. Get here quick."

"What is it?"

Another crash, then Mercedes said, "It's your mom."

44

I called Kevin Anderson on the run. He was, unsurprisingly, irritated to hear me. I heard the same weird moaning I'd heard on my earlier call with him. That bizarro pleasure-pain thing.

What is going on*? Is* Anderson *a Nespda client?*

Again, the moans lessened as Anderson got on the phone. I didn't have the time to grill him on whatever pervmania he was into, but made a mental note to do so later as he said, "What is it?"

I gave him a quick briefing on what had happened with the Lycaons, omitting the secret they'd given and their two-day ultimatum. I'm no fink.

"But I think there was more," I said at the end. "I think Moonbeam had something she wasn't telling."

"What?"

"If I knew that, I wouldn't need her to tell me."

"So what do you want *me* to do about it? Ask her pretty please?"

"Do you think it would help?" Before I could get bitched out for that[18] I added, "I need the Dead Ones' complete files on Haemon, his family, and anyone in their close circle. And same with King William, Borga, Roberta, Warine, and Eustace. Especially Roberta," I added.

Short silence, then Anderson harrumphed. "Fine. I'll have Butler print out the copies."

I paled, even as I ran. "When Butler, uh, *prints* something...." Robot Dave went around licking things, and I could only think of limited places even remotely big enough for him to "print" things. I wasn't sure even a murderer on the loose could get me to handle something like that.

---

[18] Do werewolves bitch each other out?

"With a *printer*," Anderson snarled. The moans started up again, and he ended the call – though not before I heard him say, "Calm, my pretties. Uncle Andy is here to –"

Thankfully, that was the last of it.

I was almost up to the area Mercedes had called from, but I would have known something was bad even without her phone call. I heard crashes, bangs.

Someone yelled, "Pew, pew, pew!" There was a bit of nervous laughter – more like concerned tittering from a few people who clearly didn't know what to do.

I rounded the corner and saw Mom.

45

She was still dressed in her steampunk gear, which made me oddly happy. As long as Mom looks like a weirdo, things can't be too bad, right?

Wrong.

Mom was waving her "laser pistol" – which she and Dad made by gluing a bunch of crystals to an old-fashioned brass hair dryer, topping it with the base of a plastic "champagne" glass, and spraypainting the whole thing gold.

It sounds lamer than it is. Or maybe not. Whatever – it's cool.

But it's not functional, which made the fact that Mom was going around the circle of people surrounding her and threatening them with it very weird.

"Who are you?" she said. She didn't shout, but it was loud. "What manner of strange vestments do you wear?" She looked up, hands toward the ceiling high above. "Has the alien steam-demon Gorbash caught me at last? Has he transported me from my beloved Britain of the eighteen-hundreds, with its steam-powered zeppelins and gear-laden machines which don't look like they should work but somehow do?"

Oh, lest I forget to mention: she delivered all this with an English accent. Quite a passable one, too. I might have been proud of her repertoire, were it not for the odd gleam in her eyes. She seemed nearly manic. Or maybe like –

"Pew, pew!" she shouted. Remembering the number of people I'd run into who referenced this, I wondered if she'd been acting like this all day.

Not manic, no. She seemed almost like she *believed* what she was saying. Like, one step away from the people in the park who walk around with their arms turning circles while they talk to the invisible man who keeps trying to steal their invisible dog.

Mercedes was in the circle of people surrounding my mom, and when she saw me she ran over.

"The hell –" I began.[19]

"She's been acting like this since I found her," said Mercedes. "She's disoriented, and she's acting like she...." She couldn't find the word.

"*Believes*?" I supplied.

"Yeah. Like she really thinks she's Dame Ginny McLaserbeam." I shot Mercedes a glance. She nodded. "Yeah, that's how she keeps referring to herself."

On cue, Mom said, "You'll never take Dame Ginny McLaserbeam alive!" before pointing at a guy dressed like Voltron and screaming, "Pew, pew, pew!" while shaking her gun at him. When he didn't fall down or disintegrate or disapparate or whatever, she looked down the "barrel" of the gun and shook it as though trying to figure out why it wasn't working.

Regardless of how this turns out, I'm going to have to have a talk with Mom about gun safety.

"Thanks, Mercedes."

I walked forward, hand outstretched like I was approaching a frightened kitten. A host of fears ran through my head: had someone cursed her to get to me? Had she stumbled into a spell?

Worse, had she hurt herself? Hit her head? Could this be a sneak attack by Alzheimer's or dementia or a similar vicious disease? I hoped not. Spells and curses I could deal with – at least try. But there are some things, many in fact, that neither science nor magic can treat. My wife and I took care of her

---

[19] Laura does not like me to curse, and I'm not a huge fan myself. I realize a bit of cursing – certainly more than I normally engage in – has appeared in this story, but tell me: if *you* were on the trail of a supernatural murderer who might have sparked an apocalyptic war while your mom ran around acting like a reject from Dr. Who, what would *you* do?

grandmother for a couple years as she gradually succumbed to just those illnesses.

If a disease can be truly evil, it's Alzheimer's or dementia. Even cancer doesn't come close, since at least it has the decency to finally kill mind and body at close to the same time.

Mom saw me and, sure enough, shrank away. She gave a half-hearted, "Pew, pew," then threw the gun away. She crouched into a creditable version of an attack stance.

"Come then, spawn of the Clockwork King," she snarled. She tore something away from her waist, where she wore a chain-link, steampunk utility belt.

"I shall travel with my Timekeeper!" she shouted, and flashed the time machine made of a small fuse box, some more crystals, and an oven thermometer. Sprayed gold, of course.

She twisted the thermometer, and when nothing happened she threw it away, too, and went back into attack posture. "Then come, come you coal-powered dog of the Clockwork King! I shall save his son, Max Steam, and there's nothing you can do to stop me!"

I was completely at a loss. I knew what to do if something threatened me. When my kids were sick, I could do a passable job of comforting them. When something bad happened to Laura, I was there for her.

But I don't think anyone in the world knows what to do the first time they are confronted by a parent who is failing before their eyes.

Mom was getting more agitated. She backed away from me, and fumbled on her belt for something else. I didn't know what she'd pull out this time, but I knew it wouldn't matter.

What would she do when she was out of "weapons"? Would she go back to herself? Or would terror steal her even farther away from me?

Then Mercedes started to sing. She had her ukelele with her – I don't think I've ever seen her without it – and now she plunked out a tune I'd never heard before.

Hush, my child, fall sleep
Tumble down a hole so deep.
Fall into the gentle dark,
And find within it your own spark.
Tumble down below the ground,
And find me there, where all light is found.

It was a short song, nothing epic or passionate or funny. But there was magic in it. Even the crowd, none of whom had found the World, weaved back and forth and then moved away with smiles as the last notes fell to silence.

In Mom, the effect was more marked. Her agitation ceased with the first note. She swayed back and forth with the rest of the crowd, but when the song ended she kept swaying, a contented smile on her lips and the look of someone who has found a peaceful field with thick grass to lay upon.

I moved forward. Mom didn't shy away. Just kept dancing to that silent music. Mercedes swiveled her uke behind her as she walked forward, too. She touched my mother's shoulder, and then closed her eyes.

A succubus controls people by manipulating memory and emotion. To do that they have to know how to find the mental backdoors that let them in deep, and how to crack the locks that so many people use to keep themselves away from the darkest and brightest parts of their souls. Like any other sneak thief, the succubus can't work well when separated from her target – that's why physical contact is so important, and why they won't be able to control you without hugging you (or doing even more intimate things). But even with a touch, Mercedes might be able to see inside Mom – at least deep enough to give me an idea what was going on.

It was a big deal: Mercedes hadn't used this aspect of her magic for years. But she was breaking that rule to help Mom.

"You feel anything?" I said.

Mercedes didn't answer for a moment. We stood there, we three, in the middle of the crowd that moved back and forth on the second-floor walkway. A few looked at us. Most didn't. I was glad.

I thought for a moment I saw one of the beasties from the Other Green Room – a nix. He grinned as he passed by. Not a friendly grin, but one that showed he was aware something bad was happening and he was glad of it. I decided that if he and I ran into each other I'd have a gentle word with him that would involve smashing his face into something hard.

"I don't know," Mercedes finally said. "Could be, but...." She shook her head. "For a second I almost thought I sensed something magical."

"What was it?"

"I couldn't tell. And whatever it was, it's gone now."

"'Gone' gone, or you just can't feel it?"

She shrugged, a helpless look on her face.

Mom turned and looked at me for a second I thought I saw a glimmer of recognition in her gaze, then it faded away like a body sinking into a lake. "I'm tired," she murmured, in a voice nothing like her own. She sounded like a child.

I pulled her close, hugging her. She lay her head on my shoulder. She'd done that before, but this was different. Not the motion of family, but the way you or I might fold into a firefighter's arms if too exhausted to get out of the house on our own.

It chilled me.

"Michaelbrent? What are you going to do?"

I looked at Mercedes. Mom murmured, "Tired," again so I said, "I'm gonna call an ambulance."

I pulled out my phone. A hand grabbed it out of mine. Blake.

"Blake, give it back," I said tightly. Mercedes stepped back as though she could sense the imminent violence.

Blake could break me in half without breaking a sweat. But no way was I going to let him do *anything* that would hurt my mom.

"I can't, Michaelbrent," he said in a low tone. "You can't leave until you find who killed the princess."

"My mom –" I snarled.

Blake cut me off. "Your mom is a great gal. I like her. But this is bigger than her. How long do you think she'll last if war breaks out?"

I shook my head. "That's a possibility. This," I said, nodding to Mom, "is a reality. So give me the phone, or –"

He put the phone in his pocket. I considered rushing him, but that would mean letting go of Mom. And for some reason, I couldn't will my body to do that. She was leaning on me, and I wasn't going to let her fall.

I looked away from Blake as dismissively as I could. There was an emergency exit at the near end of the walkway, and I headed over there with Mom. Blake ran ahead and inserted himself between me and it.

"Collings," he said, "don't."

"Get out of my *WAY!*"

I shoved past him, got to the emergency door, and hit the crash bar. A loud alarm whooped, but Blake was already on the phone and a second later the alarm went off.

I took a step out.

Mom began screaming. I think. I almost couldn't hear, because I was screaming, too.

46

Hands yanked me back through the crash door, and through pain-blurred vision I saw my mother pulled back as well.

As soon as we crossed the threshold back into the convention center, the pain ceased. My mom was crying on the floor, but again, it was the cry of a child. Innocent and nearly empty.

Blake stood over me, then helped me up. Mercedes was doing the same thing for my mom – they must have been the ones who pulled us back. I saw that Mercedes was gritting her teeth and huge beads of sweat rolled down pasty white cheeks.

That told me what had happened.

Maybe he thought I was too wiped out. Maybe I caught him by surprise. Maybe he just *let* it happen. Whatever the reason, I launched a swift fist at Blake's face and for the first time ever it actually connected.

It wasn't a great punch – the pain still throbbed through my body and threw off my aim. I just hit him a glancing blow across the temple that slid over the cartilage of his ear. It still knocked him back.

"You sonofabitch, you Contained *me*!" I screamed. "Worse, you did it to my mom!"

He didn't respond with his own attack. Just held up his hands and backed off. A few people were gathering. Nothing supernatural to see here, so they were seeing what they could see here.

Mercedes noticed the attention. She pulled out her ukelele and started plunking strings. They sounded random, but people started walking past with uneasy looks on their faces, like they'd just seen someone peeing on the wall.

Blake shook his head. "I didn't Contain either of you," he said. "Neither did Kevin."

"Then how come we can't leave?" I shrieked. I pointed at my mom. "You *hurt her*, you sonofa –"

"He didn't do it."

I spun. Anderson was there, frowning. He walked to the door and opened it. Stuck his hand out, then stepped out himself. His frown deepened.

"Neither Blake nor I would do something like that to –" He stopped and shifted a bit. "Well, we'd do it to *you*. But not your mother." He smiled. "I like your mother."

"I completely believe you," I said, and debated whether to land one on *his* kisser.

Anderson's smile disappeared. "Mr. Collings, I would never do this. It's not my way."

"Then how do you explain what just happened?" I gathered Mom back to me. Mercedes had her hand to her mouth, fear for my mother painted in broad strokes across her face.

"I can't," said Anderson. His face darkened. "But I will."

He disappeared.

I blinked. I'd never seen that before: it wasn't the kind of thing he would do in public normally – even with the mental adjustments people make to deal with magic in their midst, it could have caused problems – but he must have known Mercedes' magic would cover him.

I rounded on Blake again. "What am I supposed to do about my –" I began. A small voice interrupted me.

"MB?" said Mom. She was looking at me with a semblance of the normal light in her eyes. "What happened?" She winced. "I feel like I had a bad attack."

My mom has rheumatoid arthritis. She normally works around it, ignoring the pain as much as possible. But every once in a while she has an "attack" – a level of pain so high that all she can do is lay flat in bed and pray for the ceiling to fall on her.

I stared daggers at Blake. "I. Didn't. Do it," he said.

And I believed him. The words weren't accompanied by a scowl, a look of irritation, a threat about my contract, or a flurry of punches, all of which were his normal conversational medium when dealing with me. He just looked a bit worried, apologetic. Even embarrassed.

I nodded, then started moving Mom toward the elevators. "Come on, Ma," I said.

"Can we... can I get someone to help?" asked Blake hesitantly.

"I think I've had enough of your help for the moment," I said. "Besides, if you didn't do this, and Anderson didn't do this, then it sounds a lot like someone in the Dead Ones isn't using the same play book, so I'm not about to trust any of you with her."

Blake paled at that. He nodded. "Yeah. Okay."

"Hi, Blake," said Mom, seeming to notice him for the first time. "How are you doing? You look tired, you should get some rest."

That's Mom for you. Hurting, confused, and her first impulse is to help someone else.

"I'm good, Judi," he said. He tried a smile. It only partly worked. She nodded and smiled back, then put all her attention back into moving.

We walked away. I thought dark thoughts. I believed Blake: he hadn't done this, and neither had Anderson – nor did they know who had.

But someone did it. And I was going to find out who and make him very *very* sorry.

You don't mess with my mother. Not if you want to live.

47

I took Mom back to the hotel, thanking Heaven we'd booked a room here instead of the Motel 6 a few blocks away. Mercedes told me she'd closed down the table, and handed me the cash box and a bag.

"What's this?" I asked.

She looked woeful. "It's all that was left there."

I peeked inside. A defaced copy of *Crime Seen*, and the two books Kevin Anderson had "sold" me. Of course, *his* books had come through all this just fine.

Mercedes saw the storm brewing in my gaze. "If you want, I –"

I shook my head. "Thanks, Mercedes. You've been a life-saver." I looked at Mom, who was painfully putting one foot in front of the other. "Maybe literally."

At that, Mom looked at Mercedes. "Hey, Cadillac," she said as brightly as anyone can when they're gritting their teeth that hard.

Mercedes rolled her eyes, but the worry was still there. "Hey, Hootie."

"It's *Judi.*"

"And I'm *Mercedes.*"

They both smiled good-naturedly. I got the feeling this was a ritual for them. Mercedes darted away, then returned with my mom's discarded steampunk gun and time gizmo. She dropped them into the bag with the books, squeezed my arm, then said, "You take care, Cootie," to my mom.

Mom nodded, "You, too, Beamer."

She left. I got Mom – slowly, painfully – to the elevators. We went down, then passed through the concourse outside the convention floor. I took her through the walkway that joined convention center to hotel. I didn't see any Otherworlders – which was a good thing, because I was in the mood to get into it with someone.

At our hotel room, I dropped her onto the bed. I took off her top hat, then helped her lay down. I loosened her bustier – she was wearing a blouse under it, so don't get any inbred hillbilly *Hills Have Eyes* ideas. After that I took off her boots and removed her chain belt.

Mom was already asleep.

I looked out the window. It was totally dark out. I hadn't realized how late it was, or how famished I had gotten. I tore into the supplies we had brought, and came out with a bag of Gummi Bears and some teriyaki jerky. I popped a hunk of jerky into my mouth, and was about to yank open the Gummi Bears when I thought better of it and used the hotel phone to call the concierge.

A few minutes later a fresh-faced girl appeared at my door. I handed her the bag and asked her to drop it off at the door of the convention center surveillance room. She looked unsure, but a ten dollar bill got her nodding. I told her where the room was.

"Who should I give it to?" she asked.

"No, just drop it on the floor outside the door. Seriously."

That unsure look returned. Another five bucks made *it* disappear. Then the girl disappeared, too, and I leaned against the closed door. Gandhi would smell the candy like a tiger tracking a bleeding gazelle. I really wanted to eat the candy myself – some junky sugar seemed like just what the doctor ordered – but I'd promised him.

I went back to the phone and considered calling my dad to tell him what had happened to Mom. Decided against it. I'd wait and see what the night and the morning brought.

Dad is a great guy. He and I work together on a lot of things. Not writing together, but he looks over my work and vice-versa. He was the Creative Writing Director at Pepperdine University in Malibu for thirty years, and along the way he also became a world expert on Stephen King, Dean Koontz, and knew more about horror and monsters than anyone I knew who wasn't in the World. He was in demand at conferences for a lot of years – lecturing on writing, poetry, and the dark worlds that they so often try to illuminate.

A year ago, Dad stopped coming to cons. His health just wouldn't permit it. He's diabetic, nearly deaf, and has major depressive disorder and a few other mental quirks, some of which I had inherited myself. Any one of those is dealable, but mix them all up in one person and you get someone for whom conventions are an exhausting and sometimes terrifying experience. In his seventies now, he finally decided to take it a bit easier.

That was part of why I didn't call him: I was worried about what it might do to him. Telling him "something" was wrong with Mom would put him in a worse state than letting him know she had a rare, deadly, but very specific disease. His mental issues thrived on the worst torture of all: just not knowing.

So no, I wouldn't tell him unless she was physically injured or I could figure out exactly what was happening with her.

Fine. I made another call. Again, I used the hotel phone. When Blake answered, I told him I wanted *my* phone back and to send Dave Butler to my room with it.

Blake must have still been feeling guilty, because he didn't respond acridly, just said, "Yeah, okay."

I sat down on the semi-soft chair that took up three-quarters of the floor space not already covered by the two twin beds. My mom snored softly. I smiled at that.

Be okay, Mom.

I didn't want to go out and do any on-site sleuthing. Lots of Otherworlders like wandering around at night, but with the convention closed for the night and a Containment spell locking everyone down, most of them would be in their rooms. They wouldn't try anything with people in the hotel, either: the Treaty was still in force; and even if it weren't, they wouldn't want the heat or attention a bunch of weird murders in a single hotel might bring.

More important, I didn't want to leave my mom alone.

"Okay, what've we got?" I said.

The answer was easy: nothing. Or too much, which was worse.

Calista was supposed to marry Eustace at the signing of the treaty Saturday night. Everyone seemed to think she was a pure, chaste thing – except for the Nerdfather, Harold Kumar. Yet she was operating out of Nespda, doing things the madam there had implied were the stuff nightmares were made of.

A princess with a double life. Princess by day, cosplayer/booth babe/monster prostitute by night. But without the day and night – she apparently mixed them up without regard for the position of moon or sun. She even had a glamour token – the star on her hand – tattooed into her skin in order to change her appearance when she was messing around as "Lani."

So who would want to kill someone like that? The answer: everyone.

Eustace might have motive if he didn't really want the treaty to succeed, or if he had found out she wasn't really pure as the driven snow. Anyone in the High Court might have the same motive. I didn't know if they'd rage to find out she was a hooker, but certainly a lot of vampires would not want to cast their die with the lycans.

Plus, there were Calista's half-siblings. Warine was apparently a jealous twit who was petty enough to hate anyone more powerful than he, and if he really felt as impotent as I'd been given to understand... well, those kind of people sometimes whimper and cower until they suddenly break inside and lash out at anyone nearby.

And let's not forget Roberta: she hated the idea of the treaty, and she was eager to undermine her mother.

That was a bright spot, I supposed: Borga was probably not the killer. She had a lot invested in the success of the treaty.

She had implied that, should she fail, her position as queen and her life itself might end shortly after. And Gandhi had verified her alibi. Which didn't mean she hadn't arranged for the killing to occur, but if that was the case then I still had to find the actual wetworks person before I could link back to her.

The prince's various alibis for the time of the murder hadn't been confirmed yet, but I believed he hadn't known about it, and hadn't had anything to do with it. Still, if he had found out about Calista's extracurricular activities... well, more than one supernatural fiancée or family member had killed someone involved in that kind of life.

Which reminded me of what Eustace had said about Nespda being part of a trafficking ring. Could Calista have seen or found out something? Another visit to the madam might be in order.

The only other member of the royal family was King William. I had no froikin' clue what he was thinking. I thought it likely no one did, other than he himself. I wanted to talk to him, but couldn't for the life of me figure out a way to make that happen.

Then there were the lycans. The vampires, I had to admit, were higher on the suspect list. Part of that was because of the way Calista had been found: arms stretched out, wounds on neck and inner thighs, exsanguinated. Part of it, I had to admit, was just that I liked the lycans better – or, at least, didn't dislike them as much.

With the lycans, again, everyone thought Calista was the light of all life. I was fairly certain King Haemon really loved his daughter, and he had logic on his side as far as really wanting the treaty to go through. I hadn't verified his claims about werewolves' breeding cycles or that they were in danger of losing the conflict with the vampires, but if it were true then certainly he had everything to gain by the treaty going through.

Moonbeam? I'd have to put her in my "look at very carefully" list. She said she loved her sister. But she kept giving those shady looks, and the expression that flashed over her when I mentioned Calista's star tattoo definitely indicated she knew something she wasn't telling.

How about Aseas? I assumed he was still in a coma, since I hadn't heard anything to the contrary. But why was the Lycaon Peacemaker meeting in secret with a princess of the High Court? What had happened during the meeting? What did they talk about? Had Aseas killed her, then done something to cause his own coma?

That last sounded doubtful. If he was so involved in the treaty, why would he do that? And he loved Calista like she was part of his own family. He might lash out same as anyone about her double life, sure, but failing that, why? Of course, if he didn't kill her that created an even bigger problem: how did someone else sneak up on a Peacemaker? Impossible, right?

I might get some answers if I could see the security feeds. But those led to only more questions: how had someone bypassed a dwarf's security measures? What wouldn't just block a feed, but make it completely disappear? What was up with the tiny markings on both the security cams and Gandhi's computer?

And the last person in the puzzle: SuperGhoul. Why did the booth babe run when Larry and I went into the Other Green Room to talk to Pixela? What did she know, and where had she gone?

Then there was Calista's phone, my only real physical evidence. I brought it out. I used the same kind of plug as mine did, so I plugged it into the wall and turned it on.

The lock screen stared at me. I moved my thumb across it a few times, and I have to admit that I hoped the gods of Rorschach doodles would smile on me. They did not. The phone remained locked.

Okay, Collings. Time to actually think about it.

What did I know about Calista herself? She was a princess. She was a liar and someone with an apparent proclivity for doing things that would make most supernatural beings throw up. Her preferred client at Nespda was the Nerdfather. She was a supporter of the vampire/lycan treaty.

Actually, I didn't know that last. She might have been slated to be the bride who would help seal the treaty, but as for whether she truly wanted to act that part, she was an enigma.

So: liar. Pervert. Nespda. Nerdfather.

I doodled a few racy pictures on the phone. I will not tell you what they were, because frankly you're not equipped (inadvertent pun!) to handle them. The way a slythgodin reproduces would give you nightmares.

Regardless, the doodles resulted in a locked phone.

After I exhausted my representations of "pervert," I moved on to Nespda. I traced the word itself. I traced a long slide. I traced more racy doodles – this time focusing on female monster... uh... stuff.

Nada. Zilch.

I tried the Nerdfather's favorite symbol: that of the Green Lantern. And even though I hadn't expected it to work, I still felt disappointed.

I knew I was going at this wrong.

What was she? What would she have as her lock symbol?

What was she?

What is she?

I kept coming back to that. Circling it over and over, and coming up with liar. Or at best a compulsively secretive person.

Okay, what do secretive people do?

They keep secrets!

And the man wins... a brand new car!

Secrets. Secretive.

Secretive people – and liars – try to hide their secrets. Of course. So go with that. Who would she most want to hide them from?

There were the girls at Come and Play – but I discarded that. Sure, they were just as grossed out by the Nespda dealings as anyone in the World. But they were far from the ones Calista would be most concerned about.

That would be her family – with her sister, Moonbeam, likely at the top of the list of people she wouldn't want digging into her life.

Who else?

Easy: the High Court. What would a bunch of angry vampires do to her if they found out she was not only cheating on their prince, but doing it in the most disgusting possible way?

Yikes.

Blood would be drained, that was certain.

Just like it had been. Just like happened *to her.*

So… she would want her family out, and the vampires out.

I stared at the lock screen for what seemed like an eternity.

A knock came at the door, for which I was grateful. I felt like I was drowning in a sea of questions, waiting for the lifeboat of answers to throw me the round floaty thing of inspiration.

I checked the peephole, then opened it. Dave Butler came in the room when I opened the door, then handed me my phone, followed by a folder full of papers. "Kevin asked me bring these to you." He cocked his head. "Do you know why I'm the errand boy all of a sudden?" Then his eyes widened and he added in a whisper, "Sorry, didn't know your mom was sleeping."

"It's okay," I whispered back. "She's had a rough day."

"Anything I can do to help out?"

I shook my head as I looked into the folder, which was full of printouts: the Dead Ones' files on the players in our murderous drama. "No," I said. "Just problems with her arthritis."

Dave understood Mom's arthritis – as much as an outsider can. He knew I thought "asshole" was spelled "arthritis."[20] He nodded. "You must grow in patience when you meet with great wrongs, and they will be powerless to vex you." Then, for the dumb ones in the audience (meaning me), he added, "Leonardo da Vinci, 1492 to 1519."

"Who uses words like 'vex'?" I responded. "Michaelbrent Collings, usually between one-ninety and two-ten."

Dave grinned at that. He's very smart, but he puts up with my lowbrow jokes, which is nice of him.

We chatted quietly for a minute. Dave did not mention losing out on a half-million dollar book deal, which I'd been worrying about. I made a few offhanded comments designed to lead him to the subject, but from his responses he had no knowledge of anything that had happened during his Robot Dave phases – or, apparently, for a few minutes before or after.

Dave took off after we promised to catch lunch or dinner at some point during the con. I was lying, but I think he knew I was, so it was okay.

Then we said goodbye. I walked Dave to the door, and pinched his butt on the way out. I'm not into Dave, you understand – at least, most of the time[21] – but he's so tall his butt is pretty much perfect height for pinching, and I thought it would get a good expression out of him. Funny. I needed some funny.

Off his growl, I said, with wide-eyed innocence: "Sorry, man. Did I vex thee?"

He growled again, but there was a smile behind it. Again, Dave gets me. Or at least tolerates me with good grace and humor. A friend.

"Vex," he muttered. "I'll show you vex."

---

[20] I'm not going to apologize for this one. Arthritis can bite me.

[21] That one's just to keep Laura on her toes. See, I've got *options*, baby!

I almost added, "Hey, at least you're not burning crosses into yourself. Now *that's* vexing," then realized I wasn't talking to Robot Dave.

I said goodbye. He headed out.

The image of the crosses being burnt into Eustace's skin stole all the good feelings of Dave's visit. I'd never seen something like that. Never –

I froze. So completely I'm pretty sure my blood stalled in my veins for a moment before everything started up again and I ran the few feet to Calista's phone.

Secrets.

Secretive.

What was the one thing she could put as a passcode that none of the people she most worried about would ever use.

Only one thing. The thing her family abhorred for what it might remind them of.

The thing that would actually *hurt* the people even more likely to come after her if they knew what was in here.

I swiped a cross over the face of the phone. And…

… nothing.

I almost threw it across the room. I actually had my hand up to chuck it against the wall – yeah, Mom was still snoring, but my frustration overwhelmed my desire to let her rest – then I looked at the phone again.

I'd swiped a cross. Crossbeam, long vertical beam. But what if….

This time I swiped it like a good Catholic. "Spectacles, testicles, wallet, and watch," I murmured to myself. I'm not Catholic, but I had a friend who was, and he told me this little ditty.

Up to down, left to right.

The phone unlocked.

48

I was walking through a foresty area in Paraguay, South America once. Long story why I was there.[22] I was following railroad tracks, and this awful stench started to assault me. I kept walking, because it was literally the only way to get through the jungle without a machete. The stench got worse and worse, to the point that vomiting wasn't a threat, it was a reality.

Finally found out what it was. A cow or a bull had wandered on the tracks and gotten plowed by a train. It was shredded to pieces and scattered over a two-mile stretch of rails.

Then left there to decay. Which, in a place where you hit one hundred and ten degrees and one hundred percent humidity, creates some of the worst levels of rot you'll ever (hopefully never) see.

The cow bits were almost as revolting as the smell. But guess what? I spotted every one, and looked at it closely as I passed. Couldn't help it. There's just something in our bodies and minds that cries out to look at the things we abhor. I couldn't look away and, on a primitive, ugly level, I didn't want to.

What I found on Calista's phone was like that.

I flipped through the contacts first. There were the expected ones: Haemon, and a few members of the Vampire High Court: Eustace and Borga. Surprisingly, she had Princess Roberta listed as a contact, too. I'd have to talk to Roberta about that when I finally got around to chatting with her.

Even more surprising, most of the calls were to her sister, Moonbeam. Moonbeam had said she adored Calista, but I frankly didn't believe a lot of what Moonbeam said. And if Moonbeam had been so disgusted with Calista about the impending nuptials, didn't it make sense that they'd have talked *less* recently?

---

[22] Not really, but it *is* a story for a different time.

Huh. I'd have to examine that, too.

On to her social media.

Nothing on Facebook. No Twitter. No surprise, really.

On to the big guns.

FiendFace.com is *the* social media for the World. Creatures post about everything – parties, solstice events, the equivalent of flash mobs only with much more blood. It was similar to Facebook, sure, but when you saw a picture of someone's lunch posted on FiendFace, that lunch was much more likely to be bound, gagged, and crying for Mommy.

Did Calista have an active presence? Hoo, boy, did she ever.

The phone auto-logged me on as Lani, her Come and Play name. She had the max amount of friends, and when I checked she also had a Celebrity page with followers well into the five figures.

Of course. Because the Facebook fanpage of a mere author (mine is at facebook.com/MichaelbrentCollings – sign up today!) is not nearly as interesting as that of a booth babe/cosplayer/bargain-priced hooker.

"Lani" was everywhere – she went to all the cons, she posed with just about everyone who wanted to be in a glam-shot with her. Pictures with smiling men, women, and children, all posing beside Prostitute Ninja or Schoolgirl Phantom of the Opera. The Come and Play girls were often in attendance, lined up beside whatever unsuspecting nerd wanted a pic with the beautiful "girls."

I got a chill as I read some of the captions. Many of them just laughed at whoever was posing with her. A few, though, had markings like, "Room 203C – and he's all alone with no friends or family, so if he were to go missing...." I cross-referenced the dates on other feeds that had tagged "Lani," and was beyond dismayed to see how many times that poor guy or girl ended up in one of the "check out my lunch!" photos.

And no, it was never as a guest. Unless "guest" can be defined as someone whose dismembered fingers are the first course, and whose head watches as a centerpiece.

Still, for Otherworlders this was nothing *too* surprising. It bugged me, but other than revealing Calista's "Lani" alter-ego, this was actually pretty tame.

So where's the grody cow part?

Okay. You asked for it.

After a while moving through FiendFace, I decided to move on. Maybe I'd have Robot Dave or Gandhi look for more information later – they'd do it faster and be less bored/horrified by it all.

I went to the phone's home screen. One of the widgets was "Gallery," and I clicked it.

I tried really hard not to wake my mom up. But it's hard to puke quietly.

Mom was still snoring when I came back, picked up the phone with shaky hands, and forced myself to continue.

There were lots of pictures. And they were all shots of Calista – as the blond booth babe Lani – doing nasty things. Not "murder" nasty – apparently she took pictures while doing her work at Nespda.

An astounding number of shots paraded across the screen – all Lani, all in poses that would make a hardened pornographer quit his job and move to Africa to do charity work for the rest of his life.

Sometimes Calista was in her human guise in the pictures, other times she was fully wolfed out. They were all taken selfie-style, too: it was clear that Calista was the one taking the shot in every one. Though not always with her hands. I'll just leave it at that.

The other person in the shot – or sometimes people – was always male. Always, to the best of my observation, a human.

I'm not a cop. But sometimes I understand why so many of them struggle to find a way where they can both do their jobs and maintain a grip on their humanity. Every picture I looked at left me feeling a little dirtier, a little more stained. I knew I wasn't looking at them for fun, and that someone had to view them in order to find out if any clues were hiding here, but... it cost me. It made me feel like maybe I wouldn't be able to hug Laura or the kids next time I saw them. As though just being this close to what had happened might be enough to cast me out of the Heaven of my own home.

I pushed on.

A large number of shots featured Calista's body parts in gravity-defying positions against (or in/out of/through) someone else's body. A large someone, a person with a body so huge that it sometimes threatened to actually envelop Calista's hands/feet/head/tail/muzzle/naughty bits. The person in those photos clearly had great strength, because there is *no* way some of the things I saw could be done without such strength. He was also covered in some of the curliest black hair I've ever seen. Not "werewolf-levels" covered, but certainly, "Dude, get a *razor*" covered.

His face was never shown, but there was no doubt this was Harold Kumar, the Nerdfather.

I wondered how he'd react if I showed him the pictures Calista took of him. Or how he'd react if I showed him the *rest* of her pictures.

On, on, on. Hundreds – maybe thousands – of shots. I started flipping through them more quickly; looking at them closely was something I could perhaps leave to Robot Dave, since he wouldn't remember any of it when it was done.

Until then, however, I kept going. Two more visits to the bathroom.

And then one that was like a breath of fresh air, if only because it was different.

The other shots had all been so close that only Calista and her paramour(s) were visible. Sometimes it was even closer, showcasing some new "move" that was close to biologically and physically impossible. There was little context for where the pictures occurred, though there was occasionally a glimpse of a dark bedside table or a mirror, which gave me the impression they were either in bedrooms or in one of the dedicated "activity" rooms Nespda likely featured.

This view *was* inside Nespda. But not a bedroom. It was the front lobby. The bar was visible, as was the right half of the witch bartender I'd pissed off on my earlier visit. She was talking to someone at the bar, only the back of his head visible.

"Lani" was sitting behind a small, circular bar table. She sat on the lap of someone I hadn't seen in any of the pictures before. I recognized his face – just about everyone in the world probably would. I am a classy, discrete guy, so I won't say who it was, but it rhymes with Shmesident Shmill Shlinton.

I was surprised by how *un*surprised I was by that. Or by the fact that his hand was doing very naughty things right on camera.

Still, that wasn't what really drew my focus.

It was the fact that this picture – unlike every single other one I'd seen – wasn't taken by Lani herself. Both her hands were – ahem – busy. And this one was taken from farther away than the others. Most telling, there was a hand on the table – one that belonged to neither Calista nor her special friend.

All the other pictures had been taken by Calista. And now I thought of it, in her FiendFace posts she hadn't responded to comments made on her fanpage or her personal page. People go on social media to be *social*. Lani, though, went there not to interact, but to… what?

To brag. To show off.

That was it. This was a girl who said little as "Calista." Lots of secrets, and no confidants that I could tell. Either beaten down in some way, silent as a whipped dog who fears further attacks; or simply silent because she didn't really see herself *as* Calista.

Lani, though, was a pathological exhibitionist. She didn't come to interact with her "friends" and fans – at least, not in the sense that interaction was an open communication. She came only to show how sexy and wild and fun and generally amazing she was.

I flipped back to her FiendFace feed. Noticed now that she *had* interacted somewhat: under each picture or statement she posted to show how amazeballs her life was, she'd pinned all the comments that simply boiled down to "You're amazing and much better than I'll ever be!" to the top of the feed. Comments that just said "You're amazing!" without the "better than me!" part came next. And after that....

I frowned. After that there was nothing. Not a single person asking to get together, asking for her phone number, asking questions about the beautiful and mysterious Lani. Otherworlders are secretive in certain respects, sure, but among their own kind they are as catty and gossipy as anyone. For someone with as many friends and fans as Lani to have not a single question, invitation, or anything else could mean only one thing: she had deleted all of them.

This wasn't a social interaction. It was a shrine she had built to herself and to the fact that she was better than anyone else.

What did that say about her? Secretive about anything of substance, but open about her alter ego.

Not quite right.

My subconscious niggled at me, and I finally realized what it was trying to say. Calista wasn't secretive about anything of substance; there was *nothing* of substance about her. She was an empty shell that existed for thrills, for adoration. A creature whose entire focus was herself, and the instant gratification of adulation.

She also did shocking things. That was important, too. People who repeatedly engage in activity that society at large deems scandalous or appalling generally break down into two categories: people who need attention, and people who are psychologically broken.

I would bet the farm that this was an instance of the latter.

I flipped back to the picture of Calista and "the other person" in the bar. Didn't focus on either of them, though; just on the hand of the man who took the picture.

It wasn't Harold Kumar, I was sure. The hand was too white, and there was a complete dearth of pelt on the back of it. But there wasn't much else to go on. It was just a hand on the table. Big, with thick knuckles that looked like they'd probably broken their share of noses, but the only thing that stood out about it was a pinky ring, which looked like gold with a small red ruby.

I continued through the photos. Mostly the same gag-inducing kind of shots I'd already seen. Other than the one with the "Shmesident," the only face that was ever in the pictures was Lani's, which spoke again to pathological narcissism. Even the one she *had* allowed someone else to show up in was of a person so famous it would inherently showcase her own unparalleled value to the universe.

Interspersed here and there, though, there were now a few other shots of Calista taken by someone else. I assumed it was the nameless man. Usually they were of Calista modeling outfits designed to drive men to distraction – and some of those men were clearly distracted only by dominance and the giving or receiving of pain. Any rooms I saw were Nespda rooms – brown wood and red trim. Few details, and certainly none that were helpful.

Once I actually thought I had a breakthrough. Calista was standing in front of a mirror – again, in an outfit that was illegal in fifty-two states.[23] Calista's back was turned, revealing very little clothing and some very weird bodypaint.

The big thing, though, was that I saw another body in the mirror's reflection. I zoomed in, trying to make out the details. This could be huge.

Or very small. The more I zoomed, the worse the resolution got, obviously. Things started getting blurry way before I got close enough to make out details. All I could really make out was that the person was in a white outfit, and that from the angle of the reflection whoever I saw in the mirror must have been the one who took the picture. Which, because I of my amazing detective skills, I had already inferred from the presence of the picture itself.

I flipped over to the FiendFace page. Maybe if I correlated some dates.

Nothing useful. The Fiendface posts listed dates she was at conventions or other locations, but they didn't particularly correlate with anything helpful on the pictures' date stamps. Even if they had, it didn't mean much. There are a lot of ways magic can get you instantly from one place to another, so it's not like just because she was in Topeka for FlySwatPaperCupCon (yeah, they were both invented there), it's not like she couldn't have zapped herself to Albuquerque for WrongTurnCon.

It was getting late, but I felt enervated. I felt like I'd been spinning my wheels up to now. Getting information, sure, but not adding myself to any of it. I'd been a sponge. Now it was time to be a bit more of a Warden.

I turned back to the pictures. Scanned through a few. And looking for something specific, I got some interesting answers.

---

[23] I know there are currently only fifty. I can only assume this outfit will be outlawed in the future when we finally make a state out of Puerto Rico and then eventually invade and annex Canada. We all know that war is coming.

The earliest photos on the gallery were, of course, of Calista. The one where she stood in front of the mirror, with the odd body paint on, was only the third one in the camera roll, and the first two, though of sexual acts, were much tamer than the others had been.

I checked the date stamps: December twenty-third, twenty-fourth, and twenty-fifth of last year.

"Merry Christmas," I murmured. I flipped back to the first shot I'd seen that was taken by Mr. Mystery. It was in February of this year.

So... three months. Three months, and Mr. Mystery disappears from the picture. Why? What happened? Falling out?

And now I was following that line, I realized that the first pic he'd taken *was* important. Not necessarily because of what it shared of him, but because of what it said about Calista.

I flipped to FiendFace. A quick scan of her posts showed me they dated back about five years.

Back to the picture of her looking in the mirror. The two pictures before that had been relatively tame, and now I looked closer, the dress-up picture seemed a bit... nervous. Calista/Lani was close enough to the mirror that I could see her expression well. At first blush it was just a face, but then I noticed the subtle creases. She was worried, maybe a little afraid.

The first picture with Mr. Mystery showed a fearful Calista. What was she afraid of? The picture itself? No – she'd already taken pictures before, of more compromising situations.

It was what she was doing. This was when it started. I bet if I asked the madam at Nespda – and assuming she answered me truthfully – she would tell me that Lani had started working at the bordello right around the end of December. Could Mr. Mystery be Calista's pimp? Had he gotten her started at Nespda?

Calista's FiendFace posts showed that her vanity – a vanity I suspected hid a lot of self-loathing – had begun years ago, and might have gone on forever just the same.

But in December, something changed.

In February, something else shifted.

What? What could have happened three months –

Oh.

I put the phone down and went to the folder full of documents Dave had brought by. I was pretty sure I remembered the dates, but just in case....

It was on the top page, along with a scrawled note from Anderson reminding me I had only until Saturday night. The night of the treaty.

The treaty that had begun negotiations in December of last year.

And then, a few months later – February, to be exact – Calista had been betrothed to Prince Eustace.

So when the treaty became a possibility, Calista, through Lani, upped her game and began acting out on literally criminal levels.

And when it became more of a reality with her betrothal, there was a falling out with Mr. Mystery – but Calista kept on working at Nespda. After a quick look, I verified that the pictures after that point were much more graphic and horrifying.

I glanced back at the shot of her with the ex-president – oops, did I say that out loud? – and Mr. Big Hand. I noticed something more.

I looked away from those photos. Put Calista's phone in my pocket.

Picked up my own.

I knew what the next step had to be. I just hoped I would live through it.

49

I was out the door by the time I got the number dialed. Mom seemed to be sleeping normally, and I'd be back quickly. I hoped.

Kevin J. Anderson answered my call on the fourth ring, picking up and snarling, "What?" into the phone.

I checked the time. Oops. I'd been at the slide show longer than I thought. It was after three in the morning. Still, Anderson didn't sound like I'd woken him up. Just....

"Geez, man, what –" I managed to cut off the rest of the question. Asking my more-or-less boss why it always sounded like he was in a slow-burn orgy would be a bad idea right now.

Instead, I told him what I'd found. What I noticed in the last photo. And what I now intended to do.

"Absolutely not!" he whisper-screamed, as though others were listening and he wanted to be angry without them *knowing* he was angry. "You don't have any evidence to –"

"No evidence?" *I* didn't have to be quiet; mine was a full-throated yell. "Didn't you hear a word I said?"

"That's not evidence, that's guesswork. And if you guess wrong, we're looking at an even bigger incident than the one that already threatens."

"Really? Because from what I understand the current one threatens life as we know it on the planet. How can it get much worse than that?" I mock gasped. "Is Roseanne Barr getting a new television show?"

He made a noise I found rather funny – so long as I was far away. Then he said, "Do. Not. Go. To. The –"

"*Skchidkhd*," I said. "Sorry, it's… *sdhrkeh*… -ignal dying… *shkckekd*… into a tunnel or… *shekdkc* –"

"Don't you dare, Collings! Don't pretend –"

I ended the call and kept walking. Actually, I ran. I didn't know if Anderson would actually try to intercept me, but I didn't want to take the chance.

I got into the elevator. Noted that the button I needed wasn't there. I had figured that to be the case – last time I went here I heard a key, not a card.

Above the banks of floor buttons, there were several openings for keys that would be used by hotel maintenance, fire fighters, and police. The one I needed sat right there in the middle.

I pulled out my magically-enhanced key card.

What, you thought it only worked on electronic locks?

I swiped it over the keyhole and there was a click. The elevator doors started to slide closed. A tired-looking guy in a business suit ran for the elevator and almost got his hand in. I punched his fingers and he yelped and let go. I didn't feel bad: the dude did *not* want to go where I was going.

Okay, I felt a *little* bad, so I yelled, "It's not you, it's me!" as the doors closed. That line had always worked on my ex-girlfriends, so I was sure he'd be fine.

A few seconds later, the elevator gave that tiny lurch it always does and the doors opened. I left, and heard the doors close behind me. It sounded like I imagine it must sound when crypt doors close – and you're on the inside.

I stepped out of the small elevator penthouse, and found myself on the roof. It was very dark. So dark that I jumped a good seven feet straight up when a voice hissed out of the darkness, "It would be better for you to return during the day."

I looked over and saw Rathton, the captain of Queen Borga's guard.

I told you how the sun narcotizes and mellows vampires. Here before me was a vampire of the un-sunny variety. Not just the irises, but the entire eyes had succumbed to the blood ring that only hinted at their nature during the day. The teeth stood out against his lips, all jagged and sharp as a mouthful of broken glass, with the canines so long I could see holes where they punched through his lower lip.

He also seemed bigger. He *wasn't* – I have a pretty good eye for spatial relationships, and he was still just as big compared to me as he had been earlier. But there was a looming presence about him that made me want to shy away, to curl up and crawl into whatever safe place I could and wait for the day to return.

He saw it in my face. Saw my surprise, my fear. He liked it.

Once, when I was a kid, I had to have a minor surgery in my shoulder without any anesthetic. When the doctor came at me with his scalpel, my mom holding tight to one hand and my dad holding tight to the other, that was beyond terrifying. The doctor looked at me and said, slowly and deliberately, "Hold absolutely still."

I did. But only because I knew that being cowardly in this instance would result in something far harder than the pain that my bravery would cost.

I had that same feeling now. Everything in me screamed to run, flee, *escape*.

Instead, I drew myself up to my full medium-height, and said, "It's better whenever I say it is, Dr. Teeth."

Rathton's smile disappeared. He lunged at me, fingers that had grown razor claws outstretched to rip out my throat. Perhaps he intended to do what had been done to Calista. She had been drained with care, with a certain *grace*.

But I was pretty sure Rathton intended simply to yank my head from my shoulders and bathe in whatever gouted out of the stump.

I didn't shrink.

At the last second – and I mean that, his fangs were a centimeter from my throat – a loud noise sounded. It was like a giant's hands slapping together, and at the same time a bright pink and purple firework exploded between us.

Rathton cried and cringed away, holding his burnt fingers in his good hand.

I leaned in close. "Queen's Blessing," I said.

The Blessing of the queen or king of the High Court isn't just a request for courtesy. When she gave it, she rendered me impervious to attack from any in her power. Until she rescinded it, which, based on Rathton's glare, he would look forward to like a kid waiting for a bloody Christmas.[24]

C'est la vie.

I left him there, and went looking for the rest of the court.

I found them well past the pavilion they had stood under during the day. Past where Borga and I had found Eustace sobbing behind some machinery.

The vamps were all in a group, hunched over something. They swayed slightly, and I could hear muffled voices and even lower sounds that I couldn't identify.

On the outskirts of the vamps was a strange sight: a variety of Otherworlders, all of whom were frenziedly drawing pictures by the illumination of small lights they each wore. At least half a dozen different kinds of Otherworlders – some of them with enough extra hands and/or eyes to work on several drawings or paintings at once.

What the –

I moved forward a bit more, but before I could make out any real details, one of the vampires broke away from that central group. It was Borga. Like Rathton, she was fully in vamp mode. I know they can control that when they want to, but there was no one around here but them (and me), so why bother?

She didn't bother shifting back to her less-pointy demeanor when she saw me, either. "What is it?" she said, and there was an edge to her voice that hadn't been there during the day. The sun was gone, and so was any pretense at humanity.

Her teeth, I noted, were stained. Blood.

---

[24] Not every kid looks forward to bloody Christmases, but trust me: the ones that do, *really* look forward to it. So the simile works.

All this made what was coming up that much harder. But it had to be done, and it had to be done now.

"I need to see Eustace," I said, and started toward the vampire throng that huddled in the darkness beyond us.

Borga put her hand on my shoulder. Squeezed so hard I swore I could hear my bones creak. "You should go," she whispered.

"I have to talk to him *now*," I answered. I tried to take a step, but she yanked me back, pulling me as easily as I might yank a puppy on its leash.

"It would be better for you not to see what happens beyond," she said, nodding at the vampires. "Remain here, and I will bring him."

She was as good as her word. In only a moment, Eustace stepped away from the indistinct mound and walked toward me.

He was very different now. The sobbing was over, the drugged appearance utterly gone. He had changed his pants and now wore a pair that I could tell were expensive, even in the dark. No shirt, though, which let me see the musculature that had only been hinted at before. His hair was immaculate to the point he could have done Paul Mitchell commercials. As I had suspected, he was just as good-looking as the rest of the court.

Except for the blood that completely covered the lower half of his face, slicking well past his chest and dripping down the furrows in his washboard stomach.

I now knew why I'd been warned off, and what the other monsters with their sketch pads and canvases were up to. The vampires were holding the equivalent of a wake. And everyone knows the only two things you absolutely need for a wake are a dead person and food. Apparently they were mourning for Calista – unheard of since she was a lycan – while eating something they thought it would be better for me not to see.

I probably should have asked about what was on the menu – I was a Warden, after all – but I decided to focus on one thing at a time.

I also understood what the other Otherworlders were doing here. This wasn't just any wake: it was a wake by vamps for a lycan. Unknown in history. Plus, it was the High Court doing the waking.

The Otherworlders on the outside were paparazzi. The monster equivalent of celebrity photographers. You want to publish pictures of an event, but most of the creatures at it don't show up on film or digital video?

So you draw them.

"Huh," I said to myself. The World is endlessly weird and fascinating and scary and darkly wonderful. Just like ours, I suppose.

"What is it?" asked Eustace in an imperious tone. "Why do you summon me like this, creature? What have you found of my love's killer?"

"Well," I said, and swallowed. "I have a prime suspect."

His claws grew an inch, and snapped together. "Who?" he said. "Tell me so I can make him suffer an eternity."

"You might not want to chuck him in the sarlacc pit just yet," I said.

He pointed at me, and that simple movement held more threat than a primed block of C-4. "Who," he said darkly.

I grimaced. "Well, uh… you."

50

In case you haven't figured it out at this point, I'm not super-subtle as an investigator. There are people who have it down to half art, half science. People who spin suspects around until they're dizzy, then get the truth from them so adroitly they don't even know it's happening. But those people have a few things I don't:

1) training, and
2) some kind of desire to actually do what they're doing.

Neither of these was on my resume. I was pretty good at some things, but very often had no idea what I was doing, and generally I wasn't sure why Blake had even bothered to make me a Warden. Sure, I could fight okay; and yes, I knew more about monsters than Joe Average (thanks, Dad!). But I was hardly Sherlock Holmes. If there were a show about me it would be called *Bull in a China Shop, P.I.* My method could be summed up as "break as much merchandise as possible, then see who comes to pick up the pieces."

That was why I came up here like this, and dropped a direct accusation on the prince. Sure, it might get me killed, but it also might get me answers – either from a tear-ridden confession (Ha! Fat chance!) – or from the honest expressions that tend to leak out when people or Otherworlders are truly surprised.

To my amazement, Eustace didn't try to mangle me. Nor did he wave his hands around and say, "No, you've got it all wrong!" Thankfully, he also didn't slice me to bits (though I have to admit, I never would have tried this without Borga's Blessing giving me some protection).

Instead, he laughed. Hard, and long, and without malice. He laughed like I'd just said the single stupidest thing in history.

Another group broke away from the center mass. Before they came close enough to see any details, I knew these weren't vampires. Vampires move a certain way – a near-glide that lets them travel with ghosty stealth. The figures coming now had more of a slink to them. No less silent, but much lower and careful. They moved not like Otherworlder nobility, but like dangerous animals.

I realized it an instant before they stepped close enough for me to see.

"Who's laughing, man? It's my baby's funeral, have some respect," said Haemon, King of the Great Pack.

"Great," I said to myself. Because this wasn't already hard enough.

Prince Eustace ignored the lycans. "Well," he said, and now his smile faded to something smoldering and dangerous. The reds of his eyes drank in the darkness and burned the world. "Why would you accuse me of this? Why would you accuse me of murdering my love?"

More vampires drew near. King William, Princess Roberta, and Prince Warine. The paparazzi had noted the shift in activity, and were following them at a discreet distance.

Haemon saw me looking at the photog – er, illustrators. Pallas stood nearby, and Haemon nodded at the tall, bespectacled Lycaon. Pallas moved off without a sound and a moment later there was a concerted rush by the illustrators in every direction but ours.

Pallas didn't return, but I could feel him in the darkness, watching and waiting. Ready to protect his pack. I figured he must be the de facto Peacemaker until Aseas woke up.

A few of the Otherworlders had watched Pallas do his thing, but now everyone turned their full attention to me.

"Why you got my baby-girl's phone?" asked Haemon quietly. Moonbeam was there, too, and she started to growl deep in her throat. I looked at her because I recognized the tone of her voice, and was surprised to see someone else looking at me through dark, angry eyes.

"Talk, you grungy little pig," said the girl – and it was definitely Moonbeam. Only she looked... beautiful. The girl's features were still built off the same model – some obvious similarities of feature and shape – but it was as though God had finally gotten around to ironing out the kinks in the original prototype.

She must be wearing a glamour, like her sister had. She didn't want the outside world seeing her real face. The only reason I'd seen it was probably because she was wearing that stormtrooper costume on the con floor and didn't bother putting on her token before leaving – then when she returned to find me with her father she was too angry to worry about her appearance.

I felt very, very bad for her. What would it be like for the world to see you only through a lens of lies and illusions? Or, worse, to think that was the only way they *should* look at you?

I was suddenly ashamed beyond measure of my first, unkind reaction to her.

Now, though, she was beautiful, and very angry. She reached for Calista's phone, which I still held. I yanked it away. Looked at Eustace, his family, and Haemon and his pack. Debated whether to do this now.

Time's a-tickin'.

Screw it.

"Talk, man. You better have a reason for your grody hands being on my perfect princess's phone," said Haemon.

"Yeah, that's just it," I said. I turned it on, ran my fingers in a cross over the screen, then brought up the pictures. "Because she wasn't that perfect."

I held up the phone. Its screen shined in the night, and it would have been easy to see even without the supernatural vision everyone but me had.

A gasp. I'd keyed up one of the worst pictures: might as well dive in with both feet. I knew it didn't look like Calista, but I made sure you could see her token: that star tattoo, front and center on a hand that was doing something that would haunt my dreams forever.

I passed my thumb over the screen. Brought up the next picture.

As I did it, I watched the others. Very carefully. This was the moment I'd get some answers: who knew about this; what they truly thought.

It was pretty easy to read most of them. King William and Queen Borga put hands over their eyes and made signs that looked like the vampire equivalent of warding off the evil eye. They looked sick, and King William gagged.

Prince Warine and Princess Roberta had completely different reactions: they leaned in close, grinning so widely I was worried they might give themselves a bad case of TMJ. Warine started to giggle, and Princess Roberta looked like she was trying to decide whether to follow suit or start hissing through her smile.

Moonbeam fell down. I mean, *literally* fell down. Her legs wobbled, then they went right out from under her and she sat down hard on the rooftop. She looked like she'd been belted by a Larry Correia-sized fist made of extra knuckles.

Haemon shook his head. Just shook his head, back and forth and back and forth. He was mouthing something, I couldn't tell what. But I could see the wretched anguish in his face.

I kept turning the pictures, moving from one to another to another. Watching for changes, for moments where truths might be revealed.

Prince Eustace had, aside perhaps from Moonbeam, the most graphic reaction. The vampiric features disappeared immediately: the red of his eyes fell away, the teeth and talons yanked back and were gone. He was still caked in gore, but now he looked less like a monster and more like one of those survivors you see in pictures of wars or terrorist bombings.

After I scrolled through a large number of achingly explicit pictures, Eustace finally yanked his gaze away from the screen and looked at me.

"This is Calista," he murmured. "This is Calista, Calista...." He said it a few more times, then added, "Why... why would you show me this?" His voice was that of a lost child. "Why would you do this? Why would you think *I* –" He broke off. "You think I knew about this?" He sounded horrified.

I shook my head. "No. I *know* you did."

51

"I got a great view of the back of your head earlier today, when you were sun-wasted and crying in your mommy's arms," I said. I turned the phone toward me and flipped to the February shot. Mr. Big Hand, Calista, a certain serial philanderer, and in the background: the witch barkeep, and.... "That," I said, turning the phone around to all of them and pointing at the person the witch was talking to, "is you."

I said it all as mean and nasty as I could. Bull in a China Shop, P.I., on the case. Doing this had already told me a lot, and I was going to ride it to the ugly end.

What it had told me so far: I thought King William and Queen Borga were out as suspects. One of the hardest emotions to fake is utter surprise. That's because someone who *wants* to be surprised at something always hesitates a moment. The brain says, "Hey, isn't that –" and then it cuts itself off and yells, "Not now, idiot! Act surprised!" That subtle instant of indecision kills the façade. Not only that, but Borga and William were surprised *and* disgusted, which was even harder to do.

Warine and Roberta, now.... I still didn't know about them. Their reactions seemed genuine, but overtly crowing about the misfortune of a rival wasn't exactly a Get Out of Jail Free card. Murder is, first and foremost, about motive. Who will profit most?

Warine and Roberta would profit. Maybe not the most, but enough to murder someone who was already a hated rival – a Lycaon? Very possibly. Maybe probably.

Haemon and Moonbeam were every bit as shocked as William and Borga. More so. I could tell from his shell shocked gaze that Haemon's world had just collapsed – his girl was dead, her body gone, and now that he was seeing her it was in a strange face and doing things that no father should ever see.

Because I am a father myself, I ached for him. Because the world needed this murder solved, I pushed on.

Moonbeam looked as upset as Haemon. She had said she loved her sister, but at the same time hated what she was doing with the vampires. I had a problem with that earlier, since there aren't a lot of people who can bifurcate like that, and hate something a person does without hating that person. Now, though, I believed her. She was wearing a skirt, and now had handfuls of the fabric held in fists clenched so hard the knuckles glowed in the night. She swayed as though she was going to pass out, then managed to right herself – and her gaze never strayed from the screen of the phone.

Eustace's reaction had been one of shock to this point, of quiet rage that I would do this to him filtered through the overwhelming grief that had controlled him since he got the news of his "beloved's" death.

But I had withheld judgment on him until now, because I knew this photo would be the real test.

The shots up to now had all been explicit, but this was the first one that showed Nespda. Everyone's reactions stayed the same, but the emotion behind them quadrupled as the photo explicitly showed not just what Calista had been doing, but what she had chosen to *become*: something worse than a human-lover; she was what almost every Otherworlder thought of as a whore.

"I didn't realize this was you at first, because why in the world would a *vampire* show up so easily on camera? But then I realized: Nespda caters exclusively to human males." I cocked my head. "So you got your hands on a spell to turn yourself human, at least for a bit. Long enough to slum around and sample Nespda's wares... or maybe just kill a cheating fiancée?"

King William and Queen Borga screamed and fell back as one. They actually grabbed each other's hands – an expression of clutching affection in the midst of something too horrible to be borne.

Roberta and Warine also clasped at one another. Not in fear or disgust, but in simple, avaricious glee. Again, not the reaction you want to show to someone who thinks you might have murdered your sister. But in a way, it also made me think it improbable that either of them was the murderer. Whoever had killed Calista had done it with a great deal of care, control, and planning. The more I saw of Warine and Roberta, the less I thought either of them possessed *any* of those qualities. Just spoiled, power-hungry children in a family led by people greater than they could ever hope to be.

Haemon and Moonbeam started weeping. Haemon knelt and clutched at his remaining daughter, holding her face to his breast and so protecting her from what was on the phone.

Even Rathton, Borga's guard, seemed shaken to the point it was hard to believe he was faking it. He had been on the outskirts of the group – not a member of the family, but not willing to let them be close to me without his protection, either – but now he stood forward and placed his coat over Borga's shoulders. A moment later he held William's hair as the king vomited up large bits of whatever he'd been eating earlier. As he did this, Rathton glared at me, and there wasn't a trace of guilt in his eyes. Just rage at what I had done to his king and queen. And a promise that he would see much worse done to me.

All the reactions were unspoken protestations of innocence, emotions that provided clear reasons each could not have been behind Calista's murder.

Eustace, though… his reaction damned him.

He had acted shattered up to this point. And it was a good act – maybe a great one. But when I flipped the screen to show the inside of the Nespda lobby, he froze. The act disappeared, the grief instantly gone. He looked from the phone to the others with a jerky gaze. "No," he said. "No, I didn't –"

He didn't say more, because a huge shape lunged at him, wreathed for an instant in a nimbus of red light as Haemon shifted to his wolf form in the blink of an eye. By the time the light of his change faded, he had Eustace's throat in one great, paw-like hand.

"You... killed... my baby-girl," he growled, the words almost undistinguishable. His muzzle pulled back and he bared all his teeth.

Rathton moved now, letting go of William's hair and rushing at the lycan.

I didn't think. If I had, I probably wouldn't have done what came next, because I'm not nearly that brave.

Rathton was fast, but he was a few steps farther away than I was. I dropped the phone and darted forward and inserted myself between him and Haemon.

"Stop!" I shouted, and there was a really spiffy flash of light that made me look terrifically heroic (at least in my head) as Rathton's hands hit me instead of Haemon. He fell back with a hiss.

Borga had managed to straighten up. She drew herself to her full height, and looked from Haemon to her son to me to Rathton, then did the whole round again. She snarled, and through long, pointed teeth she said, "You dare?" She pointed a talon at me. "My Blessing is revoked."

Rathton moved to his feet. About to pounce, but now another person entered the fray. Moonbeam, also a wolf – and though ugly as she was in human form, her wolf-shape was a vision of beauty. Muscular but limber, her fur a pale gold that shone like a moonbeam (and now I knew why they named her that! Hooray for me!). She got between me and Rathton. Now it was Haemon holding Eustace in the Darth Vader Suspended Stranglehold[25], me next, then Moonbeam, then Rathton. Warine was still laughing like an idiot, and Roberta was smiling an evil little smile that showed how much she hoped there was a brawl and that her step-mother was one of the first people killed.

William, for the first time, had shown interest in the proceedings. He stood, wiped off his chin, and said, quietly, "Let my boy go. Now."

---

[25] Please don't sue me, Lucasfilm! Or Disney!

He made a gesture, and suddenly the roof around us was crawling with vamps.

At the same time, a form bounded toward us, breaking through the group of vamps. I had an instant to see horn-rimmed glasses, thinning hair, and wild eyes. Then the golden glow obscured my vision for a moment. When it faded, Pallas, too, was in his wolf form. As big as Haemon and Moonbeam put together, the Pallas batted a vampire out of the way without visible effort. The vamp flew ten feet through the air, hit a pipe jutting out of the roof, and was silent and still.

Pallas moved close to Haemon, who was still slowly strangling Eustace. The crowd of vampires came closer, their red eyes like bloody wounds on the face of the night. William and Borga moved forward, fangs and talons extending to their fullest. Roberta stepped back, still grinning and the hope that she could gain a throne without having to Challenge Borga nearly stenciled across her face.

And through it all, Warine laughed. The cackle of chaos in a moment poised on the brink of mayhem – and perhaps war.

Okay, I admitted to myself, maybe the Bull in the China Shop method wasn't the best way to go.

52

"Everyone. *Just. STOP!*"

One of the first things you develop as a dad is the ability to shout loudly enough to be heard over anything – three televisions at once, a crowd of my oldest's friends in an argument about which *Minecraft* mod is the best, or a party at Times Square. If one of my kids has to be found, instructed, or disciplined, my voice literally has to rise to the occasion.

Bull in a China Shop, P.I., disappeared, and Dad In Command reared his head.

It worked. Everyone stopped. At least for a second. Even Haemon let Eustace down far enough that the prince could support himself on his tippy toes – though Haemon's big paw still wrapped around Eustace's neck.

They all looked at me. Which, I realized, might not be super-awesome for yours truly.

I gulped. "You're angry," I said. "You're all angry, because there's a killer on the loose. But if you move forward like this, it will be war."

I turned to Haemon and looked him in the eye. Not easy to do when it's a massive werewolf on the other side of the stare. "You want war?" I whispered. "With what you told me about your people?" I leaned in as close as I could and whispered even quieter. "This is your last hope, King Haemon."

Haemon just stared at me for a moment. His wolf eyes were gold; cold and unblinking. Then, with a chuff he let Eustace down far enough the prince could fully stand.

"Release him!" shouted William. "Release him or –"

"Or what?" I asked. "If he killed Princess Calista, he deserves to be turned over to the Great Pack. Unless you want war to come, here and now, on this rooftop." I nodded to him, a deep nod that I hope conveyed respect and a genuine hope for his people's best. "You are a wise leader, King William. Strong and careful. Do not let your strength lead you to a lack of care."

Warine was still giggling, and William grabbed his son by the arm and hurled him away. "Shut your stupid cackling," he snapped as Warine flew a good six feet and then hit the roof hard enough to knock an air conditioning unit off its moorings. The violence seemed to sooth William, though, and when he turned back to me I could see a modicum of control in his still-red eyes.

"What would you have us do?" he said carefully. "Would you have us wait for this creature," he said, gesturing derisively at Haemon, "to kill our son, with no proof he deserves such?"

"No. But let him hold Eustace, until I find proof – either that he is innocent, or that he did it."

"And if you don't?" asked Moonbeam. She didn't look at me, but I sensed her hatred of the vamps and a nearly equal dislike for me.

"Then I guess...." Crap. I *really* have to start thinking things through before I do them.

"No," said Borga. She slashed the air with her hand, so fast I could hear the wind whistle around her talons. "I will not let *anyone*," she said, looking at Haemon, "take my son from me."

"Then this is the end," said Haemon. He growled the words, but there was an undeniable note of sadness in them. "The prince must be held, but you refuse, so –"

"*I* will hold him."

Anderson strode through the circle of vampires that closed us all in. A few of them moved to intercept him.

Huge mistake.

Anderson gestured, made a movement with his hands that was too fast to see. A whisper, and glowing bands encircled the vamps that had dared try to interfere with a Dead One.

Anderson was always imposing – at least to me. But now he was different. Cloaked in the full measure of his power, and now I understood how a small group of men and women had been able to hold the forces of darkness at bay for so long.

I knew some things. Things that gave me a certain measure of power.

But this, what I was seeing... it *was* power.

Everyone oriented on Anderson, the entire tableau shifting in his direction. I probably would have fallen over and started sucking my thumb had this happened to me. Anderson didn't even blink. He just turned to Borga and William and bowed low.

He was dressed in what he must have been wearing when I called: just sweats and a t-shirt. He didn't even have shoes on, just black slippers with a crimson design on the toes. But when he bowed, I swear for a second I saw him in robes. Not robes like he'd just finished his bath, but robes like he was about to lay down some serious mojo and had gotten out his sorcerer's best for the occasion.

Everyone else reacted to his power just as I had. There were a few gasps, a few vamps and lycans stepped back.

Borga, William, and Haemon seemed unfazed. But they faced him with a lot more respect in their gazes than I'd warranted.

Borga's teeth were still bared. "What do you say, wizard?"

Anderson straightened from his bow. "There has been a murder. A murder that affects the path of two great and noble people," he added, nodding at the King and Queen of the High Court, then at the King of the Great Pack. "Justice must be done, and like it or not, Prince Eustace seems the likely culprit."

William made an ugly, gurgling noise of rage. "No one –" he began.

Anderson held up a hand. "No one of the lycans should have hold on your son. I agree. Yet for you to hold him would hardly appear right, as circumstances now stand. Don't you agree?"

A long, long moment. Then William nodded slowly. Anderson nodded back. "So let the prince be remanded into my custody. I will attend him and see he is not mistreated."

King William looked at his son, and it seemed like the whole world held its breath. "Father, please –" croaked Eustace.

William nodded. Anderson instantly held up one hand, making a small gesture with his other, and something jerked Eustace away from Haemon's grasp. Moonbeam growled and started toward the floating form of the prince.

Anderson spoke quickly, but he aimed his comments at Haemon. "It must be this way, my Lord."

Haemon swiped at Moonbeam. A cuff that would have killed me, but to her it only registered as a "calm down, kid." She stopped, though her teeth were still bared so widely it looked like they circled her entire head.

Anderson made another gesture. Eustace's head nodded and his eyes closed. He turned sideways, now floating on his back. Anderson gestured at me to follow him and started toward the elevator penthouse. For once, I swallowed any smart-aleck observations and just moved.

A voice halted us. King William. "You are right, wizard. Justice must be served." He leveled a finger at both of us, then that finger settled on me. "And if there has been a mistake, it will be served on him." Haemon and Moonbeam growled their agreement.

Anderson nodded.

Sure. Easy for you to say.

We left.

The second the elevators closed (Eustace's body wouldn't fit perpendicularly, so he was now sort of propped at an angle against the wall, like the sofa everybody has had when moving into their first apartment with the Ridiculously Tiny Elevator all first apartments are required to have), Anderson lost his cool.

"What the *hell* do you think you were doing?" He snarled. I got as far as opening my mouth before he screamed,

"Forget it. Don't talk. I'm too angry, and I'm tempted to let one of the them have at you."

"The thems are probably still full from eating the princess."

Wrong thing to say. The robes reappeared as Anderson leveled a finger at me. "The only thing keeping you alive right now is the fact that bringing in a new Warden would present its own problems. So you will find the murderer, and find him fast. Or I will turn you over to the High Court and the Great Pack, and Lord have mercy on your soul."

I gulped. Nodded. "I'll just have to talk to Warine and –"

Anderson laughed. Hard and loud. "You think I'm letting you anywhere near either of the royal families again? And even if I thought it a good idea, how long do you think you'd last with them?"

"Then how am I –"

"You're the Warden," he snapped. The elevator dinged and the doors opened. He stepped out, Eustace bobbing along after him. "You figure it out."

The doors closed. At the last second he tossed a piece of paper into the elevator. I picked it up. Sighed at what it said.

Fees For Services of Kevin J. Anderson
International Bestseller, Publisher, Dead One

Services Rendered: *General Consulting*
Spells cast (two)
Saving incompetent Warden

Each line item had a subtotal, with a grand total at the bottom that ate every last hope of this con being a money maker. Life sucks sometimes.

53

Let's recap.

I have to find the murderer or:

1) Blake will be mad at me (no change there).

2) I suffer the consequences of breaking my contract... I think. Though I don't know what those are.[26] Just that they're bad.

3) Supernatural war (this one is definitely bad).

4) Said war may consume the earth (slightly higher on the Bad Scale).

5) My family and I will have angry Otherworlders and the Nerdfather on our tails until we are killed – probably after extended torture sessions (HIGHEST BAD SCALE RATING POSSIBLE!).

But that's okay, right? Because all I have to do is find the murderer. By the time the treaty between vamps and lycans is supposed to be signed. Which is tomorrow night.

The only problem was that I had no idea what to do next. I had a bunch of people in naughty pictures, and I supposed I could go back and talk to the madam and find out if there were any people she could identify by looking at their naughty bits. But that was spinning my wheels, I knew it. Even if she cooperated, which was doubtful given how much her business relied on discretion, I didn't think anyone in the pictures was going to end up mattering. Even if any of them were actually at this con (also doubtful), what were the chances they knew anything or had anything to do with the murder? Nil.

No, the murderer was someone I'd already talked to. I knew it.

Was it the prince? Yeah, probably. But I couldn't prove it yet. And I had bupkis to go on. All I had were my suspicions, a phone, and a bunch of naughty –

---

[26] Blake's never actually let me *read* the contract.

I was walking down the hallway to my hotel room when the thought hit me, and man did it hit me. I stopped so fast I could swear I heard my shoes squeak. My back jolted, and I realized it had been too long since my last pain pill, so I dry swallowed one before yanking out the phone and cuing up the pictures.

And there it was.

I looked around. I needed a big empty space.

"Not here," I said to myself. Then realized I was now talking to myself – not unusual for a writer, but I try to keep all my voices on the inside. I giggled, then giggled louder when I realized I'd giggled.

Then I ran. First to my room, to grab something I keep on hand for occasions like these, then back to the elevator. I pressed "L" once I got inside, and waited to the not-at-all soothing sounds of a Muzak version of Celine Dion's Greatest Hits.

When I got to the lobby I grabbed a trash can in the corner. One of the employees approached, no doubt wondering what a nice guy like me was doing in a place like this. I stopped him with ten bucks and a whispered explanation of what I wanted him to do. He looked dubious, but ten bucks was ten bucks.

I kept moving. The employee followed a few steps behind, and barely made a sound as I grabbed the second trash can.

I went into the hall where the ballroom and several large presentation rooms were located. The ballroom would have been best, but it was locked. I settled for the Arclight room, which held probably three hundred people when packed. Good enough.

I reminded my new assistant what to do, then closed the doors after giving him another five bucks to ensure his assistance. I didn't want to get into trouble with the hotel, on top of everything else.

There were two rows of chairs on one side of the room, which didn't get in my way. I had plenty of space to chuck the contents of the garbage cans all over the floor. I spread it around as much as possible, then shouted, "I'm going to make a *huge* mess! This ain't nothin', I tells ya!"

Yeah, it was a bit hammy. But that was more effective in this situation.

Right on cue, the hotel employee – a short man with dark complexion and a mustache that would be the envy of any motorcycle cop or porn star – marched in. "What are *you* doing?" he said. The right words, but he accented the words oddly – not a great actor, even with the easy lines I'd given him. "Why, *now we* will have *to* clean all this *up*."

I stood in front of him. "Get back, you... you... *cleaner*. I swear, I will not let you clean, nor shall I ever stop messing up the floor. And then...." I rubbed my hands together like a good Snidely Whiplash. "I shall make a mess of all your hotel! Bwa-hahahaha!"

Mustache Man shook his fist at me in rage. "I guess *I* can't *do any*thing a*bout* this." Then he leaned in close and whispered in a normal voice, "You *are* gonna clean this, right?"

"Yeah," I whispered back. "Come back in ten minutes and if it's not all cleaned up I'll give you another twenty bucks. Now scram."

He scrammed, with one more wave of his fist for good measure.

As soon as he was gone, I added the *coup de grâce*, sprinkling a few of the crumbs I'd brought from my room.

I waited.

And they came.

"If you mess it, they will come," I said.

Brownies tend to follow large groups of Otherworlders. And they're very handy, since they can't abide messes. All you have to do is make a mess, have someone else try to clean it, and stop that person while shouting your intention to make another mess of apocalyptic proportion – which, the observant reader will note, is exactly what I just did with Officer Burt Dangle (insert disco music). The brownies will arrive quickly, call you some names, then clean everything up. You have to leave a gift for them, though, or they will clean *you* up as well, taking you away. No one knows *where*, only that those who are "cleaned" never return.

The first brownie appeared. Then a second, and a third. They were all about a foot and a half tall, and they just popped into existence in the shadiest corner of the room. I knew what I would call these three, who according to brownie protocol would be the leaders/head janitors.

"Hello, Footloose," I nodded to the first. "Hey, Tremors. What's up, A Few Good Men?"

Something punched me in the leg. I looked down at the empty air. "Sorry, Invisible Man. I didn't see you there."

Oh, did I forget to mention? Brownies all look exactly like Kevin Bacon. Of varying ages and dressed in the outfits that go with his different movies. I don't know why this is, but it holds true everywhere in the world – no matter where you go, all brownies are Bacon.[27]

In quick succession, Appollo 13, Flatliners, and Quicksilver all showed up. Then a few more whose outfits I didn't recognize because no one human can keep up with all the variations on the Bacon theme.

First they all converged on the crumbs I'd left out – my gift to them to keep them from carrying me off to the Big Cleaning Supplies Warehouse in the sky. The crumbs were just little dark bits that were barely visible on the floor, which was covered by the stain-resistant industrial carpet that every hotel

---

[27] Though I have heard of a lost tribe of brownies deep in the wilds of the Amazon who all look like Samuel L. Jackson. These are only rumors, however, and unsubstantiated to date.

conference room uses, but the brownies zeroed in on the brownie crumbs instantly.

Yes, brownies like to eat brownies. You leave a gift of brownie crumbs, or you get washed away to oblivion.

Footloose danced his way over to me, then started shrieking, a high-pitched whine that made no sense because brownies live at a different speed than you or me. If I'd recorded his voice and played it back at 1/100th speed, it probably would have sounded like, "You bag of jock straps! Why you gotta mess things up! I'm so angry I can't even feel the beat!"

"Sorry, Footloose," I said. "It had to be done."

A few of the brownies headed for the trash, white bags and trash pickers appearing in their hands as they grumbled at dog whistle levels.[28]

I got between them and the trash, arms wide. "No way," I said. "I can't allow it."

They screamed at me. I think A Few Good Men began a one-man court martial against me.

I ignored it all. "No," I said. "I'm obsessed with trash and I'm going to make messes forever."

Now they really freaked out. Footloose went into an interpretive dance of rage, a bicycle appeared beneath Quicksilver and he started doing angry wheelies. I felt hands batting at my legs as Invisible Man assaulted me.

"Hey, I know!" I said. "I'll make you a deal!" I held out Calista's phone. On the screen was the picture of Calista in Nespda, the bar behind her, Mr. Big Hand's one big hand in the picture.

---

[28] A (very) few of you may have noticed similarities between the brownies and the rock creatures in my book *Billy: Messenger of Powers* (find it at michaelbrentcollings.com!). I *told* you – books of "fantasy" and "sci-fi" may not be ingenious inventions. More like reporting on reality with a few embellishments to boost sales.

I zoomed in on Mr. Big Hand. Closer and closer until the ruby ring on his pinky dominated the screen. I showed it to all of the brownies, who leaned in with a mixture of curiosity and desperation.

I pointed to the ring. "You promise to find that, to bring it to me and tell me where you got it, and I'll let you clean all this up."

Footloose and A Few Good Men started keening. I said, "Yeah, and I'll provide more brownie crumbs on delivery."

They nodded with satisfaction, and started toward the trash. In a matter of seconds, the garbage was gone, the floor was scrubbed to its original brightness, and even the trash cans had been spit-shined.

The brownies turned back to the corner they had appeared from, with more than one irritated backward glance. A Few Good Men – one of the most hard-hitting brownies – gave me the middle finger.

"Oh, one more thing!" I shouted. They all stopped. Quicksilver forgot to watch where he was going and drove into a wall. "You may be tempted to renege. Especially you, Invisible Man." I aimed a glance at an empty spot and hoped he was there. "But if you do, I promise on all the brownies I have ever cooked… I will make a mess. A mess like none you have ever seen. And then another and another, until the whole world cowers under a mountain of garbage so high it can engulf us all!" I raised my hands as I spoke and let out a mad scientist cackle at the end. Brownies react well to melodrama.

They cringed, then bowed and scraped. The Following brownie – I could tell it was him from the dark colors, the slightly older face, and the little "FBI" badge on his jacket – shook his head and took out a tiny nine millimeter which he waved in my direction.

But it was all empty threats. It always was.

They popped out of existence.

I opened the door and Officer Dangle was waiting. He looked into the room, his eyes widening as he saw the new sparkle everything had. He looked into the closest trash can, and I could see him wondering where all the garbage had gone.

He looked at me. "Don't ask," I said, then belched and added, "But the coffee grounds were delicious."

I smiled at the expression on his face. Then headed back to my room.

Now all I had to do was wait.

54

Gandhi the dwarf called me on my way back to my room. "I checked the other royals."

"Which ones? What?" I said blurrily. After everything that had happened in the last few hours I felt like I had used up my allotment of brain cells for the night.

"The royals," said Gandhi grouchily. The sugar high from the Gummi Bears I'd sent must have worn off. "You wanted me to find out where they were during the murder."

"Oh. Right. And?"

"Well, Haemon was in his room, near as I can tell. Princess Moonbeam was at a meeting of the 501st."

"The 501st?" I asked, then added, "Oh, yeah, I know –"

Gandhi was already talking. "They're that group of *Star Wars* cosplayers that dress up for charity events and show up to visit kids at hospitals, things like that. Good people."

A bit surprising to hear that Moonbeam was a member of the 501st Legion. I hadn't pegged her for a charitable type. I guess looks can be deceiving.

I was also surprised to hear Gandhi call them good people. He usually doesn't think that of anyone who's not actively supplying him with food or cast-off clothing. "You know them?"

"A few. Guy named Ryan Simmons is one of them. He does some animation for my YouTube channel, and his wife tosses me the occasional hand-me-down from their kids."

"You have a YouTube – Forget it. What about the rest?" I asked.

"Borga and William…."

He went into fairly detailed accounts of everyone else's schedule for the few hours before and after Calista's murder. They were all good alibis, all solid. And I'd already verified Prince Eustace's whereabouts. Everyone was in the clear. I even had Gandhi check on the Nerdfather – much easier for him to do since Kumar was a normal and wasn't wearing a disguise or simply invisible to the cameras.

"Game room," said Gandhi. "From the time it opened to the time you went in. He didn't even leave to pee."

"Okay, Gandhi. Good work. Get some sleep. I'll do my best to send up some Gummi Bears tomorrow."

"Awww," he said. "You don't have to do that. You already have me on retainer, and...." His voice got very soft. "You've been nice to me. I got your back."

He hung up before I could say anything. I was stunned. How little it takes sometimes, for someone to become invested in you. To move from business contact to something approaching a friend. A kind word, a bag of treats.

I walked the rest of the way to my room. I still had nothing – less than I had a few moments ago, in fact, given that just about every credible suspect I had had a rock-solid alibi. Even so, I walked with a bit more pep to my step.

How little it takes to make a friend. And how little it sometimes takes for that friend to make a difference in our lives.

I went to my room, and it barely registered that the door was open a crack. I was that tired. I just went through, realized it in retrospect, at the same time I noted that the lights were all off – even the bathroom light I'd left on so I wouldn't knock into something on the way in – and went for the plastic gun Larry had given me.

A hand darted out of the darkness. Grabbed my arm. Another went over my mouth.

"Shhh. Your mom is still asleep."

I relaxed. A bit. The hand came away from my mouth and I fumbled around to find the bathroom light. It clicked on, and though the door was mostly closed, the light that bled out from around the edges of the door was enough to confirm what my ears had told me.

"Mercedes," I said – quietly, because Mom was asleep, "what are you doing here? How did you get in?"

She shrugged. She wasn't looking at me, her eyes downcast. "A nice hotel bellhop let me in."

"You didn't...."

"No," she nearly snapped. "I didn't use my powers. Just explained that there was a sick woman in here, and I'd lost my key."

She raised her eyes, and now I understood why the bellhop had let her in. Mercedes looked beyond distraught. I'd almost never seen her without a smile on her face, but now she was on the opposite side of that coin. Her eyes were bright and bloodshot. Her mascara hadn't streaked, but that only meant she wore high quality waterproof stuff, because her cheeks bore the streaks of countless tears.

"Mercedes, what... are you okay?" Stupid question, I know, but it was all that came to mind.

"Larry Correia came by," she said. Her voice was so strangled I barely made out the words. "He said he heard about your mom and wanted to check on you both."

I shook my head. "Mercedes, I don't care why Larry came by. I want to know why *you're* here, and what happened."

Mercedes didn't answer that. Instead she said, "I had to come tell you something."

"What? What's happened, how can I help?"

"I have a message," she said.

"What is it? From who?"

"The message is, 'The solution will be found where what was found was found to be lost. You will find her, and through her, him.'"

I frowned. "What kind of message is that?"

"An Oracular one."

I froze. "You know an Oracle?"

She nodded. "My son, Niko."

Those two words hit me like a world falling on my shoulders. I knew exactly what she was saying, and how hard it was. It was another bit of fact I'd posited as fiction,[29] and when I wrote about it I researched it: the gifts, the responsibilities, the blessings and the pains.

I hadn't known that Mercedes' kid was an Oracle, but that explained why she hadn't lost her powers the way Laura did when she had our first child. Oracles skew everything, and make the laws of magic go from hard and fast rules to very light suggestions.

They are also, without failure, autistic.

Science actually nudges close to some real answers on this one. Non-supernatural experts know that one of the challenges of autism is that people with that condition don't have brains that filter out background noise the same way you or I might. I go into a party and talk to my wife, and pretty much all I notice is Laura. Maybe that pile of delicious chocolate chip cookies on the table.

An autistic, however, will notice *everything*. The sounds, the smells, the scents, the touches. It all comes at such a person with the same force. It's why a lot of autistics are easily overwhelmed, and react frantically – sometimes violently – to their surroundings. A nice party for you or me is the equivalent to being at ground zero for Fourth of July fireworks for them.

That's what science knows. And like I said, that's pretty close to the reality, which is that autistics do see everything. But I mean *everything*. Not just the world in its totality, but the World around them as well. Men and women at a party, with all the sensory input that entails... and also with the view of the ghosts who walk among them, the dwarf who peeks out from under the floorboards in the hope someone will drop a bit of cake. The farther along on the autism spectrum a person is, the more he or she will see.

---

[29] In *Mr. Gray* – no longer on sale at the purple aisle due to the Nerdfather's criminal actions... but you can get it online! Go to michaelbrentcollings.com for more info!

And a few – a few who are blessed beyond measure or cursed beyond understanding, depending on your point of view – see everything. *Everything.*

Not just the room they stand in, but the world they live in comes into their mind. They are open not only to their surroundings, but to the entirety of reality. Our autistic at a party will see that party. And every other party now happening, every person on the earth, every event now occurring.

And of those blessed, or cursed, men and women and boys and girls, a few see not only everything now happening, but everything that has happened and everything that will happen. To their minds, time is not a line but a pool, where every moments coexists and many moments can be touched at once.

They have the knowledge of God compressed into the tiny vessel of human understanding. Many of them basically cease functioning, and no one in the World knows if that means they have shut down, or if perhaps they have become a part of time itself; if they have overcome their humanity and become one with infinity.

A few of them don't shut down. They are the Oracles. They are harder to interact with than many autistics, and when they speak it can be hard to decipher what they say. It could be incomprehensible, near gibberish. It could be "please pass the syrup."

And it could be a window to future, or to past. The Oracles see all that is, and occasionally they share that sight with us.

So when Mercedes said her son had given her a message, it wasn't just a bit of ephemera. It was a glimpse into my reality, and a hint to what I might need.

The solution will be found where what was found was found to be lost. You will find her, and through her, him.

I didn't understand. Another quirk of Oracles: they operate on a different level than you or I. Some unkind people call them "retarded," but the fact is that they have more knowledge in their little finger than every Nobel laureate who ever lived.

The solution will be found where what was found was found to be lost. You will find her, and through her, him.

No idea.

I looked back at Mercedes. "Why are you crying?" She shook her head. Didn't answer. "Mercedes, what can I do?"

"Nothing," she said between hitching breaths. "No one can do anything."

I switched tacks. Looking around the room, I said, "It doesn't seem like that time-sensitive a message, Mercedes. Why did you have to all but break in to give it to me?"

She sobbed again. "He said you'd ask that."

I got a chill at that. It's pretty weird to have an Oracular message sent to you. It's downright freaky to be the subject matter of one.

"He said if you did, I had to answer," she said.

"So what is the answer? Why now? Why give me the message at all, and why are you so wrecked about it?"

She took a deep breath, trying to compose herself. "He said if I didn't give the message right away, he would be murdered."

That cold feeling got that much worse. "By who?" She shook her head. I wasn't going to get an answer to that one. I touched her shoulder. "Well, you *did* give the message, Mercedes. So he's not going to be killed. It's okay."

She laughed at that. A frail, desperate laugh.

Then she said, "The message was *Oracular*," and moved quickly to the door. Before I could say anything else, she turned back to me. Her mouth moved and she swallowed a few times. Her eyes took on a curious intensity that didn't chase away her distress, but only compounded it. "I'd do anything for my son," she said. "I need you to understand that. Anything."

I nodded. "That's the way it should be."

And she left. Ran out the door and I could hear the slap-pad of her feet as she fled across the carpet in the hall. I thought about chasing her down, but what did I think would happen then? Mercedes was my friend, but you can't *make* a friend talk to you, and sometimes it's better not to try.

The door swung quietly shut. I locked it, using the dead bolt as well.

The message was Oracular.

It took me a minute to figure that out. Not on its face, of course: I already knew the message was Oracular; that had been the whole point.

My subconscious played with her words for a minute, then emailed my frontal lobe with a short missive. I suddenly understood.

Oracles are always right. Always. But remember how I said they are "the knowledge of God compressed into the tiny vessel of human understanding"? What that means is that you rarely get complete messages. They are always right, but that doesn't mean they're always understandable.

Still, telling Mercedes that if she didn't leave a message, her son would be killed seemed pretty straightforward. She'd delivered the message, so –

"Oh," I said. Then, again, "Oh."

Incomplete messages are the rule. Mercedes' son, Niko, had said he would be murdered if she didn't deliver the message. But he hadn't said delivering the message would save him.

Someone had his sights set on Niko, and the fact that Mercedes was as terrified as she was made me think she already had an idea what the danger was. Maybe not who was behind it, but at least the circumstances that might have doomed her son.

"Oh." Third time I'd said it, but it was all that came to mind. Everything was too big for me to verbalize. I was an author, and I had no words, other than those the Oracle had given –

(*The solution will be found where what was found was found to be lost. You will find her, and through her, him.*)
   – and those made no sense at all.

55

"Oh, *dammit*."

I'd spent a while mulling over the case and Mercedes' message. In both cases I realized that my understanding had reached levels of suck the envy of any black hole. I knew nothing, and nothing new was coming to me.

I tried to sleep, for about five minutes. No way. I was exhausted, but there was too much going on in my head to allow me to close my eyes. I've written between four and eight books a year since I started this whole writing gig, and part of the reason for that output is simply that once a thought takes hold, I can't sleep, eat, or properly groom myself until I get it figured out or written down. The words "manic" and "obsessive" come to mind. Mansessive. That's me.

Sleep: out. Mom was still snoring on her bed, so I didn't want to turn on the idiot box and maybe wake her up. I lay down on my bed and turned on the reading lamp attached to the frame, then started to read the nearest book. The two books I had purchased from Anderson under duress sat close by. I grabbed the top one - *Dune: The Butlerian Jihad* – and cracked it open.

"Now we get to find out what a hack you are," I whispered.

A few minutes later I closed the *Dune* book and opened up the other one: the book set in the *Star Wars* universe.

A few minutes after that was when the dammit came.

I'd really been hoping – really, really, *really* – that Anderson was using magic to influence his buyers. That he was a no-talent writer making it big because he had mojo to spare.

And I found instead that he was really – really, really, *really* – good. Smooth, clear sentences. Plots that moved forward at a satisfying clip without sacrificing character development. Great characters. No tricks, just a great writer who'd gotten the audience he more than deserved.

So the dammit came because yes, I can be a jealous wanker.

I just lay there, going over things in my head. Coming up with nothing good on the case, nothing good for Mercedes. The only concrete realization I came to, and which echoed over and over in my mind, was "Everyone's good at everything but me."

Pity party, party of one!

I tried to snap myself out of the funk, but couldn't. I just lay there, staring at the ceiling as the sun slowly poked above a mountain range in the distance. I'd drawn the curtains, but enough light came in through the cracks to see clearly.

I turned over.

Mom was staring at me. "Hi, Son!"

She was fine. She was Mom again, and had no memory of anything that had happened.

Actually, she remembered the whole day, in amazing detail. But the day she described bore no resemblance to reality. According to Mom, she hadn't done anything yesterday but sell books, then decide that they were safe where they were (and she didn't seem to notice how completely out of character that was for her, or that it was something she'd never done before) and go for a walk. On the walk she'd met some nice people and they'd talked about their cosplay.

At that point, she grinned brightly and said, "Guess what name just popped into my head as my steampunk identity?"

"What?" I said dryly.

"Dame Ginny McLaserbeam," she said proudly. I told her it was a great name, then we cracked open our supplies and had a nutritious breakfast of granola bars and Diet Coke – aka road trip food.

We talked for a while. Mom was animated. She said she felt like she'd slept better than she had in years. She smiled a lot.

She was, in a word, Mom again.

When it came time to plan our day – to figure out who would be covering the table when and anything else of import – I shook my head. "Don't you remember, Mom?"

She frowned. "Remember what?"

"We sold out yesterday." It was hard to keep my face pain-free. Mom didn't know about the Nerdfather stealing my books

The frown deepened, then released all at once. "Right. I remember." She grinned. "That's great! I can come see some of your panels and we can window shop!"

I shook my head sadly. "Can't. I don't have any panels today, and I made a bunch of business apointments that are going to keep me in wall-to-wall meetings all day. I'm so sorry."

Mom put a hand on my knee. "Don't you dare be sorry! That's what we came here for, right? To help your career."

That made a lump rise up in my throat. Mom and Dad were retired, and now that Dad wasn't coming to these things anymore, Mom could have stayed at home as well. Sure, she liked the cons, but I suspected she mostly came to help me, her "author son."

I have a good family. No matter what bad stuff may come my way, that can never be changed.

"Nah, Mom. Why don't you just stay in here? You can watch TV, do some crocheting." I nodded at the huge bag of yarn in the corner. Like the biddy in the booth next to Come and Play, my mom is a serious hooker, but unlike the old meanie she doesn't do it for profit. She crochets blankets for the families of children in our local hospital's burn ward to use while waiting for their kids to recover – or not. She also made great baby blankets, and each of my kids has a unique one of their own.

Mom's eyes lit up at the promise of a day to herself, full of nothing but rest and some good crafting.

I left a bit after that, telling Mom I had a meeting. She wondered at the time – it wasn't even seven in the morning yet – but I told her it was a breakfast meeting. When I walked out the door, she was crocheting away.

I didn't really know what else I was going to do. The brownies hadn't shown up with a report yet, and I certainly hadn't thought of anything new while reading Anderson's (really good, for crying out loud!) books.

I decided to call Blake and ask if Aseas had woken up yet, or if there was any other change in the lycan Peacemaker's condition. I doubted there was anything to report – Blake hadn't called me and I suspected when Aseas came out of whatever trance he was in, I'd be one of the first to know.

Still, I didn't have anything better to do, and if I was lucky I'd wake Blake out of a deep sleep and ruin a wonderful dream. The small things are what make life worth living.

I dialed Blake's number, and was about to put the phone to my ear, but before I could it flew out of my hand and jetted through the air to be caught by someone I really didn't want to see.

"Hello, my pretty," said the bartender from Nespda. The *witch* bartender. She dropped the phone and extended her hands toward me. "I have been *so* looking forward to this."

"To what?" I said, trying to smile as though I was fine with whatever.

"To killing you," she answered.

57

Witches look like people. Old, young, fat, thin, beautiful, ugly: just folks. The stories about green skin, scraggly hair, and warts on the nose is just a myth. A myth started by witches: as I said earlier, they are big fans of misdirection. Most of what you hear about them is wrong, and wrong in a purposeful way: they have hidden their strengths and weaknesses to the point that only a very few have any kind of idea how to deal with them.

I am one of those few. I'll give it to you in a nutshell.

Strengths: just about any kind of spellcasting. Not quite as powerful as the Dead Ones, but close. And they *are* more powerful when it comes to spells of violence. A witch can turn you inside out, rip your guts off your body, then shove them down your throat so even though you're inside out, your outside insides go back inside. And all without moving more than a pinky.

They're no stronger than normal people, physically, but good luck getting close enough to challenge one to an arm wrestling contest.

Specific weaknesses total exactly one: opium poppies. Which, as I said, are tough to get ahold of. It wasn't always that way, which is why people stopped hearing about – and fearing – witches: they were historically concentrated in western Europe and the United States, and in the nineteenth and early twentieth centuries, laudanum was used for everything from anesthetic to just shutting up colicky kids. Opium poppies were in every house, in one form or another, and the witches nearly went extinct.

What do they do? Well, they nullify a witch's power, first of all. You wear garlands of *Papaver somniferum* during a fight and her[30] spells will fizzle like sparklers dumped in a bucket of

---

[30] And yes, witches *are* all women. Sorry to all those who are offended.

water. And if you introduce opium poppies into their bloodstream, well… the results are pretty spectacular.

All this information was fairly interesting, but completely unhelpful at the moment. The only flowers nearby were some plastic ones in a vase at the end of the hall.

I hadn't really taken stock of the witch when I saw her behind the Nespda bar. Now she had my full attention. Short, but not stubby. Dark hair tied back in a severe bun, and silver hoop earrings that said "pirate" more than "witch." Her eyebrows were thick, but not ragged or overgrown. They gave a feeling of solidity and menace to what could otherwise have been a cute face. As she moved I also noted that she had grace and confidence. I wondered if she was Nespda's resident bouncer.

"Why do you want to kill me?" I said, stepping back as she stepped forward.

She just grinned.

"So what's your name? You know what they say, 'It's rude to kill a stranger.'"

She actually stopped. Frowned. "Who says that?"

"I have no idea. But it *should* be a saying."

She laughed the kind of laugh a praying mantis might give right before pulling the legs off a cricket. "Sure, why not," she said. "I'm Alice." Then she shrugged. "And I'm going to kill you because Prince Eustace wants you dead, and he paid me a lot of money to make sure that happens."

I was in mortal danger, facing a foe more dangerous than any I'd yet fought. Even so, a little thrill ran through me. Finally, confirmation! I could show everyone what had happened. There were still a few small pieces to put together, but Alice could help me with that.

I just had to survive.

So, of course, that's when I tripped.

My feet got bunched up in each other and I went back with a shout. I heard Alice cackle – she honest to goodness *cackled* – as I went down.

The cackle cut off, though, as she saw the gun in my hand.

I am many things, but one thing I am not: a guy who falls over his own feet.

At least, this time I hadn't. I had just pretended to fall. My back was really unhappy about it, but I told it to shut up because my ploy had worked: I was still carrying Larry's plastic paranormal peashooter, and I used the fall as a distraction to give me time to pull the weapon out of my waistband.

Alice stared at me; at *it*. "What's that thing?" she asked.

"It doesn't look like much, but it's a Correia," I said.

Most people in the World knew the kind of firepower Correia designed, and most people in the World did *not* want to get messed up with that.

"That's it, honey. Now, I'd like to ask you a few – *GLAH!*"

My cool as ice approach melted to nothing as I saw Alice's fingertips start glowing. That's what happens when a witch fires up her magical turbines, and it's almost always a precursor to disaster.

Alice had been sent by someone. I wanted to question her. But I also wanted to live, so I jabbed the gun at her and said, "Fire!" as I thought as hard as I could about shooting her. Just what Larry told me to do.

When I did this in the Other Green Room, the gun had lit up, fiberoptic cables had spun around it and the lights spelled "Game Over" in red while the Pac-Man death knell sounded – followed by a goblin who exploded like a pimple on prom night.

Now: nothing.

I pointed again. Said "Fire!" again. Thought shooty thoughts again.

Got the same result, which was no result at all.

Alice resumed her mad cackle. "You thought that would work against me?" Lightning arced between her fingers. "You obviously don't really know who you're fighting, you idiot."

She jabbed her hands at me.

Lightning streaked down the hall. I was a dead man.

58

This is the part where something jumps in front of me and saves my bacon. Or where the witch has a last-second change of heart. Or an asteroid takes out everyone but me. Because I'm the *hero*. I'm not going to get disintegrated right in the middle of the story!

Wrong. Nothing intervened. The hall was quiet, Alice still hated me, and all asteroids remained in the heavens.

The lightning hit me. It washed over me with a bright shower of sparks that dazzled me.

But that was all they did. I was dazzled, but not deaded.

The lights died, and I looked at Alice in shock. Then at Larry's gun in shock. Then back at Alice in shock. My shockometer needle was pegged out.

Alice wore the same expression I did. She looked at her hands, then pointed them at me again. She jabbed in my direction. This time, the lightning didn't even get halfway to me. And the third time, there was nothing at all.

I didn't hesitate. I jumped to my feet – well, lurched to my feet – and ran at Alice.

She was still in shock over what had just happened, so I covered most of the distance between us before she rejoined reality. She didn't run, though. Whoever was paying her to do this must be giving her a lot. Or she just hated me that much.

She pulled something out of her pocket. There was a *snick* and a six-inch blade popped out of her fist.

I had been planning a simple tackle. Alice wasn't that big, and I figured I could take her. The knife changed that.

Knife fights have been romanticized in television and movies. You see the hero and the bad guy fighting with a pair of short blades, their hands moving so fast you can't even see them, you just hear the *ting ting* of metal colliding as they thrust and slash and parry. The bad guy draws first blood, slashing the hero on the upper arm. The hero then Feels Intensely, which allows him to summon the courage to wipe the floor with the bad guy. Very neat, except for when the hero stabs the bad guy.

Reality is this: any time you are in a fight with a knife, you *will* get cut. I had a karate teacher who told me you can always tell the winner in a knife fight, because that's the person who leaves the hospital first. True words.

I had no wish to tangle with Alice's knife, but as I tried to skid around her, she jumped in my path with surprising agility. She slashed with her blade, and I barely managed to jump back with my insides still in place.

Alice wasn't shy, and she knew what she was doing. The blade followed me as I retreated, nipping at exposed skin and slowly flaying me alive.

I took it. My goal at this point was to avoid any major damage, and to wait.

It didn't work.

Alice slashed across my body. I danced out of the way, but her reverse slice was too fast. I raised my arm fast enough to avoid getting my throat slit, but she scored a deep gash across my forearm. The fingers still worked, but blood slicked my arm and I knew I had seconds to end this before I lost too much blood to fight.

Alice attacked again. This time it was a diagonal stab, starting above her shoulder and slashing down toward my hip on the opposite side.

My turn to score. I had been biding my time, waiting for my opponent to tire, to make a mistake.

Alice had gotten tired, and with that she slowed. Not a lot, but enough. As she cut down with her right hand, I slammed the palm of my right hand against the inside of her wrist. Without losing contact with her wrist, I spun my hand around to trap her wrist and hand, then used Alice's own momentum to twist her hand around. My left hand joined my right, trapping her knife hand between them, and I shoved the knife back at Alice.

I was certainly within my rights as a Warden to kill her if I wished, but I wanted information, not bloodshed. So I didn't slam the knife into her throat or chest. Instead, I turned her wrist and then moved her hand back so that the flat of the blade came down on her shoulder. I kept pressing, and the knife levered its way out of her hand.

I grinned. But Alice grinned, too. I heard another *snick*, and her left hand crashed the party: she had a second knife, and I'd been so busy stripping the first one from her right hand, I neglected to pay proper attention to what her left was up to. Stupid, and I was likely to pay for the lapse with my life.

Alice grinned as she thrust the knife at me, aiming for my gut. I twisted sideways, trying to avoid evisceration. Alice moved like a monkey, slipping around me and jumping on my back before slashing down at my chest with her knife.

We fell. I slammed down on her as hard as I could, and I was pretty sure I heard one of her ribs crack. She was tough, though, and didn't let go of me or the knife. Her free arm snaked around my throat and began compressing it painfully. She couldn't strangle me – she didn't have the leverage or strength to pinch of my carotids, which would have interrupted the blood flow to my brain and made me go night-night in about eight seconds. But she could certainly choke me. My windpipe started compressing, and I had to work harder and harder for every breath.

At the same time, her other hand – the knife hand – was still trying to find me. She stabbed at my throat, but I got both hands on her forearm and stopped the motion.

I had control of her knife arm, for the moment, but things still looked grim. I was still losing blood, and she was slowly cutting off my air supply, and I couldn't spare a hand to do anything about it.

"How'd you stop my spell, human?" she snarled in my ear.

"*Gar-flx... nug.*" It was all I could manage with the air I had left.

I could feel her smile. Darkness gathered around the edges of my vision. I felt my grip on her knife arm slipping.

Desperate, I dropped my chin as far as I could, then slammed backward. It was a terrible reverse headbutt, barely glancing across her cheek and doing no real damage. But it did gain me a second, as the arm around my throat slipped upward. I still couldn't breathe, though, since the arm had settled over my mouth and nose.

I bit her arm. Ground down as hard as I could into muscle, trying to tear a chunk of it away. Hot blood spurted into my mouth, but I didn't care – the part of me that only cared about living was in charge, an animal to whom the enemy's blood was not revolting, but beautiful.

I hoped the bite might buy me time at worst. At best, I hoped she would be so shocked that she would lose her stranglehold and her knife at the same time.

The results were a bit more... extreme.

Alice's body went rigid. Every muscle in her body contracted, so much so that the knife actually dug its way a few inches closer to me. A few more inches, and now it was buried a half inch in my shoulder. I screamed.

Alice said nothing. Her body relaxed as quickly as it had tensed. Her arm fell away from my throat, and her other hand dropped the knife.

I heard her whisper below me, "He didn't tell me it would be like this."

Then Alice exploded.

I was laying on top of her, and the force of the blast sent me flying into the air, all the way to the ceiling. I slammed into it with the same force as someone hitting a sidewalk after jumping off the second floor. My lungs felt like they blew through the sides of my ribcage, and I heard my nose crack into a thousand tiny pieces. The knife wound on my shoulder and the million tiny cuts I'd suffered during the fight with Alice were consumed in the overpowering pain of that impact.

Gravity showed up then, and reminded everyone who was boss. I fell away from the ceiling and hit the floor. Hard. I heard more ribs crack – this time my own. My arm was twisted painfully under me, wedged between my back and the floor in a way arms definitely are not designed to do.

I was vaguely aware that I was laying in a large red smear that was all that remained of Alice.

Laura's gonna kill me for wrecking her favorite t-shirt.

Was it a birthday present? I don't know. Maybe.

I better call her soon.

My mind spun madly, and a moment later I passed out. Or maybe died. Not sure which. Either way, the darkness that had floated at the edges of sight now wrapped me in a cocoon of softest velvet. I fell into it, and was glad to do so.

59

Waking up was weird. First of all, I hadn't really expected to wake up at all. My last thoughts were pretty much along the lines of, "So long, and thanks for all the fish," or something else equally final.

Second, I was awake, but I couldn't open my eyes or move. My entire body was paralyzed. Everything was dark, my body was not under my control.

Still, I knew I was alive. And that was something.

How am *I alive?*

I couldn't even blink, let alone call for help, so my brain did what it does best: worries about stuff. Specifically, why I was still alive, how it had happened, and what inevitable badness it would bring to me in the future.

I have never been accused of an excess optimism, and given all that had happened what optimism I did have was disappearing fast.

The witch had tried to spell me to death. Not sure what spell it was, but I *was* sure she intended it to be fatal. Not just pretty lights.

The next spell fizzled even harder. And then she couldn't do anything at all.

The only thing that could do that was the opium poppy. And I sure didn't have any of those on me so...

... so someone else must have been nearby. Someone who knew about witches, and had brought enough of the flowers to nullify her spells even at a distance.

That would have to be a lot of poppies. And what about –

Thought disappeared as pain flooded through me. For a moment it was as though every injury I'd suffered – the cuts, the bruises, the broken bones, the suffocation – all returned.

I would have screamed, but my body still wasn't listening to me. I wondered if this was the rest of my existence:

locked in the dark room of my own mind, with no one else for company.

Maybe I *had* died. Maybe this was Hell.

The pain left my body. All at once, leaving behind not so much as a twinge when it departed. Even my back and my neck felt great, for the first time in a long time.

I gotta find out what kind of medicine they're giving me.

Great medicine.

Wonderful....

I still couldn't move, but suddenly I laughed hard and loud in my mind. I thought the laughter echoed a bit, which says sad things about how much extra space I've got in there.

Still, the laugh felt great. Everything felt a bit brighter in the darkness.

My back felt good. Like I'd gotten the best medicine in the world. That was the hint I'd needed to figure out what happened.

Witches' only real weakness: the opium poppy. I'd had severe back and neck problems for years. I popped more pills every day than you'd find at an average birthday party for a Hollywood child star.

I didn't have any poppies. But my body was utterly saturated with narcotics. Which have as their base... you guessed it. Opium poppies.

I had so much of the stuff in my system that I was immune to Alice's spells. And when I bit her, the amounts in my saliva alone were enough to do her in with extreme prejudice.[31]

Sweet. The Last Witch Hunter *my butt – Vin Diesel's got nothing on me.*

---

[31] Yeah, I know that doesn't really make sense. But it sounds awesome. Adding "with extreme prejudice" to *anything* makes it sound awesome. "Would you like fries with that, sir?" "Yes. With extreme prejudice." "[Gulp.] Yes, sir. And here's a free drink. Please don't extremely prejudice me!"

The laughter in my head grew and grew, and then broke free. With it, so did the darkness. As I laughed, my eyes opened. I was laughing aloud, and my voice sounded strong and hale.

The first thing I saw was the ceiling, of course. Looked like one of the conference rooms in the hotel. I was laying down, and I turned my head sideways. I saw something furry on a bed beside mine. Not a dog, not a lycan. My thoughts were still a little muddled, and before I could really identify the form that was wrapped in blankets and a white sheet, something inserted itself into my vision.

"You're awake. Good."

I blinked. I knew that voice, but I couldn't believe I was hearing right. I had been sure I was hallucinating, but when I finally got my eyes working, I saw that it really *was* Kevin J. Anderson.

He put out a hand. I took it, and he levered me up into a sitting position. I was on a hospital cot – or near enough – and when I looked around I saw that I was, in fact, in one of the hotel's conference rooms. But it had been converted to a makeshift hospital. Other cots like mine lined the walls, each with an occupant. A few were human, but most were Otherworlders, and most of the things in here were in visible pain. Festering wounds, infections, supernatural plagues. They all moaned and wept.

The moans were familiar. I looked at Anderson. "Holy crap, you're a doctor, not a pervert."

Anderson frowned at that. "I thought I took care of the head wound. Are you still injured?" he said.

"No, just...." I shook my head, trying to clear it. My neck twinged when I did that, but other than that and my ever-present back pain, I realized I didn't hurt. A quick glance showed that I was in a robe, and when I opened it I saw no wounds, no scars, no sign of any kind that I'd been involved in a knife fight.

I looked up at Anderson, a wide smile on my face. "You *liar*," I said.

His frown deepened. "What did you call me, Collings?"

I shook a finger at him. "Oh, no, Anderson. No way. I know your secret now." I gestured at the room. "You've been taking care of all these Otherworlders and people. You're...." I gasped as the full realization came. "You're a *nice guy*."

Anderson grabbed my robe and hauled me to him. "You tell anyone and you're a dead man. You hear? Dead."

I nodded, but my grin didn't disappear. "Is that why you're such a moneygrubber? You're using all your cash for this?"

Anderson moved to the next table over and checked a machine that looked like a cross between a heart monitor, a Ouija board, and a rubber chicken. Come to think of it, so did the thing in the bed.

"Running places like this takes cash," he said.

"You really run this, this *MASH* unit?" I frowned. "Wait, does that mean I'm Hawkeye or Hunnicutt? I don't want to be Hot Lips. That just – wait, plac*es*? There are more of these hospitals?"

"Of course. Every convention in the United States, and most of the ones in Europe, have a room or a suite of rooms like this. A place where Otherworlders in the area can come to have their wounds and maladies looked after. Not the sniffles or a simple case of DeLorian eighty-eight. At WordFire Clinics, we focus on those members of the World who are in mortal physical peril, and do our best to help them."

I blinked. The idea that... that Kevin J. Anderson... that *he* was... was... *nice*.

"Your books are great," I said. Not what I meant to say, but my brain was busy short circuiting.

Anderson nodded. "Yes," he agreed, "I know. And a good thing, too." He moved to another bed, this one occupied by a moaning mothman, and adjusted something that looked suspiciously like a bug zapper on a baby's mobile that hung above the monster. The mothman's antennae quivered in appreciation.

"Why?" I said.

"Why what?"

"Why all this? You're one of the Dead Ones. The keepers of the peace, the last line of defense *against* these things."

He nodded. "Yes, and most of my brothers and sisters feel just as you do. But I think there are many ways to keep the peace, and I believe that strength is shown as much through mercy as through mayhem."

I had no pithy response, no sarcastic comment. A noise drew my attention and I realized that there were a few others working with the "patients." I didn't know most of them, but I recognized Orson Scott Card in the corner, leaning over a prone form he was clearly working on. I vaguely recollected Anderson mentioning Card was at the convention, but to see the author of *Ender's Game* – and also a Dead One – in this particular room was a shock.

Blake Casselman, of all people, looked like he was assisting Card with his patient.

Is everyone *secretly nice?*

I felt like some unpleasant but critical part of my world was falling apart.

I squinted as I caught a glimpse of the person Blake and Card were working over.

Is that –?

I slid off my hospital bed and moved in their direction. Card didn't look back at me, but he must have sensed me coming. He waved a hand in my direction and muttered something, and when I took my next step it felt like I walked face-first into a wall. I couldn't move.

It was moments like this that reminded me how deeply over my head I was in. One wave from a Dead One and I'm a plastic figurine.

I'd look good as an action figure.

Blake glanced back and smirked. "Hi, Collings," he said. "How's the sylphilis?"

I growled out a response that mentioned certain of his ancestors and what they enjoyed doing with lawn gnomes. Blake laughed, but it was obviously because he enjoyed seeing me stuck.

So, he's not nice. Good and charitable, maybe, but not nice.

For some reason, the thought made me feel better. Maybe my world wasn't completely upending itself after all.

The cot's occupant moved, and Card made a sign over him while he chanted in a low tone. Blue fire erupted from his fingers, outlining the moaning figure on the bed.

Aseas. The Great Pack's Peacemaker, who had been found unconscious beside Calista's body.

He was still unconscious, but it looked like he was trying to move. Perhaps coming out of it. Blake handed Card several things – what looked like a string, a bone, and a Tickle Me Elmo doll. Card wrapped the string around the doll and the bone, tying them together, then murmured an incantation. More light flared, and Aseas began mumbling. Still asleep, though.

"They've been working nearly non-stop to wake him up," said Anderson. "We need Aseas to figure out what happened."

"I already know what happened," I said.

Anderson eyed me dubiously. He glanced at Orson Scott Card. Card was turned away, but some kind of Dead One telepathy must have happened because without turning toward me Card waved a hand, and I could move again – though I didn't attempt to get closer to Aseas. Clearly Card wanted his space.

"What happened, then?" asked Anderson. "All we know is that you called Blake, then there were sounds of a struggle, and when we found you you were unconscious and injured in a sea of gore." His nose wrinkled. "You would not believe how many brownies it took to get that cleaned up."

I told him what had happened. About the witch's attack. Anderson couldn't believe I'd beaten her at first, until I told him about my meds. Then he laughed a bit. "Vin Diesel, eat your heart out," he said.

"That's what I thought!" I nearly shouted.

"*Last Witch Hunter* is a fun movie. Not good, but fun, and it didn't deserve the critical thrashing it received," said Anderson.

We actually grinned at each other. It felt weird.

Then I told him what Alice had told me before she tried to carve me up like a Thanksgiving chicken.[32]

"'I'm going to kill you because Prince Eustace wants you dead'?" said Anderson. "She really said that?"

"Yeah." I looked around. "Where are my clothes? We gotta get moving."

Anderson put a hand on my chest. "Moving where?" he said quietly.

I looked at him like he'd lost all his marbles. "Where?" I said. "Wherever you're hiding the prince. Where do you think. We have to give him to the Great Pack."

Anderson shook his head. "Not going to happen," he said.

I drew back. A sneer curled my lips. "So all that stuff about justice being done was just grandstanding. Tell me the truth, Anderson: how much did the High Court donate to your little MASH unit to keep Eustace in the clear?"

"Listen, Collings –"

I ran right over Anderson's words, ignoring the dark cast of his eyes – and the large part of me screaming at myself to shut up. "Or was it Eustace himself? Did the prince pay you *before* he killed Calista, or did he come to you when the job was done?" I glanced at Card and Blake. Card was still focused on the lycan

---

[32] Fine. My family couldn't afford turkeys when I was a kid. Now you know. *Happy?*

in the bed, but Blake was staring shards of broken glass in my direction. He actually took a step toward me, his body language showing his intent to lay a beat-down on me. Anderson held up a hand, and Blake held himself in check. "That's right, Blake," I said. "Stay there like a good little dog." Rage had filled me past reason. All this work, all the suffering, all I'd done, and now....

I spat on the floor at Blake's feet. "You guys aren't trying to wake Aseas up, are you? You're trying to keep him asleep! I –
"

Anderson said something short, sharp, and guttural. A single syllable, but I felt like a huge fist had just hammered me between the eyes. My whole body went numb, and only Anderson's magic kept me from toppling over. I tried to speak, and found I couldn't. The only thing I could move was my eyes, which tracked over to Anderson.

He was staring at me, wrath blanketing his features. "I know you mean well, Michaelbrent," he said quietly. "But sometimes you just don't know when to shut up." The twitch of a finger, and I spun in the air, turning to face Aseas. "You really think all of us would be required to make sure the Peacemaker doesn't wake up? We're trying to save him, and we're trying to figure out exactly what happened."

I jerked back around to face Anderson. I tried to speak, but still couldn't move anything but my eyes. I thought about blinking, "Screw you," in Morse code.

Note to self: learn Morse code.

"What do you have?" said Anderson. "You have a bunch of pictures that show a young woman engaging in questionable acts with scores of humans. A young woman, not a princess. The person in the photographs has a tattoo like Calista, but when people are looking for proof, they're going to point out the likelihood that other people have that same tattoo. They're also going to point out that Prince Eustace doted on Calista, and are going to ask what the likelihood is that he turned on her for any reason, even assuming the pictures are really of Calista, which we can't prove since Calista's body is – er, gone."

Anderson glanced at Blake when he said that. And yes, it was childish, but I grinned inside thinking of Blake getting in trouble with the Dead Ones.

Anderson continued. "So what proof – real proof – do you have that Eustace did it?"

Suddenly my tongue was free. "The witch said he sent her!" I blurted.

Anderson nodded and folded his arms. "Yes. A witch that you conveniently detonated before anyone else could hear that, or even verify her existence. For all anyone knows, you just blew up a bag of puppies in there."

"I'm not the one who blows puppies, Anderson."

You know when a book says, "His eyes were ablaze" or "There was fire in his gaze"? Well, they're usually not talking literally. I am. Anderson's eyes *literally* shot fire: six-inch tongues of flame that burst out of his face and stopped just short of frying the eyebrows off my head.

I would have shrunk back, but the spell was in full force again. I couldn't move, speak – heck, I could barely *think*.

Anderson leaned in so close I could smell his last meal (thankfully, the eye-fires died a bit so I didn't get the *crème brûlée* treatment). "Listen carefully, Michaelbrent," he whispered. The whisper was scarier than any scream I'd ever heard. "You are actually a pretty good Warden, for someone so new. But you lack patience, wisdom, and an understanding of when to keep your mouth shut." He drew back, and the light in his eyes dimmed a bit more as he got himself under control. "You think Prince Eustace did it? Well, so do I. So does Blake. So do all the Dead Ones. But *there is no proof!* And if we make a move without solid proof, then it will start a war." He looked at me carefully. "Do you have a family?"

The spell loosed. I still couldn't speak, but I was able to nod.

"Yes, I know you do," he said. "And I know you love them. So are you in such a hurry to find the murderer that you'll put them – and every other human being alive – in danger?"

I looked away. The only answer I could give, and answer enough.

The spell fell away. No one spoke. After a moment I looked up, and saw Blake staring at me with no irritation or anger whatsoever. Just quiet resignation, a hint of sadness. "Sorry," he mouthed. I wasn't sure what he was sorry for – the situation? Anderson yelling at me? It could have been anything.

The fact that he said it at all, though, rocked me. I didn't know if I could handle a world where Blake was kind to me.

I looked at Anderson. He held my gaze. I finally looked away and said, "Okay."

Anderson put a hand on my shoulder. "Good."

After a moment, I looked at him. "Can I have my clothes? I'd like to…. I don't know. But I don't want to sit around in a robe."

Anderson shook his head sadly. "I'd love to let you get dressed and go, Michaelbrent. But truth is, I don't really trust you right now."

"You don't trust me? I thought you said I was right."

"I think you are," he agreed. "But you're impatient, and lack wisdom, and…."

He tapped a finger on the side of my head. The world started to get hazy. Everything swirled around like an eighties-era flashback, and I heard him say, "And you lack the wisdom to know when to keep your mouth shut."

Hands caught me as I fell. The world dimmed still more, and someone – I don't know if it was Blake or Anderson or even Orson Scott Card – said, "Sorry, but if you go around stirring up trouble again, it might be the final straw."

Another voice, and I was sure this one belonged to Anderson. "If you tell anyone I'm nice, or do charity work, I will turn you into a dung-humping zombie who works at the DMV."

I had only a moment to scream silently at the magnitude of his threat.

Then, once again, darkness stole over me.

And stole me away.

60

Memories.

Memories are funny: they have heat, but can be so cold. They bring us joy in bad times, but are often the source of our greatest sorrows. Hope is a thing for the future alone, but regret is found only in our past. Time dips into our minds, and leaves traces of itself behind in the form of ethereal images that we can rarely access with any completeness and never with objectivity.

Memories. The birthplace of our current selves, the images that we construct *as* "ourselves." The place where all our knowledge comes from, but which at the same time so often strips us of our reason. They are the sum of our experience, because anything that we don't remember – on some level or other – might as well never have happened.

The darkness reminded me, for some reason, of the first time I saw Laura. She stumbled into my view and my heart changed inside me. I knew this was the woman I would spend my life with. I knew I was done with dating, with spending time in that hurried state of frenzied melodrama we call "single life." I knew this was *her*, and the magic I felt was only partly because she was an Otherworlder.

The darkness reminded me, too, of losing our child. The experience was one of jagged edges: sharp sorrows and pains like spikes through my and Laura's hearts. But time softened it. Melted the blades into something else. Still hard, but no longer painful. A framework to hang onto, a structure of sorrow that would become the basis for hope.

I remembered Laura. I remembered her smile. I remembered the horror when I saw my first Otherworlder and thought I was going insane. Then the greater horror when I realized I *wasn't* insane.

Magic. It was all, so….

"Magic," I whispered.

The word was real. Not blanketed in the velvet nothing of near-oblivion. I said it out loud, and as I did I fell away from memory, falling like an angel from Heaven to the profane realms of reality.

A hand under my back. It lifted me.

I opened my eyes. Found I was still in Anderson's hospital. And that Larry Correia was standing over me with a concerned expression on his face.

"Geez, I've been looking for you everywhere," he said.

I tried to say something witty and delightful back. But my throat was dry and I just ended up coughing. Larry pounded my back with his hubcap-sized hand – one of those cures that's probably worse than the disease.

I raised my own human-sized hand to ward off further bone-breaking "soft smacks" by my friend.

"Wh... where?" I managed.

"You're in Anderson's...." Larry looked around, obviously unsure what the place was. "His free clinic for monsters?"

"I know," I managed. "I mean, where's Anderson?"

Larry shook his head. "Haven't seen him. I just hadn't seen you all day, either, so I went looking for you in case something happened." He put something on my lap: my clothes with the plastic gun on top, along with my phone and Calista's phone. The clothes were all fine: clean and in good repair. Apparently they'd "healed" my outfit as well as my body.

Larry eyed Calista's phone. "I didn't really peg you as a rhinestones guy. More a faux alligator skin type."

I picked up the gun. Larry ducked away as the barrel pointed his direction. "Whoa, man! Sorry! You can be a rhinestone guy if you want, whatever. I don't judge." When I waved the gun a bit he added, "That thing's loaded!"

"It doesn't work!" I yelled. Or tried to. It came out as a scratchy, cracked jumble of syllables. "I tried to use it and it almost got me killed."

Larry frowned. "Not possible." Without further ado, he peeled it from my hand, aimed it at a box of donuts on a table in the corner of the room, and whispered, "Fire."

The fiberoptic cables at the end of the gun spun out, the words "Game Over" appearing as Pac-Man's death throes sounded. Before it was even over, the donuts had turned white and then exploded.

Larry shook his head. "Nothing seems to be wrong with it," he said.

He handed it back to me, and I pointed it at a bottle of coffee creamer that had been sitting beside the donuts. "Fire," I said, and imagined bullets hitting the creamer.

It exploded just like the donuts.

I looked at the gadget. "Then what the – She must have enchanted it."

"Who?" said Larry.

"The witch. She couldn't kill me, because of my back. But she must have gotten to the gun."

Larry frowned. I could tell from his expression that I wasn't making as much sense as I thought I was.

"Forget it," I said. Then I noticed that the bed Aseas had been in was empty. I pointed at it. "Where is he?" I asked.

"Who?"

"Him. The guy." My brain was still a bit muddled, but I managed, "Aseas!"

"I don't know who Aseas is," said Larry. "And whoever he is, he's probably keeping a low profile right now."

I had begun to throw on my clothes, but the way Larry said that stopped me with one leg in my jeans, the other hanging in air as I hopped around with all the dignity of Kanye West at the Grammys. "What do you mean?" I said. "What's going on?"

"The lycans arrested the killer," said Larry.

I wondered what new evidence Anderson and Blake had dug up that motivated them to finally move forward. "Where is he?" I asked. "What are they going to do to him?"

Larry squinted at me. "He?" he said. He shook his head. "The murderer is a she."

I had both legs in my pants, thank goodness, or I would have fallen over for sure. "She?" I said. "Who? Who's she?"

Larry got that look you get when dishing something especially juicy to a friend. "Princess Moonbeam," he said. "Can you believe it? Calista's *own sister* killed her." He chuckled. "I guess that's it for an all-out war between vamps and lycans," he said. "Though I guess the lycans might just tear themselves apart over this."

"You say it like you'd prefer a more all-consuming destruction."

He winked, "Hey, I like to shoot things, right?" Then, seriously, he said, "You don't look so hot, Collings. You okay?"

"No, I'm not. What's going to happen to Moonbeam?"

He shrugged. "There's going to be a trial."

"When?"

"Don't know."

"And if she's found guilty?"

He shrugged again. "Pack Justice."

Pack Justice is the ultimate deterrent. Werewolves are loyal to each other, but there is the occasional breakdown, the rare moments where one lycan harms another, whether physically, emotionally, or financially. If that happens, the lycans have a trial. But there are no lawyers, no judges. There is just the Great Pack – the ruling class of Lycaons, all of whom were already here at the convention. Tidy.

The Great Pack discusses what's happened. They receive evidence, both for and against the accused, without anything an outsider would see as rhyme or reason. But it works, because at the end of every trial, the Great Pack is always unanimous. If the accused is not guilty, he or she is freed. If guilty, then Pack Justice is dispensed.

Again, the Great Pack discusses the options, and often this part lasts longer than the actual trial. The point is not to punish the guilty, but to punish them with as much or more pain as they caused others.

Here's what makes Pack Justice so terrible: the punishment is always *just*. Most people say they want justice in their lives, but most people haven't really thought that through. Not just getting what they think they deserve, but a tally of every wrong they have ever done, every feeling they have ever hurt, every lie told, every wrong committed in their *entire life*. That is what the Great Pack discusses, what they use as the measure of pain the guilty must suffer for Pack Justice to be done.

What would happen if the Great Pack found Moonbeam guilty of murder? And not just any murder, but a murder of the royal family, by her own sister. Fratricide… and a fratricide that put the entire lycan race – and perhaps the whole world – at risk of extinction.

Moonbeam wouldn't be killed for her crimes. Pack Justice would not permit such an easy exit for someone responsible for so much pain and danger. They would keep her alive as long as they could – and ensure that every day was a study in torment. They would rip her body to pieces, would destroy her mind, would torment her soul. And they would do it for decades.

I started moving again. Threw on my shirt, yanked on my socks and shoes. My back hurt when I did that – I guess even magic can't cure some pains – but I checked my pocket and found my pills still there, so I swallowed one. I couldn't spare time for so much as a single "ouch" in the coming minutes and hours.

"Hey, MB," said Larry. "Easy, man. Slow down."

"Can't." I got my shoes on. Looked around and started for the door at the end of the room.

"Why not? What's got you so worked up?"

"They're going to convict the wrong person."

"How do you know?"

"It couldn't have been her." I told him about the witch, Alice. How she attacked me, how I got out of it – and this time I was coherent enough to explain the connection between her fizzled attacks and the opioids in my system. Most of all, though, what she had said.

"She actually *said* Prince Eustace sent her?" said Larry.

I nodded. "Yeah. I have an eyewitness, and they go off on some stupid evidence –" My hand was on the door out, the crash bar half-depressed under my palm. Larry's words stopped me.

"MB, your witch may have said what you believe she did –"

"What do you mean believe? I heard her. I was *there.*"

"Hey, I'm on your side. But even putting aside the fact that you were in a fight with a *witch* – which makes most people concentrate on not pissing their jeans more than what's being said around them – you have an assassin with a mouthful of hearsay. They have an eyewitness who was actually at the scene of the murder."

I froze. "Who?" I said. Though I already knew the answer.

"The Lycaon Peacemaker."

"Aseas," I said dully.

"Oh, that's who Aseas is? Well then, yeah, I know about him. Anderson showed up at the Great Pack's penthouse with him in tow a little while ago. I guess Aseas got whammied during the murder, so he doesn't remember everything, but from what I understand he reported seeing Moonbeam go into the area of the murder. He followed her, and...." He shrugged. "The rest is history."

"So all they've got on Moonbeam is that someone saw her in the vicinity of the murder?"

Larry shook his head. "No. They also found out she's been lying about her activities over the past few months. I guess Haemon was busy doing his own little investigation this whole time, and discovered that Moonbeam's been claiming to do all this charity work –"

"The 501ˢᵗ Legion."

"Right. But turns out they never heard of her. Not her, not any of the pseudonyms she uses when she's out and about."

"Maybe she used a new pseudonym, and had another glamour put on her to hide her identity."

"Sounds good to me," said Larry. "But why wouldn't she tell her dad if that was the case? As it is, she's refusing to say anything at all, and that plus Aseas' testimony has everyone pretty sure they know who did it."

I shook my head. "No, there's no way. Gandhi verified that Moonbeam was at the meeting of the 501ˢᵗ during the time of the murder."

"I don't know who this Gandhi guy is, but did he verify she was there, or did he verify that someone in her cosplay was there? Those people are all dressed as stormtroopers, so how can this Gandhi know it was her?"

"I didn't ask, but I'd be *very* surprised if Gandhi made a mistake like that."

"Why? Who is this guy?"

"He's in charge of Otherworld surveillance for the convention."

Larry grew solemn. "Is this guy a dwarf?"

"Yeah, of course he is."

"Did he tell anyone else about all this, or just you? Anyone else who can back up what you heard?"

"How should I know? Maybe. But he'll tell everyone now, that's for sure."

Larry's eyes were closed. "He was a friend of yours?"

"Yeah, he…. Wait, 'was'?" Larry didn't respond. "Larry, what happened to Gandhi?"

"I don't know if it was him, but I heard that all the feeds from the con have been wiped. And there was something about a dwarf who'd been killed, too."

"When?"

"No one's sure. They went in and a few lycans offered to sniff it out, but someone had left a Vortex in the room. The first person who walked in –"

"I know." I waved him to silence. Vortexes are essentially hurricanes, tsunamis, and tornadoes all mixed together. They devastate an area, leaving nothing behind but kindling. They're hard to make, too – not the destructive part, but the containment. A Vortex is designed to lay waste to everything in a specific space. Bigger ones are actually easier to make, since that type of energy doesn't want to be restrained.

"Did it only destroy the room?" I said.

"The room and everything in it – nothing bigger than a toothpick was left after it went off. The surveillance equipment and files, and what was left of...." He didn't finish the sentence.

What is going on*?*

Anyone who could create a room-sized Vortex meant business, and was someone whose skills ran hard to murder and mayhem. Dangerous.

Could it have been Moonbeam? I didn't think so. This wasn't her style. She might rip out a person's throat, but she didn't strike me as a saboteur or assassin. I remembered her on the roof, putting herself in the line of fire to protect her father. Brave people can be assassins, of course, but in my experience someone who stands to fight in public will rarely stoop to killing from behind.

Of course, appearances can be deceiving. I had to look at what was, not what appeared to be.

I knew I was trying not to think about Gandhi. He and I had worked together enough that we'd become... friends? Certainly I'd grown fond of him. And someone went and killed him to cover up a crime that was getting more muddled the longer I looked at it.

"I was going to give him another bag of Gummi Bears," I muttered to myself.

336

Larry probably didn't understand the details of that, but he must have understood my tone. He put a big hand on my shoulder. "Need help killing someone?" he asked.

I nodded. "Probably."

61

The room turned out to be a second floor assembly room in a part of the convention center not devoted to the FanFamFunComCon, so I started walking as fast as I could back to the main floor. Larry fell into step beside me, his long legs easily keeping pace with my hurried stride.

Gandhi was dead, and had taken all his surveillance files with him. Prince Eustace was off the hook because the lycans were sure Moonbeam had killed her sister, based on an eyewitness account of their Peacemaker and her failure to provide an alternate alibi or a reason for her long-term lies about her activities.

But Aseas hadn't seen Moonbeam actually *kill* Calista. He'd just seen her in the area of the murder. Even with the loss of her alibi on Gandhi's security footage, it didn't make sense to peremptorily arrest the Great Pack's princess. Underneath the carefully-cultivated hippie persona, King Haemon struck me as a thoughtful, cautious person. His admission of the relative weakness of his people was proof of that, given that most lycans would give up the chance to murder Stephenie Meyer[33] before they'd admit they were anything but the prize-fighting champs of the World.

But he had to have approved Moonbeam's arrest. There was no way anyone could arrest the Great Pack's remaining princess without his approval, so –

I stopped. Larry had a pair of guns out instantly, moving so fast I didn't even see the draws. Both guns looked bloated and black, like ticks after drinking their fill.

---

[33] I have nothing against *Twilight*. But don't offer to take your werewolf friends to a showing. The part where [SPOILER DELETED] makes them upset since they think it makes lycans look like a bunch of pedophiles. And by "upset" I mean "they will murder you, strip your skull of flesh, then poop in your eyeholes." If you're lucky, they'll even do it in that order.

"What is it? What'd you see?" he asked, looking quickly around.

I waved him to silence.

What if Haemon didn't believe she did it? What if he *had* to arrest her?

He'd told me how weak the lycans were. That the treaty might be their last chance to save not just their position, but their existence.

"Does the High Court know about Aseas?" I said.

Larry frowned, then his guns disappeared as if by magic as he apparently decided there was no threat worth shooting at the moment. "Yeah," he said.

"And they found out *before* the arrest, right?"

Another frown. "Yeah. My sources told me that Anderson brought Aseas to Haemon, and a few minutes later the whole High Court was at the lycans' door, demanding justice."

"And they already knew what Aseas had told Haemon?"

Larry thought. "I think so. You think Anderson told them? Maybe Blake?"

I shook my head. "No, I think someone leaked the information to the High Court so that they'd come running."

"Why?"

"To force Haemon to act. To make him arrest his own daughter, because if he didn't do that he might risk all-out war with the lycans."

"But he wouldn't actually execute her, would he?"

That was a good question. I got the impression that Haemon was a good father, and a good king. He loved his daughters, and he loved his people. Which would weigh more in his mind? Would he sacrifice his last daughter to save his people, or would he rather see his people's blood flow to save his remaining child?

"I don't know," I said. "But I'm going to talk to him. And her."

Easier said than done. I went to the hotel, then up to the ninth floor. Larry wasn't a Warden, and he looked impressed when I used my all-purpose code key on the elevator. "That opens everything?" he said.

"Pretty much." I looked sideways at him. "Don't worry, I won't get into your gun safe. I did take your car joyriding, though. To impress the ladies."

He snorted. Larry drives a beat-up SUV. Yes, he's extremely successful, and yes, he could afford better. But he's less interested in looking pretty when he drives than he is about how much artillery he can fit in the trunk.

"You're welcome to it," he said. "Damn transmission's about to go on it."

"Poor baby."

The riffing was forced, but it felt good. I retreat into sarcasm and inappropriate humor when worried or afraid. It's why I don't get invited to any of the funerals with the cool kids anymore.

The door opened at the ninth floor, and Larry and I stepped out. The door that led to the ninth floor hallway opened to my key as well, but this was where the trouble started.

The hall was full of lycans and vampires. Normally not something you would see crammed into a hallway together, but there they were: a good dozen of each. They didn't look terribly happy about it – no one was high-fiving or laughing – but the Lycaons were all in human form and the vamps' teeth and nails were sheathed. Their eyes were mostly red, but it wasn't the full-red of an enraged vampire ready to start murdering everything in range. Suspicion and tension coiled in every muscle in that hall, but they were all in check. For now.

I tried to step into the hall, but the second my foot crossed the threshold the nearest lycan seemed to split right out of his skin and before I could take the next step I had five razor claws resting on my neck. He hadn't torn my throat out, but the claws pierced me enough that blood trickled down my neck.

The lycan's growl became a yip as something darted out from behind me. A long, dark tube rammed into the wolf's groin.

"Let go of him," said Larry, "Or I will pump your nuts so full of silver that your babies will go for twenty bucks an ounce."

The lycan froze. Then it withdrew as someone pulled it away from me.

Pallas. The tall lycan who had come to retrieve me from the High Court. "Be cool, brother," he said to the lycan, his voice still so low that the vibrations made the hall windows shudder. The lycan backed away, and another person took his place, standing shoulder-to-shoulder with Pallas.

Rathton had a lot more red in his eyes than the other vamps did, and sported a mouthful of half-transformed teeth. He had never liked me, and his grin very clearly demonstrated that he never liked me even more now than he hadn't in the past.

Larry pulled back the silver-shotgun, but he didn't put it away. When Rathton took one more step toward me, Larry flipped up the weapon, pointing it skyward to reveal the underside of its barrel, which had dozens of crosses scored into the metal.

Rathton hissed and pulled back a step. Larry said, "The Correia Monster Masher, with genuine mother-of-pearl cross inlays spanning the entirety of the 4140 alloy steel body as well as the black walnut stock which has been specially seasoned with a variety of spices and herbs guaranteed to make most faeries lose their appetite. Eight-plus-one capacity, with silver shot preseasoned with a mix of garlic and blessed by a Catholic priest, a Muslim Imam, a Jewish rabbi, and a Mormon deacon. Underbarrel holy water grenade launcher optional." He delivered it all with the vacuous pleasantness of a sales rep reading from the pamphlet, but there was no mistaking the way his gun barrel moved from target to target in the small hall as pleasant.

Pallas grunted. "What do you want here, Warden?" he said. I swear, his voice actually rattled the little bones in my ear.

"I need to see King Haemon and his daughter," I said.

"What you want matters nothing here, human," said Rathton. He took a step forward again, ignoring Larry's gun. He didn't touch me, but he got close enough that when he blinked I felt the wind of it on my face. His face split in a dangerous grin. "The queen has withdrawn her Blessing."

"I'm sure I'll dampen my pillows with salty tears of woe tonight," I answered. Larry let out a quiet guffaw. "Until then, I need to see Haemon. Now."

Rathton looked like he was considering mayhem. Larry's shotgun poked past me again, this time over my shoulder and coming to rest on Rathton's cheek. The vampire's skin sizzled as the crosses on the barrel came into contact with him – apparently Larry was a believer in the power of the cross. Or maybe just the power of any cross in one of *his* guns.

Probably the latter.

Regardless, Rathton still didn't withdraw. His smile only grew as his skin charred. "I shall look forward to tearing out your throat and consuming it before your wife and children. How many is it now? Four?"

For a second I saw red. I wouldn't have been surprised if my own eyes went full-vamp in that moment. I restrained myself, but only with the promise that I wouldn't forget what he'd said, and I'd make sure someday that *he* never stopped regretting it.

Pallas stepped close as well. "You need to make like an egg and beat it, Warden," he said. He didn't say it with rancor – unlike Rathton, he seemed almost sad about what he was doing. "Seriously, you gotta burn rubber, like, now."

"You don't believe it, do you?" I said, the words coming out in desperation. "You don't think she did it?"

Pallas' eyes flicked toward Rathton. Just an instant, but I noticed it. "It don't matter what I think. I'm no whiz kid, just a regular guy who tries to keep all the cats cool. Now, please go."

I held my ground. "When's the trial?" I said. "How long do I have?"

Rathton finally backed away from me – or, more precisely, from Larry's gun. He laughed. "As though anyone here would tell you *anyth* –"

"Tonight. The full moon," said Pallas.

"Don't talk to him!" screeched Rathton, rounding on the Lycaon. "Don't speak a word to him!"

Pallas eyed him calmly. "The big man told me to protect the Great Pack and the High Court. The big man told me not to let anyone in. But the big man never told me I can't talk to his personal pig or that I have to listen to a thick square like you."

As Rathton dissolved into a spitting fit of rage, Pallas turned to me and said, "You only have a few hours, my brother."

I looked out the window. I hadn't realized what time it was, how long I'd been asleep. It only dawned on me that it was late evening. With the sun going down as late as it did, it could be as late as six or seven o'clock. And that meant, what, four or five hours until the moon rose?

"Please. Please let me talk to them."

Pallas looked genuinely conflicted. Then shook his head. "I would if I could but I can't so I won't."

I bowed to Pallas and said, "Thank you, Lord Pallas." I believed he was helping me as much as he could, and the help was appreciated.

He bowed back, then leaned toward me. Larry's gun shifted to point at him, but I gestured for him to pull it back. "I don't trust them," Pallas whispered to me. Though "whisper" is a pretty loose term when you sound like you're gargling asphalt.

"The vampires?" I whispered back.

He shook his head. "*Any* of them. The lights went loopy right after Anderson showed up with the Peacemaker. Not long, just a couple quick flashes, but not five minutes later the Sucky High Court bigwigs all showed up. I think someone's snitching, and it doesn't make me like what's going on."

"Why are you telling me?"

He sniffed, then shrugged. "You've got an honest smell."

"That's Irish Spring," I said.

Pallas actually smiled. Then he leaned back. "Lay some rubber, pig. Hash out the real deal, and make some noise."

I nodded. Then turned back toward the elevator, Larry behind me.

Rathton's voice followed me out. "Oh, that's right," he said. I looked back at him. He buffed the fully-extended claws of his right hand against his lapel. "It wasn't four children. You have five, don't you? Or at least... you did."

Larry looked at me. At the expression on my face. "You want to take them?" he asked.

I shook my head. It was all I could do without losing control. If I made a single other move, then I *would* go back. I *would* attack Rathton, and whatever tenuous peace there was between lycans and vampires would dissolve as I sought revenge for a taunt against my dead child.

62

I got into the elevator, jammed a button, and was halfway down before my brain caught up to where my body was going.

I needed to get to the con floor.

"Was it true?"

Larry's voice was so soft the casual onlooker would have sworn there was no way this was *the* Larry Correia, speaking as quietly as any other mere mortal.

I didn't look at him, but I nodded. The fact that I'd lost a daughter wasn't secret – though the exact facts of that loss were something very few people knew. Even so, it's not exactly something I toss around at parties, so it wasn't surprising that Larry hadn't heard about it.

"I'm sorry," he said. Simple, and enough.

I nodded. A moment later, he said, "You really need to get to the lycan princess?"

I nodded again. A sideways glance showed me he was inspecting one of his guns –

(*Where does he* keep *them all?*)

– and had a dark gleam in his eyes.

I shook my head. "Not like that, Larry."

"I could get you in there," he said.

"Yeah, but the whole point is to solve this case in a way that *doesn't* end with all-out war between lycans and vampires. Pretty sure blasting our way in would negate that chance."

Larry looked like he was going to say something, but instead he dug a small object out of his pocket. I gawked.

"Is that a Port?"

Larry nodded. The item in his hand was a plastic circle that measured about three inches in diameter. It looked like a stargate, just like the one in the actual movie *Stargate,* or one of the TV-spinoffs.

I was never sure if the people who made the show knew about the Port, or if whatever wizard created them was a fan of the show. But I knew that what Larry held in his hand was one of the most expensive enchanted objects around. They were also incredibly rare; I'd never seen one before in the flesh, and only knew of six in existence.

Larry was successful, yeah – both as a novelist and a supernatural gunsmith. But this was a whole other level, even for him.

I was so shocked to see the Port that it didn't even dawn on me what he was about to do until it was already done. Larry lifted the Port to his eye like a ginormous monocle; looked through it; and, as he lay his free hand across my shoulder, whispered, "Moonbeam."

Remember how I wasn't sure if I got smaller or Gandhi's room got bigger? Something similar happened now, only on a much larger scale. Larry and I both shrank, or the Port grew. When it was too big to hold anymore, Larry let go of it, and the ring fell around us like an ornate hula hoop. The second it did, we passed from one world to another.

On the side of the Port we had started out in, there was only me, Larry, the elevator. The entirety of our worlds defined by the box that was the only thing we saw.

On the other side of the Port, was... everything.

It's hard to explain, because how do you use mere words to define infinity? The best I can come up with is that I suddenly felt a bit of what an Oracle like Mercedes' son must feel. The whole of creation in your grasp at once.

It was awesome. It was beautiful.

It was terrible.

We're not designed for this, so at nearly the same instant my mind started taking everything in, it also began running from all that pressed down on it. I wanted to scream – maybe I *did* scream, but it was lost in the vastness of everything around me.

Then I felt the hand on my shoulder. Larry. I looked to him, and there in the bright stars, in the lights that were every human, every Otherworlder, every plant and animal and planet and star in the universe, one glowed a bit brighter than the others.

Larry reached out with a hand that somehow spanned the infinities, and touched the star with his finger.

As he did, everything fell back to itself again. I once more stood in my place in the universe, instead of having the universe in me.

Larry still had his hand on my shoulder, and as he took it away I saw something flare in his hands, the Port dying out as they always did after their single use.

"Beautiful," he murmured, and I knew he must be thinking of the universe that had just been a part of us.

We were no longer in the elevator. We were in a hotel room I knew. The bedroom of King Haemon, in the penthouse suite the Great Pack had rented.

Moonbeam lay on the bed, mute and motionless.

The guards in the four corners of the room were neither mute *nor* motionless. All four fully transformed Lycaons stepped forward on muscles coiled to spring, their muzzles pulled back and teeth bared.

"My, what big teeth you have," I whispered. I hadn't known what Larry was going to do – certainly there was no way to guess he would be willing to spend millions of dollars to get me into this room – but even if I had, I don't know what I would have done to take down the guards. I had the plastic gun Larry'd given me, but, again, the whole point of what I was doing was to *avoid* war. And killing a bunch of Lycaons in their room didn't seem like a good call for that.

The closest Lycaon made a sound that was the beginning of a roar.

Great. The only way to make this any worse would be to get the rest of the Great Pack in here with us.

I estimated the total time remaining before Larry and I were torn to pieces at about three seconds. One second for the guards to attack, one second for the noise to bring in every lycan in the main room of the penthouse, and a third for the whole "now you die!" part.

It didn't happen. Because Larry needed *less* than a second. The instant the Lycaon started to make a noise, Larry spun. The move was surprisingly lithe for someone his size, and as he turned, his hands flung out and I saw something catch the light.

The guards all stopped moving. The one who'd been growling gagged oh-so-quietly. Then all four of them slowly folded to the ground.

I turned to Larry. "What was *that*?" I asked.

He had a huge grin on his face. He held up something: some kind of dart, about two inches long, with a clear plastic housing that ended in a needle point.

I could see silver inside the housing. Bad, bad news. "You killed them?" I said.

Larry shook his head. "No. But thanks for the vote of confidence."

"Then what –"

"Quicksilver." I frowned, so Larry continued, "Historians of the supernatural believed for a long time that when it spoke of silver as a weakness of the werewolf, it really referred to mercury, since in ancient times people thought mercury was just a *kind* of silver. Of course, anyone who knows anything knows that silver *does* kill them, and most people don't go beyond that. But I did. And I discovered that if you alloy mercury with a tiny trace of silver nitrate, you get the ultimate wolf-trank." He eyed the dart. "That actually might be a good name for this." His voice changed to that of a cheesy television announcer. "Wolf-trank – when you have to put a big dog to sleep! Accept no substitutes."

"Why are you here?"

The voice jolted me back to the task at hand. I turned to the bed after murmuring a quick, "Way to go!" to Larry.

Moonbeam hadn't moved. She still lay on the bed, but her eyes were open and she clearly knew what was going on around her. She'd obviously been crying, and for some reason the ugliness of her physical shape was dimmed by grief. The features were still just as horrific, but the eyes allowed me to see a soul that was marred and injured rather than grotesque.

I wanted to weep in that moment. Not just for Moonbeam, but for myself since I had seen so little of what she *was*, focusing so much on what she looked like.

Larry busied himself making sure the guards were all down for the count as I knelt beside the bed. Moonbeam didn't move, though she watched me through still-glimmering tears.

When I was eye level with her, I said, "When I first showed you the pictures on your sister's phone, you were shocked. I thought it was because of what was happening, but that wasn't it, was it? You were shocked because I'd found your secret." She said nothing, so I pulled out Calista's phone. I flipped to the picture of Calista in the Nespda bar, and pointed to the "man's" hand in the forefront. "This is your hand, right? And the ring's a token for the glamour that made you look like that?"

For a long moment, there was nothing. Then, slowly, Moonbeam nodded.

I sat back on my heels, flipping through the pictures as I spoke. "You went with her to Nespda the first time, didn't you?" Another nod. "And that's where you always were when you said you were going to the 501st meetings?"

Moonbeam finally spoke. Her voice was soft and gravelly. "Not always. I went to the meetings in the beginning, then went to Nespda from there. After a while, though...." She shrugged.

I got to the photo that showed Calista getting dressed, her expression in the reflection excited, uneasy, scared. I didn't show it to Moonbeam, just stared at it myself as I said, "You've been going to Nespda for a long time, haven't you?" She nodded. "Why?"

She laughed, a bitter, derisive laugh. "Do you even have to ask?" She pointed at her face. "Who would be friends with this? Where else could I go to find companionship?"

I shook my head. "But you have glamours. And your father –"

"My father loves me," she said fiercely, and I sensed that here was one of the few pillars of her existence. "But I'm his daughter, and I need more than just a father in my life. And as for glamours," again she laughed, "everyone knows they're not real. Everyone knows that under the glamour, they're getting…." She gestured to her face. "They're getting this. They know the glamour will fade, and they'll be left with a nightmare. At least at Nespda, everyone knows the appearances are a lie. And they're okay with it."

Again, sadness gripped me. I'd never really known Moonbeam, but would I have driven her to this decision of I had?

"But *Nespda*? Aren't there places that cater to… uh… lonely werewolves? You had to know what Nespda does, what its specialty is."

"And so what?" she nearly barked. "Is what they do so bad?"

"They traffic Otherworlders against their will."

She frowned. "I know. That was part of why I stopped going."

"When? In February?" She nodded. "But before that, you liked the life?" Another nod. "Is that why you introduced Calista to it?"

Moonbeam was struck utterly dumb for a moment. Then she started laughing, long and hard. I was worried she might bring in some of the lycans from the next room, but she buried her head in a pillow until the laughter subsided. When she turned back, her eyes still glimmered with tears, but half of them were born of laughter.

"Is that what you think happened?" she whispered. She snorted, then said, "Calista has been going there for years. *She* was the one who introduced *me*."

"But you said –"

"I said I went with Calista to Nespda the first time. I thought you meant *my* first time, not hers." She shook her head. "Everyone always thought Calista was this virginal angel, the perfect daughter of the Great Pack's king." She poked a finger down her throat. "She's anything but. She's a liar, a thief, a sex addict, and a pervert."

"So you killed her?"

I knew the answer already, but it had to be asked, if only because that was the next logical question.

As expected, Moonbeam shook her head. "I *loved* her. I adored my sister, and –"

"You adored a liar, a thief, a pervert?"

"I adored a liar, thief, pervert who loved *me*." The words came as a whisper, but they carried the force of a lifetime's conviction. Moonbeam finally sat up. She folded her hands in her lap, rubbing them nearly manically as she spoke. "I've always been ugly. Always… like this." She pointed at herself. If this had been my daughter, I would have pointed out that she was more than the skin she wore. But I said nothing to Moonbeam, and a bit of me wondered what kind of Hell I might earn for myself, by adding now to the Hell this girl had suffered.

"Everyone, my whole life, turned away from me. All of them. I knew how ugly I was without ever seeing myself in a mirror, because I could see that disfigurement in their eyes." She waved offhandedly. "Oh, Dad loved me. But even him… as close as he held me, as hard as he hugged me, there was always my face coming between us." She laughed, a hitching laugh that was nearly a sob in itself. "Once I came home from something – I forget what, maybe just the store. Someone there was so mean to me, and he held me and said, 'Baby-girl, you are so much more than what others see.' I remember it like it was yesterday. 'You are so much more than what others see.' And I believed it." Her eyes found mine. "I ran up the stairs, and for a second I thought everything might be all right. I thought, 'If Dad believes in me, then to hell with everyone else.'" She laughed that same laugh again. "I felt so much love for him. So much…. I turned back to say thank you, to tell him that he wasn't just King of the Great Pack, he was the best dad in the whole world. And you know what I saw?"

"No."

"He was *shuddering*. Rubbing his arms up and down like he had bugs crawling on them. Because he'd been so close. So close to *me*. So I ran upstairs, and there…."

"Calista."

She nodded. "She was in my room. She kissed me because she saw I was sad. We played tea party. She kissed me. She *kissed me*." Moonbeam was silent a moment, lost in thought, then added, "She was always a pervert. But who else but a pervert would love this?" She pointed at her face.

A sick feeling washed over me. "You said she kissed you…." The words hung there. "But you would never kill her, because –"

"Because I loved her. And she loved me."

The way she emphasized "loved" chilled me still further. Apparently the royal family of the High Court of Vampires had no taboos about incestuous relationships. But lycans certainly did.

It seemed Nespda had been far from the worst thing Calista had been involved in.

"Why did she take you to Nespda?" I asked.

"It was a game," said Moonbeam. "We both wore masks. I pretended to be a man, and she pretended to work there. We got a room from the madam, and…." She sighed, her eyes lost in memory. "That was the best weekend I've ever had."

I glanced at Larry. He was hunched over the last of the guards, apparently caught as flat-footed as I was over all this. His mouth hung open, his eyes so wide they reminded me of the T-rex eyeball scene in *Jurassic Park*.

I turned back to Moonbeam. "Then why'd you help her work at Nespda?"

"Help her work?" Moonbeam shook her head. "I don't understand."

I showed her the picture. Calista getting dressed up – or down, depending on how you look at it. I tapped the white smear in the mirror. "That's you, right? In your stormtrooper costume?"

Moonbeam stared at the picture for a long time. She finally nodded. "Calista said she had a present for me. A surprise, a new part of the game. She'd rented a room, like we always do. I was excited when I showed up, and she looked like this," she said, pointing at the phone. "Until she told me this was going to be her first 'work uniform.'" She shook her head. "I didn't understand. Even when I finally did understand, I didn't want to." She looked at me, eyes reflecting the torn spirit behind them. "How could she do that? How could she take the most magical place we'd found and turn it into something...." She couldn't finish.

"Why did she?" I asked.

"The treaty. Aseas presented it, and Dad jumped on the idea. Calista went along – she isn't a good person, but she really does want the best for our people. She wanted to help. She even loved Eustace, I think, in some ways. But when the treaty became a real possibility, when negotiations started in earnest, I think it flipped a switch in Calista. I told her none of that would matter, that she and I would be there for each other forever and that Eustace didn't have to know how important we were to each other. It didn't matter. She couldn't be tied down."

"She was already tied down to you, wasn't she? Or does that not count as tied down?"

Sometimes when I play princesses with my youngest daughter, or build block cities with her, I'll do something that earns me a specific kind of wide-eyed stare. An innocent asking, "How can you *not* understand something so obvious?" She'll remind me that I'm the Princess of Cookies, *not* the Princess of Cake, because there's no such *thing* as the Princess of Cake. Or she'll put my block somewhere else because "Silly Daddy, cars don't go there, they go in the house!"

That was the look I got from Moonbeam now. "Tied down to me? Calista was never tied down to me. She's never been tied down to anyone. She shared with everyone, and everyone was happy with what they got. I didn't own her, I didn't tie her down. I was just happy with what she shared with me."

I thought for a moment. "It got worse the closer the treaty came to reality, didn't it? For you?"

Calista nodded. "Nespda used to be our special place. Not anymore. I understood at first – truly I did – but it got harder and harder to be there with her. She did more and more... things. More and more...." She shuddered.

"And after the betrothal? In February?" I asked.

"It was like she went crazy. She ran around like she was trying to push as much life into her as possible, like it wasn't a treaty and a wedding that loomed, but her death." She shuddered. "I could barely stand to be near her when she was like that."

"But you went anyway."

"Yes. But not so often. And not so long."

"Do you think anyone else knew what she was doing at Nespda? We know Prince Eustace was at Nespda at least once, but could someone else have followed her there? Someone in the High Court?"

Moonbeam shook her head, but I couldn't tell if she was saying she didn't know who might have done this, or just saying she didn't think anyone would have done it at all. She fell silent.

I did, too, something inside telling me to wait. "My dad," she finally said.

"Your dad what? Your dad knew?"

"I think so."

"Why do you think so?"

She shrugged. "I just got the feeling that someone was watching. I figured it was him."

"Aseas says he saw you near the room where Calista was murdered."

She looked away from me. "I was there."

I thought of what Gandhi had told me: that Moonbeam had been at a meeting of the 501st during the time of the murder. "I have – had – a friend who saw you at a meeting of the 501st. How could you be in both places at the same time?"

She snorted. "I've been doing this a long time. I have doubles at every con. Not that look like this," she said, gesturing again at her face. "But that have my same body type, the same cosplay armor. I go into a prearranged bathroom stall dressed as a stormtrooper, they're waiting for me in there. We wait a minute, then they leave. I just hang out there for ten or fifteen minutes, then I leave with a different helmet – *Force Awakens* instead of *New Hope*."

"Okay, so you were at the murder scene. But why?"

"Why?"

I barely said the word before Moonbeam said, "Not to kill her!" and new tears started spilling over her cheeks.

"Then why?"

"She wanted to go to Nespda again. Wanted me to go with her. 'We can have fun like it used to be,' she said."

"What did you say?"

"I told her that I'd only go if it really *was* like it used to be. Just her and me. She told me she couldn't." Moonbeam laughed that dry, empty laugh again. "She told me that wasn't fun enough."

"How did that make you feel?"

"If you're looking for me to say 'angry,' then you're looking in the wrong place. I just felt... used up. Stretched tight and old. The irony is that after I left the room, do you know where I went?"

"Not the meeting of the 501st, I take it."

"No. I went looking for somewhere to kill myself. Some way I could 'accidentally' die without bringing shame on the Pack or on my father."

I believed her. Completely, unreservedly.

"Moonbeam, if all this is true then why aren't you telling people? Why aren't you telling your dad – especially if you think he already knows? It would at least show another side to the story, and you wouldn't look as guilty."

She gave me that wide-eyed "when did you forget the meaning of life?" look again. "I'm a lycan."

I didn't get it. So I said, "I don't get it."

"If I tell all this, my family will fall. The Lycaons might even see a shift in leadership at this, a time when our entire species hangs in the balance." She looked at her still-fidgeting hands. "I've done wrong. But I was ready to die before, and now... if I can take the blame for this, and if my father can show by prosecuting me and turning me over to Pack Justice that he is strong and fair and just before all, then maybe my house and my clan and my people can weather this." I saw strength in her eyes. Not the mad strength of anger, the stormy rage I'd seen in her face before. This was the strength only the badly broken can manifest, the strength of someone who has decided to do something greater than they are, that it will destroy them, and that they don't care if it does.

My back and legs were aching, so I finally stood. I put my hands in the small of my back and pressed forward, then said, "Who do you think killed her?" She didn't answer, so I took her shoulders and said, "Don't you understand, Moonbeam? You say you want your people to live and to thrive. Well I'm telling you now that even your death won't help that. War is coming, and if we're going to have any hope of stopping that from happening, we have to find out who really killed Calista. And we have to get justice for her. Not false justice, but the real thing."

I leaned in close to her, and didn't notice her ugliness. Just her eyes, which were sad and strong; the eyes of someone not loved enough, and who has far better to give than anyone really knew. "Moonbeam, I believe the universe takes note of our pain. I believe that when justice is done, it balances things in a way no sacrifice – however noble – can ever do. So please, help me."

Moonbeam stared at nothing. She was lost, either in memories of the past or a sick fascination for the course she had laid for herself.

I felt a hand on my shoulder. "We have to go. The darts are going to wear off soon."

I nodded. Larry pulled *another* Port out of his pocket. "How many of those do you have?" I said.

He grinned. "You wouldn't believe me if I told you."

I looked back at Moonbeam. She still stared into whatever nothing she believed she deserved. "The whole time we were talking just now, you didn't sound like a hippie at all. I think that's interesting. I think you've got a lot inside you that would surprise and delight other people."

It may have been my imagination, but I thought the trace of a smile graced her lips.

Larry held the Port to his eye and said, "Elevator," and the Port fell over and around and through us and we were gone.

63

The elevator doors opened to the lobby. Larry didn't move, just said, "Where to?"

"You get back to your life, Larry," I said.

He grinned broadly. "What do you think I'm doing now?"

"I know. But I'm gonna take it from here."

He nodded. "You sure you don't want backup?"

"I don't think I'll need it. But keep your phone on, okay?"

"You got it."

I exited the elevator. Larry stayed on, and as the elevator closed I saw him pat his head and then use the same hand to point at me. Tactical signaling, which I'd researched for *This Darkness Light*.[34] It meant "I'll cover you."

I stood there after the doors closed, looking at my spectral reflection in the polished steel. I was alone, but I had friends. I was in over my head, but determined not to give up. Bad people – and not people – had threatened to hurt my family, but I would die before that happened.

A mix of good and evil. Struggle and failure and triumph and the potential for more of any and all of them.

In other words, a pretty good example of that thing called life.

I took a breath, then turned away from myself. Time to go to work.

I headed straight for Come and Play. The booth was still empty. SuperGhoul had seen something she shouldn't have, and was laying low. As for the rest of them: if *you* found out your coworker came from one of the most powerful families in the world, who was leading a double life that may have led to her

---

[34] "[Another]winner." – *The Horror Fiction Review*

"[Collings'] latest and honestly greatest work..." – *Media Mikes*

"Such a good book! Everyone read it!" – *My mommy*

death, and you were a part of that double life... well, would you come to work after that?

No, I didn't think so.

I didn't mind that the booth was empty, though. I wasn't there for the babes.

Old Crabbypants was still in her booth, her hook flying faster than the needle of a sewing machine as she used glittery yarn to crochet a chastity belt.

"They're gone," she cackled. "Gone, and good riddance to all that flesh. People shouldn't dress like that. The only good and right way is to cover yourself up in three or four petticoats, then use a modesty curtain for reproductive necessity."

I stared at her. I had no words. She grinned as though my stare were a resounding agreement.

I tore my eyes away from her and walked into the booth. The LEDs and other lights that were supposed to illuminate the space still weren't on. Which I'd expected. I was starting to see a pattern.

When I first saw Calista's body, the exit sign in the hall flickered. The lights turned off and on when Kevin Anderson came in with Dave Butler. At the time I'd assumed that was just a bit of showmanship on Anderson's part – I've never known a wizard who didn't try to increase his mystique with that kind of parlor trick now and then. Now, I wasn't so sure.

Gandhi had complained about the surges at the con, and the light in his hole under the surveillance room had flickered almost constantly while we were down there. Pallas had said the lights went off and on right after Anderson brought Aseas to the Great Pack, and five minutes later the High Court was there. Coincidence?

I wanted to get a closer look at these places, but most were out of my reach. Gandhi's room was gone, destroyed by the Vortex. It had been made clear that I wasn't welcome near the Great Pack, so going back to the ninth floor wasn't an option, and I hadn't even thought to look around when Larry Ported us into Moonbeam's room – and even if I had, I probably still would have concentrated on talking to her, not inspecting the wiring.

As for the murder scene, I had no doubt that Blake had posted guards everywhere, and given them specific instructions to either keep me out or simply detain me so I couldn't meddle.

I couldn't go to any of those places – not right now.

But there was one more place where I'd seen lighting issues. The Come and Play booth. The lights had been off when I first went there looking for people who worked with Calista. When I returned later, to look around for Calista's things, they were out again... and the old lady with the fascination for crocheted medieval fetishware had told me the girls who worked there had gone to see "facilities management," because the lights kept going out.

(*"They were really mad. It's the fifth time it's happened today," she said, and sniffed. "The universe's judgment on whoring, you ask me."*)

I looked around the booth. The lights were all plugged into a massive surge protector, orange and black plugs sitting there like little piglets suckling at an electric teat.

I looked at the surge protector. There was a power switch, and I clicked it back and forth from on to off and back again a few times. The lights at the booth stayed dim.

"What're you looking for?" asked the old lady. It was almost time for the con floor to close, and she began closing up shop, one eye on her merchandise and one eye on me.

I ignored her. I didn't like her, and I wasn't in the mood to hide that fact.

Instead, I followed the surge protector. It was plugged into an industrial extension cord which had been taped to the floor, the whole thing then covered with more layers of tape so no one would trip on it. The extension cord ran in a fairly straight line, passing behind several more exhibitor spaces. I followed it until it plugged into an outlet at the base of a support column.

The extension cord wasn't the only one plugged into that outlet. There were three other extension cords plugged in there as well, and each one went to a different exhibitor space. A quick check verified that all *those* spaces had full electricity.

I switched the locations of the Come and Play extension cord and the one that powered the A Life Full of Henna booth. A few people at the henna space shouted as their light went out, but they went quiet once I plugged their cord back into the wall – even though it was in the socket the Come and Play space had been using.

So not the socket. The problem's downstream.

You may be asking why I cared so much. And honestly, I couldn't tell you. I was following a combination of evidence and hunch. It was also just about all I had left, so I might as well be thorough, right?

Everything was working up to the point of the wall. Which meant the problem with the Come and Play lights, whatever it was, had to be in the extension cord that led from the wall to the surge protector, or in the surge protector itself. It couldn't be in the individual lights – the idea that they all blew at once for separate reasons strained believability.

Cord, or surge protector.

To look at the extension cord would have meant ripping up fifty feet of orange cord from the tape securing it to the floor, then cracking open the housings of the male and female ends and slitting the length of the insulative plastic to see if there were any breaks or flaws in the wiring. That sounded really time-consuming and generally like a pain.

So I went to the surge protector.

I unplugged all the power cords that fed into it, then yanked it away from the extension cord that fed to the power. I turned the white box over.

"Yeah, they already looked at it," said the old lady next door.

"Oh, well, if *they* already did," I mumbled.

The surge protector looked normal. There were a few screws at either end. I always carry a Carolina tool when I'm at cons – never know when you'll need to unscrew or screw or cut or file something to get your table set up – and I took it out now and quickly opened the housing of the surge protector.

Inside, it looked pretty much like you'd expect an open surge protector to look. Fuses, braided wires, coils of copper.

"Nothing to see here, officer," I mumbled. "Everyone move al –"

I frowned. Pulled the housing of the surge protector close. It was too dark to make out what I was looking at, so I left the Come and Play booth, walking into the main aisle where it was brighter.

As soon as I did that, I could make out what had been hidden inside the housing. A scratch. I shouldn't even have noticed it – just a lucky angle of the light that let me spot it. And even now, it was barely visible.

But barely was enough.

It was a bit bigger than the one I'd seen in Gandhi's room, on the edge of the tablet he used to monitor security. But other than that, it looked exactly the same as that mark had:

A voice spoke in my ear, sending a blast of air that smelled like a mix of halitosis, denture gum, and perhaps a trace of dried meat made from wildebeest anuses. "You're not going to find anything," said the old lady. She had finished packing her booth away and now tied a crocheted monstrosity that I guessed was supposed to be a bonnet on her head. "The man already checked it out."

I took a fast step sideways, trying not to gag on the smell of her breath. If this was how she smelled every day, no wonder she was jealous of the attention the booth babes got.

"What... what do you mean?" I wheezed. My nose hairs were actively trying to retreat into their follicles.

"The maintenance man already came by. He was the one who installed the surge protector, then he happened to be nearby when the power started acting funny, and when the girls complained he told them to complain to the power grid department." She sniffed. "He looked like a fine man. Not some flesh-following whore-lover."

"Wait, so someone other than the girls installed this?" I asked, holding up the pieces of the surge protector.

The old lady eyed me suspiciously. "Of course. That's what I said. I remember because I was putting the finishing touches on a codpiece made from Solomon's knots and a trim of –"

"Sorry, not to interrupt – and I *am* fascinated, my mother crochets, too, and we both totally hate flesh – but what did this person look like?"

She frowned. "Small. Real small. Maybe five feet tall, and skinny as a crochet hook. Head like one, too, all crooked and shiny. Not a lot of hair. Sweaty. Gray uniform and wearing gloves. Seemed like a good boy." Her eyes gleamed in a way that would have put Leatherface off his lunch. "The kind of boy I could dress up to be so pretty."

"Huh." I looked at the tiny scratch on the surge protector again. "And when the lights went off, he told them to talk to the 'power grid department'?"

The question brought her back out of whatever crochet-wrapped Happy Place she had momentarily fled to. "Yep. Nice boy, like I said. He seemed revolted by all the flesh."

"How so?"

"Just really uncomfortable. Like he didn't want to be there." She sniffed. "Can't say I blame him. Whores. Whores and harlots and floozies. The world falls apart, and we dress up in our bikinis and our *longer-ray*, our teddies and cheekies and g-strings and beaded lace open crotch panties and –"

For a woman who hated "flesh," she had an encyclopedic knowledge of all the ways a woman could showcase it. I tuned her out before I got caught in her web of crazy, and stared at the surge protector. The mark on it.

I turned the surge protector a bit in my hands.

"Holy crap!"

The crazy crochet lady with enough repressed sexual energy to put the entire country of Japan to shame nodded. "Yep," she said. "Holy crap is right. I mean, they flaunt around in their bodystockings and stringbodies that showcase the evil sensuality of a woman's gracefully curved buttocks while –"

Without taking my eyes away from what I'd seen, I said, "This man, the nice boy, did he take one of the girls with him?"

She seemed surprised. "Why yes, how did you know? He offered to walk one of the girls down there and she –"

"Was it the slutty ninja?" I said.

The old lady eyed me suspiciously. "How did you know? You been watching her? You *stalking* her? You want to date her or something? Maybe watch her dress up in a merry widow and then peel it off with your teeth, leaving only a sheer satin panty to showcase the gentle curve of her young –"

"Whoa!" I practically screamed it. "First of all, no. No to all of it. Second of all, you are a weird old lady in desperate need of psychiatric attention. And third of all...."

I turned and ran. I had no "third of all," but I figured leaving like that might buy me an extra moment before she started screaming about my fleshy urges.

Surprisingly, no screams followed me. Maybe the mad crocheter had realized she *did* need help. Maybe my scream had given her an idea for a new way to crochet a Spartan jock strap. Or maybe she'd simply had a heart attack.

I didn't know, and I didn't care. I just ran to my first destination. The information booth was on the outer rim of the con floor, and a small line of people were waiting to find out where the bathroom was or if there was any way they could get a short half an hour alone with the guys from *Supernatural* or other equally critical things.

I elbowed to the front of the line, which earned me more than one dirty look. I brandished the pieces of surge protector like a club, though, and everyone shut up.

I expected that reaction: If someone threatens you with a handful of disassembled electronics, it's usually best to avoid arguing with them.

The information lady – who was approximately six hundred years old and probably couldn't answer any questions not spoken in Latin – eyed me with mild interest but didn't say anything. Undoubtedly too busy wondering whatever happened to *Golden Girls*.[35]

The information booth had stacks of papers on it, mostly schedules of the convention's daily events. I yanked one off the pile and flipped through it. Found what I was looking for.

"Yes!" I screamed. Everyone backed away from me.

I expected that reaction, too: If someone who has just threatened you with a handful of disassembled electronics now starts shouting to himself, distancing yourself is always a good idea.

I ran. I dropped the program schedule on the floor behind me. I didn't need it. For the first time, I actually understood what was going on.

---

[35] Or *Aurea Puellae*, as they called it in the good ol' days of the Roman Empire.

64

It was almost eight o'clock, which meant I didn't have a lot of time. I doubted I could get backup on deck quickly enough to help, but I called Larry as I ran. If he was still close by then there might be a chance.

I got his voicemail. "Hi, this is Larry. You either know what to do, or you're too dumb for me to talk to."

The beep sounded, and I gasped out the words as I ran.[36] "Larry, I need you to get to 403-C. I know how the surveillance feeds got screwed up, and I know how the killer got Calista alone. I'm on my way now, but I could use backup."

That was all that needed to be said. If Larry came, he'd show up the way he always did: loaded for bear and ready for mayhem. If not, well, I'd do what *I* always did: muddle through and hope for the best.

At this point you might be wondering what all the fuss is about. Because we have a few minutes to kill before I get to 403-C, I'll tell you. Remember how nice I am when my birthday rolls around![37]

The lights had been one clue. The marks another. The fact that Robot Dave keeled over when he licked Gandhi's tablet was one more. But it wasn't until I looked at the mark in the right way that I put it together. I'd seen this – both in Gandhi's lair and at Come and Play:

---

[36] I'm not including the gasps in this record. I hate it when they… write things… for ten pages… in the… style of… someone breathless… who just… needs to….

You get the point.

[37] October 25th. I accept presents, but prefer checks or money order.

Gandhi hadn't let me touch the tablet where I first saw the mark. But this time I could look at it from a different perspective. When I turned the surge protector slightly, changing the angle of the mark, I saw this:

And honestly, even that might not have been enough – it still looked pretty random. But luckily I had a friend who liked to sound smart.

(*"You must grow in patience when you meet with great wrongs, and they will be powerless to vex you. Leonardo da Vinci, 1492 to 1519."*)

After Dave said that, I hassled him about the word "vex"

–

("Who uses words like 'vex'?" I responded. "Michaelbrent Collings, usually between one-ninety and two-ten.")

– and that made me wonder if my subconscious had already put all this together and was gently trying to get my higher mental functions to catch on.

Regardless, the fact was the word "VEX" had been scratched onto all the electrical equipment that malfunctioned or just failed outright.

Vex – or, as it is said in Old English, *gremian*.

The gremian are literally "the vexing ones." They have an obsession with technology, but in the opposite way as dwarves. Dwarves conquer technology, they turn it inside out and make it do whatever they want. The gremian have a pathological need to make it *mis*behave. Everything from wagon wheels to cutting edge tech.

Never heard of them? Sure you have. *Gremian*, like most other Old English words, changed during the transition to the English we speak today. Just as *eald* became old and *brodor* became brother, *gremian* turned into gremlin.

Gremlins aren't little small, scaly beasts like you see in the movie *Gremlins* (or the underappreciated *Gremlins II*). They look completely human, with one glaring – but easily hidden – exception. Finding one in the convention would normally be just about impossible, but for once luck was on my side.

I got to 403-C, and before I even went in the room I knew I was in the right place. The light in the hallway outside the room was flickering. Gremlins physically sabotage things, but they also emit a supernatural aura that tends to interfere with electrical function, particularly lights. The aura doesn't last long, but for a few minutes after a gremlin passes through the area the lights tend to act wonky. When they mark something – like Gandhi's computers, the CCTVs, and the surge protector, the problems become more pronounced. A big enough effect to, for example, even short circuit a magic robot who gets too close to the infected hardware.

The in the hall lights flickered again. Harder.

"Boo-yah," I said, and opened the door.

403-C was a smallish room, only capable of holding maybe one hundred people at the most. Because the con was winding down for the night, and because this wasn't one of the more popular presentations, there were only a dozen or so people in the audience. Up front, a twenty-something was talking as film clips showed on the screen behind her. A high-stakes game of pool between a man who didn't want to die and one who already had. A man dropping his daughter's doll into the trash. A man surrounded by apocalyptic destruction, and who looks thrilled at the fact that everyone he knows is gone... until he steps on his glasses.

"The reason these are the best *Twilight Zone* episodes of all time isn't just that they have the best stories, but they *say* the most important things. Talking about the nature of family, of love, of hate, of...."

She kept talking, and from what I heard it was a pretty good presentation. But I was only half listening. I was looking for the gremlin.

I knew he or she would be at the Best Episodes in *Twilight Zone* History presentation. Gremlins love watching themselves on TV, and I've never met a single one who won't move mountains to watch any part of the famous "Nightmare at 20,000 Feet" episode which pits a pre-Kirk William Shatner against a gremlin intent on wrecking the plane Shatner is a passenger on.

It wasn't hard to pick out the gremlin. I didn't even bother looking for the "nice man" who looked like a crochet hook that Lady Repression had mentioned; I had no doubt the gremlin had been disguised.

Even so, I picked the Otherworlder out with ease. I slid into the seat behind her. She looked human, of course. A trim girl who looked to be around seventeen or eighteen. Hair so dark it was nearly black, cut shoulder-length, with thick glasses that didn't really make her look nerdy but instead imparted a fairly cute emo vibe. She wore a black *Big Bang Theory* t-shirt and dark jeans that looked like they had been fitted on her legs in a zero-g vacuum. Nothing unusual about her, except the dark gloves on her hands, which didn't really fit with the "casual goth" look she was going for.

Still, not the kind of thing that would mark her as unusual, especially not in a place where people dressed up as Hairy Dude Slave Leia or Pregnant Thor. In fact, the only one who might notice it at all… was me.

I leaned forward. "I love this one," I said, pointing at the screen. Agnes Moorehead, dressed in an old-fashioned nightdress, fought off tiny "aliens." "'The Invaders' has got to be the best *Zone* ep –"

"Shhh," hissed the girl. "And the best one is *Nightmare* –"

I poked my Correia gun in the middle of her back. "Let's go out and talk." She looked like she was going to protest, so I added, "Don't vex me."

Her shoulders slumped. She knew I knew what she was, and she had to figure I had come prepared to deal with her if she got difficult.

Gremlins are a lot of things, but brave isn't any of them, so she didn't put up any kind of a fight as we left. She almost said something when the clip with the gremlin from "Nightmare at 20,000 Feet" flashed on the big screen at the front of the room. I poked her in the back with my gun, though, and she kept moving.

One of the people in the audience saw me doing that, and grinned. He mouthed the words, "Pew, pew!"

Another fan of my mom's, clearly. I grinned back at him and mouthed the same words. The nice thing about having a gun that looks like a party favor for a five-year-old is that no one it too likely to call security on you for threatening someone with it.

I got the gremlin into the hall. She kept a cool face, but the lights flickered a bit more when we got there, so I knew she was agitated.

She pulled away from me, crossed her arms, and leaned against the wall. "This is harassment, man. I haven't done anything since the Dead Ones got all over me about that little blackout in Spokane last year."

Huh. If she was talking about the "little blackout" that left over one hundred-fifty thousand people without power last winter, then I knew who this was, and both provided me leverage and made me even more worried than I already had been.

"Show me your hands," I said.

She rolled her eyes, then raised both hands over her head. "You gonna frisk me?"

Now it was my turn to roll my eyes. "You know what I mean. Now show me your hands."

She sighed. She pulled the glove off her right hand, one finger at a time. And by that I mean that she pulled one finger of her *glove* off at a time. Because there was a heck of a lot more under her glove than four fingers and a thumb. Each finger of her glove held at least a hundred of what looked like fleshy filaments, wrapped around each other and pressed into something vaguely finger-shaped. But when the glove was taken off they all spread out – five hundred "fingers" less than half a millimeter thick. It made the girl's hand look like an anemone, only instead of catching food, each of the little strands that were the girl's "fingers" could grasp tools and manipulate any kind of technology.

The girl finished with the glove. Showed me her hand.

"The other one."

Another sigh, but this one hid worry. She pulled off the glove, though, when I gestured with the gun.

As I had expected due to her comment about the blackout, this hand had only half the "fingers" the first one had.

I'd never met her, but I knew this was from an accident she suffered while doing a job for a certain dark organization that shall remain nameless – [koff] Screen Actors Guild [koff koff].[38]

"What are you doing here, Phoebe?" I asked.

Phoebe eyed me, then eyed my gun. One of her thread-fingers extended, reaching for the housing of it. "Ah, ah, ah!" I said. One finger would be all she needed to mess with the gun. Phoebe was young, but a top-level gremlin. She sold her services to the highest bidder, and guaranteed results. The highest bidder could be the CIA, ISIS, even the IRS – which most self-respecting Otherworlders wouldn't touch with a ten-foot Death Rod of Am'chtl. It didn't matter to Phoebe; it was all the same to her. She did it for the money, and where the money went, she followed.

"Talk, Phoebe," I said. "What are you doing here?"

"Enjoying the convention," she said. Another thing that set Phoebe apart. Gremlins aren't brave, as a rule, but if you got her services, they came with a promise of discretion. And I had to break her. Fast. Moonbeam's trial was looming, and if she was judged worthy of Pack Justice, it wouldn't just be an innocent person suffering, it might well upset the balance of things in the World.

"Phoebe, do you know what this will do to you?" I said, gesturing with the gun.

She eyed it. Her "fingers" felt at the air, as though tasting the technology from afar. "Honestly? Not much."

Again, surprising bravery. Or maybe she just knew that I wasn't about to start torturing an unarmed girl – or an unarmed gremlin.

I tried to sound tough anyway. "Listen, Phoebe, do you know what I am?"

---

[38] Most people think SAG is just actors. Don't you believe it. And don't ever go to a wrap party without taking someone who runs slower than you. Just in case.

"Someone with poor taste in *Twilight Zone* episodes."

"Not true. But I don't have time to debate that. I *can* tell you that I'm a Warden. And I bet if I marched you over to the Dead Ones they'd be very interested in what you're doing here."

That got her attention. "Don't," she said, waving her hands in front of her. "Listen, you can't."

"Then tell me what you're doing here."

She looked conflicted, then terror stole into her expression. Not just normal fear, but something that slithered in her brain and consumed whole portions of it. "No," she whispered. "Don't make me. I –"

A shot rang out. It didn't sound like a gun, but every magic-sensing hair on my body stood up and started doing a tango when I heard it.

I dropped immediately, then rolled away from where I'd been standing. "Phoebe, get d –"

I stopped talking. Phoebe wasn't going to be giving me any information, and she sure as heck wasn't going to get down.

Where she had been, a statue now stood. It was perfect in every respect, an exact replica of Phoebe, down to the thousand tiny fingers. But instead of flesh and blood, this replica was made of....

"Are you freakin' *kidding* me?"

Legos. She had become a masterful reproduction of herself, done in bright plastic bits. The details were all there, down to the logo on her shirt and the untied lace of one shoe. Her face was turned up, and I could see in her plastic eyes a look of pure terror.

The weapon used on her was both precise and was tailored to conventions. Whoever saw this would assume it was some kind of display, or perhaps a joke by some Lego enthusiast with a weird sense of humor and way too much time on his hands.

All this flashed through my mind in an instant. I barely noticed, though, since I was trying very hard not to be dead. I rolled across the floor, slammed into the wall, then threw myself into the closest door.

The room I found myself in was empty. The lights were on, but they blinked and flashed – the death of the gremlin must have sent out the equivalent of a low-level EMP. I pointed my gun at the door and backed up, waiting for something to bash through, expecting to have to fight in the strobing lights around me.

Nothing came in.

I pulled out my phone, intending to call Blake or Anderson for backup, or to let Larry know to be careful if he was on the way over. But the phone had also been caught in the gremlin's death throes. The screen jittered and flashed and random photos from my camera roll appeared and disappeared.

"Crap."

I tried Calista's phone, too, and got the same result. I pocketed the phones and stayed there. Not moving a muscle, just waiting. And waiting.

And waiting.

Finally, the lights slowly stopped flashing on and off. I didn't move.

My phone rang. It scared me so badly I almost vaporized the door, but managed to restrain myself.

I pulled the phone out, saw who was calling. I kept the gun pointed at the door, but jammed the phone against my ear and shouted, "Blake! I –"

"Michaelbrent," he said. Just one word, and he said it quietly, too. But it sliced through my fear and jammed its way into my heart.

"What?" I said. A thousand possibilities crossed my mind, none of them good.

He said three words. And they constituted the top thought I'd had. The worst one.

"It's your mom."

"Blake," I said, and was dismayed at how shaky I sounded. "What's happened?"

"You should get here," he answered. "You should get here fast."

65

I blasted through the door with barely a care about whether the bad guy might be waiting out there. That kind of thing was beyond my focus right now. I just knew I had to get to Mom. That was the only thing that mattered.

I ran out of the room so fast that I actually knocked into Lego Phoebe, and I may have knocked one of her feet off. I made a mental note to feel bad about that later.

Then it was just a mad dash through the convention center, until I got to the rooms that housed Anderson's Monster MASH[39] unit. Blake was waiting for me right outside the room, his hands wrapped up in each other and twisting nervously.

When I saw him, he gestured for me to get over to him, like I wasn't already running as fast as I could. I sprinted the last bit, then Blake's arm went around my shoulder in a comforting embrace – which didn't comfort me at all, considering who was doing it and how many times he's comforted me before (I'll give you a clue: never).

"Blake, what happened, what –"

Blake opened the door and ushered me into the room. "We don't know, exactly. We –"

I didn't hear the rest. I was looking at Mom, and all I saw was her and all I heard was the steady *beep... beep... beep...* of the monitor reading her vitals.

She was wrapped in bandages. One side of her face was covered, and I saw hints of charred skin beneath the bandages. Her visible eye was closed, and her purple hair – yeah, in case I didn't mention that before, she has purple hair, because she's awesome – lay lank against the pillow.

I sat down on a chair beside her bed. The bed next to hers held a Gorgon (her face was covered, so no one was in danger of going the way of the Kraken) whose hair-snakes

---

[39] See what I did there? Ha!

looked like they had contracted a grotesque fungal infection, and one of them hissed at me as I sat.

My mom's in the hospital. A hospital where half the other patients could eat her, and the other half could steal her soul.

Mom's in the hospital.

One of her hands was covered in gauze as well, clearly burned along with the rest of her. The other one was whole and unharmed, but when I took it it was shockingly cold.

Tears sprang to my eyes. Yes, I am a full-grown adult with a family of my own; and yes, I am very strong and brave and have a full chest of hair to prove that I am a Real Man. Doesn't matter. My mom was hurt. Tears happen when that kind of thing goes down.

I sensed someone behind me. "What happened to her?" I asked.

To my surprise, it wasn't Blake but Orson Scott Card who answered. "We're not really sure yet. Bystanders saw her walking around with a laser gun –"

"Pew, pew," I said listlessly.

"Just so," he agreed. "But after she 'shot' several people, she apparently wandered away and then returned an hour or so later with several bags in her hands. Chemicals of some kind. She mixed them together, and there was an explosion."

"Why is she here?" I asked.

"I thought I already addressed that."

"No." I turned to him. I didn't know Card all that well – he was as standoffish to mere Wardens as any of the other Dead Ones – but I knew he wouldn't have brought my mother here under normal circumstances. "Why is she *here*? Why not at a normal ER?"

Card shrugged. "It's my understanding that she's held back by the Containment spell."

"Oh." That's right. I had forgotten that neither I nor Mom could leave. I looked back at her. Was she always that small? "Okay, so what's wrong with her?"

Card read off a list of injuries, which boiled down to "she's burned a lot and she's got a lot of broken bones."

"Is she going to be all right?"

"Physically? Yes. She should recover. We got her here in time to repair the worst of the physical injuries, and the rest will just require time."

"Why do you keep saying 'physical'? What other injuries does she have?"

Card glanced to his left, and I realized that Kevin Anderson had come in the room. Blake was at his side, and the three of them – Blake, Card, and Anderson – exchanged looks.

"There's magic involved," said Anderson.

"What does that mean?"

He shrugged. "I don't really know. It feels like she's been enchanted somehow, but not in a way I'm familiar with."

"Is that what's been making her act odd? Will she get better? Is there something I can do?"

Anderson sighed. "As to the first two, we're working on it. I don't know yet what's going to happen in the end, but Card, Blake, and I are all hopeful."

"What about the last part? What can I do?"

"Nothing," Blake finally said. "We'll let you know if something comes up, but until then...."

I turned back to Mom. *Beep... beep... beep* went the monitors. Every electronic ping felt like someone punching me in the spine.

"What can I do?" I said, not to the three men behind me but to Mom. "How can I make this better?"

A hand touched my shoulder. "You should call your father," said Card.

I looked at him. My dad had written several critical studies of Card's work, so I had figured Card knew my dad and vice-versa, but it was odd to hear one of the Dead Ones telling me to call him.

Not odd. Scary.

I called Dad.

66

I mentioned before that my dad is mostly deaf. This creates problems in a phone conversation. I called my parents' house, and got the machine. Not a surprise. It was late enough I knew he'd be home, but why should a deaf person answer the phone?

So I called again. And again. And again.

On the seventh try, the phone picked up. "Hello?"

"Dad."

"Hello?"

"Dad, I –"

"Hello?"

"*DAD, HI. IT'S ME, MICHAELBRENT. YOUR SON.*"

I yelled so loud that the gorgon's snake hair all started hissing, and a yeti in the corner bed sat up and started growling and making threatening gestures. Blake dealt with it by leaning close and whispering something into its ear. The yeti gulped and lay back down. Then Blake grabbed something off a table and tossed it at the gorgon. The snakes each grabbed one of the baby mice he had thrown and started wolfing them down.

Two thoughts hit me:

1) If gorgon snake-hair eats, then where does the food go? The snakes must poop *right into her skull!* No wonder gorgons are so pissy all the time.

2) Blake wasn't just putting up with me. He was watching out for me. By far the weirdest thing that had happened to me. But nice.

"*DAD, I HAVE TO TELL YOU SOMETHING!*"

This is how most phone conversations with my dad go. First, the verbal fumbling until he realizes that yes, someone *is* talking to him, and until I realize how to pace my voice so he can pick up as much as possible. Then it's just a long, slow scream on my end.

He gets to sound normal. Some people have all the luck.

"What is it?" he said. He sounded calm but quiet. He *always* sounds calm. I told you as well that he's got some mental health issues, but other than when his depression gets the best of him, I don't think I've heard him sound anything but calm and in control for well over two decades. Still, his voice was so quiet I ended up turning on the speaker full blast to hear him. It made it so everyone in the room could hear him speak, but I opted for clarity over privacy in this situation.

"Dad, it's Mom.[40]"

"What about her?"

"She was in an – she's been hurt."

He still sounded calm, though there was an edge to it. "In what way?"

"She got burned. There was a chemical explosion."

"At the convention? Are you okay?"

"No, Dad, I'm fine. It wasn't just a random explosion. She... they think *she* caused it."

Silence. I started to wonder if Dad heard me, and got ready to re-scream that last bit. Then he said, "How was she dressed at the time?"

That took me utterly by surprise; the last thing I ever would have expected him to say. I tell my father that Mom's been in a serious accident – which she may have intentionally caused – and he wants to know what she was *wearing*?

"Uh, I think she was wearing her steampunk."

"Her tree trunk?"

"No, Dad. Her steampunk. Her. STEAM. PUNK."

"Her steampunk?"

"Yes!"

"Oh, okay, then everything's fine."

I stared at the phone like it might be the one at fault for this entire surreal moment. I returned the phone to my ear and

---

[40] I will refrain from writing out the rest of my side of the conversation in all caps. Just remember that I'm shouting.

said, "Dad, didn't you hear me? I mean – that is, didn't you understand? She's burnt all over –"

"Is she going to be all right? I assume she got picked up by Kevin Anderson or Orson Scott Card or whichever of the Dead Ones is manning the convention, so the burns shouldn't be too much of a problem." My mind was reeling so hard at this point I didn't even blink when he sighed and added, "I guess we'll have to restrict her to Mrs. Claus."

"Dad," I finally managed, after several long seconds of my jaw and tongue trying to make words together, "what are you saying? What do you mean? Why would Kevin Anderson or Orson Scott Card being here matter?"

My dad chuckled. Another rarity for him. He smiles plenty, but he's just not a big laugher. Then he said, "Oh, son, did you think you were the only one in the family?"

"The only one what?"

"The only one in the World?"

I sat there for what seemed like six or seven hundred millennia. "You know?" I finally managed.

Another chuckle – a red-letter day. "Know what?" said Dad. "Know that Laura's a sylph? That you got an STD from her? That you started seeing monsters about fifteen years ago and have been a Warden for the last few of those? Yes, I have an inkling of all that."

"But... how?"

"Again: you're not the only one in the family. Your mother got hit by something when she was younger. We're not sure what, but I think it was probably a siren or some other creature whose primary metaphysical strengths lie in psychic intrusion."

I parsed that out. I think. "Okay, so Mom got attacked by something?"

"Correct. The effects grew worse with time, and by the time you were about eight she was having serious psychic reverberations."

"What does that mean?"

"It means her identity became a bit more fluid than most. Something inside her dissociated, and she would forget who she was."

"Like, amnesia?"

"Partially. But then she would assume the identity reflected by her outward appearance."

"Her outward appearance?" I frowned. "She looked like Mom, so how could she assume her own identity?"

"She couldn't. But if she dressed up – say, for Halloween – she occasionally ended up lost in the belief that she was whoever or whatever she had dressed as. Never for long, but it could be awkward. One time, for example, she put on this marvelous little geisha outfit –"

"Gah! No! Delete! Fast forward. Skip this part!"

He chuckled again. "As you wish. At any rate, she assumed the identity indicated by her ensemble. It's part of why she started dressing up exclusively as Mrs. Claus during Halloween. You know your mother, it would kill her not to be able to participate in the holiday, but we decided that being 'Mrs. Claus' would lead to far less dire consequences in the event of one of her 'fits' than if she were to dress as a zombie or a witch or Genghis Khan."

"Dad, I... I don't remember any of this."

"No, you don't. Because we didn't want any of this coming down on you or your brother or sisters. But you do remember her having periods of time where her arthritis was so bad she would shut herself up in her room?"

"Yeah," I said warily.

"Sometimes it *was* your mother in the room, suffering greatly. Other times I would do my best to reason with Mrs. Claus and tell her that our room was the best place to wait until her husband got back from the North Pole."

"Wow," I said.

"Indeed."

"Why?"

He understood my question, immediately and completely. "You kids had quite enough to deal with without having to cope with a mother who assumed different realities."

I noted he said different *realities*, not different *identities*. Whatever hit Mom hadn't just altered her perceptions, it altered who she actually was.

This is why we got caught by the Containment. Mom and I couldn't leave when the wizards could – because even though they see the World, they're still human. But Mom and me... we have a bit of the World in us. Enough to catch us in the same trap.

"All right," I said, "then why was she trying to blow something up?"

"Did she have her laser gun?"

I already knew I was beyond exhausted at this point, but the proof was that I nodded at the phone instead of answering, then got irritated because Dad hadn't heard me. "YES!" I screamed as loudly as I could.

"An SCD," he said.

"SCD? What's that? Sickle cell disease? Scottish country dancing?"

"Supernatural cognitive dissonance. Her mind, in this instance, is that of a steampunk time traveler with a laser gun. The laser gun does not work properly, so she seeks out materials that will create the effect she desires. In effect, she's acting as both the star and the special effects department of the movie in her mind."

"So she thinks she's this steampunker, Ginny Whatsername –"

"Ah, Dame Ginny McLaserbeam. Wonderful girl, born just outside of Leeds if I recall correctly."

Maybe it was the presentation earlier, but I kept hearing the *Twilight Zone* theme in my head at this point.

"Right, Dad. Ginny. So Mom thinks she's Ginny, and when her gun doesn't work some part of her splits out and makes her get materials that will make it *seem* like it worked? And you let her dress like a steampunker, even knowing this?"

"Well, it's been nearly twenty years since she had one of these attacks. We thought they were behind us." He sighed. "I suppose we'll have to restrict her to dressing as Mrs. Claus again. All in all, though, that's fine. She's a true pleasure to chat with, and makes astoundingly good hot cocoa."

My head hurt. Was it time for another pain pill?

Yes. Yes it was.

I fumbled the pill out of my pocket, then took the cup of water Blake extended to me –

(*Still being nice. My mom is Ginny McLaserbeam, my dad enjoys chatting with Mrs. Claus, and Blake is being nice. It's like I'm living the book of Revelation.*)

– and washed the pill down with a mouthful of water.

"Dad, are *you* in the World?"

"I do have my own Supernaturally Transmitted Disease. Not quite the same way you contracted one, but there was this three-day weekend quite soon after we were married, and she and I –"

"NO NO NO NO! No details! Please, Dad, I've had a day you wouldn't believe, and I don't think I can handle more horror."

He was silent, but I could hear his laugh even in the silence. Some people have no respect for others' pain.

Then in a serious voice he said, "Yes. I'm in the World. It's what sparked my interest in horror. A lot of great literature in the world of the darkly fantastic, true, but much of my interest was simple survival. One cannot properly protect oneself or one's family against that which one does not fully understand."

"Story of my life," I murmured. I knew he wouldn't hear that, so I said, louder, "So what do we do?"

"Well, please give my best to Scott and to Kevin. I suspect they're nearby, so they've no doubt heard your side of the conversation. I think Scott suspected I knew more than I was letting on, but this should come as a shock to Kevin. I'd like to see his face."

I glanced at Anderson. His face *was* pretty funny – I don't think I've ever seen someone's mouth make a more perfect circle.

"Regardless, please let them know I would prefer this information not be made generally public. All that I've done has been in furtherance of helping my family stay below any Otherworlders' radar. More people in the World knowing about me or Judi would not further that. Thus, their discretion would be appreciated."

I looked at them. Anderson and Blake nodded with the same semi-glazed look of surprise. Card nodded, too, though I could tell my dad was right: he had already suspected, if not known. Maybe that was why he encouraged me to call Dad in the first place.

"Well, I'm sure you've plenty to think about, and we all know this mode of communicating isn't the most pleasant for anyone, so I'll sign off. Unless you need anything else?"

I think I said no. Everything had gotten pretty dreamlike at this point, so I couldn't be sure.

"Call me if there's any further problem. Otherwise, kiss your mother when she wakes up and I'll see you both in a few days."

Something touched my leg. I looked down, surprised at what I saw there. "Hold on, Dad," I said into the phone, then knelt beside a small man dressed in a green, ribbed tank top. I almost didn't recognize him at first. There are so many, it's hard to place the specific sub-classes. Then I got it.

"Hey, Friday the 13th Bacon," I said. "What's up."

He held something out. Moonbeam's glamour token: the ring I'd sent the brownies to find, along with a written report. The report was tiny – about the size of a credit card. Even as small as it was, though, they had written it in large (for a brownie) font. I flipped through the report, and it basically said, "We found the ring in Princess Moonbeam's stuff."

Which, since I'd already figured out who the "man" in the photo in Calista's photos was, was neither surprising nor particularly helpful.

Them's the breaks.

Friday the 13th held out a small hand. "A deal's a deal," I said to him, scrounging around in my pockets for the brownie bits I'd left in there for this purpose. The deal had been that they'd get the ring in return for my tidiness at the con, and a few more brownie crumbs. You do not want to renege on brownies, and I had a moment of terror when I realized that my clothes had been fixed up – and what if whoever or whatever spell did that also got rid of the crumbs?

But they were there, and I made sure to give Friday the 13th Bacon extra crumbs – so many that when he disappeared, he actually left behind some bits of chocolate on the floor. Not much, but a huge mess for a brownie.

"Hey," I said as he walked toward the corner, where he would no doubt disappear to rejoin his brothers. He turned. "Everything's better with Bacon, right?"

He nodded, and gave me a thumbs-up. Then he was gone.

A voice came out of nowhere and it actually took me a few seconds before I realized it was Dad, still on the phone. "Anyone there? Am I still on hold, or is this just me being deaf?"

"Sorry, Dad. I had to do something." I looked at Mom. The singed remains of her steampunk corset lay on the table beside her bed. I couldn't help but smile a bit. Her particular "curse" was actually kind of perfect for her. "Ginny McLase –"

The world seemed to stop. I whispered something, but it must have been a *loud* something, because Dad said, "What was that?"

I said it again, louder. Much louder. Looking at Mom, at "Dame Ginny." I looked at the others in the room. At Kevin

Anderson, Blake Casselman, Orson Scott Card. None of them seemed to understand the light I knew was shining in my eyes. Into the phone, I said, "You were wrong, Dad."

"About what?"

"It wasn't a siren that got Mom." I added, quickly, "I'll call you back," then hung up and turned to the three still-watching men.

"I know who did it."

67

I opened the door to the ninth floor hall. My friends and the Dead Ones were there – Robot Dave, Larry Correia, Blake, Anderson, Card. It had been quite the crunch to get them all in the elevator, and they clustered behind me as I opened the door.

Rathton was the first one, of course. Waiting in the doorway as I opened the door. His fangs bared when he saw who it was.

"I told you to stay away, Warden," he snarled.

"I need to talk to the High Court and the Great Pack. Now."

He laughed, a deep, dangerous laugh.

"Is that a no?" I asked.

The laugh got deeper, darker, and even more dangerous.

I punched him in the nose. Normally not a good idea with a vampire, but I'd slabbed garlic over the knuckles. It was enough to bloody his face and knock him back a few steps.

It also probably wasn't the way to try and get what I wanted, but the scumsucker had threatened my family, and I wanted him to know that was definitely in the no-no column.

Rathton screamed and fell back. The other vampires jumped forward, rushing toward me as one. The lycans joined in. I wasn't sure if they were worried about their orders to let no one pass, or if they just didn't want the vampires to have all the fun. Didn't matter, I guess. All that mattered was the eight or so tons of monster coming at me.

Something whizzed over my shoulder. Darts embedded in the first four lycans and down they went. "Reloading," said Larry from behind me.

One of the vampires reached for me. Not Rathton – he was still down and sputtering – but someone else with equally red eyes, equally long fangs, and equal rage in her eyes.

I got ready to fight.

And I didn't get the chance.

Before I could move, Blake pounced. He was a *blur*. Seriously, like faster than anything I've ever seen. The vampire should have taken anything human apart, but I was no longer entirely sure that Blake *was* human.

The vampire looked like it had fallen into a pinball machine with blenders instead of bumpers. He bounced back and forth, skittering madly and his flesh flaying off his body under the force of Blake's blows.

He was alive when Blake finished with him. But he wouldn't be getting up for a few minutes.

Sadly, that was when one of the lycans grabbed Blake. I suspect Blake could have taken the werewolf as well in a one-on-one fight, but he got sucker-punched.

The werewolf swiped its claws across Blake's back. Robot Dave jumped in. I didn't know what he could do – he wasn't armed like Larry, he didn't have Blake's fighting chops.

But, it turned out, robots are incredibly precise. Dave extended a pair of fingers and jabbed them into the werewolf's eyes. Then, while it reeled, he pursed his lips and blew.

I heard nothing. But all the lycans went nuts, clapping hands over ears and baying in pain. No normal person could have done it, but Robot Dave apparently could precisely craft the interaction between air, soft palate, tongue, lips. He became a human dog whistle. Well, a robot human wolf whistle. Close enough.

Two more vamps bounded forward. Reaching for Robot Dave and Blake in a coordinated attack. Robot Dave took up a position over Blake's moaning form.

"Enough."

The voice was soft. It should have been barely audible. Nonetheless, it penetrated to the core of every person, Otherworlder, and robot guy in the hall.

I felt a blast of power wash past me. The lycans slammed up against one wall. The vampires against the other.

I turned and saw Anderson and Card extending their hands casually. "Holy *cow*," I muttered. "Remind me never to piss you guys off. Again, that is."

Neither of them spoke, but Anderson winked, and there was a definite twinkle in Card's eye.

I turned back around, and came face to face with Rathton. Somehow the queen's guard was resisting the Dead Ones' spell. He reached for me, and I was so surprised I didn't even put my hands up. A cold, cold hand encircled my throat.

"I've been looking forward to this," said Rathton. Then he added, "*Arglefargle!*" as he was hurled through the air, slamming into the wall with his compatriots.

I thought it was the Dead Ones' spell. Then I realized there was one more Otherworlder that had resisted their efforts.

Pallas stood tall and huge against the storm of spells. Rathton had slid down the wall. Now he started to stand. Pallas slammed a huge fist against his head and said, "Stay down," in a voice like an earthquake with a head cold. Rathton went down… and stayed down.

Pallas looked at me and my friends. He nodded, then gestured for me to pass.

"Why?" I said as I moved by him.

He grinned a toothy, deadly, but not unkind grin. "You've got an honest smell."

"I get that a lot. It's Irish Spring."

I went to room 902.

68

The door was locked, but hello! Magic key card!

I opened it and moved into the room. The others didn't follow at first, because the penthouse room seemed to have more Otherworlders than a Brandon Sanderson book signing.

Of course, that was just what it looked like at first. There *were* a lot of Otherworlders, but they were crushed up against the walls in a nearly-impenetrable ring.

Inside the ring: the royalty of the High Court: King William, Queen Borga, Prince Eustace, Princess Roberta, and Prince Warine. Beside them stood King Haemon.

And before them all... Moonbeam.

She was in human form, and she hung from a rope mechanism that had been strung through the ceiling.

They are so going to have to pay extra for damages.

Though she was untouched, it was clear that was about to change. She had a coat of silver mail over her shoulders – enough silver to keep her from changing or otherwise using her powers. And Aseas – the Lycaon Peacemaker who had been found with Calista – stood in front of her with a bat wrapped in silver barbed wire.

He looked at the royalty of the High Court. The vampires all gave a thumbs down. Prince Eustace was there, too, so either the High Court had forgiven him patronizing Nespda, or they were going to revisit it later. Whichever it was, he was apparently part of the judging body, and now leaned forward and spit upon Moonbeam. "How could you?" he whispered, the depth of his loss apparent in every syllable.

Aseas looked to Haemon. The Lycaon King's shoulders slumped. He looked at Moonbeam, then whispered, "May this preserve the peace," in a broken voice before nodding.

Aseas drew back the bat. This was the first – and easiest – trial of Pack Justice.

Moonbeam just stared at him, and I didn't see anything of ugliness in her. Just sadness, and a damaged spirit... and a nobility all the greater for those things.

Aseas growled and changed to wolf form. He looked uncomfortable beside the silver on the bat, but there was no question that he would fulfill his duty as Peacemaker.

"Stop!" I screamed.

The assemblage all turned to me. Queen Borga was the first to respond. "You!" she screamed. "You have not my Blessing! You will die for this!"

"Right. Death, slaying, blah blah blah." I tried to ignore everyone who crowded in on me. And their fangs. And teeth. And muscles.

Please don't die, MB.

I'll do my best!

"You can't kill her!"

"Why not?" screamed Prince Eustace, and tears of blood tracked down his cheeks, born of crimson eyes that now spoke only rage.

"Because you've got the wrong guy. Girl. Wolf." I pointed at Moonbeam. "She didn't do it!"

"And who did?" snarled Aseas. He took a step toward me, the silver club still raised.

I blinked at him. "You did, Aseas."

69

After the furor subsided – a bit, at least, enough to make my case – we all went for a nice, friendly walk. Because that's what you do on the eve of the apocalypse, right?

At first, no one was quite sure where we were going. But it was easy enough to figure out. A word or two to the front desk with a little dose of magic, and *voilà*! Up we went.

Using the elevator was out of the question, of course. Me, my friends, the High Court, the Great Pack. *Way* too much to pack into one little box. And probably not a great idea to put them all together in close quarters even if it had been possible. Tensions were high. So we took the stairs.

I was… a bit tense myself. Probably had something to do with the fact I'd been given exactly twenty-five minutes to prove what I'd told them – coinciding, not too coincidentally, with the time the treaty had originally been scheduled for execution.

Now it was *my* execution on the line. Not to mention my family's since both Haemon and William had quietly mentioned details about my house. The inside of it. No outright threats – classy kings! – but the fact that Haemon asked where I got my youngest daughter's Princess Aurora nightlight,[41] and William mentioned how much he liked the wedding photo Laura and I had hung over the mantel, was pretty clear.

When Queen Borga mentioned that they had a "family dinner" planned in case this didn't work out, it was even clearer.

Yikes.

I had chewed my nails down to the elbows by the time we got to the fifth floor. I was in the lead when we tramped out of the stairwell. The two Kings were right behind me, flanked in turn by the Dead Ones. Blake, Dave, and Larry came right behind *them*, then Prince Eustace, Pallas, Aseas, and Rathton.

---

[41] At a garage sale, for the record. Official Disney merch, so it was a steal at two bucks.

The rest of the vamps and lycans trailed down the stairs like the worlds hairiest and toothiest wedding train.

We got turned around on the way to room 535 – seriously, has *anyone* ever managed to go directly to the hotel room they want? Eventually we figured out that the numbers apparently skipped around in various factors of prime numbers. After that it was easy.

Room 535 was around a corner, beyond a small room with an ice machine and a vending machine where you could get a Coke for the bargain price of seventeen dollars. The door to the room was inset quite a bit, out of sight of the main hall until you were right on top of it.

We all moved as quietly as possible – which is pretty quiet considering the glidey, lurky, hunty nature of those involved.[42] No one wanted to spook our target.

We needn't have worried. She was waiting for us.

Mercedes stood in front of the closed door. She wore a black skirt, a black blouse, and held a black clutch in her hands. She even had a black cocktail hat with a birdcage veil on it. The only things that kept her from looking like something out of an Audrey Hepburn movie were the deep crimson skull print on her skirt, and the bright red Wonder Woman boots.

Mercedes eyed us as we came in sight of her door – and her. She seemed a bit paler than usual – though that might just have been an illusion caused by her bright red lipstick – but other than that she appeared not at all surprised to see the menagerie.

"You look lovely," I said. I eyed the boots. "Those the boots you bought yesterday?"

She nodded and smiled wanly. "I wanted to wear them at least once."

Silence. No one else spoke. Everyone in the strange group wanted to know if I'd been right.

---

[42] Or... *super*nature. Heh. I crack my butt up.

"At least once?" I prodded.

"Before I die."

At that, a murmur rippled through the crowd.

"Did Niko tell you we'd come for you?"

She nodded. "Yeah." She tittered nervously. "Great thing about having an Oracle in the house. He was even pretty clear this time. He said, 'Justice will be at your door tonight at eleven forty-seven. Dress nicely.'" A tear rolled down her cheek. "He said he loved me, too. That was nice."

"So...." I didn't really know what to do here. I mean, I've caught the bad guys before, but not like this. Not a friend.

Mercedes let me off the hook. "You know how I did it?"

"I think so."

She turned to the group. "I pretended to know Aseas," she said, nodding at the Peacemaker. "He was confused enough to let me hug him." She looked hard at him. "You truly love your family, sir. I'd heard that, but if you hadn't... this wouldn't have worked."

"You used your magic," I said. "Hit him so hard his mind broke a bit."

She nodded. "How did you figure it out?" Then she answered her own question. "That's what was happening to Judi."

"Yup. Another succubus got to her when she was a kid." I looked at Aseas. "You were dressed as a vampire, and in that outfit you became a vampire." To Mercedes I said, "You knew Calista was going to be there?"

She sighed, then nodded. "I got him in deep, then left when I knew she was coming. Aseas saw Calista – and he was no longer the Peacemaker with his beloved princess, but a vampire in a solitary room with his natural enemy. She never expected it, never saw it coming."

"But there was no blood in her body. The marks were those of a vampire," said Prince Eustace. His eyes still shone with tears.

"That's how it works," I said, my eyes still on Mercedes. "He wasn't a vampire, but his mind split a bit, so he killed her in a way that perfectly mimicked a vampire slaying of a lycan. Easy to slash her throat, cut her legs as though with talons, since he had claws."

"And the blood?" demanded William. "Where did that go? She was killed in that room, and there's no way –"

"That's what kept me thinking all the wrong things, too," I said. "But Aseas could easily slash her throat, her legs, then hold her upside down and drain her."

"That would have been a slaughterhouse," said Anderson with a shake of the head.

"It was," I said. "And that created a cognitive dissonance inside of Aseas: a vampire – a fussy, fastidious vampire – would have left an immaculate scene. And he did, except for a few dots on the carpet that I thought were blood."

"Brownie crumbs," said Card, understanding.

I nodded. "Not hard to get a troop of brownies in there, and when it was done, you had a perfect scene with a vampire's victim at the center. Then Aseas lost consciousness – just like after Mom did when she turned into Dame Ginny McLaserbeam."

"Who's Dame Ginny Mc –" someone whispered, but I heard the distinctive sound of an elbow to the ribs, and whoever it was shut up.

Back to me. "Even after sixty years, after my mom's episode she was out like a light. So after Aseas' episode, same thing, only stronger." I eyed Mercedes. "You really hit him hard, by the way. He's been out this whole time, and didn't remember anything before or during his little episode."

She nodded, then did an odd little curtsy toward Aseas. "Sorry about that."

"Sorry?" he growled, his voice strangling to nothing before he got anything else out.

"You also blew it when I talked to you then, though I didn't notice it." Mercedes' eyebrows rose in confusion. "You said you knew Calista in her cosplay guise. Told me about her eyes, her hair, her exotic features. But you couldn't tell me more because she always wore her mask. But if that was true, if you never saw her without her mask... then how did you know she had exotic features?" I shook my head. "You knew because you'd just seen her, and were targeting her."

King Haemon had had enough. He walked forward and slapped her. The hit rocked Mercedes, knocking her into the wall. But Haemon could have rendered her unconscious, or even killed her if he wished, with that single blow. Mercedes screamed, and I saw blood spurt from her mouth and nose, but the fact that she remained standing was terrible. Haemon didn't want to hurt her badly.

No, that would come soon enough.

"You killed my baby," he snarled. "You made me doubt my other baby." He backhanded her again. Mercedes screamed again. Haemon caught the front of her blouse, his hand shifted into the clawed paw of a Lycaon. "You will pay for this. Forever."

I leaned in close. "Why?" I said. "You've worked so hard to be Mercedes, so why did you return to the life Rcham Bt'Agra, Spy of Samael, Slayer of the Living?"

Mercedes didn't answer. Just smiled a strange smile.

I waited. Waited.

Then I pulled back, and that was why the bullet hit me instead of her.

70

The Big Bang – that first moment of infinite, nuclear, explosive force – had nothing on the mayhem that erupted in the hall.

A clot of Otherworlders converged on Larry and one of the werewolves. The lycan had a chrome gun clenched in his fist, and Larry had his own fists clamped over both the gun and the lycan's gun hand. The gun fired into the ceiling, then the lycan pushed it toward Larry.

Larry let go of the gun long enough to whip a dagger out of nowhere – presto! It's the Amazing Larry and his magic of mayhem! – and slashed it across the wolf's throat. The dagger must have been silver, because the effect was immediate. The lycan had never turned into his wolf form, so there was no turning back to his human shape. He just gurgled once, then fell to the floor in a boneless pile.

Aseas was on top of Larry in two strides. The Peacemaker shifted on the first stride, and on the second he knocked Larry to the ground. I heard the crack of my friend's nose breaking.

By the time he hit the floor, of course, Larry had produced –

(*And now for my next trick!*)

– the Correia Monster Masher, and had the shotgun shoved deep into Aseas' gut.

Aseas didn't even seem to notice it. He leaned toward Larry, slavering and drooling. "You totally killed a lycan," he growled.

"No, I totally tried to save the girl, which I assumed you'd prefer since you probably have about six lifetimes of pain to dish out." He looked like he disapproved of that, and I couldn't blame him. "Though I probably should have just let him kill her."

"That was no reason to kill him," said Aseas.

"No, that came when he tried to kill *me*."

Aseas moved. The Peacemaker was *fast*. The shotgun was wrenched out of Larry's hands so quickly I was pretty sure I heard a small sonic boom.

Aseas pointed the shotgun at Larry. His huge finger moved to the trigger.

"Enough," said Haemon. "Everyone stay cool."

Aseas turned to his king. "Lord?" he said.

Haemon looked at Mercedes, who was standing again, blood coating her face.

That's never gonna come out of her blouse.

"There has been enough Bogarting of our Houses," he said to King William. The lycan looked exhausted in every way. I knew that look. It was the look of a father who has lost his child.

The vampire looked confused, as did everyone else who wasn't a lycan. Haemon clarified. "Enough hurt for tonight," he said.

The vampire nodded. He looked at his son. "What do you want, Eustace? You have lost so much."

Eustace smiled. He looked at his father, then at Haemon. "I want her to suffer."

"No problem, son," said Haemon. He gestured, and Aseas and Pallas stepped forward and took Mercedes' arms.

"No," said Eustace. He put a hand on Haemon's arm. "I want her to suffer for as long as I will. I want her to suffer *forever*."

Haemon shook his head. "I doubt it'll be more than a single lifetime, son."

Eustace smiled. His fangs extended, and he touched one thoughtfully. His red eyes ablaze, he said, "I suspect I could find a way to lengthen that time a bit."

Haemon grinned, his fatigue burned away for a moment, and I saw the wolf hiding behind his eyes. "Now that is a choice, killer, rockin', *righteous* idea."

Haemon nodded again, and Aseas and Pallas hauled Mercedes through the hall, the members of the royal family of both houses following close behind. Pallas' low, rock-like laughter trailed them out. Mercedes glanced at me once through her veil and her curtain of blood.

Then she was gone.

That's right, she glanced at *me*. Did you forget about me? About me being shot? Thanks a lot. After all this time together, just –

Oh, forget it. I'm too tired to be mad at you.

I moaned as Mercedes was dragged by, and someone finally remembered I was there. Nice, eh?

Larry hurried over to me. He had a roll of gauze in one hand, a thick handkerchief in the other.

Where does he keep all his stuff? Amazing.

He knelt down beside me, putting the bandages on the floor, then flicked open a karambit – a wicked-looking folding knife with a curved blade – and sliced my shirt off.

I was still in shock, so the pain hadn't really hit. But it did now. I said, "Oooowwwwwwww!" to let everyone know where I stood in the scheme of things.

Larry leaned me forward and started packing gauze against my my back. "Looks like it missed any arteries, but I can't be sure. Bullet's still in there, so it likely hit some bone, maybe broke something." His eyes flicked to the knife on the floor. "You want –"

"No!" I croaked. "Let's leave it in for now, okay?"

A hand fell on my shoulder. Anderson.

I screamed again. "Dude! Do you not see the bullet hole back there?"

"Shut up," he murmured. As soon as he said that, he began incanting something. Warmth spread through my body, and I felt something roll down my back. Anderson leaned down and picked it up. Held it in front of me. It was a bullet, silver highlights peeking out from under the slick coat of blood. "Good bullet," he said, and shoved it in his pocket.

"I want it," I complained.

"Who are you going to show it to?"

I shut up. Nothing good ever happens to me.

He clapped me on the shoulder, which only hurt agonizingly, then looked at Larry. "If you can keep pressure on it for a few minutes, it should heal completely in an hour or so."

Larry nodded. "Got it."

Anderson leaned close to me. "You did well, Warden." Then he straightened up. Sighed. "I have to leave."

I nodded. Just because a murderer had been caught didn't mean there was no more work to do.

There's always more work to do.

71

Everyone left. The lycans and vampires had been leaving this whole time, following their leaders to the beginning of what promised to be exceptionally horrible judgment. Robot Dave followed Card and Anderson out. Neither of the Dead Ones spoke, and I realized they *hadn't* spoken to each other in any of the time I'd seen them. I wondered if they didn't like each other.

Big mystery. I'd have to solve that one eventually, right? 'Cause of my mad detective skills.

Blake left, too, but not until he touched me on the shoulder and asked solicitously, "You gonna be okay?"

I was touched. "Yeah. Thanks."

"You sure? Because what with the sylphilis weakening your system and all –"

I actually took a swipe at him. And I maintain that it would have connected if it hadn't been slow, weak, and compounded by the agony of a wounded shoulder.

He laughed as he left. I couldn't tell if it was a nice laugh or a malicious one. Were we friends now?

Another mystery.

"Screw it," I said. "I'm done detecting for the night."

"What was that?" asked Larry. He was still pressing both hands against my back.

"Nothing." I tried to dig my phone out of my pocket, but it hurt too much. "What time is it?"

Larry actually wore a watch, so he didn't have to move his hands to see. "A couple minutes until midnight."

Still on duty.

"I don't work Sundays," I said, and giggled.

Larry didn't ask what I'd said this time. He just kept holding my back.

"Huh," I said after a minute.

"What?"

I shook my head. "Sorry, I keep talking to myself."

"It's cool."

Another moment of silence. Then I said, "What did you do?"

"What do you mean?"

"To get Mercedes to kill the princess. How did you make her do it?"

Everything went very quiet. The hands left my back, and Larry sat down beside me. "Threatened her kid," he said.

"Niko?"

"Yup."

Something very cold crawled inside me. "Not very nice. Would you have actually done it?"

"I don't know. I hoped it wouldn't come to that." Silence again. After a moment, Larry said, "How'd you figure it out?"

"A bunch of things. They just didn't come together until now." I laughed. "Turns out that getting shot is clarifying." The laughter died. "One of them was Niko himself. Did you already know he was an Oracle?"

"Not until tonight," Larry admitted. "What'd he say?"

"*'The solution will be found where what was found was found to be lost. You will find her, and through her, him.'*"

"Wow. *That's* vague."

"Yeah. But it makes sense now. The solution – the answer to who killed Calista – was found at the place 'where what was found was found to be lost.' The thing that was found was Calista, and we found her body but it got lost after."

Larry chuckled. "Yeah, I heard about that. Blake pulled a real boner there."

"And the last part: I found Mercedes, and through Mercedes I found you. Because I couldn't understand *why* Mercedes killed the princess. She did it, yes, but she has no motive that I can see. Why would she do that, when she's worked so hard for over a decade to just be human again?"

Larry shrugged. "Otherworlders don't always *have* motives."

"True, but still.... Then there were the other things. SuperGhoul ran away." Off Larry's confused look, I said, "The ghoul in the Other Green Room? I thought she didn't want to talk to me, but now I think it was you she was avoiding."

Larry sighed. "Been looking for her. I thought someone might have heard me talking to Mercedes when all this started. Wasn't sure, though." He shook his head. "Spilt milk."

"Mercedes was scared of you, too. She said you came by the night she was watching my mom –"

"Glad she's feeling better, by the way."

"Thank you. When Mercedes said you came by, she had a weird look in her eye. She was terrified, though I didn't realize it at the time.

"Then there was the gremlin. Mercedes has her powers and a uke that she can do some nifty things with. But a gun that turns gremlins to Legos? That was something very specific – something a supernatural arms dealer might actually have." Larry nodded. "You had a number of Portals, which is how you must have found Gandhi when you heard I was looking at the security feeds. Vampires and lycans don't typically worry about things like that – lycans are too direct for that kind of thought process, vampires don't worry about showing up on video, and I *know* neither of them were aware they were being watched. But you did. You told Phoebe to sabotage his feeds, then when I was getting too close, you took *him* out."

"It's actually a compliment. I didn't originally think you'd get that close."

"Well, thank you very much," I said with as much sarcasm as I could muster. Far as I could see, it just rolled off Larry. "Then when you told me about Gandhi, you even asked if I'd told anyone else about what I found. Worried about copies?"

He nodded.

"You found out no one else was privy to the information I'd gotten, but when you found out I was aware of the gremlin –

because I am an idiot and I told you myself – you hustled over there and killed Phoebe before she could tell me about you."

Larry was silent now. Just looking into the distance.

I said the next thing very quietly. "You sent the witch to kill me, too."

He nodded. "Sorry, MB. You are a great friend, but you were getting too close."

"You gave me a crappy gun so I'd more likely die."

He shook his head. "No, I gave you a *great* gun. I just didn't tell you that it doesn't work when *you* want it to, it works when *I* want it to."

Damn. Looking back, every time the gun worked had been in his presence. How did I miss that?

"But you didn't manage to kill me. In the end you tried to kill Mercedes, though, so she wouldn't tell anyone that you were behind all this. I'd already figured it was you, but trying to shoot Mercedes was the bit of proof that sealed the deal. The bullet." He cocked his eyebrows, a *Go on*. "It wasn't steel or lead. It was *silver*. But why would a werewolf, of all people, be carrying a gun loaded with silver bullets?" I looked at Larry, watching his reaction. "The gun you used was silver-plated, too, wasn't it?" A nod. "So when everyone was focused on Mercedes, you tried to shoot her. Then you jammed the gun in the closest lycan's hands. The silver weakened him, so you could wrestle the gun to look like he was trying to kill you before you killed him."

Larry wore a smile of pride in his craftsmanship. "Correct on all counts." He gave me a sincere look. "I really do regret sending Alice to kill you, and setting you up to die. If there'd been any other way...." He shrugged. "Sorry, again."

"Apology *not* accepted." A pause, then I said, "I get it, though. I get why you'd send her, to stop me from getting too close to answers. And you even fed her the line about Prince Eustace being behind it, in case I survived, right?" He nodded. "Which brings me to the big question, Larry. *Why*?" I nodded to the little – useless – gun he'd given me, clipped to my hip.

"Everything you did was to try and get Eustace nailed for the murder. You set up a murder that looked like a vampire had done it, you made sure there was no proof on the surveillance feeds that he actually was where he'd said he was – another reason you wiped out Gandhi and all his stuff. You helped me, but only when it looked like I was going to clear Moonbeam's name – which again would have put Eustace in the crosshairs. You even hunted me down when Moonbeam got brought in, and helped me get to her to gather evidence that she wasn't the killer. You were trying to start a war, weren't you?" He said nothing. My lips drew back, my teeth exposed in anger. "I thought you were my friend, and here you are nothing better than a war profiteer."

Larry laughed. "That's what you think?" he said. "That this is all about *money*? Michaelbrent, I'm the author of the *Monster Hunter International* series, of *Son of the Black Sword* and the *Grimnoir Chronicles*. What do I need *money* for? "

I will admit to complete and utter confusion at this point. "Then why?" I asked. "What could you possibly gain –"

"How about life?" he asked, in a tone so ferocious it was nearly a snarl. "How about life for my family? How about life for every human on Earth?" When he saw my expression, he laughed again. "Michaelbrent, I wasn't trying to start a war, I was trying to stop peace."

"I'm not seeing the distinction."

"Of course you're not." For the first time in our relationship, Larry looked absolutely disgusted with me. And it's one thing for my kids to occasionally look at me like that, but a friend? Ouch. "You're not, and neither is that good-for-nothing group of namby-pambies, the Dead Ones." He had shifted, and now knelt in front of me. "Everyone worries about a war between lycans and vampires. They worry that it will become an apocalypse. Well I say *welcome* the apocalypse. Because the alternative is extinction for you, me, every human on the planet."

"Larry, we can't know –"

"We *can* know. The lycans and vamps have kept each other in check since either of them existed. Together, they take command. Together, they become the ultimate apex predator. How long do you think it will take for a united lycan/vampire nation to take over the world? The lucky humans die, and the rest are put into pens and kept like veal." His eyes burned with conviction. "I don't want war. But I do want a chance." He looked down at his hands. Quietly added, "This was the only way my kids would have to grow up."

"Larry, you shouldn't –"

He steamrollered me, his voice raising to levels even higher than his usual "shake the foundations of the universe" volume. "I won't even ask if you're on my side here, because I know you well enough to know you're not. But you are on the wrong side. This is the only way. And it can still happen, if I push a few people just right. Which is why *this* has to happen." He leaned in close. "Again, sorry."

"Again, apology not accepted."

I tried to move, but my shoulder was only half healed. I did get the other hand up, but Larry batted it away and that same silver knife flashed in his hands. I saw it for a moment, still streaked with the dead lycan's blood, and then he plunged it at my face.

72

The knife stopped moving, hanging in the air so close to my eye that the point was pretty much all I could see. I shifted to the side a tiny bit – just enough to see Larry struggling to ram the knife home.[43]

"Is that good enough?" I said.

Something shimmered, like a heat wave across the desert. The empty hall suddenly wasn't empty at all.

"Quite," said King William.

"We are rockin'," said King Haemon.

Larry turned and saw them, along with the Dead Ones, Blake, Robot Dave, and all the vamps and lycans who had "left" the hall a few minutes ago.

"Do you really think I'd sit down and just chat with you about the details of your plan without some reason behind it?" I asked. "That's what you see in an Agatha Christie novel. But I'm not Jacques Clousea."

"I believe you mean Hercule Poirot," said Robot Dave.

"Shut up," I told him. Then, to Larry, I said, "I made a deal with them." I pointed to where Anderson, William, Borga, Eustace, and Haemon stood close together.

"And you delivered," said Queen Borga. "I must admit that I didn't think you would be able to provide absolute proof,

---

[43] One of the biggest problems with stories like this is that *obviously* I'm going to survive. Otherwise, you'd have to write the ending with a Ouija board or something, and no one has time for that.

But let's pretend I *did* die. Let's pretend that Larry stabbed me and then went on with his devious/actually pretty sensible plan. Would you be sad? I don't want to sound needy or anything, but would you? And if so, would you be "bummer, dude" sad, or would it be more of a "I can't see through my grief everything is dark and why should I go on myself" sadness?

Okay, keep it together. When you can see through your tears again, go on back to the story. I appreciate your love. [sniff!]

but...." She shrugged. "First-hand confessions will be quite enough to satisfy the High Court."

"And the Great Pack," said Moonbeam, stepping out from behind her father. Her face had transformed to that of a wolf and she licked her lips with a long red tongue.

I looked at Haemon. "Mercedes should be let go."

"Absolutely not," said Eustace. "She was a part of this and –"

"She will be," said Haemon. I knew he would agree to that, and I knew he would convince the others to go along. No one understands family like Mormons, Catholics, and lycans.

Larry had been trying to stab me this whole time. I think he knew he couldn't, but I also think he might have blown a gasket in the last minute or so.

I looked at him. "Sorry, bud."

He grimaced, still pressing down on the dagger.

"Apology not accepted."

Then Haemon and William both gestured, and two Otherworld houses descended on my friend.

73

You heard that right. I said, "my friend."

They didn't kill him, but he did get roughed up quite a bit, and life promised to be… unpleasant for him from here on out.

And because he *was* my friend, it was hard to watch. Even harder because I worried that he might have been right. The lycans and the vampires worked well together as they pounded him like a cheap hamburger. What if they turned that kind of energy on all of us?

Worst of all, I caught Haemon's eye while it was happening. He wasn't participating in the beat-down, but he watched with obvious glee.

As though he sensed my attention, he turned and smiled.

I'd been impressed by Haemon. Loyal, strong, and definitely more laid-back than I'd ever manage to be. He'd seemed almost like a friend.

But when he grinned like that, I knew that friendship had never had any part in his heart. He had seemed friendly because he needed an ally. He had treated me with respect because he must have sensed that would be the fastest way to get me on his side.

Now, though… he had what he'd wanted. And there was no friendship or respect in his gaze. I was a mere human. I was, at best, a toy. And more likely food.

His smile widened, and he shifted to his wolf form. Still staring, with golden eyes that told the clear story of his intentions.

I will save my family, said those eyes. *I will save my people. I will join the vampires. And then, together, we will come for all of you.*

I looked away, and in that moment if you had asked me to do it all over again, I might well have helped Larry instead of getting in his way.

74

They dragged Larry off a bit later. He'd taken it all, absorbed it, and never cried out once. The only sound he made was as they pulled his loose body past me. He looked up and said, through a mask of blood and a mouth with only half its teeth left. "I'm not mad, MB. But Bridget probably will be."

Every chill I'd felt during the investigation rolled over me. Bridget. His wife was a very nice gal. Pretty, intelligent.

And at *least* as dangerous as Larry. I'd be very surprised if he was in custody more than a few days before she went after everyone who'd dared to hurt her man.

Maybe war would come after all.

People left again. This time for real. Blake was the last one out. He knelt down to help me up. I waved him off. "I think I'll just stay here a while."

"Probably for the best." I pulled out my phone as Blake spoke. "You wouldn't want to make your sylphilis worse. It'd –"

Looking at the phone, I held up a single finger. "It's midnight, Blake." I grinned at him. "I don't work Sundays."

"Well, you –"

The same finger went up. "Which means I don't have to listen to you, either."

Blake looked like he was on the verge of hitting me. I smiled as prettily as I could.

And he turned around and left. No violence. Maybe we *were* becoming friends.

I waited.

12:01.

The phone rang. I held it up to my ear. "Hey, lovely lady," I said. "I had a feeling you'd be calling."

"Hey, sweetie," said Laura. "I'm so sorry to call so late, but we didn't touch bases yesterday and if I didn't talk to you before I tried to hit the sack, I'd have worried too much to sleep."

"No worries, hon," I said. "Everything's fine."

"You sound pretty happy."

"How could I not be? I'm talking to my best friend." I heard something break, and frowned. "Are the kids still up?"

"Oh, boy. Number four has been a monster."

"A monster, huh?"

"Like you wouldn't believe."

I laughed quietly. "You might be surprised."

More crashing. It sounded like glass broke. The sound of a family. It actually made me believe what I had said.

Everything is fine.

And, for the moment, that was true. I was a Warden, a monster-hunting detective, a horror author trying to make it. I was a father. A husband.

My name is Michaelbrent Collings.

This is what I do.

Epilogue

Mom and I packed up and left the next morning. Headed home.

I offered to take Mom's bags for her, but she said she was feeling more than well enough to haul her own gear. She looked great, too; around four in the morning someone from Anderson's MASH unit brought her to my room, as good as new and remembering nothing about the day before but that it was lazy, relaxing, and refreshing.

When we checked out, there were a few items waiting for me. I told Mom to head out to the car – I had a suspicion what they might be.

The first thing was a package – and a very nice surprise. When I opened it, a small note fell out.

Thank you for your service, my friend. I must point out that I desired you to kill the person behind my love's murder, and should also point out that you did not do so. Normally I would take such a failure personally, but as the culprit is doomed to suffer for a very long time, that will suffice.

As a token of my appreciation, please find the enclosed. I hope that you will look upon me as a continuing friend, and remember our friendship should I ever come to you with a request for a favor.

- H.K.
Nerdfather
Game master
Keeper of the dice

PS I am enjoying The Ridealong, *though I must admit I suspected the twist.*

416

Under the note sat several stacks of twenty-dollar bills. Not exactly a king's ransom, but it more than paid for the stock his goons had stolen. I didn't like the idea of being Kumar's "friend" – but I needed the money. The bills went into my suitcase.

The next thing that waited for me was a short note from Queen Borga.

> *You found Princess Calista's killer and turned him over to us and to the lycans. For this, I grant you your life.*
>
> *You revealed my son's flaws for all to see. The world is no longer his for the taking. He is derided and scorned. For this, I grant you my undying ire.*
>
> *Enjoy your life. Enjoy your family. And when next we meet, you will be my enemy.*

It was unsigned, but there was no question who wrote it. Queen Borga's cursive was fluid and elegant, the handwriting of someone who had had centuries to practice her penmanship. The handwriting of someone who could wait patiently to strike, and would do so at the most painful moment.

There was nothing from Haemon, and for some reason that worried me almost as much as Borga's note. I was not a friend, I was not a helpful human, I was *nothing* to him.

Maybe Moonbeam would help keep him off my back. I *had* saved her life, and when I told her I thought there was more of her than her hippie speech… I think that got to her.

Or maybe I was deluding myself. It wouldn't be the first time.

Blake had called in the morning. He spoke in a subdued voice, and told me the Dead Ones were sending some people to my and my parents' houses to set up wards that would keep out

Otherworlders. He told me the treaty had been signed. The lycans and vampires were a single, unified force for the first time in all history.

Cthulhu had been right: before the weekend drew to a close, I had known fear and pain. And I suspected it was just a small taste of what lay ahead.

The world had shifted, right here in the middle of a comic book convention.

It looked like my work as a Warden was just beginning.

But for now... for now I threw away both notes, and took my bags outside. It was time to go home.

If you would like to be notified of new releases, sales, and other special deals on books by Michaelbrent Collings, please sign up for his mailing list at http://eepurl.com/VHuvX.

(ALSO, YOU CAN GET A FREE BOOK FOR SIGNING UP!)

And if you liked *this* book, **please leave a review on your favorite book review site**… and tell your friends!

*

ABOUT THE AUTHOR

Michaelbrent Collings is a full-time screenwriter and novelist. He has written numerous bestselling horror, thriller, sci-fi, and fantasy novels, including *The Colony Saga, Strangers, Darkbound, Apparition, The Haunted, Hooked: A True Faerie Tale,* and the bestselling YA series *The Sword Chronicles.*

Follow him through Twitter @mbcollings or on Facebook at facebook.com/MichaelbrentCollings.

NOVELS BY MICHAELBRENT COLLINGS

Made in United States
Orlando, FL
13 September 2024

51464500R00241